34320000091499

D0852311

The Trinity Game

Text copyright ©2012 by Sean Chercover

All rights reserved.

Printed in the United States of America.

Published by Thomas & Mercer
P.O. Box 400818
Las Vegas, NV 89140

ISBN-13: 9781612183503
ISBN-10: 1612183506

The Trinity Game

A novel

SEAN CHERCOVER

THOMAS & MERCER

For my father
Murray H. Chercover
(August 18, 1929 – July 3, 2010)
I love you, Dad.

"For nothing is hidden, except to be revealed..."

Mark 4:22

In 1983, Pope John Paul II officially abolished the Office of the Devil's Advocate—the Vatican's department responsible for investigating miracle claims. Only, he didn't. The ODA continues its work, unofficially and in secret, to this very day...

Prologue

New Orleans, Louisiana...

The Deceiver had not yet arrived, but the multitudes preceded him, and Jackson Square was packed. A sea of clamorous believers stretched from the rocky bank of the Mississippi River all the way to the microphone stand set before the blazing white façade of Saint Louis Cathedral. A turbulent sea of believers, jostling and sweating under the oppressive midday sun.

Some in the crowd carried placards.

REPENT AND BE SAVED
PREPARE FOR THE RAPTURE
TRINITY SPEAKS FOR THE TRINITY

Idiots.

The man wondered if he would get a clean shot. *It's in God's hands.* He stepped back from the window and again checked the action of the well-oiled rifle that had been left here in this room for him. *Clack-clack.* Smooth.

There were cops everywhere, of course. National Guard too. And media. News vans below and helicopters above. The timing had to be perfect. No one would see him at the window, so long as he was quick and careful. The lights inside the apartment were off, and the sheers—yellowed by years of sunlight and nicotine—were duct-taped to the wall against any wayward breeze. This too had been done for him in advance.

He had set up a table with a sandbag rest, four feet back from the window. This far back from the sheers, he wouldn't be seen from the street outside, yet with the scope, he could see right through them.

The crowd outside roared to life. It was time. The man lifted the rifle from the bed, seated the magazine, and racked a round into the chamber. *Clack-clack*. He carried the rifle to the table, set it firmly on the sandbag. He wiped the sweat from his forehead with a sleeve and put his eye to the scope.

His target had arrived. About a dozen cops cleared a path to the small stage that had been set up in front of the cathedral, and the Deceiver followed in their wake, carrying his famous blue Bible from the television. He wore a shiny silk suit, which picked up the highlights in his wavy silver hair. His skin glowed with a deep salon tan. The tan contrasted with his brilliant smile. His teeth looked like dentures, or implants.

Perfect, and perfectly fake.

The Deceiver hopped up on the stage and waved to the cheering horde with both hands. He approached the microphones and signaled the multitudes into submission. The cheering subsided.

All at once—*divine providence?*—the cops backed away, providing a clean shot.

It's in God's hands.

The Shepherd had said not to pull the trigger before one thirty. He checked his watch. 1:34.

The man mopped his brow with his sleeve one more time, put his eye to the scope, and carefully positioned the crosshairs, center-of-chest.

Flicked off the safety.

Put his finger on the trigger.

"State of grace," he said. He took a deep breath, held it, and squeezed the trigger.

1:

Lagos, Nigeria – four weeks earlier...

Daniel Byrne didn't notice the boy with the gun until they were standing face-to-face, six feet from each other in the quiet alley behind the fruit stand. Before he saw the gun, Daniel Byrne had been enjoying the best day of his trip.

First day off in two weeks, seventh in the nine since he arrived in Africa. A day free of commitments or obligations or expectations. A day he didn't have to live up to his rep as Golden Boy of the department. He spent the morning working on his tan, reading a novel on the beach, and swimming in the Atlantic Ocean, bathtub warm and salty soft. Back in his executive suite on the top floor of the Federal Palace Hotel, he showered, made the executive decision to give his face a day off from the razor, and dressed—light chinos, a plain black silk Tommy Bahama shirt, and deck shoes, no socks.

Out on the balcony, Daniel stood with the salt air caressing his face and looked out over the white sand beach, the sparkling blue ocean beyond. He leaned forward until the balcony railing pressed against his waist, just above the pelvic bone. Then he leaned farther, keeping his hands free, bending over the railing, looking down at the concrete patio and swimming pool below.

He started to get the tingle.

He leaned even farther. There was a little give to the railing, but it was unlikely to give way completely. Unlikely, not impossible.

The tingle grew into an adrenaline rush. Heart racing, Daniel imagined concrete screws shredding mortar, imagined the sudden jolt of the railing ripping free of its mooring. Imagined falling. Like the dream of falling that jerks you back from the edge of sleep.

But the railing held.

He straightened, blew out a breath, went back inside, and checked his e-mail one more time—all quiet at the office—and grabbed a taxi to Jankara Market.

He wandered among stalls of corrugated steel and sun-bleached canvas, navigated around the beggars, dodged the occasional moped, stopping at the stalls of the artisans, thinking he might find a gift for his boss, who had a birthday coming up. Folk art was always a safe bet.

In the stall of a juju man he found a stunning crucifix—the cross carved out of ebony, polished to a high gleam. But the corpus was real ivory, so he let it go.

He moved on, taking in the bright colors and rough textures, shrill sounds and pungent smells of the seventh largest metropolis in the world. Second largest, on what was, but a few generations ago, referred to as the Dark Continent.

The aroma of charcoal-grilled meat, peanuts, and hot chilies drew Daniel to a smoky green tent across from the voodoo shop, sandwiched between a stall brimming with colorful jewelry, hand-beaded in Nigeria, and one selling counterfeit Gucci and Louis Vuitton handbags, made in Southeast Asia, bribed through customs, and liberated off the back of some transport trailer.

An old man sat in the swirling smoke, skin dark as ebony and beard whiter than ivory, shifting wooden skewers of various cubed meats around on a rusty hibachi, calling out:

"Suya, Suya!"

Hanging on the canvas wall, a menu of sorts:

PORK

CHICKEN

BEEF

GOAT

Beside the menu hung a line drawing of a snake coiled around a pole, cradling a large egg in its open mouth. *Damballah Wedo.* The Source— Creator of the Universe, chief among the *loa* for the Yoruba practitioners of the Ifa religion, and for practitioners of new-world offshoots like Vodun in Haiti, Santeria in Cuba, Voodoo in America.

Daniel had been warned not to purchase any animals—dead or alive, cooked or raw—in the market. The meat of cats and carrion birds sometimes masqueraded as chicken, dogs and hyena as beef. The rumor of what passed for pork was too horrible to contemplate. Goat was the safest choice. Goat meat had a taste you could train your tongue to identify, and goats were plentiful, cheap to raise—probably not worth faking. Daniel always ordered goat. He held up two fingers.

"Eji obuko, e joo." *Two goat, please.*

The old man offered a gap-toothed smile and held out two skewers.

Daniel handed over some bank notes—the equivalent of about twenty-five American cents. He'd have been happy to pay five bucks, but that would've been an insult to the man's pride, so he just paid the price listed on the menu.

"E se," he said. *Thank you.*

The old man held up a hand. "Ko to ope. Kara o le." *You're welcome. Good health.*

Daniel dodged through the crowd, spotted a quiet alley behind a fruit stand, made his way there, and sat on an empty crate to eat. The *suya* was delicious, maybe as good as that served at the Ikoyi. And he was pretty sure it was goat.

He wiped his fingers on the rough paper napkin as he stood, turned, and then he saw the boy, six feet away.

Saw the boy before he saw the gun.

The boy couldn't have been more than thirteen. Skinny kid. Too skinny, wearing cutoff jean shorts, two sizes too big and held up with a rope belt, and a once-white T-shirt, threadbare and stained. A small gold cross on a thin chain around his neck. Complexion almost as dark as the *suya* man, eyes set far apart. Eyes more desperate than afraid.

And then Daniel saw the gun. A snub-nosed revolver, pointing at his chest.

"Gimme your wallet."

Daniel dropped the paper napkin, raised the index finger of his left hand, and slowly fished the wallet from his back pocket, nodding his head the whole time.

"No problem, I understand." He kept his tone casual, his face placid. He finished chewing the last bite of lunch, swallowed. "Here's my wallet." He opened the wallet, showed its contents. "No plastic, but I've got two hundred Yankee dollars, and you're welcome to it."

"Hand it over."

Daniel locked eyes with the boy. "Well, now that's the problem. You can have the money, but only in exchange for the gun."

"What?"

"I'm offering you the money, but I'm buying the gun. It's a purchase."

The kid stared at him, processing. "Then I just shoot you, take the wallet anyway. How you like that?"

Daniel held the kid's stare. "I really wouldn't like that at all. Have you done it before?"

"Plenty times."

"No," Daniel put compassion in his smile, "you haven't," he drew the bills from the wallet, "and you don't want to start now." He pointed at the cross hanging from the kid's neck. "You really want my blood on your hands? Carry that with you for the rest of your life? Answer for that, when your time comes?" He slipped the empty wallet back into his pocket. "Give me the gun, and you can have the money."

The kid bit his lower lip, shook his head. "I give you the gun, you shoot me, take your money back."

"Fair enough." *Keep the head nodding and the tone soothing and the message positive:* "Here's a solution. Take the bullets out, and *then* hand me the gun, and that will make you happy." Of course, he could pistol-whip the boy into submission with the empty gun easily enough if he wanted to, but he didn't want to, and he figured the kid could see the truth of his intentions. Just as he was betting that he could read the kid. "Two hundred, American. Just give me the gun and it's yours." *Always be closing.*

The boy thought for a few seconds, then flipped the cylinder open and dumped the bullets into his left hand and shoved them into his jeans. He held the gun out and said, "Same time."

They executed the trade by simultaneous snatch, and the kid ran away. Daniel took the gun to the back of the alley. If he gave it to the police, it would be back on the streets before nightfall. He cocked the hammer, used a rock to break off the firing pin, smashed the hammer until it bent and wouldn't snap back into place, and tossed the now useless weapon into a trashcan.

A voice behind him said, "You really are a sucker."

Daniel knew that voice. He turned around. "How long were you watching?"

Father Conrad Winter pulled at his clerical collar, letting a little air in, and grinned. "Long enough."

"Thanks for the help."

"Any time." The priest pulled at his collar again, wiped a handkerchief over his forehead, pushing back his damp blond hair. "Hot as a bitch out here, let's find some shade."

2:

Conrad Winter snapped his fingers at a waiter, and the waiter put a two-hose hookah on the table, went away, and came back with a copper pot of sweet Turkish coffee.

Daniel didn't want this meeting but Conrad's position as head of the Office of World Outreach was of equal rank to Daniel's boss, Father Nick. Refusing to meet was not an option. At least the café was cool, with open walls all around, massive ceiling fans turning above. He reached for the hookah, picked up one of the hoses, and puffed. The hookah burbled, and his mouth filled with the taste of coconut. He blew out the smoke.

"What brings you to Lagos, Father Conrad?"

"The case you're working on."

"I've got six open files, three more on deck. I'm afraid you'll have to be more specific."

Conrad sipped some coffee. "What is it with you, anyway?" He gestured at his collar. "It's a powerful symbol, makes you a *minor god* to these people. Why not wear yours?"

The last thing Daniel needed was people putting on more of a show for him than they did already. But he wasn't about to take the bait. "Too hot," he said.

"Tell you one thing," Conrad puffed on the hookah, "that kid never would've pulled a gun on a priest." He blew out a white cloud. "I'm curious. How much did you give him?"

Daniel shrugged.

"And how much does a gun cost on the street? Forty, fifty bucks?"

Another shrug.

"So what did you achieve? He'll just buy another gun, with cash to spare."

And the kid probably would. But what the hell. Daniel had resolved the situation without hurting the kid or getting shot, and as a bonus, he'd taken one gun off the street.

And maybe he'd given the kid something to think about.

Maybe.

He puffed on the hookah. He said, "Which case?"

"The girl."

"Which girl?" He knew perfectly well which girl, but he wasn't giving anything away for free.

By way of explanation, Conrad held his hands out, displaying his palms. "South of Abuja. We need this one."

So Conrad had access to Daniel's e-mails. Only way he could've known his personal persuasion was necessary. Another fun-filled day of Vatican office politics.

"The investigation was fair," said Daniel. "The girl is not a miracle."

"A lot at stake here, Golden Boy."

"Especially for the girl."

Conrad shot back the rest of his coffee, sludge and all, brought the cup down hard. "You think you've got the moral high ground? You don't. We're at war, and this girl lives on the front lines. *Thirteen* provinces have gone over to Sharia Law, soon fourteen, and it's spreading south. You see that one girl, you want to save her. Hypocritical. What about the millions of other young girls unfortunate enough to be born in this place? What chance will they have, if the tide keeps rolling? You think God wants us to trade all their futures for that one girl, so you can wallow in your integrity?"

"This isn't about me."

"The hell it isn't."

Daniel swallowed his first response. "Father Conrad," he said, "I agree with the goal, but this is not the way to get there. The ODA is independent for a reason, and we don't knowingly certify fake miracles."

"From what I hear, *you* don't certify *any* miracles."

A little below the belt, but Daniel didn't flinch. "Not yet. Still looking, though."

"Then step down off the cross and look a little harder at Stigmata Girl. The parish has been flooded with converts since she started manifesting." *Manifesting.* That's what they called it back at the Vatican. "Did you even read the Outreach brief on Nigeria before going native and eating the bush meat?"

"It was goat."

"Boko Haram is acting on its promise. The head count is over a thousand and accelerating."

"Father Conrad, I read the report."

"Then consider this: despite everything, and because of this miracle, we're winning hearts and minds up there."

"I wish you success in keeping them, but my orders are clear. I follow the evidence where it leads." Daniel put back the rest of his coffee. "And I don't work for you."

Conrad reached into his jacket and came up with an envelope, handed it across the table.

Daniel turned the envelope over, and his heart sank. The flap bore the red wax seal of Cardinal Allodi, the direct superior of both Conrad and Father Nick. Daniel had long suspected Allodi favored the political mission of World Outreach over the more esoteric duties of the ODA.

Daniel broke the seal and read the letter.

Fr. Daniel:

Due to departmental workload fluctuations, you are hereby on transfer status from the Office of the Devil's Advocate to the Office of World Outreach. You will report to Fr. Conrad Winter until further notice.

In faith, we serve.

"Cardinal Allodi told me about Honduras," said Conrad, "so don't act like you're above this."

Daniel's blood rose. He pictured breaking Conrad's nose with a hard right, followed by a hook to the ribs and an uppercut to...He reined it in, refocused on what the man was saying.

"...you can't just pretend it never happened. People *died* because of you. I guess we'll never know exactly how many at your hand, but—"

"Three," said Daniel. "I killed three. And you already know that...or are we pretending you haven't read the case file?"

Conrad's mouth tightened very slightly. "Watch yourself, Daniel."

Daniel nodded, not an apology but a grudging acknowledgment of his station.

Conrad's tone turned conversational. "You'll enjoy your time in Outreach. We have many pencils that require sharpening, and you're just the man for the job. We'll cure you of your sin of pride, and you'll be a better priest when I decide it's time for you to return to the ODA." He flashed Daniel a grin that said: *Checkmate.*

3:
==

Rome, Italy...

Daniel picked up his Honda Shadow from long-term parking at Leonardo da Vinci Airport, hit the Autostrada, and pointed the motorcycle toward the lights of Rome, barely seeing the road, his mind replaying scenes from Nigeria.

The obsequious parish priest, angling to parlay his local miracle into a promotion to the big city. The grandparents and parents filled with pride because "God has chosen our little Abassi to bear the wounds of Christ." And the teenage girl with endless brown eyes, manic energy, and a handful of three-inch twisted-shank roofing nails hidden under her mattress.

Daniel had caught her in the act. He knew she was self-mutilating, but he played dumb for a few days, interviewing the girl and her family with softball questions, lulling them into a sense of security. Every few hours, the family would contrive to leave the girl alone. "She needs to rest, this is so hard on her," one of them would say, and all would agree with pitying nods of the head, wringing their rough country hands. They would sit in the kitchen and drink tea from chipped china, and when they returned an hour later with a cup of tea for the girl, their footfalls were loud and they paused a little too long between knock and enter.

Willful blindness. He tried not to hate them for it.

On the third day, during one of the girl's "rests," Daniel excused himself from the kitchen table and headed for the bathroom, exactly as he had done the previous days. But this time he walked straight to the girl's room and threw the door open.

She sat smiling on her bed, quietly singing "Jesus Loves Me," while jabbing a nail straight through the palm of her left hand. Then twisting the nail, enlarging the hole as blood dripped into her lap.

Conrad wasn't wrong about what was at stake. The twisted, fundamentalist brand of Islam that Boko Haram was selling in Nigeria was beyond regressive—it was violent, misogynistic, and apocalyptic. Their name meant "Western education is sacrilege." They'd vowed to kill all the Christians living in their territory, and they were making good on it. They'd already killed over a thousand, burned over three hundred churches. Last Christmas Day, they slaughtered forty-two Catholics. The moderate Muslims struggling to govern the country in cooperation with the Christian minority were losing ground to the Islamist radicals, and after years living under the imminent threat of civil war, no one wanted to admit that the war was in fact well underway. The politicians still used the term *insurgency*, but it came out sounding like wishful thinking.

Of course there was no argument with Conrad's goal, and yes, faking a miracle might help win the current battle, but it could very well lose them the longer war. And the mandate of the ODA was to always take the long view and evaluate miracle claims honestly.

And then there was the girl with the holes in her hands, the girl who needed help from a psychologist, not validation of her neurosis from the Vatican. Calling this a miracle would only guarantee her complete destruction.

Conrad was willing to jettison this girl—condemn her to a life of mental illness—for the *greater good*, and call it collateral damage. Call *her* collateral damage. But to Daniel, you cross that line and now you're cutting God's grass. It's one thing to try and do God's will, quite another to start making His decisions for Him. If pride was Daniel's sin, it seemed a little less monstrous by comparison.

Daniel said a long prayer for the girl, crossed himself, and returned his attention to the road ahead.

✤ ✤ ✤

"I can't believe you're letting this happen."

Father Nick, head of the Office of the Devil's Advocate, shrugged broad shoulders, leaned back in his chair. "Out of my hands. His Eminence oversees both departments—if he wants you in World Outreach…"

"I'm an *investigator*—I have no business over in Outreach. You know that."

"Easy, Dan. Your skills as an investigator are not in question." Nick gestured at a chair across the desk. "Sit."

Daniel sat. "It's politics, isn't it? Conrad's pissed because I won't fake one for him, and he got Cardinal Allodi to go along."

"That would be my theory," said Nick. "His Eminence didn't share his deliberations with me. I lobbied for you, but…" He rose to the antique mahogany wet bar, poured golden Armagnac into a couple of crystal snifters. "I've skimmed your e-mails on the case. You say there's no miracle."

"No miracle. Just a messed-up teenager sticking nails into her hands and feet when everyone's back was turned." Daniel took the offered glass. "And their backs were turned a lot. Everyone wanted it to be real."

Nick sat. "OK. I know it's rough sometimes."

"The girl started self-mutilating at twelve. For *three years*, the whole town—family, friends, even her priest—treated her like a gift from God. I spent three days in that madhouse, and I can tell you, that girl is seriously broken." He took a long swallow of brandy. "And we're the ones who teach them that stigmata exists."

Father Nick fixed the younger priest with a firm stare. "Just because you haven't seen it yet doesn't mean it isn't real."

But in a decade investigating miracle claims for the Vatican, Daniel hadn't seen *anything* yet. Ten years of stigmatic self-mutilators and schizophrenics hearing voices and con artists pumping salt water through hollowed-out statues of the Blessed Virgin. Ten years of oil drum rust-stains that look *kinda-sorta-almost* like Jesus if you squint your eyes just so and hold your head on an angle and harbor an intense desire to see Jesus in a rust-stain.

Ten years.

Seven hundred and twenty-one cases.

Not one miracle.

It wasn't as if Daniel wasn't hoping for a miracle. But even setting aside the principles involved—even if he were willing to start down the slippery slope of *ends justifying means*—the girl in Nigeria would never stand up to scrutiny; she'd be exposed as a fraud. And putting the Vatican's stamp of approval on a fake could lead to the kind of PR the Church didn't need in the war for *hearts and minds*. "You're not suggesting I change my verdict on this case, are you, Father Nick?"

"No. There are those who wish you would, but I'm not one of them, and I already made that fact clear to all interested parties. But you need to face reality—the cost of that choice is I now have to loan you to Conrad for a while. I'll continue to lobby His Eminence, and hopefully your exile will be brief." He sipped some brandy and forced a smile. "Ah well, if God wants a miracle in Nigeria, He'll just have to make one Himself."

"Come on, Nick, there's gotta be something you can do. Conrad's a first-class prick, I'll go crazy working for him."

"You haven't walked in his shoes," said Father Nick. "The horrors he has to deal with…but you're right, he is a prick." Nick looked into his snifter for a long while, then took a slow sip. "Actually, there is a case I could claw you back into the ODA on, citing special circumstances, but—"

"Special circumstances?"

"That's the problem. The very reason I don't think I should assign the case to you."

"I'll do it. Anything."

"I think it could be bad for you, kiddo. I've seen you get personally involved in cases before—"

"One case." Daniel fought to keep the anger out of his voice. He'd done his penance for Honduras, but Vatican memories are long. Here they forgive, but they never forget. "*Four years ago.* Come on, Nick, I'm fine. I can handle it."

"I dunno." Nick held eye contact. "How's your faith holding?"

"I'm working on it, as usual." Nick didn't respond, so Daniel quoted the older priest's familiar phrase back at him, " 'Faith is a choice, not a state of being.' " He smiled. "I keep making the choice. That's what matters, right?"

"You're not working on it, you're running around looking for proof. You don't think I know? Believe me, I know. You made a deal with God a long time ago: you'd pretend to believe, and He'd show His face, and then you'd *really* believe. And you know *how* I know? Because that was me as a young man. But time's ticking, you're not getting any younger." Nick finally smiled for real. "Look, you're my doubting Thomas and I love you for it. I hope someday when I'm old and senile enough, you'll be sitting here in the big chair. But you do have to work on your faith. I shouldn't have to tell you that."

Daniel shook his head. "What do you want me to say? I keep making the choice, even when I have to make it several times a day. I'm fine, really. I want this case, whatever it is. And the fact that we're still discussing it tells me you could really use me on it."

Father Nick conceded the point with a nod. After a long silence he said, "OK. We've got a…well, an anomaly, let's call it. And it has to do with your uncle."

4:

D aniel played it twice over in his mind until he was sure he'd heard it correctly. A defensive snort escaped before he could rein it in. He followed with, "My uncle is a *con man.*"

Father Nick held up his hands. "I know. I know, and that makes you perfect for it. You're the best debunker in the business, *and* you know his particular tricks." He picked up a television remote from the desktop. "Have you seen his show recently?"

"It's been a while," Daniel said.

Nick aimed the remote at a wide, flat-panel television perched on the antique credenza, and the screen came on blue. He pressed another button, and the blue screen was replaced by video of the *Tim Trinity Prosperity-Power Miracle Hour*. "This was taped last week," he said.

On the screen, Reverend Tim Trinity stalked the stage like a large predatory cat, right to left, left to right, pausing occasionally to connect with the camera, never fully at rest. The stage was dressed up like a pulpit, complete with faux stained glass windows (backlit, of course), balsawood columns painted to look like mahogany, and a clear Plexiglas lectern, downstage-center. Trinity wore a royal blue silk suit, white leather cowboy boots and matching belt. On his left wrist, a chunky gold Rolex, its face wall-to-wall diamonds. A wireless microphone curved around from his right ear, like he was God's own telemarketer. On his right hand he balanced an open Bible, its pages edged in silver, its cover made of fine leather, dyed blue, the same bright shade as his suit.

Daniel wondered if the suit had been selected to match the Bible or the Bible to match the suit.

Trinity spoke with a pronounced New Orleans accent, and his patter flowed like brandy, perfected over more than twenty-five years on the tent revival circuit and in churches, then on television for the last fourteen. The man had his act down cold—didn't even need the Bible, but for its value as a prop. And that was no small value. He brandished his blue Bible to maximum effect, flipped pages with a flourish, and punctuated important words by *thwacking* the pages with his left hand, calling attention to the bling on his wrist with each *thwack*.

"Friends, I have some very bad news for you," said Trinity, still smiling. "I've been called upon this day to reveal a hard truth. And I ain't gonna sugar-coat it—*thwack*—NO, sir! I'm here today to tell you, most people who call themselves Christians have a fundamental *mis*-understanding of the nature of *sin*." He stretched it into a two-syllable word.

Trinity stopped at the lectern. His eyes fell shut and he pulled his chin to the right, offering his profile as the camera cut to a close-up. He held the Bible to his forehead for a few seconds, then lowered it, faced forward, and opened his now watery eyes, blinking rapidly. A man of God, on the verge of tears.

"Forgive me. I must share with you what happened last night as I prepared today's sermon. I was sitting in my study, pen in hand, and the Devil came calling. Yes, the—*thwack*—Devil! The Devil came to me last night and said, 'Reverend Tim, stop what you're doing.' He said, 'The people are not ready for this, you must not reveal it. Seal up these things and do not write them.' Oh yes, and he presented himself to me as an angel of the Lord…but you and I know that the Lord would never stop a prophet from speaking the truth. So I said, 'Get behind me, Satan!' and his white robes fell away and he stood before me as a naked beast." Trinity blew out a long breath. "Was I afraid? You know it, brother! You bet I was. But more than afraid, I was—and I know that it wasn't me speaking, but for the power of Christ, I know it was God speaking through me—I stood up from my desk and I shouted, 'You Devil, go straight back to Hell! Take one step closer and I will *strike* you down—" Trinity slashed at an imaginary devil with his Bible "—and I will *kick* you down—" he stomped hard on the stage "—and I will beat you like a redheaded stepchild!"

Daniel had seen his uncle's act thousands of times and had hoped never to see it again. "What's the point of this, Nick?"

Nick kept his eyes on the television. "Keep watching."

Trinity held the Bible to his chest. "And just like that—glory be to God—the Devil disappeared, leaving behind only the stench of a goat." He smiled and waved away the stench with the Good Book, and the camera cut away to the congregation as they laughed on cue.

It was not the megachurch of a Joel Osteen or Creflo Dollar, but Trinity's flock was not small. Daniel estimated about five thousand in attendance, give or take a few lost souls.

Trinity let the laughter play out just the right length of time, then turned serious. "I know in my heart, my life was saved last night. Saved by God, so I could bring you this truth about *sin*. See, most folks think sin is bad behavior. You break God's laws, and you have committed sin. But that is a *mis*-understanding of sin's true nature. Those bad behaviors are not sin, not in the true sense. They are the *result* of sin. Sin is not something you do. In reality, sin is a *demonic force* that acts upon you, *causing* you to break God's laws."

Trinity flipped a few pages and glanced at his Bible. "Romans 3:9—we are under the *power* of sin, 6:6 and 6:17—we are *enslaved* by sin, and 5:13—'sin was in the world before the law.'" He waved a finger in the air and grinned like Clarence Darrow on closing summation to the jury, knowing he'd proved his case. "In the world, *before* the law. If sin was in the world before the law, then it is not caused by breaking the law, it *precedes* the law. You see? Sin is a *demonic force* that has power over us, enslaves us, and causes us to break God's laws. Get back, Devil! Powers and principalities!" Trinity swatted the air again with his Bible. "Glory to God, I am telling the *truth* today! Sin is a demonic force that causes *all* our suffering."

Pacing the stage again. "People ask me, they say, 'Reverend Tim, do you mean that poverty is a sin?'—*thwack*—YES! Poverty is a sin. God don't want you to be poor of spirit, and He don't want you to be poor of material comforts. God loves you—why would He want you to suffer? And poverty *is* suffering. Only the Devil wants you to be poor." The toothy smile flooded his face once more. "But here is the good news: If you *really* want to live in abundance—abundance is yours for the taking! Word of God. All you have to do is act *in faith*. When you act in faith, God will return it to you *one-hundred-fold*. But you must sow your seed, or you cannot expect to reap the harvest of God's riches."

Trinity stopped pacing, dropped the smile, looked straight into the camera lens. "I'm calling on you, *right now*, to make a thousand-dollar vow of faith to this television ministry. You know who you are—I'm *talking* to you. You don't have a thousand dollars right now, in the material world, but that's OK—you *vow* it, and you start *paying* on it, in faith, fifty dollars, a hundred dollars, two hundred dollars, five hundred dollars at a time… and as you pay on your vow, God will take the measure of your faith, and He will begin to work *miracles* in your life! Word of *God! Hallelujah!*"

Father Nick lowered the volume as Trinity assured viewers they could use any major credit card to sow their seeds of faith. "You know him better than anyone," he said and gestured at the screen.

"*Knew* him," said Daniel. "Twenty years ago."

"Just tell me what you see."

"I don't see anything. It's the same old snake oil, and he still sells the crap out of it. Just a fancier package…nicer suit, bigger watch, better hairdo. The man knows his scripture, and the way he twists it, it always comes out *Send Me Money*. That's all I see." He searched for something else to say. What *did* he see? "He's got a lot more followers now. Oh, and he's had a facelift."

"Really?"

"He's sixty-four, and he's a drinker. He's had a facelift."

"What else?"

Then it hit him. "Ah, he's not speaking in tongues anymore. He used to sprinkle a lot of gibberish in with the rest of the pitch."

"Watch." Nick paused the video. "He still does the tongues routine, but not as often. And it's different now." He hit play.

Trinity continued his money pitch for another minute or two. Then he froze, mid-sentence, like an epileptic having a *petit mal* seizure. He stood stock-still for a few seconds. Then his lips began to twitch. His entire body lurched to the left. Then jerked again, harder, like he'd just stuck his finger in a light socket.

And the tongues began. It was still gibberish, but Nick was right—it had changed. The tongues that Trinity used to speak sounded like a bad parody of some West African language, spiced with a little Japanese inflection. But what Daniel heard now was very different. The sounds coming from Trinity's mouth were not like any language Daniel had ever heard. In fact, like *nothing* he'd ever heard. He couldn't even imagine how to make them.

Father Nick shut off the television. "What do you think?"

"It's different, all right," said Daniel. "Very dramatic. Weird. I don't know how he does it."

"It goes way beyond just sounding weird," said Father Nick. He put on his reading glasses and moved a thick file folder to the center of his desk blotter, then reached for the telephone. "Here's where it gets *really* weird."

5:

Nick picked up the telephone receiver, punched a single button, and spoke to his secretary. "George, send Giuseppe in."

As the door behind him opened, Daniel turned in his seat and nodded hello. The ODA's top linguist, Father Giuseppe Sorvino had consulted on a handful of Daniel's cases over the last decade. They only knew each other slightly, but he'd struck Daniel as very bright, and also deeply sad. He'd lost his left arm below the elbow five years earlier while working on something in Israel, but he never talked about it. Whatever the cause of the sadness, it was evident long before.

Giuseppe wore the left sleeve of his jacket folded, the cuff pinned to the outside of the shoulder. This always struck Daniel as strange. Why not just have the sleeve cut and cuffed at the elbow? It was as if Giuseppe were holding out hope that the forearm might suddenly grow back and sprout a new hand. Then he could just let down the sleeve and get on with life.

Father Nick gestured and Giuseppe sat in the empty chair next to Daniel.

"Tell him," said Nick.

Father Giuseppe bobbed his head and let out an embarrassed smile. "Sometimes on my lunch breaks I like to watch the television evangelists who pretend possession by the Holy Spirit. They are very bad at it, always good for a laugh—"

Nick cut in. "Please, Giuseppe, we don't need the lunch break. Just what you learned."

The linguist's face flushed a little. "Yes, sir. So I was watching Tim Trinity's tongues act on my lunch break, and I suddenly realized his tongues had a definite linguistic structure. I recorded it and played with the tape, you know, speeding it up, slowing it down, noting patterns." He rubbed his stump with the palm of his right hand as he spoke. It always seemed to itch more when he was nervous. "Then I remembered the rumor that went around the world when I was a kid. Remembered playing Beatles albums backward on the turntable in search of messages about Paul being dead. Backmasking, they call it. Putting those messages on records."

Father Nick drummed his fingers on the desk.

"Yes, I'm sorry. Anyway, I played the Trinity tape backward. It sounded like English on Quaaludes. I sped it up by a quarter, then a third." He stopped rubbing the stump and his hand swept up in a triumphant gesture. "And there it was! Trinity was speaking English backward at two-thirds normal speed. Amazing. I recorded every broadcast since. Whenever he does his tongues act, they manifest the same phenomenon."

"Thank you, Giuseppe," said Father Nick. "That'll be all."

The abrupt dismissal set Giuseppe to rubbing his stump even faster as he took his leave. Nick watched him go and didn't look at Daniel until the door had closed behind.

Daniel shrugged. "So Trinity's upped his game, learned a new parlor trick."

"And he's very good at it, which makes him dangerous," said Nick, pulling a mini tape recorder from the case file. "Listen. This is what it sounds like." He pressed play.

The crowd noise in the background was now strange, but Tim Trinity's voice sounded natural. He was saying, "...on the south coast of Georgia, there will be an unexpected thunderstorm tomorrow in the late afternoon. So all you folks down by Brunswick, all the way up to Darien, be sure to pack an umbrella..."

Father Nick clicked the tape off.

"You have got to be kidding me," said Daniel. "If this were anybody but you, I'd expect the door to fly open and the *Candid Camera* people to come in."

"I told you it was gonna get weird," said Nick.

"OK, weird. But a *weather report*?"

"Not exactly the kind of message you'd expect from God."

"Not exactly. What else does he say?"

"He says a lot of trivial crap. A few bigger things too, things that are going to get him noticed. Nothing earth shattering. Thing is, he makes predictions. Sometimes he's gonna be right—law of averages. He lucked out on that weather report, for example. We checked. And he guessed the winner of the Superbowl. He also gets things wrong, but it's like reading your horoscope in the paper. You forget all the days it didn't make sense and remember the times it resonated."

"OK, so he's got a new con," said Daniel, "but I don't see our interest here. We already know he's a fake, and he's not even Catholic."

"Think about it, Daniel. Think about how it'll play out if Trinity isn't exposed as a fake. He'll just keep going on like this, and soon he'll have a pretty big record of correct prophecy. And when he does, he'll reveal how to decode what he's saying. People will go crazy. Not a few people, *millions* of people. Catholics, Protestants, Mormons—it won't matter. People are hungry for miracles, and they'll be led away from God—they'll follow a false prophet. We need him debunked before that happens. Question is can I trust it to you? I know things ended badly between you two, and I don't want you to take the case if you don't think you can handle it. This can't be personal. It isn't about what happened between you and your uncle."

Twenty years ago, when Daniel was just thirteen, Tim Trinity had been the closest thing to a father that Daniel had ever known. A lot of water under the proverbial bridge since then, but some wounds never fully heal.

"Personal involvement won't be an issue," Daniel said. "I have no problem exposing Tim Trinity as a fraud."

Nick removed his reading glasses. "Then we may just be able to outflank Conrad after all. I can sell His Eminence on my need to assign the case to you, based on your knowledge of Trinity. And if you can nail this case shut fast, I think it'll convince him that you're indispensable to the ODA."

"Thank you."

"Just don't make me look like an idiot for assigning it to you." Father Nick pushed the file folder across the desk. "Transcripts are in the case file—you can read them on the flight to Atlanta."

Daniel took the folder, stood, and walked to his boss's four-centuries-old oak office door. Carved in the wood was Saint John, the Baptist, kneeling in the Jordan with his arms open, while Jesus instructed him to fulfill all righteousness.

And a voice came out of the heavens, "You are my beloved Son; in You I am well-pleased."

6:

After completing his morning prayers, Daniel skipped rope for fifteen minutes, working up a good sweat. Then he donned the gloves and worked out on the heavy bag that hung in the corner of his bedroom, enjoying the electric jolt that ran up his arm each time he landed a particularly vicious blow. The bag bucked and the chains rattled and the feeling of power spurred Daniel on. He put even more into his punches, employing his legs, his lower body, and the bag bucked harder and the chains rattled louder. He kept at it until his shoulders and wrists begged for mercy and the muscles of his arms began to twitch from fatigue.

As he pulled the gloves off, his gaze fell to the framed photo on the dresser. From the center of a boxing ring, eighteen-year-old Danny Byrne looked back at him with a prideful grin. The teenager wore silk trunks—purple and gold—and his bare chest, not yet as hairy as it was now in the mirror above the dresser, glistened with sweat. He held a Golden Gloves trophy above his head.

Sometimes it felt like yesterday. Sometimes, a hundred years ago. Daniel couldn't decide which feeling was the sadder.

Daniel drank espresso in the first-class lounge, waiting for them to call his flight, thinking: *One week, at most, and you can wash your hands of the man again.*

Usually he was thrilled when a case brought him back stateside. He loved America, always missed it, occasionally ached for it, often fantasized about someday returning "back home" for good.

But this case did not thrill him one bit.

One week, he told himself again. *Get in, debunk, get out.*

Turning toward the flight-status monitors, Daniel caught a glimpse of the pretty redhead from the check-in line, now sitting three tables away. She'd been standing directly behind him in line, and she'd asked to borrow his pen. The skirt of her Chanel suit stopped a couple inches above the knee and the jacket hugged her narrow waist. She looked about his age—thirty-three—but her manner suggested late thirties as she took the pen and smoothly launched into small talk. She was a buyer for a chain of upscale women's clothing stores—twenty locations spread across the South—and she loved expense account trips to Rome but was happy to be heading home to her papillon and her yoga classes, both of which she missed terribly whenever she was away. She was clearly single, and interested, and he'd tried to be friendly without encouraging further interest.

And now she sat three tables away, watching him over the top of her *Marie Claire,* trying to be just obvious enough that he'd get the feeling of being watched, look over, make eye contact. This was the downside of not wearing his clerical collar. And, if he was honest, it was the upside as well. Daniel wasn't devoid of ego and it was nice to be reminded that women found him attractive. But it was also a bitter reminder of the woman he'd left to join the priesthood, the love he'd cast aside and tried so hard to forget. And the truth was he didn't need a reminder.

Because he thought of her, every damn day.

Daniel's father confessor was the only other person who knew. They'd talked about it countless times, most recently just a month ago...

"God doesn't expect you to be perfect, Daniel," said the father confessor. "You're supposed to *emulate* Jesus, not *be* Him. And as He was tempted, so are you. This woman is your temptation."

"It's more than just a passing temptation. I'm still in love with her."

"So that's your cross to bear. You love her, but you choose to love God more."

The words rang hollow in Daniel's ears.

7:

Singapore…

Chulia Street was so perfectly paved the airport limousine seemed almost to float as it cruised along, the soft hum of its tires the only evidence of contact with the road. On either side, young trees rose from evenly spaced planters along spotless sidewalks. As the newly built Sato Kogyo-Hitachi building slid by on the left, Conrad Winter set his watch ahead to local time.

Seven hours ahead, twelve spent in the air, for a net loss of five hours. A negative way to frame it, no doubt, but Conrad was not looking forward to this meeting. At least he'd have a night in Singapore before flying out again.

Conrad loved Singapore for all the reasons he didn't love Rome. Rome was a city that fetishized the past, lived in the present, and made no plans for the future. But Singapore was *all about* the future. Singapore tore down her outdated relics and built gleaming new skyscrapers at a furious rate, always thinking big, always looking forward. The seven-hour time difference between the two cities might as well be seven centuries. No wonder the council kept its headquarters here.

There were many good men at the Vatican but, like the city that surrounded them, they were not sufficiently forward-focused. They were wearing blinders that obscured the future. Most of them, but not all. Besides Cardinal Allodi, Conrad knew five other council operatives within the Holy See itself, although there were surely others as yet unknown to him. The council was not the sort of organization that published a list. The Church demanded undivided loyalty, and affiliation with the Council for World Peace was grounds for excommunication. But that was a rule made by the good men wearing blinders. Conrad's loyalty was not divided. Conrad's loyalty was to God.

And God would never leave the fate of the world to good men wearing blinders.

The council had operatives everywhere and introductions were on a need-to-know basis. So he couldn't say who had alerted the director to the setback in Nigeria, but someone had and now he would have to explain himself. It was just as well, since he had other, more important news to report.

The limousine pulled to the curb and Conrad instructed the driver to take his bag on to the Raffles Hotel. He stepped out into the hot, muggy air and headed toward the entrance of UOB Plaza One, stopping briefly, as he always did, to look at the large Salvador Dali bronze, *Homage to Newton*.

The grotesque figure stood rigid, arms stretched out to its right, a sphere hanging from its right hand by a thin metal thread. This sphere was supposed to be Newton's proverbial apple, the one that hit him on the head and taught him about gravity. There was another sphere, representing the heart, suspended in Newton's wide-open torso, and there was also a gaping hole in his head. Art critics said this represented "open-heartedness and open-mindedness."

To Conrad, it mostly looked painful.

Inside, the building's atrium was all granite and glass and brushed steel and high ceilings. Conrad plucked the fabric of his shirt away from his chest, moist from the brief time outdoors, made clammy by the arctic air conditioning. Stepping into the elevator, he remembered his last visit, at the conclusion of a successful project. The deputy director had taken him to lunch at Si Chuan Dou Hua on the sixtieth floor—they'd ordered honeyed lotus root at the chef's suggestion, and it was excellent—and the director himself had joined them for a drink at the end of the meal to thank Conrad personally for his work on the assignment.

Conrad's finger moved past the restaurant level and pressed the button for the sixty-seventh floor. Today there would be no celebratory lunch.

✤ ✤ ✤

The director of the council stood behind a vast marble desktop. Through the floor-to-ceiling windows, the surface of the Singapore Strait glittered like a field of broken glass. He did not extend his hand or offer a chair. He said, "Your last report indicated the project was on schedule."

"Yes, sir," said Conrad. "I'm taking care of it."

"But this investigator…" The director waved his hand in the air for a prompt.

"Daniel Byrne."

"He refused to certify."

Conrad nodded. "Any other investigator, we'd have been fine. Bad luck we got him. But it had to look like a routine case, Cardinal Allodi couldn't insert himself without signaling an agenda."

"The insurgents are getting smarter, targeting infrastructure. If we lose the town where that girl lives, the oil stops flowing. Unacceptable."

"We'll hold the town. I always had a Plan B in place, and it's now in motion. A few days at most." Conrad said it with enough confidence and the director seemed somewhat mollified. "But sir, a much bigger issue has come up. Another anomaly has surfaced—as strong as the one we had last year in Bangalore—and this time the Church knows about it."

The director let out a long breath. "Where?"

"United States. Atlanta. A television evangelist named Tim Trinity."

"He's on *television*?"

"Yes, sir, it's not good. And Nick has assigned the same priest to it."

"Really? Is it possible that this Daniel Byrne is working for the foundation?"

"No sir, I've been keeping tabs on him. He doesn't know the foundation exists, or the council for that matter. I'm quite sure he doesn't even know the *game* exists."

"All right, wrap up Nigeria ASAP and make Trinity your top priority."

"Will do."

"Top priority," the director repeated. "If you need backup, call for it. Any sign of foundation involvement, you send up the alarm, straight to my office."

Conrad had heard it said that the Fleur-de-Lis Foundation had almost as many operatives embedded in the Church as did the Council For World Peace, and he had suspicions about a few of the fathers, but he'd seen nothing conclusive. "Sir, I don't think they—"

"Don't make the mistake of underestimating your opponent, Conrad. The foundation threatens our very existence. And despite his genteel façade, Carter Ames is the most dangerous man you will ever meet."

8:

Atlanta, Georgia...

For years, Daniel avoided hotels like the one he was staying in now. The luxury had just felt inappropriate for a man who'd taken a vow of poverty.

The meth-lab fire in Detroit changed his mind.

Daniel had flown there to investigate a spontaneous cancer remission that turned out to be a misdiagnosis. At the airport, he rented a Toyota Corolla. He checked into a generic chain motel near the freeway. Late that night he sat in his motel room, reading his e-mail, when there came a muffled *whump!* and a flash of light outside his window.

The room directly across the parking lot was ablaze, black smoke pouring from the open door. A man staggered out of the burning room, carrying the porcelain lid of a toilet water tank, cradling it like a baby. Daniel ran to help. The man saw him coming, wound up, and heaved the lid at his head. Daniel ducked the flying toilet tank lid and it shattered on the blacktop. It was then he saw the wild look in the man's eyes.

Fire—crappy motel—meth-lab fire—crazed junkie all raced through his brain in the moment it took for the man to draw a knife from a belt sheath and close the distance, slashing at the shrinking space between them. Daniel broke the man's nose, dropped him with a kidney punch, and took the knife away from him.

After giving his statement to the cops, after the firefighters had come and gone, Daniel lay on his lumpy motel bed with the smell of burning chemicals lingering in his nostrils.

Thinking: *Screw it.*

Thus ended Daniel's acetic rebellion.

In the three years since, he'd made peace with the luxury. It wasn't as if the money he'd saved was being diverted to orphanages, he told himself. And he had to admit that his previous austerity had enabled him to indulge in that pesky sin of pride.

One of the seven deadlies. And one of the three to which Daniel remained vulnerable, the other two being lust and wrath.

Daniel sat at the desk in his executive suite at the downtown Atlanta Ritz-Carlton. To his side, the room service tray held the remains of dinner—filet mignon and Caesar salad. He was not a glutton and always left some food on his plate. He opened his notebook and reviewed his shorthand version of Giuseppe's transcripts.

Reverend Tim Trinity had done a lot of weather reporting during his tongues act and had given a few traffic and sports reports on the side. And sometimes he got lucky. He even predicted a ten-car pileup on the southbound I-95, just outside Savannah, which came to pass. Of course, pileups happen every day, and usually during the morning rush, when commuters haven't had their morning coffee. So the prediction was a high-percentage bet on Trinity's part. And, as Nick had mentioned, he got the Superbowl right, but so did most football fans, since the underdog lost.

"Trivial crap," Nick had called it. A true assessment, but far from complete. It wasn't all crystal ball stuff. Trinity also dispensed sage advice to anyone who could understand English spoken backwards at two-thirds speed.

He proclaimed Mahatma the best brand of rice for making jambalaya.

He cautioned against carrying a balance on high-interest credit cards.

And he said that human beings should love each other as brothers and sisters.

I told you it was gonna get weird.

Daniel put the notebook aside and moved his laptop to the center of the desk. He tapped on the spacebar, waking the computer. He'd left the browser open, and as the screen came to life, his uncle still smiled at him from the home page of the Tim Trinity Word of God Ministries website.

The website featured the standard evangelical *prosperity ministry* crap, illustrated with staged photos of clean-cut, healthy couples (white, black, brown, but everybody please stick to your own race and the opposite sex, the photos said) and their clean-cut, healthy, racially unambiguous children.

Everybody smiling like the world contained no injustice, no misery.

God wants you to be rich. God wants you to be well dressed, and He wants you to spend your leisure hours fishing, horseback riding, or strolling through the park with your family on a sunny day. God wants you to live in a gated community McMansion, drive a Mercedes, fly first class.

All this can be yours. All *you* have to do is sow that seed of faith by making a vow, and then start sending your money to the Tim Trinity Word of God Ministries.

And prosperity shall rain upon you like magic fairy dust.

Daniel knew the whole grift by heart. Knew every inch of it, snout to tail. After all, he was raised in it.

Uncle Tim was the twin brother of Daniel's mother. He had been Daniel's closest relative since the day Daniel was born. The day Daniel's mother died giving birth to him. The day his grieving father threw himself off the Greater New Orleans Bridge and into the Mississippi River, taking his own life and leaving Daniel orphaned.

There was a bio page on Trinity's website, and Daniel clicked through to read it. The biography waxed nostalgic about Trinity's years traveling the Southland in a Winnebago, town to town, tent to tent, healing the sick and saving souls. Alongside the text, there was a photograph of Trinity standing beside the rusty RV, taken when Daniel was seven. Daniel was not in the photo, but he recognized his shiny new bicycle leaning against the front bumper. Trinity had given him the bike for his seventh birthday.

He scrolled further down the page, moving past the photo, moving through the years, moving to where Trinity's life and his life were no longer intertwined. He stopped scrolling after Trinity quit the tent circuit and built a permanent church in the Mid-City neighborhood of New Orleans.

Trinity's church quickly grew prosperous, and he established the largest soup kitchen (the website called it a "nutritional center") in New Orleans, nourishing body and soul in the deeply impoverished Lower Ninth Ward. He still took his show on the road regularly, but the road was a series of airports and he rented arenas instead of pitching tents. A few years later, the *Tim Trinity Prosperity-Power Miracle Hour* premiered on late-night television across Louisiana, and pretty soon Trinity was buying time on cable networks with national reach.

In addition to running the soup kitchen, the Tim Trinity Word of God Ministries built fifty schools and dug five hundred clean-water wells in Africa and built a medical clinic in Haiti. A tiny fraction of the haul, Daniel figured, but just enough to make Trinity look legit and protect his tax-exempt status with Uncle Sam.

The bio said that God spoke to Reverend Tim after Trinity's church was destroyed by Hurricane Katrina and instructed him to relocate to Atlanta. Trinity obeyed.

At the bottom of the page was a quote:

"The righteous one, my servant, shall make many righteous, and he shall bear their iniquities." Isaiah 53:11

It was a strange choice, because it was a passage from the Old Testament. Or, as Trinity had always jokingly called it (behind closed doors), "the Jew book." But what was really strange, the thing that stopped Daniel cold, was that Isaiah 53 was held by Christians to be a prophecy of the life of Jesus, and placing it in this context, at the end of Tim Trinity's biography, seemed like an attempt to apply it to Trinity himself.

9:

Almighty God, whose blessed Son was led by the Spirit to be tempted by Satan: Come quickly to help us who are assaulted by many temptations; and, as you know the weaknesses of each of us, let each one find you mighty to save; through Jesus Christ your Son our Lord, who lives and reigns with you and the Holy Spirit, one God, now and forever. Amen.

—PRAYER FOR LENT

10:

Rome, Italy...

As he told the taxi driver to take him to Piazza del Popolo, Father Giuseppe Sorvino was careful to speak in broken Italian with a heavy German accent. He barked the destination as an order, waving a tourist map in the air between the seats, and he did not say please. Giuseppe's brother was a taxi driver and had complained about German tourists often enough—they were supposedly the only ones ruder than Americans. Accurate or not, that was the stereotype, and it fit Giuseppe's need to come across as a *type*, not an individual. Just another tourist. Forgettable.

But it's harder to be forgettable when you're missing an arm, so Giuseppe was wearing his special windbreaker. The left sleeve below the elbow was filled with foam rubber and a tennis ball was glued inside the elastic cuff and pinned inside the left pocket. It wouldn't pass close inspection, but if you stayed in motion, moving through people's field of view, you didn't jump out as an amputee. Otherwise he was dressed as any other casual tourist, with nice blue jeans and a lime-green polo shirt under the windbreaker. Nothing to identify him as a priest.

Sticking with bad Italian and still holding the map out, he added, "I know where it is, so do not get the idea to take me for a long ride."

The driver sneered and turned to face the road. "*Si, mein Führer,*" he said as he threw the Fiat into gear.

At the west end of the piazza, Giuseppe told the driver to stop, paid the fare, and got out beside the fountain of Neptune and his two pet dolphins. He walked—not too quickly—toward the center of the vast oval, which had served in centuries past as a favorite location for public executions. Reaching the center, he put on his sunglasses and stopped at the Egyptian obelisk of Ramesses II.

The obelisk had been brought to Rome by Augustus in 10 BC and later moved to this spot in 1589, and every Roman knew its history. Giuseppe had seen it thousands of times, but he stopped and pretended to be a German seeing it for the first time. He walked slowly around it while scanning the tourists milling about the piazza to be sure he wasn't followed. Then he shoved the map in his windbreaker and pulled a pack of cigarettes and a lighter from the back pocket of his jeans. He strode to the east side of the piazza, where he lit a cigarette and puffed away, not enjoying it. He normally smoked Marlboro Lights, but for the next taxi driver he would be French, and so these were Gitanes Brunes, which carried a distinctive odor that would linger in his hair.

This time he spoke French, with a perfect Parisian accent. *"Je vais a la Trinità dei Monti, s'il vous plaît."* He checked over his shoulder as the taxi pulled into traffic. No one was following. He breathed slow and deep to calm his nerves, again fighting the urge to touch the stump end of his left arm.

It happened whenever he was particularly tired or stressed, this feeling of the phantom limb. Years ago it had been painful, like paper cuts on his fingertips, bee stings on his forearm. The pain had faded over time, but what lingered was the aggravating feeling that he *had* fingers, a hand, a forearm, where there were none. The doctors had told him to apply sensory stimulation to the skin covering the stump whenever the phantom limb reappeared. They said this would train his brain to stop imagining the missing appendage. And it worked, temporarily, but the damn thing always came back. After five years, Giuseppe had just about given up hope that it would ever go away completely.

The driver stopped in front of the French church. Giuseppe waited until the taxi was out of sight before crossing the street and descending the Spanish Steps, navigating around tourists and college kids, all the way down to the Piazza di Spagna and past the Fontana della Barcaccia, which to Giuseppe's eye was the least interesting fountain in Rome. He crossed the square and rounded the corner to a small newsagent and tobacco shop—the sign above the door read *Edicola Moderna*.

Giuseppe entered and browsed magazines while the old man behind the counter announced he was closing for lunch. Once the shop was empty of customers, the old man looked at him and said, "Lock the door."

Giuseppe locked the door and stepped forward to the counter, now rubbing his stump through the windbreaker. "I need to speak with Carter Ames."

The old man shook his head. "You have something to report, you file a report, let it work its way up the chain. Foundation protocol."

"This is not just a report. And we don't have time."

The old man looked at him for almost a full minute. "Do you know what you're asking?"

"I do." Giuseppe scratched his stump harder, willing his phantom hand to recede. "I do understand. But it's already in motion and they've sent a priest to investigate. Tell Mr. Ames it is about a preacher named Tim Trinity. And tell him I've never seen anything like it."

11:

Emory University – Atlanta, Georgia...

Professor Cindy Elder, head of Speech Pathology at Emory University, led Daniel into her book-lined office and offered him a seat. "I haven't spoken to Father O'Connor since my wedding," she said. Then she peered over the rims of her elegant glasses. "Sorry to say, I'm a bit of a lapsed Catholic."

Daniel smiled. "We're all lapsed, in one way or another. Anyway, I came for your professional advice. I promise I'm not here to measure your faith." Then he added, "I told Father O'Connor I needed the best."

The professor seemed appropriately flattered. "Well, I'm happy to help in any way I can."

Daniel opened his notebook. "If I wanted to learn how to speak backwards, how would I go about that?"

Cindy Elder's eyebrows rose. "I beg your pardon?"

"Speaking English backwards, say, so if you recorded it and played it in reverse and sped it up a bit, it would sound normal."

Cindy Elder shook her head and smiled. "I'm guessing you don't know anything about speech pathology."

"You're guessing right," said Daniel.

She picked up the telephone receiver, punched in a number. "Gerry, is the sound lab free? Great, meet me there in five. Thanks." She hung up the phone and stood. "Let's go," she said.

✠ ✠ ✠

The lab looked like a scaled-down control room at a recording studio—a large mixing board on a counter, facing a window that looked onto a small room with microphones and sound-deadening foam lining the walls. Alongside the mixing board was a computer screen and a panel with various recording devices and visual sound monitors and other gizmos.

Cindy Elder introduced Daniel to Gerry, a graduate student who looked like a California surfer dude. Daniel told Gerry what he was after—a way to speak English backwards at two-thirds speed so it sounded natural reversed and sped up.

Gerry laughed, incredulous. "You serious?"

"Sure. Why not?"

"'Cause it's not possible, Padre." He caught himself. "Mind if I call you Padre?"

"Whatever makes you comfortable."

"Cool." Gerry smiled. "I could tell you were one of those hip priests." He flipped a couple switches on the mixing board, brought up a couple of faders. "Here, check it out." He pointed to a microphone on the counter. "Say your name into the mic."

Daniel leaned forward, said, "Daniel Byrne."

Gerry tapped on the computer keyboard, and Daniel's voice came through the monitors. Gerry tapped some more. "Here's what it sounds like backward. Listen carefully, I'll play it a few times."

Daniel listened as Gerry played his name, in his own voice, backwards, five times. Gerry pointed at the microphone again. "Now try and say what you just heard."

Daniel did.

"Again."

Daniel did it three more times. Gerry tapped on the keyboard some more, recording Daniel's efforts. "Now I'll run *that* backward," Gerry said.

It didn't sound close to natural. It didn't even sound much like his name.

"But with practice," said Daniel, "I'd get better."

"Not better enough. With practice, you could speak it so we'd understand your name clearly, but it would never sound natural. And your name is very simple, no problematic consonant digraphs like 'st' or 'th' or 'dl'. Add to that, you want to speak it, what? Slowed down by a third?"

Cindy Elder said, "Gerry's right. You could work with a speech pathologist for ten years, and you still wouldn't be able to pull it off. I just don't think it's possible."

Daniel pointed at the computer screen. "Gerry, can you access the Internet on that?"

"Can do, Padre."

After giving them a quick summary of the Trinity Anomaly, Daniel directed Gerry to the Tim Trinity Word of God Ministries website, to the page where Trinity's broadcasts were archived as Quicktime movies. Checking his transcript notes, he said, "April twenty-third broadcast, beginning forty-two minutes in, lasting for a minute-thirty. Can you record that?"

Gerry did, and they all watched as Tim Trinity did his tongues routine.

"Audio manipulation?" asked Daniel.

"Must be," said Cindy Elder.

"Looks smooth too," said Gerry. "But you can't fool *el waveform monitor*." He flicked the switch on a little round monitor, and the screen glowed green, like an old radar screen. Then he tapped on the computer keyboard, brought the downloaded video to the end of the tongues act. "Speed it by a third, you said?"

"Yeah, he speaks it at two-thirds normal speed."

Gerry let out a broad smile. "Whoa, dude."

"What?"

"Two-thirds. That's 66.6 percent. Number of the Beast." Then he made a noise like a cartoon ghost. "Oooh, spooky."

"Gerry, please," said Cindy Elder.

"Just sayin', is all," Gerry shrugged. He tapped the percentage into his computer, spoke to the video image of Trinity on the screen, "Get ready to be busted, Mr. Holy Roller." He hit the enter key.

Trinity gave the same weather report Daniel had heard in Nick's office, his inflections sounding completely natural.

Green lines danced around the screen of the waveform monitor, mapping the audio profile of Trinity's speech patterns. Gerry stared hard at the screen, and his smile disappeared.

"Damn," he said.

"What do you see, Gerry?" said Cindy Elder.

"That's the problem. I don't see anything. Can't believe it, but I don't see any evidence that the audio's been messed with."

"There must be a mistake," said the professor. "He just said 'thunderstorm.' Impossible to say backward. Would never sound natural."

"I calibrated the monitors this morning. I'm telling you, this is for real."

Daniel stood stock-still, feeling like the floor had just been removed from under his feet. Like the dream of falling that jerks you back from the edge of sleep.

12:

Las Vegas, Nevada...

William Lamech sat behind bulletproof glass in the wood and leather lounge of his Bentley limousine, a crocodile-skin briefcase on his lap. Inside the briefcase was something more explosive than dynamite, more dangerous than powdered anthrax.

Inside was something that could take down the entire gambling industry, or at least the sports books. And William Lamech was *not* going to let that happen, whatever the fuck he had to do. He'd been in the gambling business fifty-three years, had survived the cowboys and mob wars and the F-B-fucking-I, all while quietly building a personal fortune of over one hundred million dollars and earning many times that amount for his employers. He had a talent for turning peril into opportunity, and he thought he'd seen it all. But he'd never seen a threat remotely like the one now sitting in the briefcase on his lap.

Lamech was not your average septuagenarian. At seventy-three, he still swam lengths in the casino pool an hour each morning, did crunches and push-ups in reps of fifty, and worked with weights three days a week. People often said he wore his age like Clint Eastwood. He preferred to think of himself more like Jack Palance, but most people had already forgotten Palance, a mere fifteen years after the great man's death.

You're here, you're gone, and no one remembers. Not a complaint, just a statement of fact. While Lamech intended to stick around as long as he could, he wasn't afraid of melting into the sands of forgotten history when his time came. In fact, he'd already started melting.

Time was, everyone in Las Vegas knew his name, and the important people in Chicago knew it too. Time was, he was a celebrity in this goddamn town. *Feel like a little gambling, Mr. Lamech?* A nod of his head, and a tray of checks would appear. *Dino would be honored, Mr. Lamech, if you'd drop by his dressing room at the Sands for a drink before the show.* And to have William Lamech seen in your restaurant was always worth a complimentary surf-n-turf and a bottle of your finest champagne.

And then Las Vegas changed. Wall Street muscled out Chicago, and now corporate accountants ran the joint. Many of the better restaurants still refused to present Lamech with a bill, but outside the sports books, most of the younger casino workers didn't know who the hell he was. They knew they *should* know, knew he was important, and always treated him with respect, but the days of widespread fawning were long past. And that was OK with him. He'd enjoyed the high profile of his middle years, but at a certain age it befits a man to gracefully yield the spotlight. Anyway, he'd never really been in it for the fame; it was always about the money.

And he was still making a pantload of money, from both his legitimate casino operation and from the less legitimate network of backroom bookies he personally bankrolled in over a dozen cities.

The corporate accountants now running Las Vegas didn't much care for the old-school Chicago guys, but the sports book was the one part of a casino that couldn't be managed by numbers alone. To maximize profit, you needed a deep and practical understanding of both gambling psychology and the dynamics of group behavior. And you needed a reliable network of informants to let you know when the fix was in, who was hiding an injury, and the sordid personal troubles of various athletes.

Each year more than three billion dollars was wagered in Las Vegas sports books, and the books held onto 4.5 percent of it. If your hold dropped below 4 percent, you found yourself looking for a new career. If it hit 5 percent, you were a superstar. William Lamech's sports book was one of the largest in town, with more than thirty massive screens on the wall and plush seating with personal monitors at each station. And Lamech's book averaged a 5.6 percent hold. He was the best there was, and the corporate accountants just had to shut the hell up and kiss his ring. Much had changed in the Nevada desert, but gambling was still gambling and money was still money, and William Lamech had faced all comers for fifty-three years and hadn't lost a fight yet.

Whoever was behind this strange new threat had miscalculated, Lamech told himself. And whatever leverage they thought they had, it wouldn't be enough. He was a tough old bastard; if they forced him to prove it, he would prove it.

And woe be to them.

☘ ☘ ☘

"Well I think it's bullshit," said Michael Passarelli. "I don't believe it for a second."

"I don't buy it either," said Jared Case. "It must've been recorded after the game."

"A new variation on past-posting," added Pete DeFazio. Heads nodded around the boardroom table as the others murmured their agreement.

William Lamech knew that the hardest part would be getting them to believe it. Nobody rises to the top of a sports book by being a pigeon, and these were twelve of the sharpest and most skeptical minds in the gambling business. Before playing the DVD and the decoded backward audio, he'd warned them it would seem incredible.

"It's not past-posting," said Lamech, "I had the broadcast dates verified independently. He's actually predicting the outcomes. And he's always right." He paused to let it sink in. "I know how you feel—I couldn't believe it either, at first. And I still don't know how he's doing it. But he *is* doing it, and if this breaks public..." Lamech zapped the television off. He took his time, made eye contact around the long glass table. "You all know me. I don't play jokes. This is for real."

DeFazio whistled through his teeth. "Goddamn," he said. "Where'd you get this?"

"Couple days ago, one of my bookies in Atlanta. Customer of his—some kid, audio engineer with a gambling problem—stumbled on it, brought it to the bookie, hoping to settle his debt with it. He didn't believe the kid, naturally, but the kid played the tapes for him, and he was smart enough to call me in on it. It checked out."

"What's Trinity's game?" said Darwyn Jones from the other end of the table. Next to Lamech, Jones was the smartest man in the room. Maybe just as smart. "You think it's a shakedown?"

"He hasn't contacted us," said Lamech.

"Who's backing him?" asked Passarelli.

"We don't know," said Lamech.

"Well, that's just great."

"Goddamn," repeated DeFazio. "We can't just wait. I mean, he predicted the fuckin' *Superbowl*." He picked up the sheet of paper on the table before him—his copy of the decoded transcript—and read it over. "He got it *exactly*. He even nailed the over/under. And he said it ten days before game time. If that had gotten out…"

Jared Case broke the silence. "It woulda killed us. Our margins are tight enough in this economy."

"We need to act now," said DeFazio.

"Act how, exactly?" said Sam Babcock.

"I think," said Darwyn Jones, "that William has an idea." All eyes shifted to Lamech.

"I do." Lamech sipped some Perrier; made them all wait for it. "We're in the information business, gentlemen. So let's get some. The preacher must have his own sins, everyone does. Let's find out what they are, and see what leverage that gives us with Trinity."

"I like it," said Darwyn Jones.

Once again, heads began to nod around the table.

"You think the preacher will play ball?" said Case.

"I don't know the man, and I don't know what leverage we'll find. But one way or another I think I can convince him it would be better to work with us than against us."

"And if he refuses?"

"If he refuses…we'll jump off that bridge when we get to it." Lamech gave the men a reassuring smile. "But one way or another, we *will* silence Tim Trinity."

13:

Atlanta, Georgia...

It was starting again. Tim Trinity felt it bearing down on him, like the dull ache before a heavy rain, pressure building inside his head, scrambling his thoughts, blurring his focus. Then the voices, quiet at first, but growing steadily louder and more critical. It always started like this, and he knew the tongues would be on him if he didn't take action soon.

How long since he'd called his connection? He checked his watch. Ten minutes. How long did he say it would take? Half an hour. OK, another twenty minutes to wait. He could hold off the tongues another twenty minutes, couldn't he?

He did, barely. Pacing furious circles around the living room of his Buckhead mansion, sweating profusely, peeking out between the front curtains every minute or two. By the time his dealer arrived, he was twitching and starting to babble. But he got the transaction done fast, and the dealer didn't stay for conversation.

Trinity's movements were becoming spastic, but he managed his way into the den, got the small Ziploc baggie open, and poured two parallel white lines onto the coffee table. He rolled a twenty-dollar bill into a straw and shoved it into his left nostril. Snorted the first line and was immediately rewarded with an icy explosion of cocaine clarity, coating the inside of his skull from front to back.

The voices faded away.

The pressure dissipated.

His head cleared.

He switched to his right nostril and snorted the second line.

The Second Line. No parade permit, no responsibilities, just twirl your umbrella and dance all the way to the French Quarter. The second line. Laissez les bon temps roulez...

But no. The cocaine was medicinal, not recreational. And New Orleans was the past. It wouldn't be the same anyway, even if he could go back.

Not after that bitch, Katrina.

✤ ✤ ✤

When the voices began, in the aftermath of the hurricane, Trinity put it down to a delayed stress reaction. It seemed everyone who stayed through the storm was suffering from post-traumatic stress disorder. Why should he be immune? Cops and firefighters and doctors and nurses stayed because they were required to stay. The infirm also stayed, some abandoned in their homes or at the entrance of overcrowded hospitals, others attended by loved ones who couldn't bear to leave them behind. And then there were those simply too stupid, too crazy, too lazy, too stoned, or too poor to leave.

Trinity fell into another category. Too greedy. He'd stayed for Andrew in '92, and it earned him a lot of credibility with the *po' folk*. He figured if he rode out Katrina, he could be on-scene for the reopening of his soup kitchen in the Lower Ninth Ward, and he could snag some good press. Hell, if he played this right, he might even get interviewed by Anderson Cooper or that Soledad babe, get on CNN.

Something to shove up the ass of the IRS, next time those fuckers questioned his *legitimacy*.

But it didn't play out like that.

New Orleanians are no strangers to weather, and while Katrina remained a category three storm, there was much talk about who would be hosting the hurricane party on each block. But as the storm passed through the Gulf, she gained strength, and talk turned to evacuation.

Trinity never seriously considered leaving. He owned a six-thousand-square-foot stone mansion in Lakeview, and he could ride out anything nature cared to send his way. He did urge his congregation to evacuate, and they did. But before they got out, he conscripted a half dozen of their strapping teenage boys. The boys hauled 120 jugs of Kentwood Springs water from the neighborhood Rite Aid to Trinity's mansion. They boarded up the massive ground floor windows and helped him secure the storm shutters on the second and third floors. They sandbagged the front of Trinity's three-car garage. When the boys' parents picked them up, Trinity gave each a thousand dollars in cash, for "traveling money."

On August 28, 2005, Katrina was upgraded to category five. At ten a.m., just twenty hours before the storm would make landfall, Mayor Ray Nagin held a press conference and made the evacuation mandatory. The National Guard was being called in, and the Louisiana Superdome was being set up as a shelter-of-last-resort for those who couldn't get out in time. About ten thousand would take refuge there, and many of them would later wish they hadn't.

It would be a bad storm, but the roads out of town were already jammed, and Trinity's mansion was thoroughly battened down. In addition to the stormproofing, Trinity had Robért Fresh Market deliver enough non-perishable food to feed a family of a hundred for a week. He had a portable shortwave radio and a waterproof flashlight and a ton of batteries, a Colt .45 semi-automatic pistol and seventy-two hollow point bullets, if it came to that. He was ready.

During the long night that followed, Trinity buzzed with anticipation, unable to sleep. News reports suggested that maybe one hundred thousand people would be unable to get out in time. There would be plenty of hungry mouths to feed when he re-opened his soup kitchen in the Lower Nine.

The wealthy of New Orleans had long since evacuated and Tim Trinity was the only soul left in Lakeview. But the "Hurricane Party" is a venerable tradition, so as the black sky lightened to gray, he mixed a very large Sazerac—to the original recipe, with real absinthe, and cognac instead of rye—and proceeded to get thoroughly drunk in preparation for the show.

Katrina made landfall at 6:10 a.m. on August 29, 2005, with sustained winds of 140 miles per hour. For a while, the radio said she was veering east and everything would be OK. But then the radio announcements changed, and Katrina slammed into the Crescent City with a storm surge of twenty-two feet.

People say a hurricane sounds like a freight train. It doesn't, not exactly, but the analogy is close as dammit. Tim Trinity ambled through his mansion, from empty room to empty room, listening to the approach of nature's freight train, sipping Sazerac and congratulating himself on his place in the world.

His dad had been an ineffectual door-to-door salesman—vacuum cleaners, encyclopedias, aluminum siding, whatever he could get a job peddling—and his mother had been a poor housewife, because Dad wouldn't cotton to a wife who worked outside the home, even though he never earned a decent living. Tim and his little sister Iris never knew real hunger, but they knew red beans and rice, not just on Mondays but sometimes three, four days a week. They knew the shame of having to lie to bill collectors on the phone, saying, "My daddy ain't home just now," while Dad stood quietly to one side, grinning like it was a game. And they lived their childhood in threadbare clothing that had been worn hundreds of times by older kids and donated to the VOA thrift shop. They grew up, cheek by jowl, in a cramped Uptown shotgun that Mom kept ruthlessly clean.

Young Tim grew to hate his father for how easily the old man resigned himself to failure. He vowed to make a million, and he had, many times over. The rickety childhood house on Ursulines would probably not be standing after today. But this place would shrug Katrina off like a bad idea.

Trinity refreshed his drink, wandered downstairs and faced the front door, which rattled a little against the gusting wind and lashing rain. But the door was three-inch cypress and it wasn't going anywhere. He raised his glass in a toasting gesture.

"Fuck you, storm," he said. "Do your worst. You can't touch me."

He took a long swallow from the glass and realized that he was drunker than he'd intended to be. Walking back upstairs required some concentration.

He missed the rest of the storm. He'd passed out, fully clothed, atop leopard-print silk sheets on his king-size bed in the second-floor master bedroom.

But he dreamed the fury.

14:

In his dream, Trinity lay on his back, lengthwise in the middle of the railway tracks just riverside of Tchoupitoulas, while a freight train thundered over him, inches from his face. The sound was earsplitting and the turbulence threatened to jostle his body against the wheels. His heart pounded against his ribs, and he forced himself to breathe. Then there was another sound, like an elephant groaning, and he turned his head to the right, looking through the blur of rushing wheels toward the mighty Mississippi. A wave rolled down the length of the river, cresting the banks. Then another, and another, and with each wave the river swelled over the embankment, and now water flowed steadily into the basin of the rail yards, toward the track where Trinity lay. It seemed the train would never end. He guessed that maybe twenty cars had passed over him, but he couldn't raise his head to look down and see how many more cars were still to come. The water was flowing fast now, splashing against his side. If the train didn't end soon, Trinity would surely drown.

And in a flash, he knew. The train would not end in time, and he would drown. And he knew why. Trinity knew this was God's punishment for his unbelief.

He woke from his nightmare in the silence that followed the storm and realized it was the silence that woke him. The storm had passed. He shook off the dream's residue, grabbed the flashlight, and staggered to the bathroom, his head pounding. There was a box of BC headache powders in the cabinet, and Trinity fumbled a couple out of the box and poured the bitter powder onto his tongue. He spun the faucet and stuck his mouth under the tap. Nothing.

Then he remembered. *Right, of course. There wouldn't be.* He reached for the jug he'd placed next to the sink and guzzled warm spring water.

The house was like a sauna. Out in the hallway, he aimed the flashlight down the stairs, expecting to see a little water. He saw a lot. The entrance hall was waist-deep and rising. He watched as a chair floated by the staircase. *Shit.* He moved back to the bedroom, opened the hurricane shutters, and stuck his head outside.

The sky was a solid sheet of blue, the sun white-hot on his face. The air was thick and heavy and smelled of salt and mud. Aside from the soft murmur of moving water, there was no sound. No barking dogs, no chirping birds, no human voices, and no machinery of human civilization. Nothing. Most of the trees on the street were down, and those that stood were stripped of their leaves, naked limbs hanging down like broken arms. There were no power lines, and the poles stood at odd angles, like drunken sentries guarding the abandoned neighborhood. The entire street was a lake, and the muddy water flowed so quickly he thought he could see the level rising as he watched.

So much water.

Trinity craned his head to the left. The water was about chest-high against the doors of his garage. Behind the doors, his tricked-out Cadillacs would be underwater, ruined.

He turned away from the window, switched on the shortwave radio. The radio told him that the worst had indeed happened. The Seventeenth Street Canal levee had given way, and Lake Pontchartrain was now fulfilling its destiny, annexing Lakeview and flooding on into Mid-City, Carrollton, Gentilly, City Park…

Fifty-two other levees were breached, over 80 percent of the city now flooded or flooding.

So much water. And it kept on coming.

A few hours later, Trinity's entrance hall was completely submerged, the water halfway up the staircase. Outside was still silence, occasionally punctuated by the whirring blades of a Coast Guard helicopter and the patter of distant gunfire. A dead German shepherd floated down the street. A few minutes later, a ten-foot gator swam by.

"OK, joke's over," Trinity said aloud. "This shit ain't funny no more." He'd planned on camping out for a few days, was well provisioned, but now he just wanted the hell out. He could come back later.

Trinity set up on the balcony off the front guest room, and the next time he heard a helicopter nearby, he started shooting flares into the air.

No luck.

The pistol fire continued in the distance, more frequently now, and the radio said New Orleans had slipped into a state of anarchy. The radio said tens of thousands were stranded on rooftops, and no one was picking them up. Where the hell was the government?

It was a long night.

The next day passed like the first. Trinity ate canned food and drank warm bottled water and fired a flare whenever a helicopter came close. Then, as the sun settled on the horizon, another helicopter came near, and this time they spotted the flare, lowered a line, and raised him into the sky.

Below him, the city—*his* city—was drowning and burning at the same time. Trinity counted the buildings ablaze above the muddy water, until he couldn't stand it anymore and had to close his eyes.

A young man in a Coast Guard uniform got Trinity strapped into the copter, and the side door slid shut, cutting off the din of the blades. He gave a thumbs-up to the pilot, and the bird veered west. The young man took a long look out the side window and yelled to the pilot, "Incredible, isn't it?"

The pilot yelled back, "Incredible don't come close. It's fuckin' *biblical*, man."

The helicopter flew low over Trinity's ruined city, but he kept his eyes shut until they put down at Louis Armstrong New Orleans International Airport, in the suburb of Jefferson Parish, where a triage center had been established. Trinity was quickly examined by a medic and put on a refugee bus to Baton Rouge, where he sat next to a very old black woman who'd lost her wig and apologized profusely for her bald head.

"Not a thing," Trinity said as the bus rocked into gear. "Hell, if 'Fess were still alive, he'd be signing songs about you." He laughed with good nature and held his hand out to her. "Tim Trinity."

The old woman gasped. "Oh, lordy, you're Reverend Tim!"

"Yes, ma'am."

She took his hand. "Thought you looked familiar, but I gots me some bad cataracts, can't see for shit no more." She smiled at him, lips pulled back from dark gums. She'd lost her dentures in the storm too. "I'm Miss Carpenter. You call me Emogene."

"Good to know you, Miss Emogene."

Miss Emogene looked out the window at the dark road ahead. "You got kin in Baton Rouge? I'm blessed with a daughter, lives up this way."

"No, ma'am. But I'm not staying long, couple days maybe. Soon as they let me, I'll be back to doing the Lord's work. Got me a soup kitchen in the Lower Nine."

The old woman's face grew haunted, and her smoky eyes filled Trinity with great terror. "I just came from there. I mean to tell you, you ain't going back there."

"Sure I am."

"Boy, you don't understand. There *ain't* no Lower Nine no more. It's… *gone.*"

Miss Emogene retreated into her sadness and they rode on in silence. Trinity looked around and now saw that he was the only white person on the bus. A middle-aged man across the aisle turned on an old transistor radio, and the bus went quiet as all strained to hear the latest.

It was bad news on top of bad news. The old woman was right—the Ninth Ward had been wiped off the map, and the list of devastated neighborhoods included most of the lower-income parts of town.

It was at that moment Trinity realized he was finished as a prosperity preacher in New Orleans. His income base had been cut off at the knees. The market had collapsed. They say there's no man so poor he can't find a few dollars to spend on whiskey and salvation, but this was something else entirely. This was about survival.

The Lower Nine was gone, but now the whole city needed a soup kitchen. Sure, Trinity could go back in a few days and look like a hero on CNN, but what would it gain him? There'd be no income from the locals, probably for years. And the infrastructure was decimated. How long before he could get his show back on the air to draw money from the rest of the country?

A long time, if he stayed.

By the time they reached Baton Rouge, Trinity had made the decision to start over in Atlanta. He had plenty of money in the bank, could be up and running in a month or two. And he'd always flattered himself he could compete with the big boys in the big city. This was his chance to prove it.

In Atlanta, Trinity bought a large warehouse in the impoverished Vine City neighborhood. Within a month it was decorated with a stage pulpit and audience seating, outfitted with cameras and lighting and a video control room. He was back in business. In the second month, he built his flock, and by the end of the third month, he was back on the air. His new church was an instant hit, and the money poured in like never before.

But he hadn't counted on the voices.

When they started, he put it down to stress, and an Atlanta doctor prescribed Valium. When that didn't work, the doctor tried him on Ativan, then Xanax, then Serax. When none of the anti-anxiety drugs worked, he moved on to anti-depressants: Prozac, Zoloft, Effexor. They didn't work either.

After over a year of pharmaceutical futility, Trinity resigned himself to living with the voices. But then the voices strengthened, and soon they brought the tongues. Tongues that came upon him like epileptic fits, completely beyond his control. The fits often came during his sermons, and they were good theater, but they also came upon him when he wasn't doing his act. In the shower or driving his car, seemingly at random. They often woke him in the night, and he became exhausted. He knew he couldn't keep going this way much longer. Something had to give.

Then one night, Trinity sat in front of the television, flipping channels, afraid to fall asleep. He stopped on a documentary about addiction, and he heard a cocaine addict say that coke silenced the voices in his head.

Trinity had never wanted anything to do with illegal drugs, had never even smoked grass, but he'd never in his life felt this desperate. He made his first drug buy the very next morning. And that night, when his head started pounding and the voices came upon him, he snorted his first line.

The voices disappeared.

15:

Daniel stood in the shadows of Tim Trinity's backyard, snapping photos through the window of his uncle's den. Snapping photos of his uncle taking cocaine. He lowered the camera slowly, thinking: *What the hell did you expect?*

But whatever he'd expected, he sure as hell hadn't expected this.

Daniel had seen enough, and it was getting late. Time to terminate surveillance. He scaled the fence, dropping down into the wooded ravine that backed onto Trinity's property. He moved quietly through the brush, listening to the singing of frogs and crickets, the chatter of distant coyotes. Moved to the ravine's public access way, at the end of the street.

He walked among silent mansions to where he'd parked his rental car, wondering what could've gone so wrong in Tim Trinity's life that he was now snorting coke. He'd always been a drinker, sure, but for Southerners—and especially New Orleanians—alcohol is like mama's milk.

In all their years together, Daniel had never seen his uncle do anything as flagrantly self-destructive as what he'd just witnessed.

What could've gone so wrong?

✤ ✤ ✤

Back in his hotel room, Daniel sat on the bed, propped up by huge pillows, his Bible open in his lap. An e-mail had come in from Nick. The e-mail read:

Dan,

Maybe I shouldn't be, but I'm worried about you. I know being with your uncle will be difficult, and I feel somewhat responsible, having allowed you to take this case. But I need you to stay focused on your assignment, whatever personal issues arise.

Read the Book of Job tonight, and meditate on it.

That's an order, not a suggestion.

Hang tough, kiddo. I know you can do this.

–Fr. Nick

Daniel had struggled with the Book of Job in his youth and had never really come to terms with it. Reading it again didn't help any. To Daniel, the God presented in Job was like a little boy pulling the wings off flies, just to watch them flail about. He seemed shallow, cruel, and ego-driven. He caused Job, his most righteous servant, to suffer excruciating pain and unfathomable loss, for no good reason. No, worse. For a juvenile, self-indulgent reason: because God had the cosmic equivalent of a bar bet going with Satan.

Daniel did not like this God very much.

The priests who took Daniel in at thirteen had tried to reframe the Book of Job for him. They said that the story does not tell us *why* the virtuous suffer, it tells us *how* to suffer. It doesn't explain the existence of evil, but it tells us that the existence of evil is one of God's many mysteries.

The priests were big on God's Many Mysteries. It was their default response to the most troubling of Daniel's many questions. But Daniel had not come to the Church to embrace mysteries. He'd come in search of a miracle.

He'd lived the first dozen years of his life believing that his uncle was a real apostle, working real miracles on God's behalf. For a boy who'd killed his own mother while being born and caused his father's suicide, this was no small thing. God had chosen Tim Trinity as His messenger on earth, and He'd chosen Daniel to be His messenger's companion. That meant God did not despise Daniel. It meant Daniel was worthy of love, despite everything.

That was how his uncle had explained it, and it did make things better. It became the One True Thing that Daniel could hold on to and feel good about, despite the ugly way his life had begun. Trinity told the boy that God loved him, and Trinity always treated him with love, even when drinking. And he wasn't a bad guardian either. He always made sure the boy did his schoolwork on the road, made sure he passed his exams when they returned to New Orleans.

It was a strange childhood, but not an unhappy one. There were other preachers' kids to play with on the tent revival circuit, and Daniel learned many things on the road. Tim taught Daniel how to talk his way out of a jam and—*if that don't work*—how to slip a punch and run away and—*if that don't work*—how to deliver a punch and—*if that don't work*—how to shoot a pistol. "Man who lives on the road gotta take *responsibility* for his physical safety." And so Daniel learned things, shooting tin cans and sparring with Tim, that the kids in school would not learn until they were adults, if ever.

But as Daniel grew, so grew his doubts. By the time he reached age ten, willful blindness was required not to see the flimflam, the con artistry and sleight-of-hand at work behind the miraculous healings Trinity performed. Living in a perpetual state of denial was exhausting. After a few years, at the age of thirteen, he just couldn't keep it up, couldn't *not* see it for what it was. One day something just snapped, and it all came crashing down. Like a house of cards.

He swallowed the pain, hiding it from his uncle, until they got back home to New Orleans. The first night home, as Tim slept, Daniel slipped silently out his bedroom window and shimmied down the drainpipe. He walked to the nearest Catholic church, knocked on the door, and declared himself an orphan, looking for a miracle.

The priests took him in. They called in a doctor, who looked the boy over and pronounced him physically fit, and over the next few days they administered a series of tests to assess his psychological condition—*intellectually curious, emotionally guarded, spiritually deprived*—followed by exams to assess his academic standing, which allowed him to skip a year in school.

After a few schoolyard punch-ups established Daniel's position in the hierarchy of boys, he settled into life at the church's boarding school reasonably well. But the priests were concerned about his ongoing "anger issues" and got him into boxing. They said it would help him "work it out of his system."

Daniel's laptop speakers pinged, bringing him back from his thoughts. He reached across the bed and drew the computer near. A chat window had opened on the screen—someone was trying to make contact.

The message said: **Daniel Byrne?**

He read the username in the chat window: PapaLegba. He didn't know anyone who went by that handle, but he knew what it meant. Papa Legba was a prominent *loa* in voodoo mythology. Guardian of the Crossroads, facilitator of communication between the material and spirit worlds, between the living and the dead. A storyteller—and sometimes a trickster.

Daniel typed: **This is Daniel Byrne. Who am I speaking with?**

After a few seconds, the person on the other end wrote: **And you will know the truth, and the truth will make you free.**

Daniel typed: **John 8:32. Who are you?**

You seek the truth. Trinity is the path. We can help.

Daniel typed: **The most helpful thing you can do is to stop hiding behind a screen name. Who are you?**

Trinity is the path. Walk the path. We're watching.

The chat window disappeared. PapaLegba had logged off.

16:

Northbound I-20, near Thomson, Georgia…

Tim Trinity watched the white lines of the highway disappear under his car. He was still feeling jittery from the cocaine. He hated the stuff. Sure, it came on feeling good, silenced the voices and stilled the tongues, but it always left him edgy. Made him acutely aware of the existence of his skin.

A creepy feeling, and why anyone took this shit for fun, was beyond him.

Worse, it made him feel weak. It reminded him of so many of the people he used to see lined up at his soup kitchen, reminded him of lives broken by poverty and addiction.

Trinity had the cruise control set at sixty. It's the little things that trip you up—a speeding ticket, for example—and he was too smart for that. He kept it below the limit and didn't stop until he reached the airport six miles southwest of Columbia, South Carolina, where he rented a car. Trinity's car was a crystal-red Cadillac Escalade SUV with gold-plated trim, massive rims, and a Georgia vanity plate that read: TRINITY. Switching to a rental was a no-brainer.

Now he left the airport in a nondescript sedan with South Carolina plates. He took Platt Springs Road to West Columbia, drove straight through downtown—Triangle City, the locals called it.

Jimmy Swaggart had once owned the world, thought Trinity, and then he started acting like a complete idiot, picking up streetwalkers near downtown New Orleans methadone clinics, taking them to the hooker motels out on Airline and Chef Menteur, eventually giving most of his business to one girl.

The man was just begging to be caught, and in due course, he was.

Still, you had to give him major credit for his *I have sinned against you: I beg for your forgiveness* sermon—it was a truly masterful performance. And it worked; he got forgiveness. But just three years later, the spiritually rehabilitated, new-and-improved Brother Swaggart got busted with a hooker again, when cops pulled him over for a minor traffic violation.

Despite his stupid behavior, Swaggart was actually a very smart man. He knew he couldn't just go on television and turn on the waterworks for the cameras a second time and beg forgiveness. That shit only works once. No, the second time Swaggart got caught with his pants down, he went on television to address his critics, faced the camera and said simply: *The Lord told me it's flat none of your business.*

Ballsy move. Ballsy as hell. And it saved Swaggart's ministry. Sure, he suffered a sharp decline in his flock, but he stayed in the game, and eighteen years on, he was still working the TV preacher grift, still making millions. Of course the haul would never be what it could've been had he been a little more careful with his hookers, but he made a good living.

Trinity passed the girls on the corner without slowing and congratulated himself for being careful in all the ways Swaggart had been reckless. He knew that if he were ever caught, there wasn't a soul on earth who'd believe the truth.

You paid a hooker to do what?? Sure you did…

So he had to be careful.

He continued north across the Saluda River, then slowed as he passed the Dreammakers strip club, but didn't stop. Three blocks later, he pulled into the parking lot of a Waffle House where a lot of the girls came for a bite to eat after their shifts ended at Dreammakers.

Trinity cut the engine. He reached into his breast pocket and withdrew a well-worn stainless steel flask. Swallowed a couple ounces of bourbon, screwed the top back on. Then, as he always did, he turned the flask over and searched for the message on the convex side. The engraved inscription worn faint by so many trips in and out of so many pockets over so many years. He had to tilt the flask and catch the light just so for it to reveal itself:

To Pops—Happy 41ˢᵗ Birthday—Love Danny

The passage of years had tried but failed to erase the inscription, tried but failed to erase the pain of rejection by the boy he loved as a son. How many times had he resolved to throw the flask away? How many drunken nights had he actually tossed the damned thing in the trash, only to dig it out by the harsh light of the hangover morning?

Tim Trinity wiped his eyes, returned the flask to his pocket.

Thinking: *Fuck it.*

He looked at his watch. It was almost one thirty a.m. Dreammakers closed at one. He lit a cigarette, climbed out of the car, and leaned back against the door like a man with time to kill and money to spend.

"Lookin' for some company?" She was a bottle-blonde, with an inch of brunette showing at the roots. A silver crucifix bounced around her cleavage as she chewed gum.

"Might be, at that." Trinity offered an encouraging smile. "Just one thing I need to know."

The girl sighed. "Hand job's twenty-five, blow job's fifty, a hundred for—"

"That's not where I was going," said Trinity.

"Oh." The girl looked skeptical. "What's the one thing you need to know?"

Trinity pointed to her necklace with his cigarette.

"Do you believe in God?"

"How much you wanna spend?" said the girl as the motel room door clicked shut. Trinity pulled a roll from his pocket and peeled off five bills. Hundreds. The girl backed away. "Wait a second," she said.

Trinity held up his hands—*let me explain*—and sat on the edge of the bed. "You keep your clothes on, and so do I. No sex. I ain't even gonna touch you."

The girl glanced at the money, and when she looked back to Trinity, her eyes showed more curiosity than fear. In the light of the hotel room, her makeup couldn't quite hide the bruise under her left eye. Her fingernails were chewed beyond short, and there was a crack pipe burn on the side of her left index finger.

She said, "So what do you want for five hundred bucks?"

"OK, just hear me out," said Trinity. "You're a hooker…a stripper…whatever. Point is you sell your ass to strange men in the Waffle House parking lot. So I figure your life has gotta pretty much suck. No offense. Not judging, just laying it out there. Fact is God has not been good to you. And you still believe in the Lord, right?"

"So?"

"So I'm a wealthy man. Got everything I could possibly need. You could say God's been very good to me." Trinity let out a long breath. "And I don't believe in Him."

The girl shrugged. "We both gonna have to answer for our sins on judgment day. Don't matter if you believe or not. It's real, and it's gonna happen."

And that, to Tim Trinity, was simply awesome. That a girl like this could be so unshaken in faith. Unbelievable. "See?" he said. "That's why I need your help. Your belief is so strong."

"But what do you want me to do?"

"I want you to pray for me. See, some very weird shit is goin' down in my life, and I can't find a rational explanation. I mean, I've tried everything, and it's startin' to look like prayer's all I got left to try. But I can't pray for myself, 'cause I don't believe."

The girl stood quietly for a minute, then said, "Start to pray, and you'll start to believe."

Trinity shook his head.

The girl reached out, took the money. "Want me to pray for your soul?"

"No," said Trinity. If people had souls, he knew his was way beyond saving. "I want you to ask God to please stop fucking with my head."

17:

No heavy bag in the Ritz-Carlton's workout room. No speedbag, either. So Daniel contented himself with push-ups, crunches, and skipping rope. He spent the workout thinking about the strange contact from whoever was calling himself PapaLegba.

Probably someone who knew Daniel was from New Orleans, hence the chosen screen name. Someone with the resources to hack into Daniel's computer and take control of his Instant Messenger program. But who? And why?

Could be Conrad Winter, tossing a wrench in the works, trying to trip Daniel up.

Or not. There was no way to know for sure, given the available evidence, and Daniel resolved to put it out of his mind, not to get distracted by it, not to let it make him paranoid. He had a job to do.

He took a quick sauna and headed back to the room for a shower and breakfast.

As he downed the last of his coffee, an e-mail came in. From Gerry, the audio engineer at Emory. The e-mail he'd been waiting for.

> From: gerrymander@emory.edu
> To: d-byrne@live.com
> Subject: What we've learned…
> *Padre,*
> *You only asked me to do three broadcasts, but I kinda got carried away…took it on as a personal project. So I did all of 'em (transcripts and audio files attached). Bad news, though. I ran*

every possible test on the audio (AND video) of your fake holy man, and 1 gotta tell ya, there's no electronic manipulation here. The guy is really doing it. Kinda freaking me out, but 1've got no explanation. Never seen anything like it. If you need anything else, let me know.
   -Gerry

So Trinity had figured out a trick that had never been done before. Well, why not? There were many monikers you could hang on the man—childish, egocentric, immoral—but you could never call him stupid.

Daniel double-clicked on one of the attached transcript files, and it opened on his screen. Another weather report, Trinity warning of torrential rains in Charleston.

Torrential. Daniel couldn't remember seeing that word in the transcripts Nick had given him. He opened the corresponding audio file from Gerry, listened. *Torrential*—no mistaking it. He checked the broadcast date, pulled the corresponding transcript from his case file. In Giuseppe's transcript, Trinity never said torrential…because in the transcript, Trinity called for sunshine. And it was one of the predictions Trinity had supposedly gotten wrong.

But Trinity hadn't called for sunshine; he'd called for rain.

A chill ran down Daniel's arms as he flipped through his folder, pulling the transcript of Trinity's next failed prediction.

Two hours later, Daniel sat stunned, trying to understand. He'd checked and double-checked, read and listened and re-listened. Surfed the Internet for weather news and sports scores and more.

Trinity's predictions, so far, had all come true.

All of them.

Maybe Trinity had some meteorologist at the national weather service on his payroll…but how to explain the sports predictions? The games couldn't all be fixed, could they? And what about the traffic accidents?

Daniel thought about it for a long while. Then he hit "Reply" on Gerry's e-mail.

> **From: d-byrne@live.com**
> **To: gerrymander@emory.edu**
> **Subject: RE: What we've learned…**
> *Gerry,*
> *Thanks so much for your help with this. During the week, Trinity's show is a repeat—but there's a new episode starting each Sunday. Could you record and decode tomorrow's show? I can do the transcription, but if you could just send me the reversed audio file, that would be a big help.*
> *Thanks again,*
> *D.*

Daniel shut down his laptop, trying to make sense of things. He came up with more questions than answers. But two things seemed certain:

However he was doing it, Tim Trinity was predicting the future accurately, every single time.

And the Vatican's transcripts had been altered to hide that fact.

18:

The television studio-cum-church was packed with believers in their Sunday best, and Tim Trinity stood tall on the stage, reveling in the applause and flashing his pearly whites. The canned music faded away as he slowly brought his hands together like a prayer. The crowd fell silent.

Daniel sat in the back row, taking it all in. He had to admit, his uncle wasn't just good—he was a master. He'd seen many talented grifters at work on the tent revival circuit, many more preaching on television. But nobody *owned* the stage like Tim Trinity.

Trinity let the silence linger, then flipped a page of his blue Bible, which sat before him on the lectern. When he spoke, his voice boomed to the rafters. "*Jesus* said—Matthew 13:45—'The kingdom of heaven is like a merchant in search of fine pearls; on finding one pearl of great value, he went and sold all that he had and bought it.'"

He scooped up the Bible, grinned out at the crowd, and scratched his head in mock confusion. "One pearl of great value? Now just what in the heck is he *talkin'* about?"

The audience laughed easily.

"The pearl, my friends, is *salvation*. Salvation is the pearl of the *highest* value." Trinity started pacing the stage as a handful of *Amens* came up from the crowd. "But some of you are like the rich man who came to Jesus and asked what good deed he must do to get into heaven. You remember the one. The man was already virtuous, kept all of God's laws, so Jesus told him to sell all his possessions and become a disciple. And the rich man went away, grieving, for he had many possessions. What he failed to understand—and what y'all *need* to understand—is that spiritual salvation brings with it *all* the material wealth you could ever hope for! Salvation is—*always and in all ways*—the pearl of great value. *Seek first the kingdom of God and His righteousness, and all these things will be given to you as well.*"

Daniel shifted uncomfortably in his seat, thinking: *Here it comes…*

"So do not be afraid to give to the Lord what little you have, for it will be returned to you, one-hundred fold." Trinity flipped the pages. "Luke 6:38—Jesus said, 'Give, and it shall be given to you. A good measure, pressed down, shaken together, running over—*running over!*—will be put into your lap; for the measure you give, will be the measure you get back.' *Amen*, and *Amen*."

A blonde in a white pantsuit walked onstage from the wings. She looked like a beauty pageant runner-up, twenty years past her glory. She handed some sheets of paper to Trinity and flashed a smile to the audience.

"Thank you, Liz," he said, and she left the stage. "The telephones backstage are ringing off the hook and our telephone ministers are taking your prayer requests, so I want you to call that number on the screen. We only have time to read a few on the air, but *all* of your prayer requests are brought to my personal altar after the program is over, and I pray over each and every one." He flipped through the sheets, scanning each one and nodding, then held them against the pages of his Bible. He closed his eyes.

"Lord, we know that you hear our prayers, and prayers made in faith are answered. I ask you now, *in Jesus's name*, to work a financial miracle in the life of Heather from Virginia Beach, who just lost her job. Bring our sister Heather a new and better job, and break the yoke of poverty off of her. And we ask you to look down upon Sarah from Minneapolis and smash that breast cancer, melt that tumor away…"

Daniel scanned the crowd as Trinity rattled off more names and misfortunes. He estimated the majority was about evenly split between black and white, with maybe 20 percent Hispanic and 10 percent Asian. He looked from face to face, searching for any sign of skepticism, but found none. These people actually believed the swill Trinity served up. More than that, they loved it, and they loved Trinity for taking their money.

Some things never change. Daniel pushed away childhood memories of revival tents packed with dirt-poor farmers and laid-off factory workers who couldn't afford a stick of deodorant, but somehow found the money to fill Trinity's giant glass jars to overflowing.

Trinity stopped praying mid-sentence. "Wait!" he said. He opened his eyes and looked straight into the camera. "God has just shown me something. Some of you watching at home are wavering. Don't deny it—I have *seen* it. My words have awakened your faith, and you want to show your faith to God with a thousand-dollar vow to this ministry, but you say, *'Why should I sow my seed to this preacher on TV?'* I mean to tell you, that is the *Devil* sabotaging your faith, tryin' to keep you from your rightful inheritance in Christ!" Trinity flipped some pages and gave the Bible a mighty *thwack*. "First Corinthians, the Apostle Paul says of preachers, 'If we sowed spiritual things *in* you, is it too much if we reap material things *from* you? So also the Lord directed those who proclaim the gospel to get their living *from* the gospel.' Word of *God!* It is written, in *Jesus's* name!"

The congregation called out *Amens* as the master preacher executed a side-shuffle that would've made James Brown proud.

"See, God has prepared a *magnificent feast*, and Jesus has reserved a seat for you at the head table." He patted his belly and shook his head. "And you say, 'Thanks, Lord, but I'm not hungry, I had a big lunch. Maybe next time.'" The crowd laughed right along with him, until his smile melted away and his expression became deadly serious. "My-oh-my, you had a big lunch. That is the *Devil* talking! See, the Devil's got many tricks to play on you, my friends, and I'll let you in on a little secret: his two favorites are *doubt* and *procrastination*. More lives have been lost, more opportunities missed, more fortunes squandered, more relationships destroyed, through *doubt and procrastination*, than by any other means. They are the Devil's twin tools of sabotage."

Trinity lashed out at the air with his Bible. "Get away, Satan! You can't stop me from speaking the truth—I'm anointed by the blood of Christ!" Then he froze, his Bible in mid-strike.

He remained frozen far too long, and worried murmurs began spreading through the congregation.

His timing is usually perfect, thought Daniel, *why is he doing this?*

Trinity's entire body shuddered once, froze again, and jerked to the left, sending him sprawling on the stage. He bounced back up, Bible in hand, but the prayer requests lay scattered at his feet.

Then the tongues began, unnatural sounds erupting from his mouth and his body lurching spasmodically around the stage.

Seeing it on the television screen, Daniel had convinced himself that this was just Trinity's latest act. But it looked different in person. This was not the kind of performance his uncle would ever concoct. It looked too… *real*. Trinity was always smooth, and this was anything but. Worse than inelegant, it was ugly. There was just something *wrong* about it. Something profoundly wrong.

Daniel couldn't watch another spasm, couldn't listen to another eruption. He jumped from his seat and bolted for the exit, his skin crawling. Thinking: *It has to be an act. It has to be…*

Outside, he retrieved his camera from the car, stood in the sun and waited until the doors opened and Trinity's flock flooded the bright parking lot, chattering happily about what a great service it had been, about how they felt the presence of God today, about hundred-fold paybacks and their imminent prosperity.

Daniel wanted to grab them by the shoulders, one by one, and say: *Don't you see? He's a con man—you're being played for chumps. You should be paying off your debts and going back to school to get a better job, or building a college fund so your children won't have to struggle like you struggle—not giving it to some grifter.*

But what good would it do? All those things took real work, real sacrifice. Trinity offered these people an easy escape, a way to tell themselves that they were doing something to improve their lot, while never really having to take responsibility for their lives. All they had to do was throw money at him.

Daniel couldn't help these people. But he could bring down the con man. In his right hand he held the camera that contained digital surveillance photos he'd taken at Trinity's Buckhead mansion. Photos that exposed the truth behind the phony *Man of God* sham.

Finally.

He waited for the crowd to thin out and went back inside. A burly security guard stopped him in the empty hallway.

"I'm sorry, sir, service is over for today. You'll have to come back tomorrow."

"I need to speak with Reverend Trinity," said Daniel.

The guard smiled indulgently. "Lots of folk need to speak with Reverend Trinity. If you fill out a prayer request form, I'll be sure he gets it."

"Just tell him that Daniel Byrne is here. He'll see me."

19:

The security guard emerged from the dressing room, nodded politely, and left. Daniel stared at the door, took a deep breath. He reached for the knob, turned it, and stepped through the doorway.

Tim Trinity sat before a mirror framed by little round light bulbs, removing his stage makeup with cold cream. He caught Daniel's eye in the mirror, finished his task with one last swipe across the chin, and dropped the cotton ball on the table. He sniffed sharply, as if he had a cold.

"The prodigal son returns. Never thought I'd live to see the day." Trinity forced a smile, but the pain showed through.

When Daniel had walked out on his uncle at thirteen, it was with the firm intention of never speaking to the man again. But now, two decades later, he had to fight to hold his tongue. The weight of so much left unsaid, a weight he'd been carrying all these years. The urge to unload it, to say everything now, to dump the weight on Trinity, where it belonged. But what was the point? He was here to do a job, nothing more.

"Hello, Reverend."

"Twenty years." Trinity swiveled the chair and faced his nephew. Up close, without the benefit of stage makeup, he looked older. Still handsome, still had the salon tan, but the facelift had left his skin abnormally taut and shiny, and the broken veins of a drinker spiderwebbed across his cheeks and the left side of his nose. "You coulda at least said good-bye."

"And you could've told me the truth, instead of playing me like one of your suckers." He couldn't help himself, it had to be said.

Trinity lit a cigarette. "Shit, I tried. When you started questioning things, I tried, but… Guess I shoulda told you from the start. But you were just a boy, and…" He cleared his throat. "And you believed, and it was beautiful. And when you looked at me…I couldn't bring myself to let you down like that."

"You think I wasn't gonna get wise to the grift? You think I wouldn't recognize the shills? The deaf man in Biloxi who showed up in a wheelchair in Mobile? The blind woman in Pensacola and the one who was arthritic in Gainesville?"

"Sure, I had shills," said Trinity. "But you were there, and you saw the other ones. Some of those folks were really healed."

"Power of suggestion," said Daniel. "Placebo effect."

"Right. And it works. And who cares, so long as people get better? What about Jesus? The man always said, 'Your *faith* has healed you.' He never once said, '*I* have healed you.' You don't think He sometimes put shills in the crowd to rev up people's faith?"

Daniel said nothing.

"I was gonna tell you, I swear. I just didn't get up the gumption in time. The other preachers' kids still believed, and I guess I always told myself I had more time." Trinity tapped his cigarette on the edge of an ashtray. "Should've known better, you were always ahead of the others."

"Had to grow up fast, thanks to you."

"Hell, son, you were *born* old. Look, I did wrong by not telling you before you figured it out on your own, and I'm sorry for that, but you didn't have to run off, we coulda talked about it." He took a long drag on his smoke, blew it out, and looked up for a reaction, but Daniel gave him nothing. After a long moment Trinity said, "You remember the summer of '85?"

Daniel remembered. He was nine years old. It was the only summer of his childhood they hadn't spent on the road. "Yeah. You took the summer off from preaching. Bible study, you said. A lie, I'm sure."

"It was a lie, at that," said Trinity. "Wanna know what I did that summer? I got a *job*, is what I did. Selling homeowners insurance. See, that was the year I first saw real doubt in your eyes—serious doubt—so I figured to make a career change. For you." Trinity reached into a pocket and held out a gold Cross pen to Daniel. "Look at that." On the clip was a little plaque with a

B-I logo. "Each month, Bedrock Insurance gave one to their top-producing salesman. I got three more just like it. I mean, I wrote up a ton of business that summer. Worked the poor neighborhoods…those were my people, I knew how to reach them." He took the pen back from Daniel. "And then came your namesake."

"My—?"

"Hurricane Danny. Made landfall in Lake Charles, but the Big Easy got drenched, couple hundred homes destroyed. Including thirty-three I'd personally written up. And guess what? Bedrock welched, some technicality written into the fine print. Didn't pay out a goddamn dime to those folks. I quit the next day and gassed up the Winnebago again." He placed the pen back in his pocket. "I keep it as a reminder. Sure, I'm a grifter, but there ain't no clean way to get rich, and my grift never hurt anyone. Not like that."

Daniel wanted to say, *It hurt me,* but the words caught in his throat. "It hurts plenty of people," he said.

Trinity stubbed his cigarette in an ashtray. "OK, Danny. You come here to tell me I'm a scumbag? Mission accomplished."

Daniel shook his head. "Not a social call. I'm here on business."

"Thought you'd become a priest."

"I am a priest."

"But…" Trinity gestured to his neck.

"I work out of uniform most of the time."

"Lucky you. So what does the Catholic Church want with a man like me?"

"We want to know how you're doing it," said Daniel.

"Doing what?"

"The tongues."

Trinity's eyes went wide. "What do you know about that?"

"We're on to you. I also know about the cocaine…which is a new low, even for you." He'd planned to confront his uncle with the surveillance photos, but now he'd lost the taste for it.

"Yeah, I'm using, but that's because of the fucking voices," said Trinity. "What do you know about the tongues?"

"How are you doing it?"

"I don't know."

"You don't know? What about the predictions?"

"The hell are you talking about? What predictions?"

Trinity was a skilled liar, but there was no mistaking real desperation in the man's voice. "Your tongues act. You play it backwards, speed it up, it's English. You're making predictions. And they're coming true."

Trinity's face went ashen and he slumped back into his chair. "Jesus… Fucking…Christ," he said, between ragged breaths. "No. No, that's just not—no, it isn't…it's just not possible…"

Daniel smiled without any humor. "You can do better than that."

"No, you're lying. You must be lying…" Trinity's confusion looked genuine, but then, he was good at this. "You gotta believe me, Danny, I don't know anything about any predictions."

"Given that my entire childhood was based on a lie, you'll understand if I choose not to believe you," said Daniel. He turned to leave.

"No, wait! Please. Something strange is—I-I don't know what the hell is happening to me."

Daniel watched in silence as his uncle reached for a bottle of bourbon on the dressing table, uncorked it, and poured with a shaking hand, the bottle's neck rattling against the edge of the glass. Trinity put the bottle down and steadied the glass with both hands as he drank. He looked nothing like the big and powerful man from Daniel's childhood memories, nothing like the confident preacher on stage in front of a crowd.

"See, it's not just the tongues," said Trinity. He tapped on the side of his head with an index finger. "It's also the voices." A tear tumbled down his right cheek. "I'm scared, son. You gotta help me. I'm shit-scared."

Could this all be an act? It didn't seem like one.

Daniel took the chair across from Trinity. "I still think you're full of shit, but I've been sent here to find out what's going on with you, so I'll listen. Start at the beginning, and don't leave anything out. And be warned: if it turns out you're running some con, I promise you will be one sorry-assed con man."

20:

William Lamech sat in his expansive office, twenty-three floors above the Las Vegas Strip. The glass city shimmered beneath him as the sun moved into the western sky. He pushed a button on a control panel set into his desktop, and the floor-to-ceiling windows automatically darkened to a comfortable level. *Any sufficiently advanced technology is indistinguishable from magic.* It was the third of Arthur C. Clarke's three laws of prediction. He'd forgotten the other two, but he enjoyed this one and it pleased him to remember it.

The phone on his desk trilled softly, and he answered it.

"Mr. Lamech, it's me."

"Go ahead."

"That priest you said to watch for, he's here. Only…"

"Only what?"

"Well, he doesn't look like a priest. I mean, he's a young guy, doesn't look like a square. And he ain't dressed like a priest. But it's the name you gave me, Daniel Byrne."

"You're not Catholic, are you?"

"Baptist."

"Well, they don't all look like Max Von Sydow."

"Uh…yes, sir. I guess not. One other thing, might not be important…"

"Yes?"

"He's the preacher's nephew."

The preacher's nephew. It brought Lamech forward in his chair. "Interesting. Where is he now?"

"I took him to Trinity's dressing room, and they talked for about an hour. Then he left. I got his license plate."

"OK, good work. Keep your eyes and ears open, call me back whenever anything similarly interesting jumps out at you."

"Yes, sir. And, uh, Mr. Lamech?"

"Yes?"

"I just, you know, I've been with the company eight years, I'm dependable, loyal, competent. And..."

Lamech smiled to himself. "Ambitious."

"Yes, sir. Ambitious. I just want you to know, I could do more. So whatever you need, just keep me in mind."

"I see. We all have our jobs to do, but opportunities for advancement occasionally arise, and you don't get if you don't ask."

"That's exactly it, sir. I mean, I love my job, but you don't get if you don't ask."

William Lamech respected the ambitions of young men. "All right, good to know. No promises, but I'll keep it in mind, in case something comes up in future."

He hung up, leaned back in his chair. *The preacher's nephew.* Hell of a coincidence, and why would the brain trust at the Vatican send the man's flesh and blood anyway? Seemed like a major conflict of interest.

The computer speakers on his desk pinged. He put on his reading glasses and clicked the mouse, opened the new e-mail, and read the decoded transcript of the preacher's latest tongues act.

"Holy crap," he said. He grabbed the phone, punched in three numbers. "Steve, it's Lamech. Grab a pen. Do not take any of the following bets on the Gotham Stakes—Mr. Smitten to win, Executive Council to place, Sweet Revenge to show. Got it? I don't care what the line is, you do *not* take those bets. Good." He placed the receiver back in its cradle.

So now the preacher was predicting the ponies. And just two months until the Kentucky Derby.

Goddamn.

The time for prudence was quickly coming to an end. If the Gotham Stakes prediction came true and they had nothing yet on the preacher, information gathering would give way to action.

He picked up the phone again.

21:

The room was white. Ceiling, walls, floor. All white. No furniture. Just a white, windowless room with no door. Not exactly standing in a cloud of dry ice at the pearly gates, but this much was certain: Daniel was dead.

There was another man in the room. He was what people call ruggedly handsome. He wore black pants and a clerical collar over a white muscle shirt. A priest with serious guns.

He said, "Hi, Daniel, I'm Saint Sebastian," and held out his hand. Casual. Friendly.

Daniel shook the hand of Saint Sebastian. "I'm dead," he said.

"No shit, Sherlock." Saint Sebastian winked at Daniel. "Not exactly what you expected."

"No."

Saint Sebastian shrugged. "Peter's down with the flu. I'm filling in."

Daniel felt lightheaded. He made himself nod.

Saint Sebastian clapped him on the shoulder. "That was a joke. Lighten up, will you? Breathe."

Daniel gasped, worked to catch his breath.

"Good. In, out…deep breaths, slow down…excellent. Now just relax, everything will be clear in a minute. See, I'm here to do two things. The first is to calm you down and explain the rules."

Daniel calmed instantly. Thinking: *Impossible.*

"Now, I know what you're thinking," said Saint Sebastian. "You're thinking: *That's already two things.* And you're right. Thing is, calming you down doesn't count, they just send us to explain the rules. But if we don't calm you down first, the explanation goes nowhere."

Is this for real? But not out loud. Out loud, Daniel said, "What are the rules?"

"Rules are, we don't sweat the details here. So you can stop worrying about how many times you jerked off or if you did the right things with your life. You're either one of the good guys or you're not. And you were one of the good guys." A sly grin, like they were teenage boys sharing some locker-room joke. "Tried to be, anyway. The mixed results don't matter. You did more good than bad."

"That's it? That's the metric? More good than bad? Heaven's going to be a lot more crowded than I imagined."

"Not exactly." Saint Sebastian moved to his left. And again. Like a boxer. But his hands hung loose at his sides. "There's one more criteria. A test. Different for everybody. Well, not everybody. People aren't as different from each other as they imagine. There are a thousand different tests. One thousand, exactly, for all the souls in the universe. I looked it up." A third move to the left, flawless footwork sliding him into slow orbit around Daniel. "Anyway, the test is the second thing. And I'm here to administer it. Your test is to fight me."

Daniel pivoted, took a small skip-step back, keeping Saint Sebastian directly in front of him. The saint now raised his hands, adopting a true fighter's stance, and continued to make his way around Daniel in a tight circle. Daniel pivoted again, but kept his hands below the waist. Adrenaline leaked into his bloodstream and his heart beat faster and his hands wanted to make fists. He forced his hands to stay open.

"I'm not going to hit you—you're a saint."

"A saint who's been sent here to kick your ass," said Saint Sebastian. "Understand? Because I don't want to start this dance until I'm confident you get it. I'm about to beat the crap out of you. I would feel a lot better about it if you'd put up a defense. Sure enough, you'll be judged by your actions, but nobody expects you to take it like a dog." Up on the balls of his feet now, circling faster. "If you think it's the right thing to do, you're free to go wild on me, unleash the beast. That's your judgment to make. Or you can go all Queensberry Rules, if that's the way you roll. But don't just stand there like some used-up journeyman laying down for a bottle of Night Train."

"I must be dreaming," said Daniel. "I'm dreaming."

Saint Sebastian snapped a left jab off Daniel's nose. The pain brought white blotches to his vision. As his vision cleared, blood began to leak from his nose, down his upper lip.

"I'm trying to give you some good advice here, son," said Saint Sebastian. "You'd do well to listen and heed me. I beseech you to fight."

A sharper jab. Square on the nose.

"Ow!" said Daniel. "That fuckin' hurt." He could taste his own blood now. His hands came up. Fists.

"Game on," said Sebastian.

It did not begin well. Sebastian was a better boxer in better condition, and Daniel had no idea what to do with himself. But after withstanding an opening flurry, Daniel blocked a jab and drove a right hook into Sebastian's ribs, stepped back and snapped two jabs off the saint's nose. The right-cross caught only shoulder, and Sebastian came back fast. Daniel ducked a hook, pulled away from the left uppercut, circled in time and delivered a straight right to the solar plexus that stopped Sebastian's orbital dance. Followed with two left jabs to the nose, but Sebastian took the second one on the forehead.

Daniel moved in, pinned Sebastian's upper arms in a clinch, and sucked air. "OK, I fought you," he panted. "Can we stop now?"

Sebastian bit off Daniel's right ear, crimson-sprayed it to the floor, and broke the clinch.

"Faked you out with that Queensberry shit, huh?" He flashed a sympathetic smile full of bloody teeth. "Smarten up, son. Your only job here is to survive this thing. Got it?"

Sebastian set his feet and drove a fist into Daniel's abdomen.

Daniel's stomach spasmed, legs went out from under him, and his knees hit the canvas.

As Saint Sebastian shuffled his feet and moved in for the next attack, the bell rang, signaling the end of the first round.

22:

The alarm clock was ringing. Daniel slapped it off, swung his legs over the side of the bed, and planted his bare feet on soft carpet. The drapes were open, as he'd left them, and daylight flooded the hotel room.

Images from the dream lingered. *What the hell was all that?* He took a minute to shake off the cobwebs, then called room service and ordered breakfast. He said his morning prayers, then went through a set of push-ups, crunches, and Hindu squats, followed by a quick shower and shave. He ate while listening to the audio file of Trinity's latest tongues act, which had arrived by e-mail from Gerry during the night.

It started with a new installment of Trinity's Jimmy the Greek spiel, predicting that Mr. Smitten would win the upcoming Gotham Stakes at Aqueduct, finishing eight-and-a-half lengths ahead of Executive Council, with Sweet Revenge coming in third. Then another weather report of no consequence. But what came next robbed Daniel of his appetite.

> *"If you work at the oil refinery in Belle Chasse, Louisiana, do not go to work on Tuesday. Do not go to work. Anyone near the Plaquemines Parish refinery should get some distance. There will be a terrible accident, an explosion. Tuesday morning. Many lives will be lost."*

Daniel grabbed his cell phone, speed-dialed Father Nick's private line. Nick picked up on the second ring.

"What have you got for me on the good reverend?" said Nick.

"I'm sending an audio file. Listen to it and call me back."

Daniel hung up, forwarded the audio file to Nick's e-mail address. Five minutes later, his cell rang.

"Did you hear it?"

"I did."

"He said Tuesday morning. Tomorrow is Tuesday, we gotta plan our move."

"Oh, please. It'll just play out as one of Trinity's swing-and-miss predictions."

"You're wrong, Nick. I checked the transcripts in the case file against the archived broadcasts. Trinity doesn't miss. All of his predictions have come true. Every one."

After a very long silence, Nick said, "Are you sure?"

"Yes, I'm sure. This case was compromised before you even assigned it to me. Someone at the Vatican altered Giuseppe's transcripts to make Trinity wrong."

Another long silence. "Interesting. I'll look into it."

"My guess would be Conrad," said Daniel. "Don't know what his game is, but—"

"I said I'll look into it." Nick cleared his throat. "Now tell me what you've learned about Trinity."

Daniel started to speak, but nothing came out. He reached for the camera on the nightstand, flicked it on, and began scrolling through the digital photos he'd taken on surveillance two nights ago. Even on the camera's little screen, the photos were damning. Trinity snorting coke in his den.

"Tell me you got something," said Nick.

"I think Trinity's in trouble."

"What kind of trouble?"

"Serious trouble. Out of control. I saw him snort cocaine."

"Get pictures?"

Trinity had told Daniel everything, including the reason for the cocaine. The story had been so wild that Daniel was left not knowing what to believe. "You sent me to debunk the guy. The fact that he snorts coke doesn't debunk anything." He put the camera down. "I met with him. Can't believe I'm saying this, but I don't think he's in control of the tongues. He claimed no knowledge of the predictions. When I told him, he was pretty shaken up, and I think he's telling the truth. Maybe."

Nick snorted a rough laugh in Daniel's ear. "Trinity hasn't told the truth since Carter was in the White House. Bottom line, we have to undermine his authority and get him off the air. And you're wasting time. A coke habit will do the trick."

"What about the oil refinery?"

"Forget about it. You have a job to do."

"People are going to die, Nick."

"If that's God's will."

Daniel's blood surged, and he tamped down his temper. "You can't be serious," he said. "We have the knowledge to stop this from happening."

"Give your head a shake, kiddo. God is *not* talking through Trinity. Let's get that straight."

"I know that."

"Then the knowledge in our possession did not come from God. Which means we are not supposed to have it. You think Trinity's tongues act is otherworldly? Don't forget, Satan speaks through people too." Daniel didn't answer. "What now?"

"I don't even know if I believe in demonic possession," said Daniel. Thinking: *I don't even know if I believe in Satan.*

Nick sighed into the phone. "Whatever's happening to Trinity, it's not God."

"But—"

"Listen. Disasters happen every day, and people die every day. We can't know why that is, but if nothing else, we *must* believe God has a larger plan, beyond what we can see. Because if we can't believe that much, then all is chaos and there's no point. You need to take the larger view. If the oil refinery explodes, that is God's will. Who are you to mess with that? Don't presume to take God's place. You are not Him."

Daniel unclenched his fist, forced himself to breathe deep. "I'm not trying to be God. But Trinity's batting a thousand so far. Innocent people are probably going to die, and I find it hard to accept that God would not want us to save them."

"There are no innocent people, Dan. And you need to stop trying to read God's mind. Now go get me pictures of Reverend Trinity fucking up."

Nick broke the connection without saying good-bye.

Daniel's hand shook as he put the phone down. How could Nick be so callous? Why not step in to save those refinery workers? And—*Jesus*—he'd barely reacted to the news of the altered transcripts. *Did he already know?* And what would that imply? The questions swirled in Daniel's mind. He adopted a fighter's stance and shadowboxed for a few minutes, burning off the excess adrenaline. Still his mind reeled, and the thought of doing nothing made his stomach churn.

This was asking too much.

Daniel dropped to his knees, clasped his hands together, and squeezed his eyes shut.

I know I have been a bad son, and my faith is weak. But Father in Heaven, I need your help, even as I don't deserve it. I need you to strengthen my faith, because without it, I cannot sit back and do nothing while people burn to death. Please, give me something to hang my faith upon...

But there came no answer. No sign.

Just like always.

After a few minutes, Daniel stood up, feeling vaguely foolish, and wiped his eyes dry.

He picked up the camera again. Trinity made millions hustling poor people with the false promise of prosperity, and he did it in the name of God. He was the worst kind of con man. But as Daniel scrolled through the photos, he saw something more than a crook. He saw a man in deep crisis. And he had come away from their meeting convinced that whatever was happening to Trinity, it wasn't an act.

But what was it? The man was predicting the future; there was no way around that. Also no way around the fact that the Christian God would never choose Tim Trinity as His spokesman on earth. And that led back to the horrible, terrifying question that had been quietly plaguing Daniel for some time.

What if God isn't the Christian God?

One thing Nick was right about: This wasn't about Daniel and his uncle. It wasn't even about debunking a con man or protecting the sanctity of the Church or searching for a miracle. It was about the dozens of Louisiana oil refinery workers, who Daniel now believed would die the next morning, unless he did something about it.

23:

The head of security at the Belle Chasse oil refinery told Daniel to get back on his meds and hung up in his ear. Understandable, really. He probably would've done the same thing in the man's shoes.

He had known it might come to this, had hoped in vain that it wouldn't. But now there was only one thing left to do. So he directed his laptop's browser to the website of the *New Orleans Times-Picayune* newspaper, found the staff directory, and looked up the telephone extension for Julia Rothman, his heart racing.

Julia was an intern at the *New Orleans Times-Picayune* when they were together. She'd since worked her way up to senior investigative reporter at the paper. She was quite the maverick, had been fired and rehired more than a few times, had won several regional journalism awards for exposing political corruption in Louisiana. Her series on government failure post-Katrina had been nominated for a Pulitzer. Daniel knew all this because, against his better judgment, he'd followed her career on the Internet all these years, unable to let go completely.

His heart now pounding as he reached for the phone, his mind flooded with the memories of the headiest year of his life…

Eighteen years old, high school graduate, New Orleans Golden Gloves champion, and madly in love. She was twenty-one, unafraid, and scary smart. And the sex was incredible. Not that he had any basis for comparison—she was his first, and would be his only.

They first met at a neighborhood party in the lead-up to Mardi Gras, and the sexual spark was there from the get-go, but she deflected his first advance. He was welcome to hang out in her group of friends, she said, but dating was out of the question. It took two months of "hanging out" in a group, at neighborhood parties, before she finally got over the age difference and agreed to a real date.

One date was all it took. They fell for each other hard and fast, became a steady couple, and spent every free minute together. Daniel was taking a year off after high school, concentrating on his fighting and working at the gym, but he was slated to enter the seminary when he turned nineteen, and time was running out for them. As the months counted down, everything became more intense. The lovemaking, the fighting, the all-night metaphysical debates.

He'd told Julia all about his past, and she understood his need to believe. But to her, God was a human invention—a way for people to strike back at their fear of death. As she saw it, secular miracles were all around us, and that should be enough. Friendship and love and sex and chocolate and children were all miracles. That humans had evolved and survived and thrived in a coldly indifferent universe, had brought meaning and beauty to their lives through art and music and literature, had brought understanding of the world through science—she saw all of that as a miracle. And she saw no place in the universe for a God; didn't need one.

Daniel could see the promise of a beautiful life with Julia, and he almost backed out of the seminary. But the wounds of his childhood were too deep, and her love was simply not enough to heal those wounds...

Damn it, no. Lives are at stake, you cannot afford this right now. Focus. Daniel put the receiver down. He went to the bathroom and splashed cold water on his face, returned to the desk, took a few deep breaths.

He again picked up the phone, and this time punched in the number. After a few rings, she picked up.

"Julia Rothman," she said. Daniel tried to answer, but the words caught in his throat, so exquisite was the ache caused by the sound of her voice. "Hello?"

He fought against a resurgent flood of memories. "Hi. Julia, it's Daniel Byrne calling, we knew each other back in—"

Julia let out a throaty laugh. "You don't have to remind me how I know you, Danny."

"Well, yes, it's just, it's been a long time, so I didn't want to assume…" *You are such an idiot.*

"You still a priest?"

"Yes, yes, still a priest. You?"

"Uh, I've never been a priest."

"No, of course. I-I meant…" *Shit.* "Listen, Julia, I can't do small talk right now. Something important has come up, and I think it'll be of professional interest to you."

A couple seconds of silence. "All right, shoot."

"It's a delicate situation, and I'd like to keep our conversation off the record."

Another pause on the line. "OK."

"OK. There's gonna be an explosion at the Belle Chasse oil refinery. Tomorrow morning."

"Jesus Christ…pardon the blasphemy. What kind of explosion?"

"I don't know, an accident of some kind."

"Accident? How do you know about it, then?"

"That's the delicate part. I already called the refinery—they thought I was a nut job. But if you warn them—"

"I'm sorry if it's delicate for you, but I can't just take your word on it. I need to know how you know this."

"I understand. But we're off the record, right?"

"We already agreed on that."

"Fine. This will sound completely insane, I realize, but if you check it out, you'll know it's the truth."

"I'm listening."

"You remember my uncle, Tim Trinity?"

" 'Course I do."

"You'll find his broadcasts archived on his ministry website. You need to look at the one from yesterday. Not all of it. Just skip ahead to the speaking-in-tongues part. Record the tongues, then play it backwards and speed it up by a third."

"Are you drunk?"

"I'm serious. Run it backwards, and Trinity's speaking English. He predicts the accident at the refinery. I know how crazy this sounds, but it'll only take an hour of your time. Lives are at stake here, Julia."

She sighed into the phone. "All right, I'll check it out."

"Promise?"

"Yeah, I just said I would."

"And you'll get down to the refinery today, warn them."

"I will."

"Thanks, Julia."

"Yup. You take care now, Danny."

Julia Rothman hung up the phone, dropped her face into her hands, and didn't move for a full minute.

A reporter two desks over said, "You OK?"

"Yeah," said Julia, "that was just an old friend. Sad to say, he's become a member of the tinfoil hat brigade." She tore the top sheet off her notepad, crumpled it into a ball, and dropped it in the wastepaper basket.

Thinking: *What the hell happened to you, Danny?*

24:

Tim Trinity sat alone, drinking bourbon in the video control room, facing a wall of blank monitors. One monitor for each of the four camera feeds, three more dedicated to video playback decks. A master monitor in the center was for whichever feed was currently "hot," as the director punched buttons on the switcher to assemble the finished show. An audio mixing board sat on the table, next to the switcher. The soft whisper of the machines' cooling-fans was the only sound in the room. He'd always found that sound comforting and often spent time in the control room after the crew went home.

But he hadn't come here tonight for comfort.

The soundproof door opened and a young video technician—Trinity couldn't recall his name—entered, arms full of videocassettes. The kid put the tapes on the table, making a neat tower.

"Here's the last fifteen episodes, Reverend Trinity. Most recent on top. Anything else I can get you?"

"That'll do."

"Want me to stay and run the deck?"

"No, I got it. You can go home now."

"Yes, sir. Good night." The kid started for the door.

"Hey, kid." Trinity dug into his pants pocket and fished out a fifty-dollar bill, stuck it in the kid's hand. "Thanks for staying late."

"Thank *you*, sir. Sure do appreciate it. I'm getting married next month, and this'll help the honeymoon fund. We're going to—"

"Fine, have a good time," mumbled Trinity as he swiveled his chair away from the kid and grabbed a tape off the top of the tower. The door closed behind him, and he stuck the tape into a playback deck.

He scanned through the tape on high speed, to the end of yesterday's tongues, and hit pause. He refilled his glass from the bottle of Blanton's, took a sip. He turned the deck's jog-wheel to the left, and the tape began running backwards.

Trinity listened. And heard.

"Oh my God," he said.

The glass slipped from his hand, splashing bourbon across his white leather cowboy boots.

✣ ✣ ✣

Daniel sat on his bed, Bible on his lap, reading the Song of Solomon.

> Set me as a seal upon your heart,
>> as a seal upon your arm;
>> for love is strong as death,
>> passion fierce as the grave.
>> Its flashes are flashes of fire,
>>> a raging flame.
>
> Many waters cannot quench love,
>> neither can floods drown it.
>> If one offered for love
>> all the wealth of one's house,
>> it would be utterly scorned

As a young man, he had set Julia as a seal upon his heart, and there didn't seem to be a damn thing he could do to break that seal. Had he not tried to drown his love in holy water? Had his heart not scorned all the spiritual wealth the Church had offered in exchange?

No matter what he did, the flame still raged. Daniel had to admit that he knew it always would.

On the phone with her, he'd sounded like a jackass, barely able to speak. It was all he could do not to blurt out his feelings, not to tell her how much he'd missed her all these years, how much he missed her still. He knew hearing her voice again would hurt, but there was too much at stake.

Despite the pain, he was glad he'd called.

He flipped the pages back, took another stab at the Book of Job, with the usual results.

Twenty years since the priests took him in, and he still wasn't much good at accepting God's many mysteries. Maybe Nick was right after all. Maybe by calling Julia, Daniel was attempting to subvert the will of God. But even with his mind full of Job, he didn't feel wrong about it. If it was wrong, he would be judged for it when his time came. And he could live with that.

Because, in the meantime, he might've just saved some lives.

25:

Belle Chasse, Louisiana...

Andrew Thibodeaux sat in front of the television, flipping channels. Flipping past no-money-down real estate wealth-building systems and magic kitchen appliances, revolutionary exercise equipment and spray-on hair. Sat in front of the television, eating spicy pork cracklings by the handful and drinking Diet Dr Pepper and wondering how his life had come to this. Almost a year since his wife ran out on him with that asshole cop from Gretna, and a week didn't pass he didn't vow to forget all about her and move on.

He'd promised himself that he would make big changes in his life, go back and get his GED, enroll at community college. Maybe even become a policeman himself. He was still young enough, and he knew he was plenty smart.

He'd promised himself that he would knock off the junk food, start working out, get back in shape. All it took was a little willpower.

He'd promised himself a lot of things over the last twelve months. But he just kept on going to work, coming home, eating crap, and staring at the television. He hadn't even taken their wedding photo off the wall.

He didn't think he was still grieving over the dead marriage. At least, he didn't *feel* sad. He felt...nothing. A paralyzing numbness that rendered all his promises hollow, even as he made them. Maybe if he could sleep, his motivation would return. He'd never been much of a sleeper, but in the last year he'd only been getting a few hours a night.

God, he was tired.

He remembered something from high school science, before he dropped out. *Objects at rest stayed at rest unless acted upon.* There had to be a way to break the inertia.

All his life he'd felt that God had bigger plans for him, that his life would someday amount to something. He'd prayed for guidance, but the Lord had not yet seen fit to answer him. When his wife took off, he thought it might be a sign. But if it was a sign, it was one he couldn't read. It didn't point him anywhere.

He pressed the remote control's little button again, but the channel didn't change. He reached over, pulled a fresh pack of batteries from the end table's drawer, and loaded them into the remote.

It still didn't work.

On the television screen, Reverend Tim Trinity was talking directly to the camera. It seemed he was talking directly to Andrew.

Reverend Tim said God wanted to work miracles in Andrew's life.

Maybe the broken remote wasn't an accident. They say God's signs are everywhere but we're usually too busy to notice them. Maybe the remote control stopped working on exactly this channel for a reason. Maybe this was one of God's signs.

Maybe Reverend Tim had a message for him.

Andrew put the chair into full recline and settled in to listen.

God, he was tired.

The alarm clock woke him two hours later. The television was off, although he could not remember shutting it off. He put the chair upright, stood, and worked the kinks out of his neck, walked to the bedroom and shut off the alarm. He climbed into his work clothes, brushed his teeth, and made a couple of peanut butter sandwiches. He wrapped the sandwiches in tinfoil and put them in his lunchbox, along with couple cans of Dr Pepper and a fresh pouch of Red Man chewing tobacco.

He grabbed his hardhat and headed to the refinery.

.✢ ✢ ✢

Andrew punched in early and went to the refinery's cafeteria for a coffee before his shift. He took his paper cup to a long table, where the foreman was just winding up a story that had the guys in stitches.

"…so if I fall asleep on the job today, y'all can blame my mama," said the foreman.

"Coming in late, that sounds really bad," said Andrew.

The foreman laughed. "Get your mind outta the gutter, Andy. I was just telling the boys 'bout my late night telephone adventures. First, Mama calls in a tizzy, sayin' there's some emergency, and she gave my number to our old preacher. Then the preacher calls, goin' on about how he's had some kinda vision, and we gotta shut down the refinery. Guy sounded totally sauced too."

"Your preacher's a drunk?"

"Hasn't been our preacher for a long time. Moved away after Katrina, now he's a big shot in Hotlanta, but Mama used to drag me to his church in the city. Tim Trinity."

The paper coffee cup stopped halfway to Andrew's mouth. "Reverend Tim?"

"Yeah, you know him?"

"Seen him on TV. What'd he say, exactly?"

"The guy was goin' nuts, said this place was set to explode this morning. Asked him how he knew, he started on about speaking in tongues and everything's backwards and I don't know what all. Didn't make any sense."

But it made sense to Andrew. Last night had been a sign, after all. Reverend Tim was speaking for God. Andrew didn't know how he knew this, but he'd never been surer of anything in his life. He dropped his hardhat on the table and headed for the exit.

"Wait, where you goin'?"

"I can't stay."

"Boy, you as crazy as that preacher. Get back here and pick up your lid."

"You guys better come along," said Andrew. "You stay, you're gonna die."

"You leave, don't plan on coming back," the foreman shot back. Andrew turned away. "I'm serious, Andy. You walk out that door, you're fired."

Andrew kept on walking.

But as he moved through the sun-drenched parking lot toward his truck, doubt crept around the edges of his mind. He'd just walked away from the only decent job he ever had. Was Reverend Tim really talking for God? The absolute certainty he'd felt in the cafeteria now eluded him.

He climbed into his rusty old F-150, drove off the compound, and headed down the road a couple blocks. He pulled a U-turn, parked facing the refinery. Rolled down the windows, opened his lunchbox, and filled his right cheek with chewing tobacco. Popped the top on a Dr Pepper and settled in to wait.

Thinking: *I'm either the smartest man in Louisiana, or the dumbest.*

26:

The foreman hated the term *productivity meeting*. To him, productivity meetings were just about the least productive thing ever devised by middle management, and that was saying plenty. Those corporate frat boys were master time-wasters. Their other major skills included ass-covering, blame-shifting, and brownnosing. But he was a deputy supervisor, which made him junior management, so he had to play along.

At least the meetings were held in the cafeteria. It was the frat boys' way of showing that they were *just plain folk*. Those boys loved slumming with the men who worked for a living.

The foreman drank some coffee and tried to focus on the meeting. The IT guy was giving another general warning about sending jokes around by company e-mail. Not naming any names, but the ones who did it knew who they were, and the threat was implied, if things didn't change soon.

The foreman's ears popped as if he were in an elevator. *Sudden change in air pressure*, he thought. *Something's wrong. Something's—*

A blast rocked the building. Windows blew out of the far wall. Men screamed. Everyone grabbed the table for support…

The room went dark…

The HVAC and refrigerators and vending machines shut down, and the cafeteria fell silent…

A low rumble reverberated through the walls. Red emergency lights started flashing and the alarm began blaring, once every second. The generators kicked in, and white light strips set into the floor glowed a line to the door.

Years of monthly fire drills also kicked in, and muscle memory took over. The men abandoned their belongings and moved quickly to the door. A few put their hands on the door, testing for heat. The foreman and the IT guy grabbed the fire extinguishers mounted on either side of the door. Someone opened the door, and the foreman led the other men into the hallway.

The light strips ran left, down the hallway, to the nearest fire exit. The foreman clasped the IT guy on the shoulder and pointed left.

"You're in charge," he barked into the guy's ear. The rumbling had grown to a roar—he had to yell to be heard. "Take them out."

The group followed the IT guy outside to safety. The foreman turned right, walked through strobing red light toward the double doors at the end of the hallway.

The doors burst open and three men came out in a stumbling run, clothes charred and smoking, skin melting off faces and hands. Through the open doors, everything was raging flame. Smoke billowed into the hallway.

Two of the melting men continued lurching, past the foreman and toward the fire exit. The other man pitched forward onto the floor. The foreman dropped the useless fire extinguisher, ran to the prone man, and hoisted him up in a fireman's lift.

He ran for the exit. Another concussive blast from behind. The double doors flew open and a wave of heat rolled over him.

The hallway filled with fire.

Andrew Thibodeaux heard the blast. In the distance, a fireball rose through a ragged hole in the metal roof of the refinery's main building. The top third of the adjoining wall collapsed and more flames leapt free. Thick black smoke filled the air above and climbed into the sky.

For a full minute, he sat watching the fire grow, without a conscious thought in his head. Then his stomach tightened, and he sobbed once, twice, and again. The sobbing stopped as quickly as it had hit him. He wiped his eyes, turned the ignition over, and drove.

Thank you, Lord…thank you, Lord…thank you, Lord…

27:

Julia Rothman heard the call on her police scanner and mashed the accelerator to the floor, making record time to Belle Chasse.

It was a hellstorm. Massive black clouds billowed skyward from a wall of orange flame, and the whole scene shimmered with heat, like a mirage on the highway.

She flashed her press credentials through the windshield, and the deputy waved her past the police line. Michael Alatorre, sheriff of Plaquemines Parish, stood with one foot on the bumper of his cruiser, barking orders at another deputy. Six fire engines and an ambulance idled nearby, lights flashing impotently in the midday sun. A couple dozen firemen stood around smoking, gazing, awestruck by the blaze.

Julia jumped from her car, hooked a few strands of black hair with her little finger, and put them behind her ear.

The sheriff recognized her and tipped his hat, his expression grim. "Young lady."

"Jesus, Sheriff Alatorre, what the hell happened here?"

"Don't know yet, some kinda accident."

"How many dead?"

"Your guess is as good as mine. We can't get near it. Fire chief says we just gonna have to let it burn for a while." He flipped open his notebook. "Supervisor says he thinks there were one hundred forty-five men on shift in the main building when the thing blew, but that's unconfirmed. Far as we know, forty-three came out alive, eighteen taken to hospital in varying degrees of distress. Some were pretty bad off, probably not all of them will make it." He gestured at the ambulance. "They just stickin' around in case somebody else staggers out, but…"

They both looked back to the inferno. Nobody else would be staggering out.

✤ ✤ ✤

Julia raced back to the office, logged onto the Internet, and directed her browser to the Tim Trinity Word of God Ministries.

Thinking: *If that sonofabitch actually predicted this…*

Thinking: *What has Danny gotten himself involved in?*

Thinking: *Why didn't I—Oh my God, what have I done?*

✤ ✤ ✤

Daniel stayed in his hotel room all morning, anxiously flipping between the cable news networks, praying that Julia had been able to convince the refinery executives of the danger. This last hour was the toughest. He'd been too nervous to eat breakfast and now felt a little queasy. He checked his watch every few minutes, confirming the time displayed on the television screen. Noon could not come soon enough. He paced the floor, sat and checked the Internet news sites, stood and paced some more. He read Psalm 23 about a dozen times.

As the final seconds ticked by, he counted them down, like a New Year's Eve reveler watching the ball drop on Times Square, waiting to kiss everybody and sing "Auld Lang Syne."

Noon arrived. No disaster.

He flipped through the channels, and nothing had changed. Just the usual parade of Democrats and Republicans, shilling their talking points about a broken economy and how not to fix it. He decided to give it a little longer, to be sure.

He left the television on, shaved with the bathroom door open. And as the minutes ticked by uneventfully, his heart soared. He'd done the right thing, he was sure of it. If God had wanted the refinery to blow, it would've blown, so He must've wanted Daniel to take action. It seemed so clear now.

Daniel had spotted a nice-looking pub the previous day, just around the corner from the hotel. He decided to take himself out for a burger and a beer to celebrate.

At twelve thirty, the news was still the same. He shut off the television and headed out.

He entered the pub at 12:46. The television above the bar was running CNN, and he glanced up at the screen.

Everything was fine.

"Afternoon," said the bartender, "can I pull you a pint?"

"Thanks, I'll take a Guinness."

"Menu?"

Daniel shook his head. "Cheeseburger, rare. And fries, well done."

"You got it."

The bartender moved to the computerized cash register and entered the order, then to the taps. Daniel watched black stout flow into the pint glass, creamy head forming on top. It was a slow pull, as Guinness should be. Most pubs in America didn't use nitrogen tanks, but this one obviously did, and for that he was grateful. The extra wait would be worth it.

A voice behind him said, "Hey, Larry, turn up the volume." The bartender abandoned Daniel's half-pulled pint, grabbed a remote and aimed it at the television.

Daniel looked up. On the screen was an aerial shot of a massive inferno.

The newscaster was saying, "…details still coming in, but here's what we know so far: at 11:19, Central Standard Time, a large explosion rocked the Belle Chasse oil refinery in southern Louisiana, followed by three or four secondary explosions…"

Damn! Central Standard Time—of course.

"…The fire is still raging, and officials say it will be some time before they can move in and bring it under control."

Daniel closed his eyes to stop the room from spinning, forced himself to breathe.

Goddamnit, this was not supposed to happen. This could not happen…

The newscaster was saying, "…according to a company spokesman, the fire began adjacent to the number six silo, which was undergoing repair work, and quickly spread through a feeder line to the main unit, where the first explosion occurred. We do not have casualty numbers in yet—we do know that eighteen workers were taken to area hospitals, but most of the workers inside the main facility did not make it out. Many lives have been lost."

Many lives will be lost…

"You OK?"

Daniel opened his eyes. "No," he said, "I'm not."

He dropped a twenty on the bar and bolted out the door.

Father Nick pressed the remote and shut off CNN.

He swiveled his chair to face the large wooden crucifix on the wall opposite his desk, brought his hands together, and closed his eyes. He prayed for the souls of the men who died that morning in Louisiana and for their families. He made the sign of the cross.

He fought the urge to pray for his own soul. He would pray for others, and he would pray for the Lord's guidance, but he would never use prayer as a *Get Out of Jail Free* card. The consequences of his decisions were heavy, but carrying that weight was part of the job.

It was Nick's responsibility to always think of the big picture, even when the big picture was hard to see. If he had taken action to save the men in Louisiana, and the Trinity Anomaly had been disclosed to the world, then whatever power was at work in Trinity would be given instant credence, a papal stamp of authenticity.

And there was no way to know what Trinity might predict—or advise— next. He might tell us what brand of hot sauce works best in gumbo…or he might tell us to nuke Iran.

The Law of Unintended Consequences.

And the unintended consequences could be devastating, not just for the Church, but for the entire world.

Father Nick closed his eyes again, and prayed for guidance.

Tim Trinity stood in the middle of his home theater, staring at the sixty-inch high-resolution plasma television, unable to move. When the "Breaking News" graphic swept across the screen and the newscaster announced the explosion, he'd gone to the wet bar and grabbed a bottle. Now he stood there with the bottle in one hand. He wanted to sit back down on the leather sectional, but he'd forgotten how to operate his body. He wanted to raise the bottle and take a swig, but his arm wouldn't obey.

He wanted to look away from the blaze, but he couldn't even blink.

It looked to him like the fires of hell. Hell on earth. And sitting in the control room, just last night, he'd actually heard himself make the prediction.

How the fuck is this even possible?

Tim Trinity stood, unmoving, unblinking, staring at the screen, for a very long time.

And he began to believe.

PART 2

28:

Daniel jammed on the brakes and skidded to a stop in front of his uncle's Buckhead mansion. He pounded on the front door with the heel of his right hand. The door opened. Tim Trinity made bleary eye contact and turned back inside the house. Daniel followed him down a marble hallway, into a room with a big leather sofa facing a huge television.

The television was tuned to CNN, the volume muted.

Trinity plucked a bottle of bourbon off the coffee table, took a swig. "Yeah, I'm drunk," he said, "and you would be too, if you had a lick of sense."

"What did you do?" Daniel thrust an accusing finger at the television screen. "What did you fucking *do*?"

"I didn't *make* this happen." Trinity was indeed drunk, but still plenty lucid. "Until two days ago, I was just a guy with a mental problem. Question is what did *you* do?"

It felt like a punch in the gut. "I tried to stop it."

"Evidently you didn't try hard enough." Another swig of bourbon. "Lemme ask you something. If the archbishop of New Orleans showed up at the refinery, you think he coulda convinced them there was a problem?"

Daniel didn't answer.

"But they didn't send him, did they? So who's to blame here? Why don't you take a look in the mirror, Danny?"

"No, I-I called…I tried…"

"Yeah? Well, I called too." Trinity glanced at the television. "Wasn't enough. And your bosses apparently didn't share your enthusiasm, or they'd have put some muscle behind it." He pointed the bottle at Daniel. "You may not wear the collar, but long as you work for them, you're carrying their water. So let's cut the bullshit, boy. What does the Vatican really want from me?"

"They sent me here to discredit you. Debunk your tongues act."

"But they knew the predictions were coming true. So what's really going on? Eliminating the competition? What?"

Daniel brushed past his uncle and turned the television off. He sat down, braced his hands on his knees, and breathed slowly. "They don't believe God is working through you. They don't think it's Satan, but they really don't know."

"Oh, give me a fucking tax break, Danny. *Satan?* 'Course it's not Satan. Tell you who else it's not. It's not Santa Claus or the Green Goblin or the Easter Bunny neither. Satan's a fairy tale."

"Well, whatever it is, it's not God." Daniel nodded toward his uncle. "You're not exactly a poster child for faith."

Trinity sat on the sofa beside his nephew, spoke quietly. "That's the first sensible thing you've said since you got here." He put the bottle on the floor. "But you know what I think? I think the Church is worried that God *is* working through me. They've got a trillion-dollar business to protect, and they're gonna start looking pretty musty-dusty, with their robes and incense and Latin incantations, if a guy like me is a miracle. Not good for their brand."

Daniel stood. "I'm not listening to this. The Vatican is *not* a business—"

"Christ, son, everything's a business. Thought I'd taught you at least that much."

"And you are *not* a miracle. You're not even a fucking believer."

Daniel walked out without another word, his hands balled into fists.

29:

Daniel sat nursing a Guinness and picking absently at a Cobb salad. He didn't feel hungry, but needed the nourishment, so he forced himself to eat. It was coming up on nine o'clock. The television screen above the bar displayed a live shot of what used to be the main refinery building, glowing like a man-made sunset in the Louisiana night.

Still burning, but now under control.

The opening graphics for *AC360* swept across the screen, and Anderson Cooper's familiar voice said, "Tonight on *AC360*: 'Tragedy and Mystery in Louisiana.' Our guest is Julia Rothman, senior investigative reporter at the *New Orleans Times-Picayune*…"

Daniel's fork clattered to the floor.

"…and she has a shocking angle on this story that you are not going to want to miss."

Oh, no…

After a commercial break that felt like a year, Anderson Cooper gave a recap of the day's events, voiced over a video package showing the inferno in full blaze and night shots of firefighters at work. No final figures yet, but at least one hundred dead. An interview clip of an oil company spokesman established that the fire was a freak accident, the likely culprit a faulty pressure detector that had misread an open valve as closed.

And then there was Julia, sitting right across from Cooper in the studio. She smiled, and something fluttered in Daniel's chest.

God, she looks good…

Cooper thanked Julia for flying in to Atlanta for the show.

Daniel's heart skipped another beat.

She's here...

Cooper told viewers that Reverend Tim Trinity was a local television evangelist, originally from New Orleans. He showed a short clip from the *Tim Trinity Prosperity-Power Miracle Hour*. Then Julia gave a succinct explanation of the Trinity Anomaly and how to decode Reverend Tim Trinity's speaking-in-tongues routine.

Cooper asked how Julia had learned of this phenomenon.

Here it comes...

But Julia declined to reveal her source.

For now, anyway...

She cut to the chase, said that Trinity predicted the refinery explosion while speaking in tongues during his most recent Sunday sermon.

"Have we got the tape? OK, let's roll it," said Cooper.

Tim Trinity came on the screen. The video ran backwards, sped up by a third, and it looked like a clip from the old *Benny Hill Show*. But Trinity's voice was clear, and hearing the prediction again, Daniel cringed.

"This is simply unbelievable," said Cooper. He introduced CNN's top video engineer, who came on by remote feed from the newsroom and authenticated the videotape. Cooper shook his head, astounded. "So, Julia, what do you make of this?"

"Honestly, I have no idea," she said. "I've only had time to go through a few of his broadcasts, but he seems to be making predictions about all sorts of things, from thunderstorms to horse races, and every one I've seen has been accurate."

"You're convinced this is real."

"I'm not convinced of anything, Anderson. It could be the greatest hoax ever. Was Trinity tipped off to the outcomes ahead of time? Or has he somehow come into the ability to see the future? Or perhaps there's a third explanation. We need to find out what's going on here."

OK, so she's beautiful—Cut it out, and get your head in the game...

To the camera, Cooper said, "For the record, we invited Reverend Trinity on the show to tell his side of the story, but his office said he could not be reached." Then, back to Julia, "You know, people are going to think God is talking through this guy. You think that's possible?"

"No." Julia shifted in her chair, clearly troubled by the question.

Of course, she would be…

"Look, I'm a reporter, not a theologian. I'm extremely skeptical of any supernatural explanation, and I'd caution against drawing any kind of metaphysical conclusions. We don't know anything yet. We need to scrutinize and test his predictions, follow the story and see where it leads."

"And apparently the story leads just north of Atlanta, to Highway 403?"

"That's right. In a sermon two weeks ago, Trinity predicted that a billboard on 403 would collapse tonight—exactly twenty-three minutes after midnight—blocking two northbound lanes, but with no fatalities. Now, the fascinating thing about this prediction is that we know about it ahead of time, so it's testable. I've been in contact with the Georgia Department of Transportation, and they sent structural engineers to check it out."

"And?"

"And there's absolutely nothing wrong with the support structure. So, barring a massive earthquake, the sign should still be standing at 12:24." Julia slid an envelope across the desk. "They asked me not to reveal the location—they're concerned about spectators blocking the highway—but I've written the exact mile marker down, and the date of Trinity's prediction, so you can verify it after we're off the air. Whatever happens—or more likely doesn't—I'll be there to see it."

In a sermon two weeks ago… Daniel reached into his briefcase, pulled out the file folder, and started flipping through the tabs, looking for the transcript that would give him the billboard's location.

✢ ✢ ✢

A Georgia State Police cruiser stood in the median. A state trooper leaned back against the fender, looking bored. A few yards ahead, Julia stood talking to a young man with a video camera perched on his shoulder.

As Daniel got out of the car, Julia approached and gave him a warm, platonic hug.

"Hey, stranger."

"Guess I'm not clear on the definition of 'off the record,'" said Daniel.

"What's the problem? I kept you out of it." Julia brushed a stray hair behind her ear. "Danny, what did you expect me to do? This story is important."

"You showed somewhat less interest before a hundred people died."

Her chestnut eyes flashed fire. "Thanks for reminding me, it's been at least five minutes since I beat myself up about that. Look, I didn't believe you. OK? I-I thought you'd gone crazy. And my inaction cost lives, and that's something I will have to carry for the rest of my life."

She drew a sharp breath and looked away, and now Daniel could see the guilt she was carrying, the pain, and the effort to tamp it all down. "I'm sorry," he said, "that wasn't fair of me. You're right, it was a crazy story."

"Still, I should've checked it out," she said.

"It's not your fault, Julia. Anyone would've thought the same thing."

"Regardless, I'm not about to make that mistake again. So I'm sorry for your hurt feelings, but this isn't about you. Neither one of us has the right to suppress this thing."

She was right about that too, and Daniel knew he was doing the same thing he'd done earlier at his uncle's house: transferring anger at himself into anger at another. *He* had been the one with foreknowledge, and it was *he* who should've done more to stop the explosion. There was no dodging that responsibility.

He looked across four lanes of northbound traffic to the white van with a red CNN logo on its side, parked on the shoulder. He glanced at his watch, said, "Five minutes."

"Shooter says this is the best angle," said Julia, pointing up the median.

They walked past the police cruiser to where the camera guy stood mounting the video camera on a tripod. He secured the camera, aimed it at the lighted billboard standing across the northbound lanes, to the right of the highway, about fifty yards ahead.

At the left edge of the billboard was a giant peach, with the words GEORGIA LOTTERY in front. Next to the logo was a hip young white guy wearing a jean jacket. He had a Photoshop-stretched smile, and his face was comically distorted by a wide-angle lens. Across the billboard, a black woman with short gray hair held her hands to her cheeks and flashed a similarly impossible grin. Between them, dollar bills rained down from the sky.

The tag line read:

TODAY COULD BE THE DAY

Julia said, "Structure's far from new, but the engineer said there's nothing wrong with it. So we're really not expecting anything, and…"

Daniel watched her face as she spoke. The same deep brown eyes, still sparkling with passionate intelligence. The same luxurious lips that used to take him to the edge of paradise. Gentle laugh lines now framed her mouth and ran from the corners of her eyes. And a vertical worry line creased the space between her eyes. They transformed her face from something merely beautiful into something seriously beautiful. The pretty girl was now a woman in full bloom, with a woman's body to match. He felt an erection growing.

"Hello, Danny? You there?"

"What? Right, sorry, you were saying?"

Julia smiled. He knew that smile.

You've been busted, he thought.

She glanced at her watch, turned to the camera guy. "We rolling, Shooter?"

"Yup." Then Shooter jerked his head back from the camera and flicked a toggle switch back and forth. "Shit."

"What?"

"Chip just blew."

"Goddamnit," said Julia. "We're ninety seconds away."

Shooter snatched a ring of keys from his pocket. "Got another camera in the truck." He grinned. "College state champion, two hundred meters. Time me." He turned to the road and took off.

Daniel glanced to the right as Shooter sprinted out across the empty northbound lanes. The headlights of a car swept fast around the curve in the far lane, an eighteen-wheeler just behind it in the second lane.

"Wait!" he yelled, but the kid was already committed, didn't stop.

The car jerked to the left, tires squealing.

The semi's air-brakes locked up its massive wheels.

The truck veered, blasting its horn, missing the car by inches.

The car veered into the third lane, straightened out, flew past.

The big rig skidded, jackknifed, and went over on its side, showering sparks, slewing—right through Shooter—off the road, and slammed into the billboard structure.

Silence. Then the billboard groaned, shuddered, and came crashing down. Blocking two northbound lanes of Highway 403.

The state trooper jumped into his cruiser and took off across the highway, siren wailing, roof lights flashing blue and red. Daniel and Julia followed in his car and skidded to a stop beside the overturned truck. The trooper was out of his car and peering through the windshield of the truck's cab. He smashed the windshield with his Maglight.

The truck driver climbed out, stood up, and brushed himself down.

Daniel ran behind the trailer, searching the ditch for the remains of Shooter in the dark.

"Dude, that was some crazy shit!"

Daniel spun around as Shooter jumped down from his perch on the truck's spare tire. "I'm OK, I'm fine," Shooter said, shaking his head and grinning like a little kid. "Wild, man!"

"But how—"

"That big spare tire came at me, I just grabbed it and held on for the ride, prayin' for a fuckin' miracle."

"Looks like you got one." Daniel turned on his heel and headed back to the car, thinking: *And a shiny new polyester prophet walks amongst us. Goddamnit.*

30:

"**I** cannot believe what we just witnessed." Julia shook her head again, sipped her double rum and Coke in the dim light of the bar.

"Uh-huh," said Daniel.

"I mean, that is *not* something you could know was gonna happen ahead of time. It just isn't."

"Nope," said Daniel.

"Your uncle actually predicted the future."

"Sure looks that way." Daniel swallowed some beer.

Julia looked at him for a moment, her eyes filled with concern. "Are you all right?"

"I don't know what you want me to say, Julia. Am I being interviewed by a reporter? Are we two friends talking? What?"

"OK. That's a fair question." Julia's cell vibrated on the table. She held up a finger, answered the phone. "Yes, Herb. When, tomorrow? OK, all right, I'll be there. Six thirty, fine. Fine, gotta go." She put the cell down, made a *sorry about that* face. "My editor. They want me on *Good Morning America*."

"Congratulations." Churlish.

"Come on, don't be that way. Look, you're right, I agree, we need an understanding…" Julia sipped her drink again, then reached across the table and put her hand on top of Daniel's. She spoke with gentle authority. "You phoned me, remember? You brought me into this, and I have a job to do. But everything you say is completely off the record. I'll use what you tell me to help guide my investigation, but I won't report what you say. OK?"

Daniel needed to believe her. He needed to talk about the chaos now swirling around his head. He also needed to get his fucking hand out from under hers.

Her phone vibrated again, and her hand left his. She pushed a button, and the phone went silent. "That's what voicemail is for," she shrugged. "Now talk to me, Danny."

"OK," said Daniel. "Truth is I'm having a tough time with all this. I came here to debunk his tongues act, and the thing turns out to be..." He drank some beer. "I've been to see him, actually spoke with him. First time in twenty years."

"Must've been hard."

"And he's still a con man, same as ever, only...only this thing is really happening. His tongues act has become real. God has actually chosen this scumbag as his messenger. And what the hell does *that* imply?"

"You know I'm an atheist, right?" Like it was something he might've forgotten.

"I didn't figure that had changed," he said. "But the science you worship can't explain this phenomenon either."

"The fact that human understanding is limited is not evidence of a deity." She sipped her drink. "Anyway, I didn't mean to make this about me."

Daniel sipped some beer. "All my life I've been searching for a miracle... and now I've found one. And it's happening to *Tim Trinity*, if you can believe that. It's like some cosmic practical joke."

"I think it's a little early to be calling this a miracle."

"Really? I don't think so. You saw what happened tonight. Not only isn't it something you could know about in advance, it wouldn't have even *happened* if Shooter hadn't run into the highway. Which means it wouldn't have happened if the camera hadn't broken down or if you hadn't set up in the median for a better angle or if...Bottom line, *our presence* there tonight caused that billboard to come down. Just think about that for a second. So many unforeseeable and seemingly random events had to occur in order for Trinity's prediction to come true, there's just no way to explain it without the hand of God. And we wouldn't have been there tonight if I hadn't called you about the refinery…" He shook his head. "I mean, how far do we want to follow this chain? You wouldn't have been called about the refinery if my boss hadn't assigned *me* to this case…and *that* wouldn't have happened if I hadn't been Tim Trinity's nephew…and I wouldn't have even been there for my boss to assign if I hadn't become a priest."

Julia smiled. "And if you hadn't left me, you wouldn't have become a priest."

Damn…

The pain of Daniel's choice came back with full force, as if he were making it all over again. And with it, the guilt. He searched for something to say, but came up empty. Julia's last link in the coincidence chain hung in the air between them like stale cigarette smoke.

This time it was Daniel's phone that vibrated. The call display said *Fr. Nick*. He let it go to voicemail. "I, uh, I still feel…well, I'm sorry about how that worked out, Julia."

"It was a long time ago. Wasn't easy, but I got over you. Really, it's OK."

Daniel's heart sank. *But I never got over you*, he thought.

Julia's smile widened. "Anyway, here we are again. The Lord works in mysterious ways," she teased.

Daniel forced a smile, drank some beer. "I *know* what happened tonight is a miracle, Julia. There's no other explanation. I don't *want* to believe that God would work through a man like my uncle, but He is. I believe in God, absolutely. But I'm starting to think my religion doesn't describe Him very well."

A man's voice said, "Jesus, Julia, *there* you are." It was Shooter, coming up fast. "We gotta get you back to the scene. We're going live at the top of the hour."

31:

Back in the quiet of his hotel room, Daniel sipped cognac and reviewed the day's developments, sorting his responses into two categories: personal and professional.

Start with the professional, he told himself. Put aside predictions of thunderstorms and football games, and focus on the oil refinery. Maybe the small stuff was just a way to get our attention, a way to ensure that we act on the major predictions when they arrive.

One hundred lives could have been saved had the Church taken action. Had those lives been saved, this assessment wouldn't even be necessary. They weren't saved, but that didn't fundamentally change anything; the public now knew, and the next important prediction would be acted upon.

Professionally, the case was clear, and the billboard accident—which Trinity could neither have known about in advance, nor caused to happen—had sealed the deal. Professionally, Daniel concluded, the Trinity Anomaly was a miracle.

Personally, things were more complicated.

Twenty years earlier, the great and powerful Oz became a huckster jerking levers behind the curtain, Daniel's life became a lie, and he ran away in search of a real miracle.

Now he had one.

Yes, it was happening to the huckster—and yes, that was a problem—but the larger point was *it was happening*. And that changed everything. Because if the priesthood is a call to faith, Daniel's shameful secret was that he had never sincerely answered the call. *There can be no religion without faith.* And there can be no faith if we demand that God prove His existence.

No, that's not right. Not *existence.* Daniel had no trouble believing in God, creator of the universe. That God existed for Daniel. The proof he sought was not of God-the-creator but God-the-father.

God who loves us, who cares what we do with the world, cares how we treat one another.

Daniel had always known his ersatz faith made him less of a priest. And while he prayed daily for stronger faith, the truth was he just wanted a damn miracle. Just one miracle to prove God was taking an active interest in human affairs.

And now he had one.

Daniel picked up the phone and dialed a number that was known to fewer than 120 people on the planet. The phone was answered on the first ring.

"Facilitations. Please identify."

"Father Daniel Byrne. Devil's Advocate, clearance code: UG-8806."

"Go ahead."

"I need a plane, in Atlanta. Destination is Rome, and I need to leave in"—a glance at his watch—"two hours."

"Um, that's pretty tight, I'm not sure—"

"Just make it happen," said Daniel. "Priority One."

"Yes, sir. Anything else?"

"Yeah, get a message to the DA. Tell him I'm coming in. And tell him we've got a positive."

He hung up, shaved, showered, and dressed. He hadn't worn the uniform since his last visit to the Vatican, and as he adjusted his clerical collar in the mirror, he saw a priest looking back. In recent years, he'd felt increasingly like an imposter, the uniform increasingly like a costume.

But not anymore.

The sky was still dark as Daniel walked across the tarmac to the white private jet with a gold holy cross painted on its tail. He climbed the aluminum steps and entered the lush cabin, was greeted by the smell of fresh leather. The seats were wide and soft, and could swivel, and each had a gold cross embroidered into the headrest. Side tables of polished burl wood and silk curtains on the windows. At the back of the cabin, a well-stocked bar and flat-panel television on the wall.

As they reached altitude, Daniel reclined his seat and closed his eyes.

32:

Julia wrapped her wet hair in a towel and picked up her cell phone. The display said it was her editor at the *Times-Picayune* calling from New Orleans.

"Haven't found him yet," she said.

"Shit."

"Left messages with his office, got his unlisted number and left messages at the house too. Nothing else I can do right now on that angle."

"There *is* no other angle, Julia. Trinity *is* the story."

"I get it, Herb, you don't have to yell at me. Nobody knows where he is, what the hell do you want me to do? Anyway, you have no idea what it's like here. Atlanta's gone insane."

"Seen it on the news. What are you following?"

"Got a call in to Sheriff Alatorre. Figure I'll talk to a couple survivors, work some *human interest* to carry us through the next cycle until Trinity reappears."

"OK, I want you to get with Kathryn Reynolds, she's a producer at CNN. You'll be working with her for the duration."

"Oh God, gimme a break."

"I don't want to hear it, Julia. You know the drill—we're broke, and they offered to pay your expenses. And we need the profile. So it's either that or we call you home and send Sammy to work with them. Your story, your choice."

Julia blew out a long breath. "Fine, but I answer to you. Can't serve two masters." She wrote down the number Herb read over the phone, said, "I gotta run."

"Hey, one more thing."

"Yeah?"

"Nice job on GMA this morning."

"Thanks. On two hours sleep, but yeah, I think I did OK."

"Better than OK, you did great. The camera really likes you."

"Well, thank you."

"Look, I know we don't pay television money—hell, we barely pay newspaper money—but…I hope you'll stay with us when this is all over. I mean, you'll be able to write your ticket now—"

"Don't sweat it, Herb. New Orleans is home. And I'm a newspaper gal, I bleed ink."

She hung up, towel-dried her hair and tied it back in a ponytail, and switched on the television.

The city had indeed gone insane. Lunatics were flooding in from all over the country, clogging the streets, pitching tents in the parking lot of Trinity's church. And it would only get worse. The television outlets were having some kind of tantric orgasm over the story, decoding Trinity's past predictions, confirming their accuracy, and reporting each as *Breaking News*, around the clock, reporting each with the same breathless intensity as the refinery explosion.

This just in: Reverend Tim Trinity accurately predicted a traffic jam three weeks ago!

This just in: Reverend Tim Trinity declared that jambalaya is good!

Asinine.

Julia really *was* a newspaper gal, and she did bleed ink. Television is a possum with a tapeworm, she thought; always hungry and it'll feed on any garbage. But the newspaper industry was in trouble—many would say mortal danger—and nobody knew what the hell to do about it.

Julia watched the muted television for a minute—a helicopter shot of the congested highways leading into Atlanta. How to make sense of all these people? It wasn't really fair to label them *all* as lunatics—after all, there were hundreds of thousands of them and growing by the minute.

But really, what was going through their heads? Why were people so eager to embrace religious explanations for the things they didn't understand?

Julia was an atheist, sure. But unlike many of the other skeptics she'd known, she didn't consider herself intellectually superior to the vast majority of humans who did believe. She felt, rather, like a bit of a mutant. Like maybe 10 percent of the world's population had somehow been genetically deprived of whatever neurological wiring caused the other 90 percent to perceive this thing called God.

That didn't mean there was a God. It just meant the mass illusion was invisible to her. There was a level on which she would never be able to relate to believers, and while they might derive great comfort from their belief, that didn't excuse turning a blind eye to all the destructive influence of religion in the world.

All the wealth and time and labor we pour into propping up our respective priests and reverends, rabbis and imams, monks and gurus, building grand cathedrals, churches, temples, mosques, and mansions; sacrificing our young on the altar of war, war over whose imaginary friend is the *real* imaginary friend (might as well print *My God Can Beat Up Your God* T-shirts); the bigotry, misogyny, subjection, intolerance and guilt. All that human energy, wasted, in response to the simple fact that we know we are going to die, and we don't know what happens after, and we're afraid that this life is all there is. The question haunts us—from the chilling childhood moment when we realize that we and everyone we love will die, until we exhale our final breath. And if a kind of mass self-hypnosis called Religion helps us cope with our fear, fine, but we have to look at the unintended consequences of embracing an irrational philosophy. We don't have to look far. Ground Zero in Manhattan will do. Or the Gaza Strip, if you've got some air miles burning a hole in your pocket. While you're over there, make a stop in Africa, where the pope is preaching to a country ravaged by tribal war, overpopulation, chronic food shortage, and AIDS. The pope tells them to stop using condoms, or the all-powerful and all-loving God will cast their souls into the fiery furnace of eternal damnation. Nice.

So much for journalistic objectivity. Clearly this story was pushing all her bias buttons. She would have to watch herself, tread carefully.

Her cell phone vibrated on the table. She glanced at the little screen, picked it up.

"Sheriff, thanks for getting back."

"You may be the only civilized human being in your profession," Sheriff Alatorre groused. "Your colleagues are operatin' under the misguided notion that talking to them is my primary function. Can't get a minute to do my goddamn job around here." He cleared his throat. "Sorry. Been a long couple days."

"It's all right," said Julia, thinking: *Make him your ally*. She put a smile in her voice. "Have to admit, that's a true assessment of a great number of my colleagues, Sheriff. And I do appreciate your time."

"That's why I'm talking to you. Your message said you're looking to interview survivors."

"Yes, sir."

"Young lady, I am about to make your day." He rumbled a baritone chuckle in Julia's ear. "Get out your pen. I got a survivor you are *definitely* gonna want to talk to."

The home number rang unanswered. Julia punched in the cell number and Andrew Thibodeaux picked up on the second ring. She identified herself and asked him to repeat what he had told the sheriff. As he spoke, she scribbled shorthand in her notebook.

"Well, it's like I told the man," Andrew said. "Went to work, foreman said he'd got a crazy call from Reverend Trinity, sayin' we gotta shut down the refinery, and there's gonna be an accident. Something about visions and tongues. Foreman thought he was drunk."

"But you didn't?"

"I seen him on the TV night before. Just surfin', you know?—and suddenly my remote goes on the fritz, and I'm stuck on Reverend Trinity, and

Reverend Trinity is talking to me—I mean, *right at me*—and I got the idea he's talking for God. Don't know how I know it, but I just *know* it, like a *feeling* kinda knowing. So next morning, when I hear about the phone call, then I know it for sure, and I'm like, '*Shazam!* I'm outta here.'"

"Uh, wow." Thinking: *He's about a peck short of a bushel.* "Please, go on. What happened next?"

"That's it. Reverend Trinity saved my life, and the Lord saved my soul. I told the guys at work to come with me, but they stayed. Foreman fired my ass on my way out the door too. I left anyway. Best decision I ever made."

"Can't argue that," said Julia. "Andrew, that's an incredible story. I'm in Atlanta, but I can be in New Orleans this afternoon, if you'll meet with me." *What the hell—might as well fly back and forth on CNN's tab.* "I'd like to do a full interview, a profile piece on you."

"You can be in New Orleans, but I ain't gonna be. The Lord has beckoned me, and I'm on the road. Call ya when I get to Atlanta."

Julia put the phone down, thinking: *That boy needs a head-doctor.*

Goose bumps rose on her forearms, and a shiver rolled over her. That's exactly what you thought when Danny called, she reminded herself, and over one hundred men paid for your arrogance with their lives.

Shit…

Her stomach knotted, and for the first time in a long while, she wanted a cigarette. *Great.* After Danny entered the seminary, she'd graduated from social smoker to simply smoker, and she'd maintained that status longer than intended. Finally kicked the habit five years ago, and she was damned if she'd go back to it.

Danny…

The very topic she'd been avoiding. OK, *subconscious mind*, Julia thought, you want to talk about it? Fine, we'll talk about it.

Truth was, seeing Danny again had stirred up emotional silt, thankfully long settled and now unwelcome. But that was to be expected. He was, after all, the first real love of her life. The first and, so far, the most profound love of her life.

When he left her for the priesthood, the heartbreak was crippling, and Julia spent the next few months doing her job on autopilot and smoking pot on her days off. Her self-esteem had taken a pounding. Hard enough if a man leaves you for another woman, but Danny left her for his imaginary God-Daddy. Left her for a life of celibacy. And what did *that* say about her feminine charms? It was a rough blow.

She had no intention of grieving forever, and she soon forced herself to shake it off and get back in the game. A rebound romance with an old college boyfriend turned into an ill-advised marriage that lasted two years—two-and-a-half, if you include the engagement.

Her fault; she was never really in love with Luc. Then again, Luc had that Cajun brand of macho, allowed no woman past the wrought iron gates of his mind, wouldn't have proposed to a woman who insisted on knowing him well enough to achieve a profound love.

When she woke up to the fact that she wasn't in love with her husband, she resolved to get closer, figuring if she could really know him, she could fall in love with him. But Luc would not reveal himself, resented the pressure, and the relationship quickly went to hell.

Danny never kept her out. He had the same wrought iron gates as all men, but he opened them for her, and once inside, she had found her home. And then he'd ripped it away from her.

And now he was back.

She caught a fleeting image of the previous night, in the bar. The way Danny rotated his pint glass on the coaster, a quarter turn after each sip, an unconscious gesture that cleaned the foam from the inside of the glass as he drank. He was still doing it, fourteen years on.

She wondered what else hadn't changed. Had he really been celibate for fourteen years? Hard to imagine. He'd been a passionate lover—of course, who isn't at eighteen?—but unlike most young men, his passion included the desire to see her needs satisfied, and not just to bolster his credentials as a lover, but because he wanted her to be happy. Danny had been afraid of many things, but intimacy was not one of them.

They'd been good together. Really good. Her girlfriends thought it a bit creepy, a woman in her twenties taking up with a teenager, and she had her own moments of doubt and discomfort over the age difference, but Danny was not your average teenager. In ways that mattered, he was more of a man than most of her friends' boyfriends, and he was certainly more mature than Luc had been.

Still, however grown up Danny presented himself, he *was* only eighteen, and the relationship always felt star-crossed, fated to end on his next birthday, and she forced herself not to push too hard. It would do neither of them any good if Danny chose her over the priesthood only to resent her for it later.

All she could do, in the end, was let him go.

And now he was back. Not as a lover, but there was no denying the sexual spark—still alive for both of them, she knew—and he'd grown into quite a handsome man. And when she'd hugged him hello, she couldn't help but notice the muscles of his arms, tight and defined through the cotton shirt—

Snap out of it, girl—he's a priest.

"I believe in God," he said last night in the bar, "but I'm starting to think my religion doesn't describe Him very well." Might that mean…

Stop. You are not *going to seduce a priest. Shut it down, and focus on the job.*

Andrew Thibodeaux stopped at the tollbooth, paid his dollar, and chugged on up the Greater New Orleans Bridge. The old pickup backfired, protesting the climb, her payload piled high with the sum total of Andrew's life—at least, all he intended to keep—a blue nylon tarp tied down over everything, its corners flapping in the briny breeze, waving good-bye to the Crescent City. He had $357 in his pocket, another thousand in the bank, no job, and no idea what lay ahead.

None of that mattered. Through Reverend Tim, God had saved Andrew. Reverend Tim was in Atlanta, so God wanted Andrew in Atlanta.

It was that simple.

He pressed down on the accelerator, patted the cracked dashboard.

"You're a good old girl," he said. "You'll make it."

33:

Rome, Italy...

Daniel deplaned and crossed the tarmac in the dark, feeling energized but slightly disconnected from his body, not quite like watching himself in a movie, but as if his consciousness were hovering along, about a foot above his head.

Not unreasonable. The last week had been an emotional whirlwind, and he'd just slept through the flight—the first full night he'd gotten since the girl in Nigeria with the holes in her hands. But it hadn't been night—he'd actually slept through the day—and with the six-hour time difference, he now felt as though he were living in a parallel world of perpetual nighttime.

Even blindfolded, he'd have known he was back in Rome. The air here was softer than Atlanta, and carried a distinctly vegetal base note. Like New Orleans, Rome was (for good and ill) a proudly *aromatic* city, and that fertile base note was the constant denominator, never letting you forget that the city is a living thing.

He collected his motorcycle from long-term parking and headed up A91, through the warm Italian night, toward the bright lights of the city, leaning into the curves, gunning the throttle on the straightaways, feeling more alive than he had in years. In no time at all, he was in front of the Vatican, pushing down the kickstand, wading through waves of tourists, passing the Swiss Guard sentries, cartoon colorful but deadly as coral snakes, and bounding up the ancient marble steps.

✤ ✤ ✤

"Oh, hello, Daniel." Nick's secretary, George, was standing in the outer office. He spoke in a rough Belfast brogue and his smile showed gaps where a few teeth had been knocked out over the years. "Father Nick's been tied up in meetings, and it's getting on. He said go home, get a good night's rest, and he'll meet with you in the morning."

"I slept on the plane."

"Well, *he* didn't."

Daniel moved to go around, and George sidestepped to intercept. "Not so fast, boyo."

He was in his late forties, a little thick around the middle, but there was hard muscle under the padding. Rumor among the priests was George had been a Provisional IRA thug in his youth, and Daniel had no reason to disbelieve it. And boxing skills don't often tip the scales against a seasoned Provo street fighter.

"I need to see him, George. Now."

George put his hand gently on Daniel's shoulder and spoke soft menace. "The man said 'tomorrow.'"

Daniel spun, pivoting around George, bolted for the oak door, ripped it open, and said, "I gotta see you, Nick." As he crossed the threshold, Father Nick dropped a file folder on his desk blotter, removed his reading glasses, and stood.

From behind, George clamped Daniel's shoulder in a vise, found the pressure point on the joint, and dug in with a thumb that felt like an ice pick. He spoke into Daniel's right ear. "You investigators think the sun shines from yer arseholes. Got news for ya: It don't. So you can quit acting like you're fucking *Bono*." Then, to Nick, "Father Nick, if I may be so bold: Perhaps it's time you let me take our little rock star downstairs, teach him some manners."

"Appreciate the offer, George, but I'll take the meeting." He nodded assurance. "I'll be fine, please close the door on your way out."

The pain in Daniel's shoulder eased into a dull throb as George let go. The door clicked shut behind him.

"Didn't you get my message?" Daniel said.

"Which one?"

Daniel now heard the sharpness in Nick's tone, saw the anger behind his eyes.

"Way I see it," Nick went on, "you've been sending very mixed messages. And here's one that confuses me: Under orders to *stand down*, you instead call a member of the *press*? Who happens to be your *ex-girlfriend*?"

"Are you spying on me?"

"Looking out for you. And starting to have serious doubts. This isn't just a job, Daniel, we take an oath."

"OK, look, it's—well, complicated."

"Yeah, I bet."

"Not what you're thinking." Daniel raised his hands, took a slow breath. "I know, I disobeyed a direct order, and I'm sorry, but there were exigent circumstances, and the thing is, you'll understand once you hear my report." He pulled his notebook from the breast pocket of his jacket, flipped it open. "The thing is, Nick, we've got a real miracle on our hands."

Nick sighed, ran a hand over his head. "Holy Mother of God. I didn't send you to find a miracle. I sent you to debunk a cheap, gaudy Holy Roller, who you already *know* is a con man. And not only did you blow it—he converted you."

"It's not like that. In fact, I'm angry at God for choosing him. But I can't deny the evidence of my eyes, and they've seen the impossible. Did you even read my e-mail?"

Nick nodded. "And I think you've been played for a sucker. Trinity's got tons of cash, he could've paid the trucker to take out the billboard at a pre-arranged time."

"Not possible. You weren't there, you didn't see how it went down."

"And quite conveniently, there's no videotape."

"The chip blew in the camera. That's *why* the accident happened."

"Or that's the way it was staged. Did you check the camera?"

Daniel shook his head.

"Then how do you know Trinity didn't pay off the cameraman?"

"Stop," Daniel said, a little too loud. He started walking the floor to keep the tension out of his voice. "Just give me a chance. Believe me, if you'd been there…You can talk to the other witnesses, the state trooper—"

"Or your girlfriend."

"Goddamnit!" Daniel's entire body welled with rage. "Yes, she saw it too, talk to her if you want. And—because I know you're curious—I'm not fucking her, OK?"

Nick turned his attention to the file folder on the desk. "You shouldn't have come here tonight, Daniel. I'm not willing to discuss this while you're so emotional."

"But you're not listening to me."

"No, you're not listening to me. This conversation is over." Nick signed the top piece of paper in the folder, handed the form to Daniel without looking up. "Here are your orders: You are off this case. You are now officially on sabbatical, for spiritual renewal. You will go home and you will get some sleep. In the morning, you will fly to Florence, and from there you will be driven to Poppi, where you will engage in quiet meditation and prayer." He sent Daniel a hard look. "Get your head together. At the appropriate time, I'll bring you back to active duty."

The walls closed in on Daniel. The retreat just outside Poppi was a dumping ground for broken men—whisky priests with the shakes, spiritual burnouts addicted to online gambling, pedophiles addicted to altar boys— once you went in, you stayed until they decided you were fit for service. Some men lived there for decades. Others quit the priesthood to get out.

Nick had sent Daniel to Poppi once before, four years earlier, after Daniel returned from Honduras with blood on his hands. He spent nearly five months in counseling at the retreat before he was deemed spiritually and psychologically fit to leave.

"Nick, please, don't do this."

"Sorry, kiddo. You're gonna have to sit the rest of this one out, I just can't risk it. Probably never should've assigned you to the case, but I thought you were strong enough to handle it. I was wrong."

"This isn't like Honduras, I promise you." He held the form out to Nick, but the older priest didn't take it.

"No, this is worse. Then, I was worried about your sanity. This time, your loyalty is in question."

34:

Harsh morning light streamed through the east windows as Daniel paced between dresser and bed, filling a large suitcase with socks and boxers and T-shirts, trousers and toiletries and paperback crime novels.

Sorry, kiddo. You're gonna have to sit the rest of this one out, I just can't risk it.

But Nick wasn't just making sure Daniel would *sit it out*. There was no television at the retreat in Poppi, no radio, no newspapers. No contact whatsoever with the outside world. However this thing with his uncle played out, Nick was making sure Daniel would miss it entirely.

Was *that* God's will?

Whatever's happening here, it's happening to your uncle. God doesn't make coincidences that big. No way He'd want you to sit it out.

Was Nick even thinking about God's will? Or was protecting the "One True Church" from a Protestant/Holy Roller/con artist, the trump card?

Or was that just Trinity talking, inside Daniel's head?

He snapped the suitcase shut, sat heavily beside it on the bed. The framed photo on the dresser caught his eye, and he picked it up. Eighteen-year-old Daniel Byrne, freshly minted New Orleans Golden Gloves Welterweight Champion.

Julia had been in the stands when Daniel won the trophy. She didn't like him fighting, couldn't stand to see him get hit, but promised if he made the finals, she'd be there. And she was true to her word.

Tim Trinity was also there, standing in the back row, drinking beer from a plastic New Orleans Saints go-cup, cheering louder than anybody, cheering: *Danny, Danny, Danny!*

Daniel had refused to even acknowledge his existence, wouldn't give him the satisfaction of letting him play proud papa. Instead he used Trinity's presence to fuel his anger, and scored a knockout when he shattered the other boy's nose thirty-three seconds into the first round.

Now he looked at the kid he was, holding the trophy over his head and grinning for the camera. Grinning like he was the happiest kid in the world.

You might've fooled everyone else, but you didn't fool me...

He put the photo back on the dresser, picked up a roll of white Title boxing tape and his gloves. God, he wanted to punch something. But he didn't put them on, just dropped them in his carry-on.

Maybe they'd let him set up a heavy bag at the retreat.

Call it *aggression therapy.*

A black car idled at the curb in front of Daniel's apartment building. George leaned against it, smoking.

Daniel stepped out into the morning light, dropped his suitcase, and put on his sunglasses. "I know the way to the airport."

"Father Nick asked me to travel with you today, look after whatever needs you might have along the way." George didn't put any effort into selling the line. There was no use pretending; they both knew it was bullshit.

"He thinks I'm gonna go AWOL?"

George shrugged. "Quit yer whining, *Bono,* this is as awkward for me as it is for you." Then he let out a cruel grin. "Well, maybe not."

"Screw you, George." Daniel hoisted his bag. "Pop the trunk."

✤ ✤ ✤

So this was how far Nick's confidence had fallen. He'd never made a secret of the fact that Daniel was *favorite son* among his investigators. Heir apparent.

Now he didn't even trust Daniel to get on a plane.

I just can't risk it...

Daniel stewed and George gloated, both in silence, all the way to Leonardo da Vinci Airport, where George led the way through Terminal B, to the Alitalia check-in counter. They checked Daniel's suitcase and picked up their tickets to Florence.

They don't send you to purgatory on a private jet.

With time to kill, they found a business travelers' lounge, grabbed some coffee and croissants, and settled in a quiet corner, where a television displayed a scrolling stock ticker.

George snatched up the remote, aimed it at the television. "I'll get a news channel, give you one final chance to watch your uncle."

One final chance. What a prick.

"I don't want to see it," Daniel said. He stood up. "I'm gonna check the board, see if we're on schedule."

George also stood. "Wouldn't want you to get lonesome." They crossed the lounge to the bank of flight information monitors.

Daniel scanned down the departures list, past the Alitalia flight, his eyes stopping on any commercial flights to Atlanta.

The next flight departed in seventy-five minutes.

Virgin Airlines.

Very funny, God. That's a good one.

The cut-off time for check-in was fifteen minutes away.

Sorry, kiddo. You're gonna have to sit the rest of this one out…

Daniel watched his reflection in the monitor. Thinking: *Just get on the damn plane and do your time in Poppi. Don't throw your life away.*

They returned to the table, and this time Daniel got the remote first. He flipped channels, stopped on ESPN. *Sportscenter* was showing highlights of a thoroughbred race.

The announcer was saying, "…a shocker at Aqueduct, as Mr. Smitten—a fifty-to-one underdog—comes steaming around the final curve and passes the entire field to win the Gotham Stakes, finishing eight-and-a-half lengths ahead of Executive Council, with Sweet Revenge showing in third…"

The race Trinity had predicted, ending exactly as he predicted it.

Daniel's heart pounded, his head swam, and beads of cold sweat broke out on his upper lip.

That Trinity had nailed it was no surprise, not after everything Daniel had seen in the last week. What shook him was that they'd just come in here on a whim, he'd flipped channels blindly, and landed right on this story.

Was *this* God's will?

If God transformed Saul, the violent persecutor of early Christians, into the Apostle Paul—*Saint Paul*—the main architect of Christianity as we know it, might He not similarly choose a modern sinner against Christ to carry his message today? Trinity was many miles from being a man of God, but his sins paled when compared to Saul's.

We're supposed to believe there is no sin so great, no sinner so wicked… *No one* is beyond redemption through the mercy of God.

Maybe that was the point.

Nick refused to even discuss the possibility. But Nick hadn't been there.

Ignoring George, Daniel grabbed his carry-on bag and stalked toward the men's room. He burst through the door, headed to the sinks, dropped his bag on the white tile floor, braced his hands on the counter, and breathed long and deep.

George came in after him, stopped, and said, "What the fucking hell is wrong with you?"

"Anxiety attack," said Daniel between breaths.

George snorted. "Anxiety, is it? Well now, aren't we precious?" He unzipped and used the urinal, zipped up, and came to the sink next to Daniel, held his hands under the automatic tap.

Daniel straightened up slowly, stretched his hands over his head, breathed, said, "Sorry, I think I'm OK now," and brought his arms down with full force, slamming George's forehead into the faucet.

"Fuck!" George jerked upright and Daniel silenced him with a flurry of fists to the solar plexus, pounding the wind out of him.

As George slid to the floor, struggling for breath, Daniel dragged him into the large wheelchair stall, dragged the bag in after them, locked the door. He got George seated on the toilet, grabbed the roll of boxing tape from his bag, taped his mouth, wrists, and ankles. The cut wasn't too bad, but foreheads bleed a lot, so Daniel quickly taped the cut as well. It would take a few stitches later.

"I'd apologize, George, but the thing is, I'm not sorry."

George didn't try to answer, but his eyes were full of murder.

Daniel slid under the door, quickly washed the blood from his hands, splashed cold water on his face. He wiped his face dry with a paper towel, hooked a finger behind his clerical collar.

And took the collar off.

Sorry, Nick. I just can't sit this one out.

35:

Atlanta, Georgia...

By sunrise, the highways into Atlanta were jammed solid. Poor folks driving rusted-out beaters, pulling overloaded trailers, senior citizens peeking over the steering wheels of massive RVs, Deadheads with psychedelic peace signs and dancing teddy bears on their station wagon windows, and thousands of others along the shoulder, riding bicycles, or on foot, carrying large backpacks, carrying small children, making the pilgrimage any way they could.

Some holding hands, many singing their faith aloud.

His Eye is On The Sparrow...

People Get Ready...

I Shall Be Released...

Walk In Jerusalem...

Andrew Thibodeaux loved the singing. He loved the pilgrimage. Loved being part of something larger than himself, part of a tribe, loved being at the center of a fast-changing world.

And he loved his secret knowledge.

Because he knew what God was planning.

He inched up I-85, willing his old truck not to overheat from excessive idling. The traffic was getting worse. He switched on the radio and spun the dial to a local talk station. One of those *Morning Zoo*–type programs, a couple smart-mouth jocks yukking it up at the Lord's expense.

–"…Can you believe these morons? They come to our city, no place to stay, no thought to how they gonna look after themselves—"

–"My point exactly. And I aim to fix it. So, for any wingnuts listening: I had breakfast with God this morning. He said to tell you: 'False alarm. Go home.'"

–"Seriously though, we gotta read this update: The Atlanta Police Department has cordoned off the area around the Tim Trinity Word of God Ministries, where the parking lot has become a tent city. There's no more room, do not go there. Same thing with Centennial Park. It's cheek-by-jowl, and police are turning new arrivals away."

–"And don't even dream of going to Buckhead, 'cause you *will* get your ass kicked. Rich folk don't dig on hippies pitching tents on their lawns, pissing on the azaleas, and coming to the door begging for water."

–"Well said, brudda, and they got *mondo* private security up there. You get your ass kicked by Wackenhut, you will *know* your ass has been kicked, know what I'm sayin'? No ifs, ands, or buts."

–"And besides, the police have already confirmed Trinity is not at home and not anywhere in Buckhead."

–"He's. Not. Even. There. Get it, people? So, for your own sake—and frankly, I don't care if you do get your ass kicked—but for your own sake, please do not go to Buckhead. It's getting pretty tense up there, and some-body's gonna really get hurt if you people don't get the hell back downtown."

–"Of course, that don't mean you should go downtown. One more time, for the slow kids in the class: You should turn around, leave Atlanta, and go home. All we're saying is stay especially out of Buckhead."

–"Think we beat that point to death, brudda?"

–"Well, these people ain't exactly paddling with both oars in the water…"

Andrew shifted from neutral into drive as traffic again picked up to a crawl. The radio jocks were pissing him off with their attitude, and now he questioned the wisdom of calling that Julia Rothman woman. Maybe she was just part of the "Liberal Media Elite" that Rush was always talking about, just looking to mock the real Americans whose faith in God helped build this country.

–"Next item...The governor and the mayor have released a joint statement—probably the first time those two ever agreed on anything. It reads: 'The City of Atlanta remains open for business. If you're a business traveler, rest assured that your hotel reservation will be honored. Reserved rooms are not being given away. Conventions have not been canceled, and the Georgia High School cheerleading finals will begin tomorrow as scheduled. You will need to add significantly to your estimated travel times in and around the city, but the city is open. If, however, you are planning a trip to Atlanta because of recent media reports concerning Reverend Tim Trinity, please reconsider. There are no hotel rooms left anywhere in the metropolitan area, and we cannot have millions of people living in our parks. We're a hospitable city, but there is simply no room at the inn, and there is a limit to our patience.'"

–"Whoa. Strong statement, doncha think?"

–"I like the way they tried to thread the needle: Businessmen please come, whackjobs stay away."

Andrew snapped off the radio. None of it applied to him. He could live in his truck, he had money for food and water, and once he made himself known to Reverend Tim, he would be welcomed like Lazarus from the tomb. But there was clearly a dark side to this pilgrimage, and he was seized now by the thought that some of these people might not be true pilgrims—that something bad could happen to Reverend Tim.

As the truck crept into the city, he saw a handmade banner, painted on a white bed sheet, hanging from an overpass.

THE MESSIAH HAS RETURNED

36:

Presidential Suite – Westin Peachtree Plaza...

"**F**uck!"

Tim Trinity slammed his safety razor down on the marble countertop as blood seeped from the vertical slice he'd just carved in his chin, turning the shaving cream red. Electrical signals screamed up the nerves from his chin to his brain.

Goddamn, that stings...

He splashed cold water on the cut—might as well have been lemon juice—and reached out to grab the styptic pencil from his leather Dopp kit to staunch the flow of blood. But his hand jolted sideways and knocked the bag off the counter. Pill bottles and moisturizers and nose hair trimmers and tweezers clattered across the bathroom floor.

The high-pitched buzzing in his brain surged, kicking his headache into migraine territory, signaling the imminent arrival of the tongues.

This one's coming on fast...

Trinity snatched a face towel off the bar and pressed it against his chin as he maneuvered his body into the expansive bedroom, his movements now beyond twitchy, heading toward spastic.

He yanked open the bedside table's drawer, reached behind the Gideon's Bible and pulled out his Ziploc baggie of cocaine, convulsed his way back into the bathroom, and managed to get the baggie open. He poured the white powder out onto the smooth marble countertop and leaned forward.

Hold it. Stop right there...

Trinity straightened and looked into the mirror, and his reflected self looked back at him. The bloodshot eyes of his reflected self held an intensity he'd never seen, and he couldn't look away.

An idea rose to the surface of his conscious mind, taking on shape and texture and weight as it came into focus, like a long-forgotten memory that, once remembered, could never be forgotten again.

OK, God. You want to use me? I'm yours…

The idea gave him an instant joy, but he fully understood what it demanded and the joy quickly gave way to abject fear. A wave of regret washed over him. He wanted to take it back, to *un-say* it, to bury his nose in the mound of white powder and draw deeply its offered escape, to snort it all in one go and end the voices, the tongues, the spasms. End them all.

End them now, and maybe forever.

Summoning every ounce of his bullheaded will, and before he could change his mind, he swept the cocaine into the sink, spun the tap, and flushed it down the drain, fear growing into terror, heart pounding in his chest. He looked back at his reflected self.

I accept this curse…this gift…this obligation. I will not stop the tongues. I will bring your messages to the world…

But saying it only increased his panic, and his stomach began roiling.

He threw up in the sink. It purged the fear, not a lot, but maybe just enough. He washed his mouth out with tap water, looked back at himself in the mirror.

You can do this, Tim. You've been a showman all your life; you've got the skills. Just put on that smile for the people and bluff it through, balls-out.

But this time, you tell the truth…

The next wave of muscle spasms hit.

Tim Trinity braced his hands against the countertop and held on against the coming storm.

✦ ✦ ✦

Las Vegas, Nevada…

"If you're just tuning in, *this* is the scene in Atlanta today," said Wolf Blitzer as pilgrims flooded the television screen, pitching tents in Centennial Park, waving placards in Five Points, scuffling with helmeted police outside the Westin Peachtree Plaza. "They call themselves Trinity's Pilgrims, and their numbers are fast rising. But there are other voices, both religious skeptics and religious leaders, who charge that Reverend Tim Trinity is a false prophet at best, con man at worst." The shot changed to a split screen: Blitzer on the left and the clusterfuck in Atlanta on the right. "Tonight, John King hosts a roundtable to break it down for us. After John, CNN's own Soledad O'Brien hosts the one-hour special presentation: 'Who Is Tim Trinity?' I know you'll want to be here for that…"

William Lamech looked at the bespoke-suited men around the long glass table in the casino boardroom and zapped the television to silence. Zapped it to silence, but left it on. He wanted those images on the minds of these men, in this meeting.

Lamech turned to his bodyguard, standing in the doorway.

"Nobody gets in. No phone calls."

"Yes, Mr. Lamech."

The bodyguard left the room. Behind him, the door whispered shut.

Jared Case shuffled through the stack of spreadsheets and bank statements and tax returns, passed them along to the next man. "My forensic accounting guy tells me there's plenty wrong here, gives us plenty of leverage. But it's gonna be difficult to approach Trinity now, with the whole world watching."

Pete DeFazio snorted. "I say we get these out to the media *today*. That'll crack the halo. Then the press'll get serious, look into Trinity's finances… In a week, he'll be just another grifter with a Bible."

"A grifter with a Bible, who predicts the future," Case corrected.

Lamech locked eyes, unblinking, with Darwyn Jones.

Darwyn nodded, almost imperceptibly, swiveled his chair away to face the television screen. He spoke without turning back to the men. "Look at the television screen, gentlemen. Just look at it." He sat for another second, turned back to the table. "Millions of Americans believe in him. His sermon tomorrow is going out live, all the major cable networks running the feed, also in the UK, Canada, and Mexico."

"My sources tell me reporters are flying in from France, Germany, Australia, Spain, Brazil...every corner of the goddamn planet," added Lamech. "This story is going worldwide in a matter of days."

DeFazio lit a cigarette, said, "What if he does the backwards act tomorrow? For all we know, he could predict the Kentucky Fuckin' Derby."

"For all we know," said Jared Case, "he could say gambling is a mortal sin. He could say Las Vegas is an instrument of Satan." Case gestured out the window, where the Las Vegas Strip glittered in the pale red light of dawn. "He could call for the Strip to go dark. And the people will listen. He could kill us with one word."

"My point exactly," said Darwyn Jones with a switchblade smile.

Michael Passarelli cleared his throat. "I don't want to be the one to raise this, but we're talking about killing a man who, well...I'm not saying he's Christ, just that *something* really weird is going on with this guy. What if it has something to do with God? Sorry, but I happen to believe in God. Maybe we should just start with the financials, minimize our risk."

William Lamech sipped some Perrier. "Michael, if the preacher has anything to do with God, every man in this room can plan on spending eternity without need of an overcoat. The *pertinent* risk is that every day we waste on indecision is a day Trinity might speak out against us."

"And we don't know how long it'll take the press to expose him, even if we do feed them his financials," added Darwyn Jones. "Looks like they're having a good time with the whole Messiah story, maybe they're not in a hurry to show him as a grifter."

Lamech stood, addressed the whole table. "Obviously Darwyn and I have concluded that we need to kill Trinity, without delay. And I think Jared may be on board."

Jared Case nodded. "I'm sold. I say we off the motherfucker."

"So we vote," Lamech continued. "If we are to be Trinity's jury, we should be unanimous. This is, after all, a death sentence. If there's a split vote, we talk it around some more." He raised his right hand. "All those in favor of ending it now."

Darwyn Jones and Jared Case raised their hands, followed by DeFazio, Babcock, Reaves…all around the table, all the way to Passarelli.

Unanimous.

37:

Rome, Italy...

It wasn't every day Father Nick entertained cardinals, but there was one in his office now—and for all the wrong reasons.

"How injured, exactly, is your secretary?" said Cardinal Allodi.

"Slight concussion, four stitches, and a bruised ego," said Father Nick.

"You find this situation funny?"

It made Nick feel like a kid called to the principal's office. "No, Eminence. I don't. Just listing George's injuries, as you asked."

"And your golden boy, Father Byrne?"

"Caught a commercial flight to Atlanta. I suspect we'll find him in the company of his uncle."

"You assured me he was the man for the job. 'The *only* man,' you said." Cardinal Allodi's voice was like ice. "How could you have misjudged the situation so drastically?"

"Daniel was very bitter about his uncle, he was motivated to debunk hard and fast. We gave him a case file that undermined Trinity's predictions, and he already knew the man was a fraud—there was no earthly reason to think he'd vet the transcripts." Nick shook his head. "He's a top-notch investigator. Once he learned the predictions were accurate…"

"You should have pulled him off the case sooner."

"Yes, sir."

"Turning into quite the debacle, isn't it?"

"Yes, Your Eminence."

"I think His Holiness needs to be informed."

Father Nick nodded. "I'll report to his office at your command."

"No," said Cardinal Allodi. "You'll report to me, and I will take it to His Holiness. His Holiness does not need to be burdened with unnecessary detail."

"Yes, Your Eminence."

"And you need to fix this."

"I will."

38:

Atlanta, Georgia...

Hartsfield-Jackson airport was buzzing with excited chatter, and it seemed the only topic of conversation was Tim Trinity. Daniel picked up snatches of it as he made his way through the crowds toward the trains to the main terminal building.

"This is just so *thrilling,* I can hardly breathe."

"They say he's taken over the whole top floor of the Westin, hiding out like Howard Hughes. You can't get near the place."

"When I saw the news, I just packed a bag and booked a flight. Didn't even say good-bye to the wife."

"Hear the latest? He predicted next Sunday's Lotto numbers! Isn't that awesome?"

"Dangerous, I'd say. Just a matter of time before Big Brother puts a bullet in his head."

"I think we're in the end times."

"I sure hope so. If the rapture don't come, I'm gonna have to fly home and explain myself."

Daniel stopped at a newsstand, picked up the *Atlanta Journal-Constitution.* The bold headline read:

TENSIONS RISE AS TRINITY

FOLLOWERS PUT CITY IN GRIDLOCK

On the train to the main terminal, he scanned the accompanying story. The city was devolving into chaos. He was still caught up in the paper as he left the train, didn't notice them until they were flanking him on either side, with military precision.

Two very large men in dark blue suits and sunglasses. One black, one white, both bald-headed and clean-shaven. Guns bulging beneath their jackets.

Shit.

Daniel scanned the crowd for movement patterns, looking for an opening to emerge. But he knew it was impossible. Even if he got a couple good shots in and bolted though the crowd, he wouldn't get far. They couldn't fire on him in this crowd, but the place was jammed, and they'd be all over him before he could get to the door.

The black guy said, "Father Byrne. We've been sent to pick you up."

"Nick didn't waste any time."

"Who? No, we're from Reverend Trinity. He thought you could use some help getting into the city."

"How did he even know I was coming back to Atlanta?"

"I have no idea, you'll have to ask him. He just told us what flight you were on."

"Nothing personal, guys, but why should I believe you?"

The white guy grinned. "He said you were the suspicious type. Said to remind you of the time Judas got hit by a car. Said to tell you what he said to you at the time was wrong. Whatever that means."

Judas…

When Daniel was nine, during the summer they stayed put in New Orleans, Trinity finally agreed to get a dog. They went down to the shelter on Japonica Street and adopted a scruffy little mutt that Trinity named Judas. He chose the name, he said, because every dog he'd had as a kid had run away, and he figured it was just a matter of time before this mutt did the same.

But Judas didn't run away, and both Daniel and Trinity fell in love with him. Daniel took Judas to Audubon Park every day, and Trinity came along on weekends. Judas loved to splash around in the big fountain, biting at the water. It always made them howl with laughter.

Trinity also got a huge kick out of calling the dog's name in public.

Judas didn't run away, but on a rainy Saturday morning in early August, he crawled under the backyard fence and chased a cat across the road, just as a car came around the corner. Daniel ran to stop him, but it was too late.

Judas died in Daniel's arms.

They buried the dog in the backyard, and Trinity made a little wooden cross as a headstone.

"I know it hurts, son, and I'm sorry," he said, placing a hand on the boy's shoulder. "But you better know now, it's the way of life. Everything you love goes away in the end."

He said to tell you what he said to you at the time was wrong.

The white guy said, "Satisfied?"

Daniel nodded.

The black guy gestured at his partner. "This is Chris. I'm Samson." They shook hands. "Car's waiting, let's go."

✚ ✚ ✚

Chris drove the big limo into Atlanta, staying off the highway, cruising along industrial boulevards and residential streets. Samson sat in the back with Daniel and caught him up to speed.

"Reverend Trinity's instructions are that you get total access and full protection. So if you need anything at all, just say the word." He handed Daniel a business card. "My cell phone's always on."

Daniel put the card in his pocket. "What the hell is going on, Samson?"

Samson whistled through his teeth. "You got me, Father."

"Just Daniel, please."

"OK, Daniel. From a security perspective, it's a total nightmare. We had to get Reverend Trinity out of his home and into a controlled environment—the whole neighborhood was swarming with worshipers. And now the Westin is a zoo. Cops have it surrounded and nobody gets in without showing a card key." He handed one to Daniel. "Your room is just down the hall from your uncle."

"I have a room?"

"Reverend Trinity's orders. We've got the entire top floor, and we control the only elevator set to reach it. There's a keypad in the elevator, and we change the access code daily. We have men at the stairwells and in the lobby. We can keep him safe inside. But outside... Almost a million people in the last thirty-six hours, and they're still coming, now they're pitching tents in Piedmont Park. At first the cops tried to clear them out, but now they're just trying to keep people safe. The whole city's on edge, wouldn't take much to push it over."

"Jesus."

"They're setting up port-a-potties at the perimeter of the parks," Chris added from the front seat, "but it's not enough. The Red Cross has first aid tents up, and they're distributing water, best they can."

Samson said, "High today is eighty-two, eighty-eight tomorrow. People gonna be roasting out there, and there's gonna be a riot before this thing is over. A riot, or worse. Folks don't realize how fragile the social order is, I'm telling you."

Traffic ground to gridlock as they reached downtown. They turned onto Peachtree a few blocks north of Five Points, and inched through the sea of souls.

Pedestrians packed the wide sidewalks, sometimes spilling out into the curb lanes. Vendors stood elbow to elbow, hawking Tim Trinity T-shirts, Tim Trinity posters, blue bibles, battery-powered fans, and bottled water.

They rode on in silence as Daniel took in the scene outside the window.

People playing drums and tambourines, banjos and guitars.

People dancing and chanting.

Young people, singing about peace and love and salvation.

Old men, spewing bile about hellfire and damnation.

Some marched slowly, amidst the chaos, carrying placards.

PREPARE THE WAY OF THE LORD

USA IS GOD COUNTRY

REV. TRINITY WILL SAVE US

Daniel just stared, thinking: *Unbelievable. Un-frigging-believable.*

39:

The presidential suite was a hive of activity, people assembling desks, setting up computers, running phone lines. Flat panel televisions were scattered around the room, tuned to CNN, MSNBC, FoxNews, BBC, CBCNewsworld, SkyNews, half of them running stories about Tim Trinity.

"Danny, welcome!" Trinity called, over the sound of televisions and cordless drills and ringing phones. "Thrilled to have you back." He gestured to the blonde woman who'd appeared on stage with him a few days earlier. "Meet Liz Doherty, our public relations director." Daniel shook Liz Doherty's hand. "And over there is Jennifer Bartlett," pointing across the room where a curvaceous, pretty young woman in a conservative suit smiled and wiggled her fingers at them while talking on the phone, "my secretary." Then he made a comic face. "I mean, my *executive assistant.*" He flashed his pearly whites. "*My bad*, as the kids say. How was your flight?"

This can't be happening...

"Tim, what the hell is going on around here?"

Trinity beamed. "We Big Time, son! We on a roll." He pointed his cigarette at the television on the wet bar. "BBC, baby! Where's your suitcase?"

Daniel couldn't think, couldn't process the input fast enough. "I...uh, I don't...I traveled under unusual circumstances. I don't have it." He held up his carry-on. "This is all I brought."

"Well then, you're gonna need new clothes, supplies." He called across the room, "Jennifer, give Danny five thousand from petty cash."

"I didn't ask you for money," Daniel said.

Trinity waved it away. "A raindrop in the storm, don't trouble your mind over it. Already had to hire three more phone banks to handle calls. We're drawing a million every couple hours, 'round the clock, praise God."

What the fuck?

"You can't possibly think I find this in any way impressive," Daniel said, keeping his voice even. Trinity's smile lost an inch; he'd just been insulted in front of his people. "And how did you know I was on that flight?"

The smile returned to full wattage. Trinity gestured to the floor-to-ceiling windows, to the sun-baked city, seventy-five stories down. "It ain't just those people in tents. In the short time you've been gone, we have experienced a *paradigm shift*, my boy. I simply called my new friend, Senator Paul Guyot—who sits on the Homeland Security Committee—and asked him to let me know if your name showed up on a passenger list to Atlanta. Piece of cake. Like I said: We Big Time, baby, we on a roll."

"I just flushed my life down the fucking toilet for you!" Daniel shouted. "For *this*?"

The entire room fell to silence.

The television news channels all ran together on low volume, combining to make a white noise of background blather, punctuated with words such as *Trinity…Atlanta…Miracle…*

Trinity raised his hands to encompass everyone in the suite. "Ladies and gentlemen, my nephew is upset. We need some time. Please, give us the room."

"Yes, sir," said Samson from the doorway. Everyone filed out quietly, and Samson followed suit, closing the door behind.

Trinity crossed to the bar, switched the television off. He poured Blanton's into a couple of rocks glasses, added ice from the freezer, handed one of the glasses to Daniel. He spoke quietly. "You didn't flush your life down the toilet for me, son. You flushed it to find the truth. And the truth is, you didn't flush it at all. Hell, you've been a priest for all the wrong reasons—"

"Don't," said Daniel. "Just, don't. You are the last person on earth who gets to analyze me. And while we're on the subject, I'd appreciate it if you'd stop calling me *son*."

"Ouch," whispered Trinity. He drank down the bourbon, nodded sadly to himself, and spoke into his ice. "OK, I laid it on a little thick when you arrived, I admit that. Just wanted you to see a lot of people believe in me. I mean, believe God is at work in me." He looked straight at Daniel. "I know you think I'm a con man, and yes, I am…I was. But things are different now. Now I believe. Not saying I been saved or born again or any of that jazz. Just that now I know there *is* a God. A good God. And I don't have a clue why, but He wants to use me for something. Something important."

"What, he wants you to be *Big Time? On a roll? Drawing millions?* Well, excuse me while I call bullshit on that."

"No, no, no, that's all just the theater of it, you're missin' the purpose. And the money's just a side-effect, I swear."

"Then what is the purpose?"

"Don't know." Trinity put his hand on Daniel's shoulder, just as he'd done at Judas's backyard funeral. "But I do know He wants you here with me. Had me a dream last night. God told me He wants you at my right hand."

"Now He talks to you in dreams?"

"I think He did last night. Maybe He…maybe He wants you here, to keep me on the narrow path." He let out a wry chuckle, "You, of all people, know that ain't gonna be easy for a guy like me, and I sure could use your help. And your advice."

"My first advice is to tell you to stop acting like a carnival barker."

Trinity shrugged. "Tough habit to break after thirty-nine years. I'm working on it. Like I said, it's the theater of the thing. But I need advice about the deeper stuff, the stuff I don't understand. Hell, I got US senators callin', asking *my* advice. I gotta go in front of the cameras tomorrow and talk to the *whole world*…" he rattled the ice in his glass, "…and I don't know what to say. I need you, Danny. I need to talk it out with you."

Daniel put his untouched bourbon on the bar. "I don't know, Tim." He headed for the door. "I'm gonna go for a walk, get a chilidog."

"You're coming back, though, right?" The fear in his voice was unmistakable, and genuine.

Daniel nodded. "To let you know what I decide, one way or another."

40:

"Then if anyone says to you, 'Look! Here is the Messiah!' or 'There he is!'—do not believe it. For false messiahs and false prophets will appear and produce great signs and omens, to lead astray, if possible, even the elect. Take note, I have told you beforehand."

—MATTHEW 24:23–25

41:

Daniel sat on a red plastic chair in the Varsity Diner, reading his Bible. On the white Formica table, a Heavy Dog, large orange drink, fried apple pie…untouched.

"Hey sailor, come here often?"

Julia.

Daniel looked up. "How'd you find me?"

She sat, plopped a massive purse at her feet. "Your uncle called."

"But how did he know—" Then he smiled, despite himself. "Chilidog."

"Chilidog?"

"When I was a kid, he brought me here, probably a half dozen times a year, whenever he worked revivals in the area. Told him I was going for a chilidog." He glanced down at the food. "You hungry?"

"Starving!" She smiled with her whole face.

He slid his tray across. "Can't seem to work up an appetite."

Julia picked up the Heavy Dog and dug in with great gusto, coming away with a red chili moustache. "Such a lady," she giggled. "Napkin?"

Daniel took the paper napkin, warm from his lap.

Don't do it…don't you do it…

He reached across the table.

Do. Not. Do. It.

And wiped the chili off her mouth.

His heart set to racing. Something twinkled in Julia's eyes, and as she took the napkin, it seemed her hand lingered on his longer than strictly required to make the exchange. His pants got tight. He became aware he wasn't breathing, forced himself to resume.

"So," Julia said, "who goes first?" She drank some orange, tore another chunk off the dog with her teeth.

"You're eating, I'll go." He opened his Bible to the page he'd been reading. "*Then if anyone says to you, 'Look! Here is the Messiah!' or 'There he is!'—do not believe it. For false messiahs and false prophets will appear and produce great signs and omens, to lead astray.*"

"Lemme guess: Jesus, right?"

"Yes, Jesus. Matthew 24:23."

Julia chewed, swallowed, sucked orange drink through the straw again. "So?"

"It matches, 24:23. The billboard accident. He said it would come down at exactly twenty-three minutes after midnight, and it did. A day is twenty-four hours. Twenty-three minutes after midnight is 24:23."

"Oh, sweetie," her hand came to rest on his, "no, no, no. That way lies madness." A smile, gentle and kind and perhaps a little worried. "Numerology? Please, I know you're smarter than that. I mean it with love, but really, you can't go down that road."

I mean it with love? But that's just a thing people say, and her tone was light.

"Yeah…I know. Just feeling a little desperate for answers, I guess."

Her hand left his and picked up the fried pie.

"So how was the trip? What did your boss say?" She raised the pie to her lips.

"Careful with the fried pie, they're blistering hot inside. My boss? Well, if you mean God, I'm still waiting for an answer. But if you mean my boss at the Vatican, I'm not willing to talk about it."

"I thought we'd crossed that hurdle."

"Didn't mean it like that. I'm not willing to talk about it with *anyone*. I'm trying not to even think about it."

Julia abandoned the fried pie, picked up the drink. "Take a walk with me?"

✤ ✤ ✤

They strolled along North Avenue, past Grant Field, and up Cherry Street, into the Georgia Tech campus, all lush green trees and stately brick buildings, a world apart from the insanity taking place only blocks away.

"Been playing phone-footsie with Liz Doherty—Trinity's gatekeeper—for the last couple days," said Julia. "You know, laying out all the reasons I should be the one to interview him: I broke the story, my coverage has been fair, I'm a hometown gal…have to admit, I was tempted to tell her I was a friend of yours, but I couldn't allow myself to play that card without talking to you first. Anyway, my phone rings an hour ago, and it's him. Not his people, Trinity himself. Wouldn't agree to a sit-down, not yet, but said you were at the Varsity, and he was worried about you."

"How'd he know you even knew me?"

"No idea."

Daniel took off his jacket, slung it over his shoulder. "I'll talk to him, get you inside for a meeting."

Julia stopped walking. "You don't have to."

"I don't have to. I will. He can't hide forever, and you'll be fair."

"Thanks," her smile like an embrace. "How's he doing with all this? He sounded a little rattled on the phone."

"I don't know what's going on with him," said Daniel, "but I don't like what I see." He cleared his throat. "I came back here against orders, burning bridges, and what did I find? A world gone mad, a million worshipers outside Trinity's door, and Trinity playing it for all it's worth, raking the money in and bragging about it. He *says* he now believes, and he seems to mean it, but his actions betray him. I don't know what the hell to do."

"People don't change overnight. He says he's changing, maybe he is. Maybe it's another con. You can deal with that disappointment—you've done it before—but how would you deal with having walked away, never knowing for sure?"

They continued up Cherry, turned right onto the redbrick path to Tech Tower. Young men and women sat on the grass, in the shade of old oaks, alone and in groups, with backpacks and laptops and cell phones, studying, joking, flirting.

Another life. A youth he could've had, had he made a different choice.

"There's a bench," said Julia, "let's sit."

He kissed her. Just grabbed her shoulders and kissed her hard on the mouth. She tightened at first, but then softened into him, and their mouths opened and he pulled her closer, pulling their bodies tight.

It was heaven.

And heaven tasted like chilidog.

Julia jerked her head away. "Stop!" She shoved him back, hard. "What the hell do you think you're doing?"

"I—uh, I…You kissed me back." A lame defense, but it was all he had.

"*I'm* not a priest! I'm allowed." She hooked a few long strands of hair with her little finger, moved them out of her eyes and behind her ear. "I refuse to be the reason you break your vows or quit the priesthood or whatever the hell it is you're thinking of doing."

"Yeah, the thing is…I may have already quit the priesthood."

"*What?*"

He held up a hand. "Not because of you. At least, mostly not. Well, it's complicated." Daniel let out a rueful chuckle. "I seem to be saying that a lot these days." His face grew hot and his throat tightened. His eyes began to well, but he fought it back in time. He blew out a long breath.

"Talk to me, Danny."

"God, I'm…confused. I don't know where to begin."

"Begin anywhere. Just begin."

"Know what I wish? I wish we could stop time, just you and me, just for a day…step out of our lives, away from this madness, spend a whole day talking, you know, like we used to."

"Time marches on," she said quietly, mostly to herself. She took his hands in hers. "I care about you, but…if you decide to quit the priesthood, it can't be *mostly* not about me. It can't be about me at all."

"OK, but you do care about me." It was all he'd heard.

"As a *friend*." Julia drew a sharp breath. "Danny, it was over for us a long time ago. And it's going to stay over, even if you quit the priesthood. Don't have any illusions about that."

She turned and walked away from him. She didn't look back.

42:

Daniel sat alone, on top of Stone Mountain, wondering how the world could've changed so quickly. He sat for a long time, watching the sun set the sky ablaze. Atlanta in silhouette, skyscraper monoliths left behind by a civilization no longer in existence.

How could he have been so stupid? All those little signs—the secret smile in her eyes, the lingering of her hand on his, the casual throwaway lines—could they all have just been his projection of his own feelings?

No. Not after that kiss. OK, so it was the first time he'd kissed any woman since the last time he'd kissed the same woman, fourteen years ago.

Fourteen years. God, fourteen years. How do fourteen years pass so quickly?

Anyway. Maybe he wasn't the most qualified man to judge a kiss, but he was a man, and there was a moment—just as she relaxed, until she broke contact—when the kiss went both ways. In that moment, Julia's passion was real.

And that moment felt longer than the last fourteen years of Daniel's life. Longer, and maybe more significant.

But then she did break contact, and said: *It was over for us a long time ago. And it's going to stay over, even if you quit the priesthood. Don't have any illusions about that.*

No wiggle room in that statement. Goddamnit. It made him feel like he'd swallowed a brick.

The sun was getting low in the sky. Time to head down. With the highways jammed, it would be a long drive back to town on the side roads.

Daniel stood and walked among the rainwater rock pools scattered around the surface. Like craters on the moon. When he was a boy, his uncle said the little craters were made by God's fingertip. Said that Stone Mountain had once been a prime meeting place for the Ku Klux Klan, and whenever God saw a Klansman walking on the rock, He'd poke his finger down in a bolt of lightning and crush the Klansman like an insect.

Stone Mountain was the other Atlanta ritual. Sometimes before the Varsity, sometimes after, but Tim and Danny's Atlanta adventures had always included both.

The sun was almost at the horizon. He should go now. Instead he moved closer to the northern edge of the mountain, sat cross-legged.

One time, when he was about seven or eight—he couldn't remember exactly—they'd been caught at the top of Stone Mountain after dark, in a massive electrical storm. The Skyride cable cars had been shut down because of the storm, and the tourists scampered like wet cats down the slippery hiking trail, children wailing and women screaming and men shouting, thunder booming all around them as lightning strobed just over their heads.

Between lightning flashes, it was so dark you could barely see five feet ahead. The hot summer rain came down in buckets. A bolt of lightning struck so close the earth shook below their feet and Danny's ears started ringing and he was blinded for a full minute. He grabbed his uncle's leg in a bear hug, helpless, whimpering, sure that this would be the end. The other tourists were all down the hill by now, out of sight. But Danny couldn't move from fear.

Tim Trinity squatted down and took the boy by the shoulders, looked him in the eyes, and smiled like he hadn't a care in the world.

"You're safe with me, kid. You're always safe with me."

With the boy attached to his leg, Trinity walked calmly to the sheer northern face of the mountain, right to the edge, stood tall and spread his arms wide, like Moses parting the Red Sea. His unbuttoned windbreaker flapped wildly, like wet wings.

Trinity's voice boomed into the storm, "In *Jesus's* name, I command and declare! No harm shall come to this child of God on this night! All the angels of heaven shall guide our steps, and we will walk safely down this mountain, so that we may partake of chilidogs at the Varsity! So it shall be, and *so it is!*" He lowered his hands, winked at the boy. "OK, we're good. Let's roll."

They hiked down the mountain through the pouring rain, hand-in-hand, under the protection of angels. And, amazingly, Daniel felt no fear.

They drove, soaking wet, to the Varsity, and ate chilidogs and fried pies in the Winnebago. And laughed about the storm.

On that night, Tim Trinity was truly magic, and Danny was the happiest boy in Atlanta.

Daniel stood again, brushed his hands against his pant legs. He walked right to the edge—the sheer face of the mountain where Trinity had commanded the angels—and inched forward, until the tips of his shoes poked out over the edge.

He looked straight down, and the tingle began. Then spread his arms wide and held them there, muscles in his legs and core twitching to compensate for the buffeting wind.

He leaned forward at the waist...

> *Then the devil took him to the holy city and placed him on the pinnacle of the temple, saying to him, "If you are the Son of God, throw yourself down; for it is written, 'He will command his angels concerning you,' and 'On their hands they will bear you up, so that you will not dash your foot against a stone.'"*

Adrenaline surged, his nerves became electric. He held his position, felt for the exact point of balance—the tipping point—found it, teetered on the balls of his feet for a few seconds.

He imagined falling.

Like the dream of falling that jerks you back from the edge of sleep.

He jerked his body back from the edge, took a few deep breaths.

The sun was at the horizon. It was time to go.

43:

Conrad Winter sat with a drink in the bar of the Westin Peachtree, waiting for a text message that was fifteen minutes overdue, wondering if he'd miscalculated, if it wouldn't come at all. The cell phone rang—not a text—and the screen told him the call was coming from the Office of the Devil's Advocate.

"Nick," said Conrad, putting a smile in his voice, "an unexpected pleasure. What can I do for you?"

"You can knock off the happy horseshit, for starters. Just got some very disturbing news from Nigeria."

"Yes, I heard about that," said Conrad. "Very sad. Poor girl. A hit-and-run is what I heard."

"And you're the one who benefits."

"Actually her entire country benefits," countered Conrad. "The locals are celebrating the girl as a miracle, too good for this world, called home by God. Thousands are turning away from radical Islam and coming to us."

"You'll go to hell for this, Conrad."

Conrad stiffened. "Don't be absurd. I realize we do things in Outreach that you academics in the ODA find distasteful, but you can't *possibly* think I would *ever* sanction the death of a child." He downed the rest of his drink. "I may go to hell, Nick, but not for this, which of course—*of course*—I had *no* part in. Am I making myself clear? It was just a tragic accident. Given the situation in Nigeria, I can't say I'm sorry it happened—and I refuse to pretend it isn't good for us—but that doesn't make me the monster you imagine me to be. And if you don't believe me, if you *really* think I had anything to do with it, I suggest you file a report with Cardinal Allodi. *Asshole.*"

Conrad hung up, put the cell phone on the bar, and picked up his drink, overwhelmed by a bone-deep sadness. The girl in Nigeria would now be remembered as a miracle and no longer needed the Vatican's official stamp. Daniel wouldn't certify her, so she had to die. Regrettable, but necessary.

No, it was much worse than regrettable, it was horrible, it was monstrous.

But still necessary.

And Conrad might very well go to hell for it, among other things. But the world was at war, with the fate of humanity quite literally hanging in the balance. And war makes monsters, even on God's side. So he made that choice, a long time ago. To become a monster, to willingly sacrifice himself to hell, in order to win the war for God. People like Nick and Daniel would never understand. They'd only thank him when the war was won.

And Conrad believed that, when his time came, God might give him a dispensation for his service to the cause.

He *had* to believe that.

Anyway, the girl's death was having the desired effect, slowing the tide, buying time for the council to move their tin soldiers and weapons to where they were needed, and the Nigerian oil would keep flowing. For now.

And Conrad couldn't afford to think about it—he had more pressing concerns. Ever since the Trinity Anomaly broke public, he'd been expecting the Fleur-de-Lis Foundation to rear its hypocritical head, and he'd gotten confirmation last night from a council operative in New York City. A one-line e-mail that read: *Carter Ames leaving on foundation jet. Destination: Atlanta.*

The director's words echoed in Conrad's ears. *Carter Ames is the most dangerous man you will ever meet.* The director was not given to hyperbole, and Conrad would be careful not to underestimate Ames. But the challenge sent a thrill through him just the same.

Conrad's phone buzzed, this time with the text message he'd been anticipating:

ELEVATOR ACCESS CODE—018992

He paid the bill and headed for the lobby.

44:

There was an envelope waiting for Daniel at the Westin's front desk when he returned. No wax seal, but the stationery was every bit as fine quality as any used in the Vatican. Cream colored, 100 percent cotton, heavy stock, and it took fountain pen ink without a trace of feathering. A broad and flexible nib had laid down the emerald-green ink. The script told of a masculine hand, properly trained in penmanship. Boarding school educated, perhaps. The note said:

> *Daniel:*
> *The Vatican's response, while unfortunate, was expected. We are heartened that your loyalty is to the truth. You have chosen well; Trinity is the path.*
> *Walk the path, find the truth.*
> *But beware: There are thieves in the temple and mortal danger lurks nearby.*
> *Be very careful whom you trust.*
> *—PapaLegba*

Whoever he was, PapaLegba certainly had flair. Daniel put the note away and returned to Trinity's hotel suite. This time he drank his uncle's bourbon.

"First, some ground rules," he said, counting them off on his fingers, "One: I don't work for you, so don't treat me like an employee, and I don't follow you, so don't treat me like one of your flock."

"Agreed."

"Two: Don't ever lie to me."

Trinity raised his oath hand. "I swear. I want your help, lying wouldn't serve—"

"Three: You stand in front of those cameras tomorrow, and the first thing you do is tell the world that you are not the Messiah."

"With pleasure. I ain't applying for that job."

"OK. But what I told you before still stands. If this all turns out to be some massive con, I will make it my mission in life to ruin the rest of yours. I will expose you, with the whole world watching."

Trinity reached forward and clinked his glass against Daniel's. "I'll hold you to that." He drank the bourbon down in one gulp and refilled his glass. "Look, I understand you still suspect a grift..." He shrugged. "How could you think otherwise? But when that oil refinery blew, part of me died... I'm not lying to you. I believe in God, and this is no con."

"Then you better tell me what you and God are planning."

"Well, now you've pierced the heart of it." Trinity's hand shook a little as he sipped his drink. "I don't have a clue what God is planning. He don't tell me a goddamn thing."

"He told you He wanted me at your right hand."

"Danny. This thing didn't come with an instruction manual. I'm fumbling around in the dark here. *Help* me."

Daniel stepped back, rocked by the sudden and certain knowledge that there was no con, that it was all true...and by the responsibility it imposed...and by the enormity of what they didn't know.

He sat on the nearest chair, drank the bourbon.

Trinity's smile contained no humor. "*Now* you seein' what I see. Welcome to my hell."

OK, all right, no panic. Use the brain God gave you, figure it out...

Daniel took a deep breath. "All right, let's start with what we know. You've been given the gift of prophecy—"

"That's a stretch," said Trinity. "It just spews out of me at random, and I don't even know what I'm saying when I'm saying it."

"Maybe God doesn't trust you with it yet, but it's still prophecy. What else do we know?"

"We know it comes with money and power," said Trinity.

Daniel made a face. "Do you ever think of anything else?"

"No, you're not hearing me. It's not about my desires. I already had plenty of money, but now I got money *simple*. That may be part of God's plan, I don't know, but we can't ignore it. He musta known the dough would pour in when this went public. And the sermon tomorrow? Half a *billion* people might hear it, or read it in the paper. That's power. And it petrifies me."

"Yeah…we can't let fear paralyze us. What else do we know? We know—"

"Holy crap!" Trinity shouted.

"What?"

"I got it! I got it!" Bouncing on the balls of his feet, like an excited kid. "The answer's right there in scripture, son. *Do not worry beforehand about what you are to say; but say whatever is given you at the time, for it is not you who speak, but the Holy Spirit.*"

"You're just gonna wing it? That's your plan?"

"Oh ye of little faith," said Trinity. "I'm gonna stand up there on that stage, look into the camera, open my mouth wide, and invite God to talk."

"A minute ago, you were petrified."

Trinity swallowed the rest of his drink. "Still am. But I'm choosing to put my trust in the Big Guy. Otherwise, why bother getting up there at all?"

Daniel thought about it a long time, saying nothing, not quite successfully avoiding the thought that Tim Trinity's faith was stronger than his own. He nodded, put down the glass.

"OK, Tim. We'll leave it up to God. Get some sleep, we've got a big day tomorrow."

As Daniel slipped the card key into the door, he felt the full weight of the last twenty-four hours. God, he was tired. He figured to be asleep as soon as his head touched the pillow.

He opened the door, stepped inside, flipped on the lights.

His carry-on bag was sitting open on the dresser. He'd left it closed, on the chair.

He crossed to the dresser and looked in the bag. The case file was gone. He ripped open the dresser's top drawer. His laptop computer, also stolen. He walked to the closet, pulled the extra pillow off the shelf. The digital camera had been snatched as well.

In its place, there was a small note card. It read:

No theft here tonight.
The Church simply reclaimed her property.
–C.

Daniel crumpled the card in his fist, threw the pillow against a wall, and swore. Then he took a couple of deep breaths and began a meticulous search of the room.

Nothing else was missing, but there wasn't much else worth taking. He sat heavily on the bed. Between the case file and computer, Daniel had proof that the Vatican had been covering up the accuracy of Trinity's predictions. That proof was now gone.

And Conrad had the camera. Had the photos of Trinity snorting cocaine in his den.

Damn…

Daniel lay back, his head hitting the little chocolate on the pillow. He wondered if Conrad's break-in was what PapaLegba had meant by *thieves in the temple*. But then the note went on to warn of *mortal danger* lurking nearby. That wasn't about Conrad's break-in. That was another threat entirely.

Despite his efforts to keep it at bay, paranoia descended upon him. He had no idea who this PapaLegba was, or who the thieves in the temple were, or where nearby the mortal danger lurked. But he now felt that PapaLegba, whoever he was, should be taken seriously.

He jumped to his feet, grabbed the card key off the dresser, and strode into the empty hallway. In the north stairwell, he found Chris at his post.

"Someone's been in my room, and things are missing," he said.

Chris pressed a button behind his lapel, said, "Robert, status check." He put his finger to his ear, listened. Then, to Daniel, "No activity in the stairwells. Had to be someone with the elevator code. We'll check the security video."

Daniel already knew what the security video would show. But what would he do with it? Conrad was right; the Church had simply reclaimed her property, nothing taken had belonged to Daniel. "I'm more concerned about my uncle's vulnerability," he said.

"We'll put a man on the elevator; no one will breach the floor again, I promise you."

"OK."

Chris put his hand on Daniel's forearm. "Try to get some sleep, man. Seriously, you look exhausted."

Sleep. Not a bad idea…

45:

Tim Trinity lay in bed, sipping bourbon, watching a CNN documentary called *Who Is Tim Trinity?* Thinking: *That Soledad O'Brien is one foxy lady. You can interrogate me any time, baby...*

O'Brien was being fair—perhaps too fair—in her coverage. Then again, Trinity figured, she had to be careful not to appear disrespectful of religious belief, and false faith is hard to prove.

That's what made preaching the perfect con. Of course, if he'd known thirty-nine years ago that there really was a God, he'd have chosen a different line of work, or at least a secular grift. He wondered now if God might someday punish him for his earlier sins.

Or maybe what's happening now is God's punishment...

He didn't want to think about that, turned his attention back to the set. O'Brien was standing in front of Charity, which was fenced off and still hadn't reopened after Katrina. "He wasn't born Trinity, but Timothy Granger, right here in downtown New Orleans, at Charity Hospital. Born poor, to Claire Granger, wife of Fred Granger, a traveling salesman. Claire was descended from Irish indentured servants, but Fred Granger's background is unknown, and with the loss of so many public records in Hurricane Katrina, mysteries will remain..."

⁂

A dozen family photographs, in plastic frames, hung on the walls of their cramped living room. Photographs of people the young Tim Granger had never met, some long dead, but all held a place of honor in the family home.

Absent were his paternal grandfather and great-grandmother, and Tim's dad explained it away, saying the old man took after his mama, never did like the camera, thought having his picture taken was akin to tempting the devil.

When Tim was ten years old, he found the photo while rummaging through a shoebox of memorabilia in his father's closet. There was no question about who he was looking at. His grandfather looked much like his father, but the lips were a bit fuller, the nose slightly distended, and the hair—slicked back mercilessly—still showed kinky waves. Young Tim took the photo to his dad, who had just returned from another unsuccessful sales trip and was quietly drinking himself to sleep in the living room recliner.

With trembling hand, he held out the photograph. "This is my grandfather," he said. His father slowly put the recliner upright, reached for the photo.

"You oughtn't a been meddling in my things, son." Then he gestured to a chair and let out a long sigh as the boy sat. "But I reckon you're old enough to know." He took a swallow of his drink and put it on the side table. "Your granddaddy was mulatto. His features favored his daddy, who was white Irish, but never quite enough so's he could pass. He married a white woman, and they had one quadroon child. Me. When I was born, I came out lookin' white as any baby. So they had a decision to make." Tim's dad looked like he might cry, but he took another swallow of his drink and it passed. "They kept my daddy's name off the birth certificate, put down UNKNOWN for the father. They figured it would be better for me to be thought a bastard, better for my mother to be thought loose. Better for my father to be thought a cuckold. See, they were trying to give me the best start they could, and a white boy can do things and go places that ain't possible for a black boy. Folks thought my daddy was a living saint for staying with the white woman who strayed and raisin' up a white bastard as his own flesh and blood. When I was a little older, he let me know the truth but made me swear never to tell." He cleared his throat. "And when I was grown I moved clear 'cross town, where folks didn't know my family. See, nobody can look at your face and tell if you're a bastard. You can always leave your personal history behind. But you can't run away from your race, once you been branded."

Young Tim Granger had no idea how to feel. His parents had always taught him that all God's children were equal, that race was of no significance, but the rest of the world had sent him a very different message. Until a moment ago he was a white boy. Now he was an octoroon. He didn't feel shame, exactly, but he felt a deep unease, his sense of self suddenly untethered, in flux.

As if reading his mind, Tim's dad said, "Hear me well, son: I've passed all my life, and you look even fairer than I do. No one will ever suspect you got Negro blood in your veins. When you're a man, you make the decision to tell or not to tell, but you're not old enough to make that decision right yet, so keep it under your hat for the time being. Life is gonna be harder on you if you tell. But maybe you should. I can't say what's best."

"Yes, sir," said young Tim Granger. He stood to leave the room.

"One more thing I need you to know."

"Yes, sir?"

His dad sat looking at the photo a long time before speaking. Then he said, "I don't hide it because I am ashamed. I am ashamed because I hide it."

Trinity never did tell, although he felt no shame about it, once he got used to the idea. If asked, he would not deny it, but it just never came up. The world thought he was white, and he was…seven-eighths anyway. He considered telling his twin sister, Iris, who shared his blood and who also looked white, but decided it might be a burden for her, so he kept it to himself.

He never thought of his father without recalling that conversation. And he always thought his father's shame had been misplaced. Shame for hiding his race or shame for the race itself, either way, it was meaningless to Trinity.

What mattered was the poverty. That was shameful.

♣ ♣ ♣

She came to him in his sleep, in a peaceful dream. Came to him like an ebony Yoruba goddess, in the shade of the big magnolia, where he lay on a bed of oystershell gravel.

"Does it hurt?" she said.

"Not at all."

"It will."

He wanted to believe her. Wanted to square up his account, pay the full price of his sins, and be washed clean.

But he was afraid to die.

"Everybody dies, Tim," she said.

So she can read my thoughts…

"It goes both ways," she said, and he realized that her mouth had not moved.

Holy crap. Telepathy. Then it hit him all at once. *I got it! I got it! You're God…*

Her smile was full of pity. "Yes, but so are you. I'm God, you're God, Danny's God, and the man who audits your taxes for the IRS is God. Everyone is God. I hope you will earn that knowledge before you're done."

You almost had me, until you included the tax guy…

"You need to take this seriously. Something bad is going to happen tomorrow. Look at me, Tim."

So he sat up and looked…and liked what he saw. A black woman—at least as black as he was white—her features spinning tales of North Africa. High forehead, almond eyes, prominent cheekbones, full lips, sharp chin. Skin dark and smooth. Emerald-green eyes. Thin frame, delicate shoulders, voluptuous swelling at the breasts and hips. She wore a fire-red head wrap and a light summer dress of the same color. Around her neck a large silver crucifix and about a hundred beaded necklaces. Around her wrists, seven bracelets, cowrie shells strung on leather.

"I have much to teach you," she said, "but your life is on the line. Stay alive tomorrow, and come to me."

I don't know how to find you…

"You will. Remember—there's only one God, everything else is metaphor."

But you said everyone was God…

"Both are true." She knelt beside him, took his face in her hands, kissed him softly on the lips. "Good luck."

And she was gone.

46:

Julia had promised Herb she'd play well with others and promised herself she'd hold her tongue. But it had been a very long day, and she was working *with* CNN, not *for* them, and there were things that needed to be said.

So she said them.

And Kathryn Reynolds listened. A network news veteran in her late fifties, Reynolds was one *put-together* black woman. She'd been at work since eight that morning, and it was now creeping up on eleven p.m., but she somehow looked like she'd just arrived. Her suit was crisp, her makeup perfect, her long nails bright red and unchipped. Last time Julia visited the bathroom, she'd been more than a little startled by the rumpled, exhausted woman staring back from the mirror. The mirror-Julia had a hopelessly wrinkled jacket, flyaway hair, and dark circles starting to show beneath her eyes.

If Reynolds was insulted by Julia's rant, she didn't wince. She just moved her Peabody Awards—all three of them—from the edge of her desk to the center. Followed by the Emmy. Then she smiled, as one does at a slow child.

"Newspapers can afford to be selective." Gold hoops danced below her earlobes as she shook her head. "Scratch that—they can't, unless they want the blogosphere to go on eating their lunch." She slid her awards back to the side of the desk. "Here, we've accepted the existence of the Internet, the twenty-four-hour news cycle." Her red fingernails swept across the glass wall separating her office from the CNN newsroom bullpen…and the anchor desk, green-screens, lights, cameras, boom mics, and monitors everywhere you looked. "Gotta feed the beast. Would that it were different, but…" She shrugged.

"I get that," said Julia, "but at some point, we end up shifting focus to the freak show on the fringes of the story. And everybody loves a freak show. Then we start reporting the freak shows, even when there's no *real* story attached."

"I agree with you, the world would be better served if we ignored the freak shows, but we simply no longer live in that world." The news producer closed the blinds across the glass wall, shutting out the newsroom, pulled a bottle of Southern Comfort out of the credenza, poured a couple ounces into her coffee. "Days like today, the coffee around here could stand improvement."

Julia held her mug forward. "Much obliged." The women smiled at each other, for real this time. They sipped the sweet, boozy coffee.

"Because of women like me," said Kathryn Reynolds, "women like you are where you are. Not saying you haven't had to deal with your share of assholes. But you should've *seen* the bullshit I had to wade through on my way up. You'd have quit the business. So shut up a minute and hear me."

It was all said with good humor, and measured respect. A wave of self-awareness washed over Julia, and she saw herself from the other side of the desk and felt embarrassed all over again.

"I read your series on Katrina. You're a good reporter, and you've been blessed with serious writing chops. But you need to think about the road ahead. You could make the jump to television." She sipped her coffee. "Some networks, you compromise every principle of your calling..."

Every principle of your calling. The words gave Julia a start. She'd always felt pretentious when she admitted to herself that her job *did* feel like a calling, and she never gave the feeling voice. It's the feeling of having been put on this earth for a specific purpose. The genesis of which can be found in the neurochemistry of the human brain, but it's easy to see how people came to invent a soul, separate from the body. It's a spiritual feeling, even if there is no spirit.

"...At this network, you only make one compromise: you have to lower the bar of what constitutes newsworthiness. We need the eyeballs; it's the only way we can make the margins that our Wall Street overseers demand.

Understand? See, we're fighting for the survival of journalism; the 'Platonic Ideal' isn't even on the table. And if you don't bend, you break. You gotta stay in the game, and we only bend that one thing here. You keep the rest of your ethics intact, and you can still do stories in depth when you can justify them. Some of us have managed it before you. And for that, you're welcome."

"Thank you," said Julia. "I appreciate the advice."

"I knew I was gonna like you, once we got that chip off your shoulder," said Kathryn Reynolds. "I want you to think about what I said. The future ain't what it used to be, but it's coming right at us, regardless." She nodded, putting the subject to rest. "As for Trinity, I don't tell you what to put in your pieces for the *Picayune,* so don't tell me what *isn't* news for CNN."

"Deal," said Julia.

They clinked mugs and drank to it, Julia now glad Herb had made the deal with CNN. She could learn from this woman.

Kathryn Reynolds plucked a remote off her desktop, flicked the television on, muted it. Soledad O'Brien was doing a stand-up in front of Trinity's Lakeview mansion. Blue tarpaulin covered the roof of the main building, while the garage had a new metal roof. The front yard was mounds of dirt, and a tractor stood in the driveway.

Julia had done the research on this segment, prepared a crib sheet for O'Brien's field producer. In the weeks after Katrina, Trinity had taken the first lowball buyout offer from his insurance company, and simply walked away from the place. A record producer who'd worked with the Stones and U2 now owned it.

"Go get some sleep," said Kathryn Reynolds. "We've got a big day tomorrow. 'Trinity's Grand Sermon,' complete with all the freak-show angles."

Julia drank the last of her coffee, put the mug on the edge of the desk. But she didn't stand. "Can I ask you something?"

"You just did. Ask me something else."

"What do you think is going on with Trinity? I mean, best guess, given what we know."

Kathryn Reynolds chuckled. "Honey, I haven't the foggiest notion. Maybe he has a brain tumor, and it activated a portion of his brain that the rest of us can't access…and maybe that portion of his brain enables him to perceive one of the six or seven collapsed quantum dimensions. Information traveling backward through time. Or something like that. I'm not totally up on my quantum mechanics, but if I were you, I'd be interviewing a physicist. And an oncologist."

"I'm talking to a physicist Monday," said Julia, "but the brain tumor angle hadn't occurred to me. Thanks."

"Not that it'll come to anything. It's pretty wild."

"Honestly, to me, it's a lot less wild than the existence of a God."

"Well now, I'm a believer," said Kathryn Reynolds. She looked toward the television. "But that don't mean I believe Yahweh is sending us messages through this douchebag."

Julia stood, shouldered her bag. She stopped at the door.

"Thanks, Kathryn."

"Call me Kathy."

47:

The city was desperate to keep people from flooding the neighborhood to the point of inevitable tragedy, and the television networks were only too happy to help. They set up huge screens and PA systems in Centennial Park, Piedmont Park, Five Points, and in the parking lot of Trinity's warehouse-studio-church, with the city picking up the tab. They also sent cameras and reporters to cover the reaction of Trinity's Pilgrims to the sermon.

Trinity had remained silent during the limo ride from the hotel. It was an impressive operation, with a police cruiser in front, another behind, and six motorcycle cops zooming ahead in pairs to close intersections, then dropping back into formation as another pair zoomed ahead to close the next, in perfect choreography. The sort of display that normally would've thrilled Trinity. But he didn't seem to notice. He seemed to be slipping into a state of deep relaxation, and Daniel decided to honor the silence.

He couldn't think of anything useful to say anyway. Twice he started to tell his uncle about the stolen camera and the photos it contained, but he held his tongue. This wasn't the time; Trinity needed a clear head. Daniel would come clean after the sermon.

The motorcade made good time to Trinity's television studio, sped down a ramp and swept into a basement garage that had been cleared for maximum security. The only other car down there was Trinity's red SUV, which had sat unused for days and was starting to look a little dusty.

They were now alone in Trinity's dressing room, Samson and Chris just outside the door and a half dozen cops along the hallway. Trinity sat at the makeup table, deepening his tan, powdering the shine from his forehead.

The room had an abandoned look, Daniel thought. No, not abandoned…more like a snapshot, a still life—one moment, captured in time, made permanent, no matter what else followed. There was the bottle of Blanton's, three-quarters empty, sitting as Trinity had left it days earlier. The mountain of prayer requests and letters, dirty canvas mailbags that started at the east wall and took up a third of the room. The powders and crèmes and brushes and makeup pencils on the dressing table, and the little round lightbulbs surrounding the mirror.

Trinity put down the sponge he was using, removed the sheet of tissue paper from his shirt collar, straightened his white tie, and slipped into his shiny silk jacket.

"Ready?" said Daniel.

Trinity nodded, headed for the door. Then stopped and said, "I want you to know something. I got a feeling something bad might happen out there…"

Daniel started to speak, but Trinity silenced him with a gesture. "No, I'm still going out. But just in case…I need to tell you. And I'm not looking for anything back. Just want you to know. I love you, Danny. Whatever I am, whatever I was. I always did, never stopped."

"I—uh…I…" Daniel stared at his uncle, settled for, "Well, thank you."

Trinity grinned, opened the hallway door.

"*Rock 'n' roll*," he said. And strode, shoulders back, chest out, into the unknown.

Tim Trinity had never heard five thousand people make so little sound. He stood in the darkened wings, stage-right, waiting for his cue from the floor director. A small monitor on a plywood crate showed the master feed from the control room.

The director had done exactly as Trinity instructed. There was no opening jingle, cross-fading into canned church music; no video montage of happy, successful Christians; no sparkly *Tim Trinity Prosperity-Power Miracle Hour* graphic sweeping across the screen. Instead, the simple title card—A MESSAGE FROM REV. TIM TRINITY—faded up over black, stayed for fifteen seconds, and faded back down.

He turned to Daniel, "Wish me luck."

"Good luck."

The floor director counted down *4–3–2–1* with his fingers in the air and pointed at Trinity as the stage lights came up to blinding intensity.

The crowd roared as Trinity took center stage. He flashed his toothy smile, made calming gestures with both hands.

"Please, thank you for your enthusiasm, but no cheering. Please, really…"

The crowd fell into obedient silence.

He rested his hand on the blue leather Bible perched on the Plexiglas lectern, found the camera with red light glowing, and looked directly into its unblinking black eye. He cleared his throat.

"I know y'all want me to tell you about this…" a glance back to Daniel in the wings, "…this *gift of prophecy* that God seems to have bestowed upon me. But before I talk about that, there's something I need to make absolutely clear, so we will have no misunderstanding about who, or what, I am."

He picked up his Bible, stepped in front of the lectern. "I am not—" He closed his eyes for a moment, opened them again. "I am not…well, I'm not sure what it is God wants from me. I do think he's fixin' to reveal something important to the world, but I do not know what it is. I am not in control of the tongues, He is, and when they come upon me, I have no knowledge of what I am going to say or what I am saying. Sometimes I think God speaks to me, but he has not yet seen fit to give me direct orders."

His eyelids grew unbearably heavy, and he allowed them to fall closed.

Lord, I am a blank slate, an empty vessel…

I invite you now to speak through me…

Forward, backward, sideways, it don't matter…

I beg you, do it now…

Please, television hates dead air…

His eyes popped open and he said, "Paul was wrong, and James was right…" He wanted to open his Bible to James 2:26 and give the page a dramatic *thwack*. But that was the old Tim Trinity, and the new Tim Trinity's hands would not play along.

So he just opened his mouth again, and heard himself say, "Faith without works is dead."

He stood for a long time, waiting for more. Looked out into the front rows of the audience. A sea of faces, open, eager, waiting along with him.

Nothing came.

He closed his eyes again, although they did not feel heavy anymore.

Come on, God, you're makin' me look a fool up here. I invited you in with an open heart, what else am I supposed to do?

For the first time, he heard the voice of the Lord.

And the Lord said, "Get off the stage."

Trinity opened his eyes to the waiting world.

"That's all I have for today." He forced a smile, flashed his perfect implants at the crowd. "But stay tuned, folks, somethin' big is coming… soon."

The crowd cheered as if he'd just parted the Red Sea.

48:

Daniel stood in the wings, watching his uncle on the television monitor. Trinity was saying, "...there's something I need to make absolutely clear, so we will have no misunderstanding about who, or what, I am." He picked up his Bible, stepped in front of the lectern. "I am not—" A slow blink. "I am not...well, I'm not sure what it is that God wants from me."

Damn. He didn't say it...

The backstage door opened, drawing Daniel's attention from the monitor.

A man stood, half-hidden by the big metal door, looking in from the hallway. Daniel walked deeper into the backstage darkness. As his eyes adjusted, he got a better look at the man. Under six feet, short black hair, average build, wearing some kind of uniform. Gray polyester slacks with black piping up the leg and a red polo shirt, with black stripes. There was a logo patch on the shirt.

Daniel crept around a black curtain, came at the man from an angle, slowly closing the distance, staying behind a stack of crates, until he was just twelve feet away. The logo was a cartoon fire hydrant, with the words Bulldog Couriers. There was something under the man's shirt, tucked into his pants at the belly.

Something with a sharp corner.

Chris was all the way on the other side of the stage, too far to signal. He glanced around for Samson, couldn't spot him. He approached the man, said, "Excuse me—"

The man bolted.

The door slammed shut.

Daniel crashed through the door, into the bright hallway. The man had a good lead, but the hallway was crowded and he pinballed off a member of the stage crew and tumbled over an equipment cart, scrambled up, took off again.

Daniel flew after the man, hurdled the overturned cart, caught up with him just shy of the front lobby, grabbed his collar, and sent him face-first into the cinderblock wall.

"Ah, shit! You broke my nose!"

Daniel spun him around, reached under his shirt. "Shouldn't a run."

The man held his hand against his gushing nose, blood flowing between his fingers, as Daniel ripped the gun from his waistband.

Only it wasn't a gun.

It was an autograph book.

The man spoke in a rush of words. "My wife's a big fan and I told her I'd try to get his autograph and I used my uniform to get backstage and I know it was wrong and I'm sorry…" He spat some blood on the floor. "…But if you tell, I'll lose my job at Bulldog, and I really need this job. Please, man, let me go." He gestured to his face. "I think I've paid the consequences, don't you?"

Daniel shoved the autograph book into the man's hands, pointed to the front door.

"Go on, then. Get out."

Daniel trudged back down the hallway, feeling pretty low. He'd just broken an innocent man's nose for the crime of wanting an autograph.

Awesome move, Dan…very Christ like…

The sermon was over by the time he got back. He met Samson in the hallway.

"What happened?"

Samson shrugged. "He cut it short, don't know why. Promised more to come. We've got a disturbance out front, I gotta tend to that. You'll find him in the dressing room. Stay there, I'll come for you after we get the all-clear. Chris's waiting down at the car. We'll have you outta here in a half hour."

Trinity was in the dressing room, but he wasn't alone. There was also Jennifer Bartlett and Liz Doherty and some young men setting up a computer station next to the makeup table.

"Danny, there you are," said Trinity. "Liz, tell him what you just told me."

"Well, we've been talking with the city," said Liz Doherty, "tryin' to find a way to ease pressure on infrastructure, and it looks like we'll be doing the show from the Georgia Dome next week. The Georgia Dome! Isn't that terrific?"

"Yeah…swell," said Daniel.

"Not sure why, considerin' the giant egg I just laid out there," said Trinity. "But did you hear them at the end? They loved it."

"Don't worry, Reverend Tim," Jennifer said with a Texas twang, "I thought you were wonderful. The tongues don't happen every time, we all understand that."

"Thanks, honey."

"I had to miss it," said Daniel.

"Didn't miss much." Trinity sipped some bourbon, then chuckled, trying to shake it off. "Ah, what the hell, we'll get 'em next time." He turned to Jennifer. "Darlin', do me a favor, find Samson, find out what's holding us up. I want to get back to the Westin."

Jennifer smiled broadly, said, "On it, chief," and hip-swished out of the room.

Trinity said, "Georgia Dome's gonna be somethin' else, but ya know, I think I'm gonna miss this place, I've become rather fond of it."

Daniel wondered exactly what there was to miss in this place. There would be another dressing room just like it, another dressing table, another three-way mirror. Another mountain of unopened mailbags would accumulate just as this one had grown, dirty and gray, except for the new black one with the Bulldog Couriers logo and the—

Bulldog Couriers. The autograph book…

Oh, shit!

Daniel flew across the room, grabbed his uncle's arm.

"Everybody get out!" He yanked Trinity toward the door. "Out! Everybody out!"

Nobody moved. Trinity pulled his arm back. "The hell is wrong with you?"

Daniel couldn't get the words out. "Mailbag, some—I, a bomb, I think—we gotta go. NOW!"

Trinity's eyes went wide, a look of desperation on his face. "Where's my Bible?" Before Daniel could stop him, he'd crossed to the dressing table, next to the tech guys setting up the computer, next to the pile of mailbags.

As Trinity picked up his Bible, Daniel caught his arm again and yanked him into the hallway, yelling, "Run! Everybody run!" He got his arm around his uncle's waist, forced him to pick up the pace.

"Stairs," Daniel shouted as they ran down the hallway. Trinity pointed to a door, and they banged through it, into the stairwell.

A concussive blast rocked the building, and the stairwell lights flickered. Trinity stumbled, but Daniel steadied him. "Faster! C'mon!"

Muted screams of horror and howls of pain followed as they flew down the concrete steps and into the underground garage.

Daniel's eyes adjusted to the gloom, and he could make out Chris sitting in the limousine, just thirty feet away.

"Chris!" he shouted as they ran to the limo.

But Chris didn't move.

Chris had a bullet hole in his forehead. He was duct-taped upright in the seat, and his dead eyes stared at nothing.

Daniel jerked at the door handle. Locked. He spun to face Trinity. "Your car—"

"Over there."

They ran across the garage, to Trinity's red SUV. Trinity beeped the locks with his remote. Daniel snatched the keys from his hand.

"I'm driving," he said, yanking the door open and shoving Trinity forward. "Down on the floor, outta sight." Trinity scrunched down into the foot-well, his chest on the passenger seat.

Daniel stuck the key in the ignition, cranked it, and the engine roared to life.

Behind them, the stairwell door banged open. Daniel turned his head. Samson came running into the garage, gun in hand.

Thank God...

Samson made eye contact with Daniel—a split second that seemed to last an hour—and then raised his gun and pointed it at him.

Daniel threw it in gear, mashed the accelerator to the floor.

Tires squealed on concrete, found purchase, and the beast shot forward.

Samson unloaded at them from behind—*pap-pap-pap-pap-pap-pap*— and Daniel heard *thunk-thunk-thunk-thunk* as bullets hit the SUV, but he kept his eyes forward as they sped up the ramp and shot out into the blazing sun.

The sidewalk at the end of the driveway was full of Trinity's Pilgrims. Daniel leaned on the horn, jammed the brakes, saw a clearing, wrenched the wheel, hit the gas, and tore across a patch of grass and onto the road.

"You hit?"

"What?"

"Are you hit?"

"No," said Trinity, "fine." He wriggled up into the passenger seat, buckled his belt, as Daniel hung a hard right, then a left, then another right.

Daniel didn't let up on the gas, driving them deeper into the surrounding ghetto, no destination, just putting distance between them and what they'd left behind.

"Nobody's following," he said.

"Well, that's something," said Trinity. "Hang a right, there's a police station up on Magnolia."

"Not going to the cops."

"Why not?"

"Samson was coordinating security with the cops, and that was Samson who just shot at us."

"What?"

"It was Samson just tried to kill us."

"Shit. Really?"

"I saw him clearly."

"Damn." Trinity shook his head. "Still, that doesn't mean—"

"Another thing: When we arrived, cops all over the hallway outside your dressing room. Same thing when we went to the stage. But when I came out during your sermon, no cops. All gone." He hung a left, headed south. "You see any when we ran out?"

"No."

"Right. Maybe they've got nothing to do with it, but I say we don't make that wager."

Trinity sat in silence for a few seconds, then nodded. "Where we going?"

"I don't know. Away from Atlanta."

49:

Chicago, Illinois…

Special Agent Steve Hillborn straightened his tie as he crossed the high-ceilinged lobby of the FBI Chicago Division Headquarters. He signed in at the counter, clipped his building pass onto his handkerchief pocket, and nodded to the uniformed guard standing at parade rest as he passed through the inner doors.

Hillborn didn't usually mind being called in on a Sunday, but he'd promised to meet Fred at five o'clock at the Lakeview Athletic Club's climbing wall. They'd only been dating a couple months, and Hillborn had been putting a lot of hours in at the Bureau lately, and he didn't think Fred would enjoy being stood up…again. But that's the life of a cop's boyfriend, he thought as he stepped into the elevator, and if Fred couldn't accept it, the relationship wasn't gonna last anyway. Better to find out now.

The text message from his boss, Chicago SAC Winfield Battles, had said simply: Explosion @ Trinity church—Report HQ, 3PM.

Hillborn worked the Organized Crime desk. A week ago he'd been tasked with opening a file on the Reverend Tim Trinity, and he was glad to be working on something new. Morale had taken a hard hit after their most recent showcase prosecution went tits-up. There'd been a thorough post-mortem on the case, and nobody thought the investigation had been faulty or the evidence lacking. Sometimes you just get a charismatic defense attorney who dances the seven veils and seduces the jury. Sometimes you get a jury of idiots.

And when you get both, you don't get convictions.

So now the federal prosecutor was insisting that *more than enough* evidence still wasn't enough, and Hillborn's open files were growing stale. There were few feelings worse than busting your ass on an investigation, proudly presenting your case to the prosecutor as a slam dunk, and being told to go back in search of yet more evidence.

The new investigation was just beginning, hadn't really had time to take shape. Tim Trinity was seen as a successful player in the religion industry, who recently added soothsaying to his act. Nobody knew how he was doing it, but his predictions were bang-on, and his prognostication of professional sports had to be giving the gambling business a bleeding ulcer. Hillborn had not yet found a connection to organized crime, but it seemed a fair bet that he'd find one. So he was searching.

The terrorism guys—and terrorism was still eating most of the Bureau's resources—were looking at Tim Trinity from another angle, looking for a connection to the Belle Chasse Refinery disaster. Word around the office was they weren't finding anything.

Now, with the explosion at Trinity's church, Hillborn figured on a trip to Atlanta, a trip he'd have to take anyway to interview that reporter—what was her name?—Julia Rothman. It was Rothman who broke the story, she might provide a way in.

Hillborn stopped at his cubicle to grab the Trinity file, thin as it was, and headed up to the briefing room. Seated around the long table were Special Agents Robertson and Bock, Toronteli, Bryson, Macfarlane, and a couple of terrorism guys he knew only slightly, who'd flown in from National. They were watching CNN on the large flat-screen monitor mounted on the end wall between the American flag and the whiteboard.

Hillborn nodded hello to the others, took his seat, and poured himself a coffee as SAC Winfield Battles entered and muted the television. He planted his palms on the table.

"This is the situation," said Battles. "As you know by now, an incendiary device detonated in Reverend Tim Trinity's dressing room at his television studio this morning. We have a forensics team on site, but it's too early to say if Trinity was among the victims. Lot of meat chunks to sort through. Agent Hillborn has been looking at Trinity for…"

Hillborn's Blackberry vibrated on his belt as a new e-mail arrived. He looked at the little screen. The e-mail was from the Nevada office, a response to the query he'd sent two days ago. He read the e-mail.

"Agent Hillborn?"

"Sorry, sir, just got some information on the case."

"Good. Bring us up to speed." Battles sat.

"Yes, sir." Hillborn stood and opened the file in front of him. "Because of Trinity's sports predictions, I've been looking for an O.C. connection. Hadn't found one," he gestured at his Blackberry, "until now. Of all his predictions, his most recent was also the most unlikely—the Gotham Stakes. The winning horse was a fifty-to-one underdog."

"Any given Sunday," said Toronteli.

"Sure, but Trinity didn't just pick the winner, he nailed the whole trifecta—win, place, and show. So I contacted our offices in Las Vegas and Atlantic City and just heard back from Vegas. William Lamech's casino sportsbook stopped taking bets on those exact horses the same day Trinity made the prediction."

"What's the brief on Lamech?" asked Battles.

"He's been mostly legit for a long time, but he grew up on Taylor Street…rose through the ranks running the backroom 'books in Chicago. They called him Lucky Lamech back in the day. Anyway, he was the Outfit's guy when the mob ran Vegas, but he went corporate when Vegas went corporate and hasn't shown any direct O.C. contact in a while. I worked my contacts on this, and my impression is the old guard still holds him in high esteem, but he's bigger than they are, and they have no claim on him. I've also heard rumors that, aside from his legitimate sportsbook in Vegas, he runs an exclusive network of high-end bookies catering to the white-collar crowd. Just rumors, no evidence."

"Wait," said Robertson, flipping some pages in his notebook. "You said Lamech stopped taking those bets the same day Trinity made the prediction. That's the same show when he predicted the oil refinery accident. Two days *before* the news of Trinity's predictions, and how to decode them, went public." "So maybe the same source who tipped Trinity off about the fixed race also tipped off Lamech," said Bryson.

Winfield Battles spoke up from the head of the table. "What's bugging you, Steve?"

Hillborn sat, gestured at the file folder before him. "Trinity's predictions are all over the place—football, ponies, hockey, car races, golf…If this is happening, we're looking at the largest sports-fixing racket in history. Exponentially larger…I mean, *unbelievably* large."

"All the more reason to get our asses in gear," said Battles. "We've got a thread connecting Trinity and Lamech, and with Trinity fucking up the betting business, Lamech is drowning in motive for the bombing. The thread has two ends—we pull at both. Agent Hillborn will take lead on the O.C. angle; liaise with the Evidence Response Team in Atlanta. Robertson and Bryson go with him, Toronteli and Bock work it from this end, and K-Mac liaise with Terrorism." Battles nodded at the television screen. "Publicly this is an investigation of the bombing at Tim Trinity's television studio. But if there's a sports-fixing scam attached, we need to find it and take it down, fast." He stood, glanced at his watch. "Learjet's being fueled as we speak, gentlemen. Get cracking."

50:

Atlanta, Georgia…

Julia sat alone in Kathy Reynolds's office, willing the cell phone in her hand to ring, trying not to cry.

The day had started so well. The morning meeting was a relaxed affair, with plenty of cynical asides and a few good laughs. Television or print, young or old, Southern or Yankee, *reporter humor* crosses all lines, and Julia felt more at home than she had since she left New Orleans. She realized she could work in television if she had to. She'd stick it out until newspapers were no longer the best place to report the news, or until they could no longer pay a living wage, whichever came first. Hopefully that day wouldn't come, but if it did, she'd stay in the game, keep fighting.

They watched the live broadcast of Trinity's show in a conference room and joked about the unmitigated disaster that was his *Faith without Works Is Dead* "sermon." People were actually calling it that, without the ironic quotation marks. Trinity hadn't given the media much to work with, and just ten minutes after he left the stage, the post-game pundits started repeating themselves. Kathy made a face at Julia and said, "Cue the freak show," and after a commercial break, the coverage shifted to the tent cities of Trinity's parking lot and Centennial Park for instant-reaction interviews with hippies high on weed, bikers high on malt liquor, Christians high on the promise of impending rapture (or the promise of impending Armageddon), and the certifiably insane.

And then the fucking bomb exploded inside Trinity's dressing room.

Six people dead in the blast. At least six, maybe more.

It was not known if Tim Trinity was among the dead, but there was evidence of at least three men among the remains. The Fulton County Medical Examiner said several people were in close proximity to the device when it detonated, and consequently there were many fragments of human remains to sort out and identify. Trinity had not been seen since the explosion. A few survivors were found in the hallway outside his dressing room, but they were now in intensive care. No one knew if any would survive long enough to talk to the police.

The Atlanta PD had swarmed into Trinity's church, and an FBI forensics team arrived an hour later. Then they started carrying out the body bags. Some of the bags were mostly empty, carrying only a foot, or a head, or an arm.

That's when Julia let out a low moan. She didn't even know she'd done it—to her, it had been inside her head—but everyone in the conference room turned from the television to face her, and Kathy took her arm and said, "You look unwell," and led her through the bustling newsroom and into the office.

And now she sat, staring at her cell phone, thinking: *Goddamn you, Danny. Call me…* She tried in vain to avoid the memory of their walk together the previous afternoon…their kiss…

And the last thing she'd said to him before walking away. "Danny, it was over for us a long time ago," she'd said, "and it's going to stay over, even if you quit the priesthood."

He would have called. If he were alive, he would have called by now…

51:

Daniel's cell had gone missing in the chaos, and he'd removed the battery and SIM card from his uncle's phone so it could not be used to track their location. He stayed on the blue highways, off the interstates, and he stayed well under the speed limit.

The post-adrenaline hangover left nerves raw for both men, and Trinity didn't seem to want conversation, which was OK with Daniel. He needed the time to think. He drove without destination for a while, then climbed high into the rural mountains of northwest Georgia, where the roads became dirt. He cruised deep into the woods until he spotted an unoccupied hunting cabin, thirty miles from the nearest town. The cabin was off the grid, electricity supplied by a generator. The generator was cold, the cabin dark, and there was no evidence of a recent visitor.

Daniel jimmied a window open and climbed through, unlocked the front door and let Trinity in. The hunting cabin was nicer than he'd expected. Probably owned by an executive who liked the idea of *roughing it* but saw no reason to experience discomfort while doing so.

Trinity found canned soup and beef jerky in the cupboard, enough to keep them until morning. At sunset Daniel covered the windows with blankets and lit an oil lamp he found under the sink, and they ate soup out of the can and listened to the news on a wind-up radio.

Twelve dead at Trinity's church. Six killed by the explosion, another six trampled to death in the stampede from the building. Over two dozen injured.

"I told you I had a feeling something bad was gonna happen," said Trinity.

"This would qualify," said Daniel.

The radio told them that Reverend Tim Trinity was missing and was thought to have died in the explosion, but this was as yet unconfirmed. The Fulton County Medical Examiner's Office directed questions to the FBI, and the FBI wasn't releasing a statement until the forensic investigation was complete and next-of-kin had been notified.

Trinity put his soup can on the coffee table, reached out his right hand. "Gimme the phone."

"What?"

"I gotta call Liz, let her know I'm OK."

"Tim, Liz was still standing in your dressing room when I dragged you out." Trinity didn't withdraw his hand. Daniel shook his head. "I said no. The world thinks you're dead, and you're gonna stay dead until it benefits us to resurrect you. If they know you're alive, they'll come at you again. We need time to figure our next move."

Trinity's arm dropped slowly to his side, and his eyes became wet in the flickering orange light. He blinked rapidly, let out a long breath.

"You and Liz were close."

"Sorta off and on, but…yeah. We were close."

"I'm sorry."

Trinity pulled a steel flask from his pocket, screwed off the cap, and raised it toward the ceiling in a toasting gesture. "Glory and survival, Liz. Hell of a broad." He took a swig, closed his eyes for a moment, nodded to himself. "OK. We go to New Orleans."

"First place they'll look for you," Daniel said. "People in trouble usually run home."

Trinity pointed at him. "I'm dead, remember? They won't be looking. Your words."

"A couple days at most. And that's where they'll start."

"Then we haul ass, in-and-out before they find out. See, I know where the answer is…" Trinity held up a hand. "Last night, I had a dream. More powerful than a dream, it felt like a vision. It felt like God talking. In the dream, God came in the form of a beautiful black woman. The woman said

I was in danger. She also said she could help me. And when I woke up, I knew where to find her. She's in New Orleans."

"What's her name?"

"I don't know. But she's in the French Quarter. I know her address—633 Dumaine, just off Royal."

"You just woke up with her address in your head."

Trinity nodded. "I woke up, and in my head, I could *see* the building—white, one story, green shutters, slate roof. I could see the numbers by the door, and I knew exactly where it was. We go there, we'll find her. I'm sure of it." He took another pull from the flask. "If you wanna bail out, I understand. You never signed up for dodging shrapnel. I can drop you off wherever you like…but I'm going to New Orleans."

"This dream, it was like the dream where God told you he wanted me by your right hand?"

Trinity let out a sheepish grin. "Yeah, well, I was lying when I told you that. I just made it up so you'd stay."

"What?"

"That was *before* I promised not to lie to you. I haven't lied since, and I'm not lying now."

God, he was like a child sometimes. "Speaking of promises," said Daniel, "what happened to telling the world you're not the Messiah?"

"I tried. Honest—you saw me—the words wouldn't come out. So then I did exactly what I told you I'd do: I opened my mouth and trusted the Lord to feed me my lines." Trinity took a swig from his flask. "And you know what? I think he did." He winked. "Just wish he'd given me a little more material. Man, I felt like an ass up there."

Daniel smiled despite himself. He kicked off his shoes. "I'll go with you to New Orleans," he said.

"Thanks." Trinity held the flask out. "Care for a snort?"

Daniel took the flask, smooth and warm in his hand, and swallowed some bourbon. It went down with a welcome burn. The engraving on the flask caught his eye, and he angled it toward the oil lamp.

To Pops—Happy 41ˢᵗ Birthday—Love Danny

He looked up and his uncle nodded.

"You broke my heart, son."

Daniel took another swig, handed the flask back. "Right back at ya, old man." He lay back on the couch and closed his eyes. "Better get some shut-eye. We hit the road early."

Outside, rain started drumming hard para-para-diddles on the cabin's tin roof, and thunder cracked in the distance. Tim Trinity was quiet for a minute. Then he said, "Thanks for saving my life today."

"Go to sleep, Tim."

52:

*N*ow *I lay me down to sleep,*
I pray the Lord my soul to keep.
If I die before I wake,
I pray the Lord my soul to take.

"Sweet dreams, kid."

53:

Early morning mist rose through the Georgia pines like the souls of the dead ascending from their graves on Judgment Day. The lonely jackhammer knock of a woodpecker echoed somewhere in the distance. Daniel and Trinity rolled slowly along the muddy road, windows down, Daniel scanning cabins on the left, Trinity the right.

"Thought we s'posed to be hauling ass," said Trinity.

"Keep your eyes peeled, I can only watch one si—hold on…right there, perfect." Daniel turned into a driveway and stopped behind a battered, once-green GMC Sierra with about twenty years on it. The cabin had no electricity, much less a satellite dish. To the right of the cabin, a pile of freshly cut firewood and an axe sticking out of a tree stump. Tall rose bushes bloomed fiery red against the cabin's wall, and a massive Cracker in faded denim overalls stood cutting back excess leaves with a twelve-inch Bowie knife. He looked to be in his mid-thirties. He turned and stared at them. He didn't smile.

Trinity said, "From where I sit, this is about as far from 'perfect' as we are from Seattle. I say we back the hell outta here."

"Stay in the truck." Daniel got out slowly, closed the door. To the man with the knife, he said, "Good morning—"

The man let out a humorless snort. "*Was* good, until you showed up. Round here, folks get gutted for trespassing."

"Sorry, I, uh, didn't see a sign posted."

"'Round here, don't need a sign." He gestured to the road with his knife. "You girls best be on your way."

Daniel raised his left hand and reached for the door handle with his right. "No problem, understood." He opened the door of Trinity's truck. "Before we go, can I interest you in swapping trucks?"

"Huh?"

"Straight swap, our truck for yours."

"What am I gonna do with a pretty toy like that? I look black to you?"

"Your Sierra's worth—what?—maybe five, six hundred bucks? But fresh tires, so I figure you've kept it running OK."

The big man stepped forward, holding the knife at chest level. "So?"

"Our truck's practically new, decked out with all the options, worth fifteen or twenty times as much. Call it a pretty toy, but it's also a pretty valuable toy. You can sell it, buy a good solid truck with plenty years left in it, and pocket some serious cash in the process."

"Can't sell it if it's hot."

Daniel held the man's eyes. "It's not."

"Cross your heart and hope to die?" The man shook his head and snorted. "Big City faggots always thinkin' we just a bunch a gullible morons up here."

The blade rose, its sharp tip now pointing directly at Daniel's chin. Electricity hummed through his nerves, his fingertips tingling. In an instant, his right foot slid back into position, weight shifted to the balls of his feet, and his core muscled contracted.

"Keep waving that blade around, Clyde, and I'm gonna get the sudden urge to defend myself. Which would look a lot like me breaking your wrist, dislocating your knee, and shoving that pretty knife up your ass."

It stopped the man cold. The blade came down a few inches and he stood with his mouth half open, probably trying to decide which of two possibilities was more likely to be true. Either Daniel was insane, or...

"Don't make me prove it," said Daniel. "And you're the one making assumptions: talking about big city faggots, when I never said shit about mutant inbred hillbillies." Then, softening his tone, "Now I came in peace to make you an offer, and the offer still stands. The Caddy's not stolen, but for the sake of argument, you could strip it and sell it a piece at a time.

The catalytic converter alone would buy two of your trucks. So you wanna make a trade, or what?"

The man sucked air through his front teeth, and the hand with the knife dropped down by his side. He walked slowly to the back of Trinity's Escalade and pointed at the tailgate with the tip of the knife and said, "C'mere."

Daniel walked back, stood beside the man, and looked at the bullet holes put there by Samson Turner. One in the bumper, four in the tailgate, and one more, higher, on the pillar to the left of the rear window. Three inches to the right, and it would've exploded through the back of Daniel's head. *Three inches.* The thought turned his groin to ice.

The man said, "Who's chasin'?"

Daniel shrugged. "Wish I knew. But we can't hang around, so the offer expires in ten seconds. Yes or no?"

The windshield was stained nicotine yellow and the cab smelled like cigarette smoke and body odor in equal measure, but at least the redneck had taken care with maintenance. Daniel checked the oil as he topped up the gas and found it clean, recently changed. Brake and transmission fluids both fine, tire pressure bang-on. It would get them to New Orleans and beyond. And an old pickup on these roads was like a yellow cab on the streets of Manhattan or a Vespa in Rome. It would help them disappear into the background noise of the place.

A couple miles down the road, Trinity said, "Way you talked to that boy..." He let out a whistle.

"We needed the truck."

"Gotta call bullshit on that, Danny. That was about way more than a truck. I mean, how badly you itchin' to die, exactly?"

Daniel looked squarely at his uncle. "Don't think I'm itching to die, not really. But I do like to keep death within spitting distance. Helps me stay sharp."

"Probably not healthy."

"Coming from you," Daniel smiled, "that should probably worry the hell out of me."

* * *

They stopped in Calhoun, and Daniel ducked into the Piggly Wiggly for supplies. On the way out, he stopped at a payphone by the front doors and fed all his coins in.

She answered on the first ring.

Daniel said, "Julia, it's me, I—"

"*Jesus Christ!* Where the hell have you been, why didn't you call me?"

There was no mistaking the tremor in her voice.

"I *am* calling you. Sorry it took a while."

"For the last twenty-two-and-a-half *hours*, I thought you were fucking dead, Danny. Long time to find a payphone."

"Look, I'm glad the idea of my death upsets you, but I'm sorry you had to be upset for so long. That's the best I can offer. We had to lay low."

"Hold on." The phone clunked in Daniel's ear as she put it down. A few seconds of silence, and she came back with her composure intact. "Trinity's alive?"

"Not for the record."

"I see."

"We need to put some miles behind us. I promise when it's time to resurrect him, you get an exclusive."

"OK. I'll sit on it for now, but I need to be able to reach you. Area code 706…where are you, Columbus?"

"No, and we're not staying put. I'll get a pre-paid cell, call you with the number. And I need a favor. We give ourselves away if we use any plastic, so I need you to wire us some cash."

"Um, wow…" There was a pause on the line. "Yeah, OK, fine." A longer pause. "You realize I'm breaching my professional ethics with this. We're supposed to *cover* the story, not *be* the story."

"I'll never tell." Daniel smiled to himself. "Cross my heart and hope to die."

"It's not a joke, Danny. It'll come out eventually, and my journalistic credibility will go down the toilet."

"Yeah, that would really suck for you. Meanwhile, we're running for our lives."

"Don't be a jerk. I said I'd send it. I just want you to know what it's going to cost me."

"OK, but what do you want me to do about that, other than feel guilty?"

"I want you to stay alive."

54:

Atlanta, Georgia…

Just four blocks from the Governor's Mansion on West Paces Ferry, a sober stone mansion stands on a corner lot, surrounded by an eight-foot-high, spiked iron fence. Any casual observer would note the electronic gates across the driveway, the intercom and CCTV camera mounted on a steel post outside the gates, and the expansive lawn, green as the skin of a lime and trimmed golf course short. A closer inspection would reveal cameras mounted under the front porch overhang, high-density xenon security floodlights bracketed under the eaves, and razor-sharp holly bushes planted beneath the ground-floor windows. But unless you knew they were there, you'd never notice the bulletproof glass behind the double-hungs or the gun-port flaps beside each window.

A white stretch limousine pulled to the gate and the driver's window came down. The driver pressed the intercom call button. A man's voice said, "Confirmation code," and the driver punched it in on the keypad. The gates hissed open, and the limousine pulled to the top of the long, circular drive. The driver cut the engine, got out and opened the back door, and led Father Nick inside Southeast Regional Headquarters of the Department of World Outreach.

✦ ✦ ✦

"Nick, good to see you." Conrad Winter stood in the marble vestibule with his hand out and a smug grin on his face.

"Didn't know you were stateside." Nick gave a curt handshake, thinking: *This day is getting better by the goddamned minute.*

"Our resources are at your disposal," Conrad raised his hands in a conciliatory gesture, "but it's your show. I'm simply here to observe and consult and offer assistance in any capacity you may need."

It was a lie, of course. Conrad was Nick's counterpart at Outreach, of equal rank, and was not here to play second fiddle. Cardinal Allodi had sent him to be Allodi's eyes and ears and to take control of the operation if Nick faltered.

And they both knew it.

"Fine. Bring me up to speed, what have we learned?"

"They both got out alive," said Conrad, walking toward a stairwell at the back of the hallway. "Command center is downstairs." At the bottom of the stairs, he slid a card key into the lock, a green light flashed on, and the thick steel door buzzed open.

The room was about thirty feet square. Young priests sat at computer stations, tapping keyboards, reading screens. Others sat at desks, talking into headsets, working the phones. A massive electronic map of the southeastern United States dominated one wall. Another wall was covered with flat-panel monitors.

Nick knew of World Outreach's high-tech command centers, but he'd never been inside one before. He understood the Church's need for such operations in a troubled world and for men like Conrad to run them—but he wasn't looking forward to this.

Conrad signaled to the young man on the nearest computer and said, "Bring up the video."

Black-and-white security video of a parking garage now came up on a monitor, the screen divided into four segments, each showing a different camera feed. Conrad said, "The underground garage at Trinity's TV studio." In the top-left segment, Daniel and Trinity burst into the garage from a stairwell door and crossed out of frame, now entering the bottom-right segment, where they approached a limousine and Daniel tugged on the driver's door handle. From the high angle, there was no way to see if anyone was inside the limo, but the door didn't open. They ran out of that frame and into the top-right segment, where they got into an SUV, Daniel behind the wheel. Back in the top-left segment, the stairwell door flew open again, and a black man in a suit ran into the garage. The man had a gun in his hand. He adopted a shooter's stance and unloaded at the back of the SUV as it tore out of the garage.

The young priest paused the video and said, "It doesn't look like either one took a bullet. And no gunshot victims at area hospitals match their description."

"Who else has seen this?" said Nick.

"Nobody, sir. We hacked into the security system, downloaded the video, and wiped the drives. The police haven't even seen it."

"Good. What do we know about the shooter?"

The young priest tapped on the keyboard, and an enlargement of a Georgia driver's license came up on another screen. "Samson Turner. Fox guarding the henhouse, as it were. Trinity's head of security." Turner's concealed carry permit came up on the screen, along with his army discharge papers, PI license, college diploma. "Former Special Forces, Silver Star, honorable discharge, now works in executive protection. Employer is one of the best firms in the field; clients include Fortune 100 CEOs, A-list Hollywood actors, blue-chip law firms, you name it. Argos Security, headquartered in Nevada."

Nevada. Of course—Trinity's sports predictions… "The gaming industry," said Nick.

The young priest brought incorporation papers for Argos Security up on another screen. "That's what it appears. Argos is owned by a private, numbered company in Grand Cayman, but we know the same holding company also owns Paradise Beach, an online casino based in Antigua and Barbuda."

"OK. What do we know, after they left the garage?"

"Nothing yet, sir. Both their cell phones are offline."

"Of course they are."

"We've got a surveillance team in place at Trinity's house—"

"Waste of time," said Nick. "They're not going back to his house."

"We're also monitoring for any bank card use—debit or credit—but there hasn't been—"

Nick silenced the young priest with a flick of the wrist. He clapped his hands together twice and addressed the room. "Gentlemen, phones down, fingers at rest." The room fell silent and all eyes came his way. "You are dangerously underestimating the subjects of this investigation. Daniel Byrne is the best man the ODA has. He's not going to make it easy for us. We've got to do better than this."

Conrad spoke to the young priest. "Bryan, run that video back a bit. OK, pause it there. That's a Cadillac."

"I don't know anything about Cadillacs," said Nick. "What?"

"We can hack into GM's OnStar system," said the young priest at the computer, "it'll tell us where they are."

"Do it. I want the location of that truck within the hour. And redirect your men away from Trinity's house. I want them looking at Julia Rothman."

"The reporter?"

"She's…an old friend of Daniel's. They're fond of each other. If our other efforts fail, she'll lead us to him. So I want everything. I want her phone calls. I want her e-mails. I want her credit card activity. I want to know what she likes on her pizza and what songs she sings in the shower. Full surveillance, round-the-clock." Nick again addressed the room. "We are not the only interested party, gentlemen. Keep that in mind. We have to find them first."

"Absolutely, Nick. My men are at your command," said Conrad Winter. But his thin smile and unblinking eyes added: …*for now.*

55:

aniel picked up a pre-paid cell phone at a Kroger and called Julia, and she came through with the money, which he picked up at a Western Union in Gadsden, Alabama. Along with the cash, Julia sent a two-word message:

YOU'RE WELCOME.

He topped up the gas, then bought his uncle a pair of blue jeans and a simple gray shirt at Kmart. Trinity drew the line at abandoning the white leather belt and cowboy boots, and Daniel had to settle for partial victory.

"Just trying to keep you alive," he said as they pulled onto Highway 77, a paved two-lane heading south.

Tim Trinity grinned. "Don't think I don't appreciate it." He rolled down his window and lit a cigarette.

Daniel eyed the cigarette, said, "That's the fifth one this hour. How bad *you* itchin' to die, exactly?"

Trinity watched the smoke rise from between his fingers. "I do so love the devil sticks." He took another drag, blew it out the window. "Yes I do. 'Course I should give 'em up...but you and I both know I ain't gonna live long enough for these things to kill me."

"What the hell are you talking about?"

"I just don't think God's plan includes me living to see you and Julia make perfect little Judeo-Christian babies, that's all."

They rode in silence for half a minute. Daniel said, "How did you know about Julia?"

"How could I have missed her?" Trinity smiled. "Admired your ambition, going after an older woman like her. You did real good, boy...she was a knockout." Daniel said nothing. "Oh, come on! Don't say you don't remember, and don't say you didn't see me. I *saw* you see me. The Maple Leaf bar? Mid City Lanes? Golden Gloves? High school graduation? I stood to the side, holding the door wide open, every chance I got. You always knew you were wanted."

Daniel raised a hand. "Fair enough. I saw you. And maybe I should've thanked you for the offer and told you I wasn't interested in being an apprentice con artist."

"Never said you should take after me." Trinity flicked the cigarette out the window. "Made sure you got good grades, told you I had a college fund set aside. You coulda studied whatever you liked, done whatever you pleased. You knew that."

"Yeah, well, you also told me we were on a mission from God. Mixed messages. I was a kid, remember?" He pointed at the radio. "Find us a news station, will ya? Let's see what's doing in the big world out there."

Trinity turned the knob and scanned up the AM dial...some hillbilly music...a screaming preacher with a mind full of the "End Times"...a countrified pop station...and then he found a news station and brought it in strong.

...amazing development last night, when the Georgia Lottery numbers came up exactly as Reverend Tim Trinity predicted. But at a press conference this morning the Georgia Lottery Corporation announced that, despite the record jackpot, there were over 859,000 tickets sold with those winning numbers, so each winning ticket will pay only four dollars. For the first time in its seventeen years of operation, the lottery is being suspended pending an internal investigation. The GLC insisted that the investigation will be swift and said the lottery will resume as soon as the integrity of the game can be assured.

"Hot damn!" Trinity clapped his hands together. "That sure is something, ain't it?"

"Yeah, terrific. We can now add the government to the list of people who want you dead." Daniel turned the radio off. "Let's see, we've got the gambling industry—the mob, the casinos, and now the government—"

"Don't forget Wall Street," said Trinity. "For all we know, I might start predicting closing numbers of the Dow Jones."

"And Wall Street," Daniel agreed. "Then we've got probably a dozen religions, including various sects that compete for the title *Christian*— "

"Including your friends at the Vatican," said Trinity.

"You're too sinister about the Vatican. They just want you contained."

"Yeah, in a pine box."

Daniel waved it off. "Suffice it to say, you've got a lot of powerful groups in your fan club. What do you know about Samson?"

"Had a soft spot for Delilah," said Trinity. He followed with a just-trying-to-lighten-the-mood gesture. "I don't know anything. When the world turned upside down, I told Jennifer to ask around and get me the best bodyguards in the business. She was a bright kid, I could give her jobs like that."

Daniel thought back to Trinity's dressing room. "Not *was*. She *is* a bright kid. She left your dressing room a couple minutes before the bomb went off."

"Only because I sent her out," said Trinity. "Look, I see where you're going with this, but I'm telling you, you're barkin' up the wrong tree. Jennifer Bartlett's one of the good guys. I'd bet my life on it."

"You did," said Daniel.

"Doesn't prove anything."

"No, it doesn't. I'm just exploring different angles."

They rode in silence for a while. It was an easy silence, and Daniel felt a profound sense of wholeness he hadn't felt in a very long time. He'd always told himself that cutting toxic people from your life was essential to becoming an independent adult. Part of the process of self-actualization, as the psychologists called it. And that's what he'd done when he walked away from Trinity. But Tim Trinity was the only family Daniel had ever known. He was father, mother, uncle…protector, provider, teacher.

He was everything. Even if he was a con man.

Leaving may have been the healthy choice, but when Daniel walked away he left a lot of himself behind. He could admit that now. Being with his uncle again did pick the scabs off the old wounds, but it also forced him to remember the love he had for the deeply flawed man who loved him.

Although Daniel hadn't said a word, his uncle seemed to pick up on it.

"Look at us," said Trinity, "no silk suit, no dog collar, cruisin' down the 77 in a rusty old beater…" His hand swept across the sun-drenched rural Alabama landscape. "Just like the old days, eh?"

Daniel smiled back at him. "Yeah, kinda."

"But this time, we really are on a mission from God. That story I sold you when you were a child…" Trinity lit a new cigarette, "…it was prettier than the truth, and I wanted your world to be prettier than the one I lived in. Only so many times I can apologize for that. But think about where we are now! That pretty story—that fantasy—has become manifested in reality."

"In the fantasy, people weren't trying to kill you."

Trinity chuckled. "Well, I guess that's the downside of reality."

Daniel couldn't help but laugh. "Hell of a downside. Look, Tim, don't go getting all messianic on me. At best, you're a modern day Elijah or something. But you're not the sacrifice. I'm going to keep you alive. And I'll need your cooperation with that."

"You got it," said Trinity. "I don't want to die if I don't have to. But I'm seeing this thing through, all the way. Whatever God wants. Whatever the cost."

"Can't argue that." Daniel squinted against the sun, and a wave of fatigue rolled over him. The last day had used up a lot of adrenaline, and he'd only gotten a few hours' fitful sleep at the cabin. He pulled the truck to a stop on the shoulder and threw it into park. "Listen, you mind taking the wheel for a spell? I'm feeling a little ragged, just need to rest my eyes an hour or two."

56:

D aniel drifted with the current, just below the surface. He felt his consciousness moving through space-time, aware that he was being transported on the smell of dry, dusty grass.

It took him back to the Winnebago, back to the tent revival circuit in summertime.

It was always such a rush, pulling into the dirt parking lot next to the big white tent, looking to see which other preachers' RVs were already there, which other preachers' kids were hacking around the place. Looking especially for Reverend Auld's baby blue Winnebago, looking for Trixie, Auld's skinny blonde daughter with the freckles splashed across her cheeks and the unsettling green eyes. Hoping she was there, hoping she wasn't, fearing he'd be tongue-tied yet again.

A car door slammed, and the ride in the time machine ended. Daniel yawned, stretched. Then realized they weren't moving. He blinked and sat up straight. "What's going on? Where are we?"

He was alone in the truck. Trinity was gone, and he'd taken his Bible with him.

Daniel glanced at his watch—1:57. He held up a hand to block the sun and looked through the windshield. About sixty cars and pickups, parked on a field of dry grass…

And a half dozen RVs…

Parked beside a big white tent.

For a few long seconds, Daniel groggily considered the possibility of time travel, decided it was more likely that he was still asleep, still dreaming. *No, this is the truck we got from the redneck. This is now…*

Oh, shit.

Trinity's stopped at a tent revival.

He jumped from the truck and ran, weaving between parked trucks, passing under a vinyl banner that said:

THE HOLY SPIRIT IS ALIVE IN GREENVILLE

...and into the packed tent.

About two hundred people under the tent, some sitting in folding lawn chairs but most standing, some holding camcorders, all facing the plywood stage where a fat Holy Roller with a microphone bellowed hallelujahs through a PA system so powerful you could feel the man's voice rumble in your abdomen. Daniel kept moving, scanning the crowd as he pressed further inside.

After a few seconds, he spotted his uncle. But it was too late.

The Holy Roller stopped bellowing and stood agape as Trinity bounded up the steps at the side of the stage, bright blue Bible in hand. Several in the crowd gasped audibly. A woman shouted, "It's Reverend Tim!" And another, "Reverend Tim's alive!" followed by a "Praise Jesus!" and at least a dozen hallelujahs.

Tim Trinity waved to the crowd and flashed his thousand-watt smile. "Thank you, thank you, bless you." He made calming gestures with his Bible and the crowd got quiet. "I was just drivin' past and spotted y'all's tent, and I got to feeling that God wanted me to stop and say a few words." He shook his head. "Now, I don't...well, to be honest, I don't feel a spell coming on, and I don't know if God will choose to speak through me in tongues, and if he doesn't, I won't fake it."

Trinity stepped gracefully over to the Holy Roller and took the microphone from him with a smile and a nod of thanks. He turned away from the crowd, found a chair at the back of the stage, and dragged it to the front. He sat and blew out a long breath and said, "I hope y'all don't mind if I sit. I tell ya true, the last few weeks have been as much a trial as a blessing. But I'm trying. Trying to do the right thing. And that's why I stopped when I saw your tent. I know you've all seen me on television, but some of you will remember, before I was on television, I used to come by Greenville pretty regular."

"We remember you, Reverend Tim!" shouted a skinny old man in the crowd.

"Good. Because I have a confession to make." Trinity cleared his throat. "All those times I came here, I was, uh…well, no way to sugar-coat it. I was a fake." The crowd gasped, almost as one. He nodded, "I know, it's terrible. I was conning you, just trying to put on a good show and separate you from some of your hard-earned money. That's the truth." He stood up. "I believe God brought me here so I could make my confession. And I think he would want me to warn you that *this man—*" he thrust a finger at the Holy Roller standing to his right "*—this man* is a false prophet, just as I was."

The crowd responded with a stunned silence, as if Trinity's words hadn't quite registered or didn't make any sense. After a few seconds, everyone started talking at the same time, their voices running together in confusion and despair.

But some voices rose above the chaos to call out their disbelief.

"*No!*"

"*Not Preacher Bob!*"

"*Why should we believe you? You just admitted you're a fake!*"

The Holy Roller jumped forward, snatched the microphone from Trinity, jabbed a finger at the air between them and bellowed, "Satan!" He swept his arm, taking in the crowd. "These good people are like *family.* They *know* me, have known me for years, and you will *not* turn them away from righteousness!"

"*You tell him, Preacher Bob!*"

Preacher Bob kicked it onto high gear. "We are the children of God—*Hallelujah!*—and we will not have the wool pulled over our eyes—*Hallelujah!*—and we will not be tricked by your black magic—*Hallelujah*! In *Jesus's name*, we cast you out of this place of Christian worship! Be gone! Be gone! Be gone!"

The crowd chanted along with him: *Be gone! Be gone! Be gone…*

Trinity stood in place, his face a portrait of bewilderment and loss. "No, no, you don't understand. Wait, I'm trying to—I'm speaking the truth…" He closed his eyes and held his Bible to his chest. "Please," he said.

The crowd pressed toward the stage, chanting even louder: *Be gone! Be gone! Be gone...*

Daniel sharp-elbowed his way through the crowd, leapt onto the stage, and grabbed Trinity's wrist.

And dragged him the hell out of there.

57:

Blue Ridge Mountains, Georgia…

Conrad Winter pulled to a stop behind the red Escalade with the gold rims and the bullet holes in the tailgate. He eyed the axe in the tree stump, the shabby cabin, the big man sitting on the stoop, next to a row of rose bushes. He mentally tipped his hat to Daniel. He hadn't really expected him to mess up this early in the game, knew Daniel wouldn't be the easiest prey he'd ever brought down, but that would just make the sweet honey of victory that much sweeter. Golden Boy was now playing in *his* world, and the outcome was not in doubt.

Conrad cut the engine and turned to his assistant. "Here's the play. Get out, come around, open the door for me. Leave your jacket unbuttoned and accidentally flash your piece on your way. Then plant yourself in front of that axe over there."

"Got it."

Conrad watched the big man on the stoop, saw him notice the gun as Father Doug came around the fender. He got out and walked toward the man, and as he got close, the man stood.

He was big all right. Conrad was not used to looking up at other men and guessed this one at about six-seven. But he drank too much beer and ate too much barbecue, and he'd seen Doug's gun.

"You boys a little early for Halloween," said the big country boy. But his delivery lacked confidence.

Conrad smiled, said, "My name is Father Carmine, and my associate is Father David. I need you to tell me everything you remember about the two men who came here in that truck. Every detail exactly as it happened, and everything they said. You can keep the truck, by the way. We're here for information."

The man looked uneasy. "Why you chasin' after them?"

"Their lives are in danger, my son, and we are trying to save them." Conrad put no effort into selling the line. Now he dropped the smile. "And every minute I spend explaining things to you is a minute I am not getting closer to them." He scratched his right earlobe, signaling Doug to loom a little closer, and heard him take a few steps forward, then stop. "Now let's start again. I need you to tell me everything you remember about the two men who came here in that truck. Every detail exactly as it happened, and everything they said. Do you understand me clearly?"

"Yes, I think I do."

"Good. Understand this also: If we later discover that you lied to us, I will be displeased. And you will feel the wrath of God."

Father Nick picked up the camera that Conrad had liberated from Daniel's hotel room and, for the third time, scrolled through the photos of Tim Trinity snorting cocaine. Thinking: *He had the pictures the whole time and led me to believe he didn't...*

The betrayal stung.

Their relationship was a true double-edged sword, and it cut both ways. It had allowed Nick to experience something like paternal love, but was also a constant reminder of the road not taken. He'd have been a good dad, far better than his father had been to him. He never regretted giving his life to God, but he was occasionally visited by crushing loneliness. The love he felt for Daniel was both laceration and salve.

And now there was the betrayal.

If Daniel lived through this case, he would surely be excommunicated for his actions against the Vatican. Unless. *Unless what, exactly?*

Nick thought about how he would pitch it to Cardinal Allodi. Taking Daniel back in was the best way to keep him quiet. Of course, he would first have to help them with Trinity and return to the fold in a state of pure contrition. He would have to willingly submit himself to the punishment of the Church and then live a monastic life of manual labor and rigorous spiritual retraining, maybe for a year, maybe five. But once through, he could make a life as a priest again, albeit never in a sensitive position. He was multilingual, could teach at Catholic schools all across central Africa and parts of Asia.

Nick could probably sell it to Allodi and the inevitable disciplinary tribunal…*if* he could get to Daniel and *if* he could turn him around.

And those were two very big ifs.

The young priest who'd run the computer earlier approached at a near jog.

"Father Conrad on line three, sir."

Nick held up a finger to tell the young priest not to walk away and picked up the phone. "What've you got?"

"Daniel traded the Cadillac to a country boy who lives off the grid," said Conrad, "and I don't think Country Boy has any idea who Trinity is. They left here about eight fifteen this morning—I gave Bryan details of the truck they're now driving—but when they left, they didn't indicate what direction they were heading."

"It's all over the television," said Nick. "Trinity showed up at a tent revival outside Greenville, Arkansas. Tried to confess his past sins. Didn't go over too well with the locals."

"When?"

"About two o'clock."

"Greenville," said Conrad, and Nick could hear him unfolding a map. "That's between here and New Orleans. What do you think?"

"I think Daniel knows better than to let him run home," said Nick.

Conrad said, "Also knows better than to let him be seen in public, but there they are on television."

"Yeah, I know."

"Maybe Daniel's not calling the shots."

"Maybe not," said Nick. "All right, you head for Greenville, then on to New Orleans. Stay on the rural highways, and keep your eyes open for any tents. Maybe he'll feel compelled to stop at another one."

"Call me if anything develops," said Conrad. He broke the connection.

Nick put the receiver down, turned to the young man still waiting, and handed him the camera. "Bryan, I want you to keep track of the news channels. When the Greenville story loses steam, get the photographs on this camera to the media. Anonymously, of course."

"Of course, sir."

58:

"What the hell is wrong with you?" said Daniel as they passed a MISSISSIPPI WELCOMES YOU sign. "Are you insane?"

"Stop," said Tim Trinity.

"Seriously, is your head broken? What is it about the concept of a low profile that eludes you? Please explain how getting up in front of a dozen camcorders qualifies as *helping me keep you alive*."

"Will you please just let it go? For the eleventh time: *I'm sorry*. OK? I just…I saw the tent and I thought God wanted me to confess. I thought…you know, I flushed the rest of my coke down the sink on Saturday. But the tongues didn't come on Sunday and…I just thought, maybe, if I confessed my past sins to those people…if I denounced a false prophet…I guess I thought they'd come back faster." He shook his head, smiling ruefully. "I used to cherish the brief respite periods when the voices go quiet…a couple days here, a few days there…blessed relief, for as long as it lasted. And I used to dread their return." He gazed out the window. "Funny how things change…"

"A dozen camcorders, at least. Probably running on CNN already." Daniel returned his focus to the road ahead, and they rode in silence for a minute.

Trinity smiled. "You see the way Preacher Bob handled the situation? Gotta hand it to him. Totally blindsided, but didn't miss a beat when he saw his opening. Did that hypnotic rhythm thing with the hallelujahs, and then got them chanting. Yeah, Preacher Bob's got game, he's a real talent. He could be big on television if he smoothed out his act a little."

"Look," said Daniel, "*after* we get you safe, you can sit down with Julia and come clean to the whole world. But use your head. You just put a giant red dot on the map, halfway between Atlanta and your hometown. You just announced your destination to the entire world."

"I understand, I fucked up. Can we please shift our focus to what we do going forward?"

He was right. Daniel took a long, slow breath, cleared his mind, and considered their options. "By now, everyone thinks you're going to New Orleans. So we divert our route a little ways north. Then we hole up for the night."

"And then what? I still need to get to the French Quarter."

"*I know*," said Daniel. It came out sharper than he intended. "Give me some time to think it through. I get a bright idea, I'll be sure to share it with you."

Atlanta, Georgia...

Julia entered the office, where Kathy Reynolds stood behind her desk, aiming the remote at the television screen. She closed the door behind her.

"Saw it on the way in," she said.

Kathy nodded at the television. "Not this part. We just got another angle on it, but on this one, the tape runs longer." She scanned through to where the crowd started chanting, then let it play at normal speed. The camera jostled as the crowd pressed forward, and then a man jumped onto the stage and grabbed Trinity's wrist.

Daniel.

Kathy Reynolds paused the action on the screen. "Who is he?"

"I, uh..."

"Don't tell me you don't know that fine young man. Your face already established that you do. And given your little freakout yesterday when they started dragging bodies out of the place, I'm guessing you know him quite well."

Julia dropped into a chair. "I can't."

"Julia, this footage goes to air after the next commercial break, and the whole world will be asking the same question. It was his choice to step in front of the cameras. He put himself in the story—his choice—not your fault."

"If not for him, there wouldn't *be* a story, Kathy. He's the one who brought it to me in the first place, and I made a commitment in exchange. Beyond *off the record*, he's my Deep Throat on this whole thing. When I promise to protect a source, I stick to it." She looked straight at the veteran news producer. "Wouldn't you?"

"Shit." Kathy pressed the remote and the screen went black. "Yes, I would. Damn. You know, the answer will be found. It'll come out."

"But not from me."

Julia was keenly aware of the hypocrisy. She'd already breached her professional ethics by wiring money to Daniel, just as Daniel had breached his by contacting her in the first place.

But when the ethics of your profession conflict with your ethics as a human being, well, then there's just something wrong with your profession.

59:

Las Vegas, Nevada...

William Lamech sat in the cabin of his private jet, drinking Perrier while his pilot waited for clearance from the control tower. He picked up the Gulfstream's sat-phone and dialed the number of Vito Carlucci, head of all things profitable and illegal in New Orleans.

"Vito, it's William. The conversation we had earlier? It's happening... he surfaced, and he's heading your way...I'm on the tarmac at McCarran, I'll be touching down in about four hours. Assemble a team of your very best men. I want them at the Hotel Monteleone in six. We're going to end this, now."

He hung up, lifted the receiver again, and punched in the cell number of Samson Turner.

60:

Julia sat across from Anderson Cooper and adjusted the lavaliere mic clipped to her dress as Cooper welcomed her to the show.

"My producer tells me you've been looking into the possibility that the Trinity Phenomenon can be explained by quantum physics. But I gotta tell ya," Cooper chuckled, "we had Leonard Mlodinow on last night, and I still don't fully understand it."

Julia laughed along with him. "One thing all the top physicists agree on: Anyone who claims to fully understand quantum physics, doesn't. But that doesn't make it completely impenetrable."

"Can you give us an explanation we can understand, I mean without any parallel universes, anti-matter, or cats that are both alive and dead at the same time?"

"I know, a lot of it seems to run counter to common sense," said Julia. "But common sense tells us that the sun revolves around the earth. We think we see the sun rise and set, while we're actually watching the earth rotate on its axis." She shifted in her chair. "And for most of our history, suggesting that the earth revolves around the sun was heresy, punishable by death. The border between the known and the unknown is always perilous for science. Look at it this way: some animals only see black and white. You might be tempted to think our experience of the universe is more 'real' than theirs because we can see the color spectrum. But we only see part of the spectrum, while birds also see UV light. And there's increasing evidence that birds also 'see' the earth's electromagnetic field. Is their view of the world more 'true' than ours?" She smiled. "Luckily, evolution gave us the big brains—"

"Not everyone believes in evolution," said Cooper.

"Not everyone believes the earth revolves around the sun." Julia smiled. "Anyway, however we got them, we got the big brains. We use machinery and math and to expand our knowledge of the universe beyond what we can perceive through direct sensory input. And it's important to note that quantum physics, however strange it seems, is borne out by real-world results in the laboratory. And despite the seeming paradox, there's no actual physical law forbidding time travel. Physics makes no distinction between past, present, and future. For example, if we look at the Wheeler Delayed Choice Two-Slit Experiment..."

Tim Trinity cupped a hand to his ear playfully. "Hear that? The sound of millions of people changing the channel." He took a swig from a bottle of Dixie beer. "Hand me the box, will ya?" Daniel passed the pizza box across to him.

They sat on the twin beds in room twenty-three of a motel just outside Waynesboro, Mississippi. The television had to be at least thirty years old and the hue of the picture tube had shifted red, so both Julia and Anderson Cooper looked a little sunburned. But the picture was crisp enough. The truck was hidden behind a Dumpster in back, and Waynesboro was far enough north that nobody would be looking for them here.

This particular motel wasn't a place where anybody looked for anything. No other rooms were occupied. The mattresses probably predated the television, and the old woman in the office was practically blind.

They'd be safe enough, until morning.

Daniel finished his beer and pulled another from the six-pack and turned his attention back to the set.

Julia was saying, "...so basically, we know quantum physics makes accurate predictions—*perfect* predictions, in fact—about the world around us. The problem is it describes a world that, when looked at in extreme close-up, seems impossible to reconcile with the large-scale world we see through our eyes. Nevertheless, it is accurate, and in the quantum world it is possible for information to travel backward through time. As Albert

Einstein said: *The distinction between past, present, and future is only a stubbornly persistent illusion.*"

"You're right about one thing. It seems impossible," said Cooper.

"Yes, because—just as we experience the sun moving around the earth—the nature of time is not accurately described by our *experience* of time in our everyday lives. Time is not what it seems."

"And what does this tell us about the Trinity Phenomenon?"

"Tim Trinity is somehow predicting the future, and millions of people have decided that God is behind those predictions. But we don't really know that. It could just be a strange wrinkle in the quantum world, seeping through into the world we experience. We need to look at the phenomenon from all angles and follow the evidence where it leads, rather than jumping to conclusions."

"That's an interesting point," said Cooper. "It reminds me of something Stephen Hawking said in his most recent book. He said, 'Quantum physics doesn't tell us that God doesn't exist, but it tells us that the existence of God isn't necessary for the universe to exist as it does.'"

Julia said, "I think the parallel is apt. There *might* be a God who is behind Trinity's predictions, but there doesn't *have* to be."

Tim Trinity said, "Julia really *wears* that dress."

"Yes," said Daniel. "Yes, she sure does."

"You mind if I ask you something personal?" Trinity shook his empty bottle and Daniel handed him a fresh beer.

Daniel smiled. He knew what was coming. "Yes, Tim, I really was celibate all those years."

"Aside from regular dates with the Palm Sisters, naturally."

"Goes without saying." Daniel stared at the red-hued Julia on the television. He said, "There's a story about a couple of Zen Buddhist monks. One day they leave the monastery and walk into town to buy vegetables. Along the way, there's a stream they have to wade through, about thigh-deep. At the edge of the water, they come across a beautiful young woman wearing a lovely silk dress. One of the monks offers to carry her across, and she accepts. On the other side, they part ways with the girl and walk on in silence. About five miles down the road, the other monk says, 'I don't think it was right, what you did back there. You know we're not supposed to have contact with women.' The monk who helped the girl replies, 'I put the girl down once we crossed the river—why are you still carrying her?'"

His uncle smiled at the story. "Damn, son, you been carrying that girl a donkey's age."

"That I have," said Daniel as the television switched over to a commercial for prescription pills guaranteed to give you an erection whenever you want one. "Fourteen years."

"Danny...I never meant to bring you any harm. I never thought what I did to support us would drive us apart."

"No, you didn't," Daniel agreed. With no bitterness in his voice he added, "You were too busy thinking about the money."

Trinity took a pull on his beer and nodded. "That I was."

The commercials ended and Anderson Cooper came back on, but now there was a BREAKING NEWS banner along the bottom of the screen.

Cooper said, "I've just been handed something during the break..." He shuffled through some photographs and handed them across to Julia, but the camera stayed on him "...CNN has just received pictures of Reverend Tim Trinity. They came to us anonymously and we don't know when they were taken but they appear to be fairly recent, and I'm told by our staff that they don't appear to be digitally altered..."

Daniel felt a rush of vertigo as he recognized the photographs that now filled the television screen—shots of his uncle snorting cocaine in the den of his mansion. Guilt began twisting in his gut like an oversized worm.

"Wow," said Trinity. "Didn't see *that* one coming. You'd think they'd start with something like this, then ramp up to killing me, not the other way around."

Daniel struggled to find the words. What could he say? "These pictures didn't come from Samson's superiors. They came from the Vatican."

"Oh." Trinity lit a cigarette. "You sure?"

"I'm sure," said Daniel. "I took them."

"Oh. I see."

"Yeah. I came to Atlanta to debunk you, hard. I was convinced you were running a con, and then everything started happening and I didn't delete them *in case* it turned out you were running a con, and then the billboard came down and I just forgot about them and flew back to Rome planning to convince my boss you were a miracle."

Trinity let out a smile. "You know what the Jews say: Man plans and God laughs." He chuckled out a cloud of blue smoke. "Right you are, Rabbi."

"I'm sorry, Tim."

"Yeah, well, don't sweat it, son. I messed up a couple times myself, as you so frequently feel the need to mention." He reached sideways and clinked his bottle against Daniel's. They both drank. Trinity picked up the remote, muted the television. "So what's the plan now?"

"We drive straight past New Orleans tomorrow," said Daniel, "down into the bayou. I've got a friend in Dulac. Pat Whalquist. Worked with him on a case in Honduras."

"A priest?"

"Not hardly," Daniel let out a grim laugh. "Pat's a mercenary."

Trinity's eyebrows went up. "A mercenary? Oh, you have *got* to tell me that story."

Daniel remembered the dampness of the church basement, the fear in the eyes of the politician, the weight of the pistol as Pat pressed it into his hand. He remembered the sound of automatic gunfire above and the thundering of soldiers' boots coming fast down the wooden stairs. He remembered not knowing if he could do it, not knowing if he *should* do it, and then doing it without hesitation when the door banged open. The bucking of the pistol in his hand, the muzzle flashes and smoke and the smell of gunpowder. The blood and gore and the smell of death.

Daniel drank some beer. "Not much to tell," he said. "Pat was there to protect a politician and I was there to investigate a miracle claim. We helped each other out, I guess, and we became friends. Anyway, we'll drive to Dulac, stop with Pat one night, maybe two. See, we can't beat them to New Orleans, so we wait 'til it becomes clear you're a no-show and they start thinking about where else you might be headed."

"Then what?"

"One step at a time," said Daniel. "Pat'll help plan our strategy for getting you in and out of the Quarter without getting killed."

61:

Piedmont Park – Atlanta, Georgia...

Drums and guitars and tambourines lay silent on the grass, the time for singing and dancing now past. The Kumbaya spirit had deserted Tent City #3, and Trinity's Pilgrims were fast falling away.

Families mumbling their dejection aloud as they collapsed their tents and rolled their sleeping bags. Couples speaking sharply to each other, pushing the bitter pill of blame back and forth. Litter strewn all over the place. A girl of about fifteen, who looked like—and probably was—a street-walker, sitting under a tree, knees pulled to her chest, face in her hands. Weeping.

Andrew Thibodeaux wandered numb through the crowd, taking it all in but unable to form either thoughts or feelings in response to the input. Disconnected from it all. Disconnected even from himself.

A young man stood perched atop a milk crate, a replica Tim Trinity blue Bible open on his palm. He had the look of a straight-A student at some evangelical Christian college. He was saying, "Lest we forget, brothers and sisters—Matthew 11:19—*The Son of Man came eating and drinking, and they said 'Look, a glutton and a drunkard, a friend of tax collectors and sinners.'* Now they say Reverend Tim is a drug addict! It's the same thing! Don't you see?"

"Hush your mouth, boy," called a very large, middle-aged black woman. She stopped to face the loyal pilgrim. "Jesus didn't snort no *damn* cocaine, and you got rocks in your head."

"They didn't even have cocaine in the Holy Land in those days," he insisted.

A powerfully built white biker stepped out of the gathering crowd and came to a stop between them. He was bald and wore a horseshoe moustache and black leather pants. He was shirtless—his entire back covered by a tattoo of Christ on the cross. His right bicep featured a cartoon red devil, complete with horns, cloven hoofs, and pointed tail. A buxom Bettie Page angel graced his left. He pointed at the kid on the milk crate.

"The lady's right. Shut the fuck up, we don't want to hear it."

The kid persisted, despite the terror on his face, saying, "Please, Reverend Trinity is the Messiah. I'm just trying to help you see—"

"I'm gonna help *you* see the inside of an intensive care unit if you don't shut yer fuckin' yap." The biker stepped closer. No one moved, except the kid, who fell off the crate when his knees went wobbly. He managed to recover his footing after one knee hit the grass, and stood there, visibly trembling. The biker said, "The Savior doesn't *run away*, dipshit. Here's what happened: The going got rough, and Trinity saved his own ass."

The kid fought to get the words out. "I'm-I'm sorry, sir, but the Savior does run away. Jesus ran from the temple the first time, then he came back. Reverend Tim will return to us, and it won't be long…" Tears breached the levees of his eyelids and flooded down his cheeks. His bottom lip danced violently, and he blubbered in a very small voice, "Please, we must keep the faith."

The biker took two steps forward and swung with his right, and the kid's nose popped, splatter-painting his chest crimson.

"Don't you fuckin' bleed on me!" bellowed the biker as the kid dropped to the ground. He cocked his arm again, but froze in place. After a few tense seconds, he shook his head, lowered the arm, and started opening and closing his hands repeatedly. "I warned you." He stormed away, disappearing into the crowd. Nobody tried to stop him.

The kid lay on the grass in the fetal position, hands to his nose, blood running through his fingers, gulping air through his mouth, sobs wracking his entire body. A hippie cowboy who looked like Kris Kristofferson and the teenage hooker rushed to his aid.

Andrew continued walking through the wreckage of the tent city. Probably a quarter of the crowd had already deserted, and it looked like another quarter was making moves to pack up.

This can't possibly be God's plan...

He saw a guy he knew slightly, coming his way. They'd met two days ago, standing in line for a port-a-potty. The lines were over an hour long, and the guy was a talker. But now Andrew couldn't recall anything he'd said. *What was the guy's name?*

"Andrew," the guy said. "Dandelion, remember?"

"Right, yes, of course." Now he remembered. Dandelion was from Canada. His mother was full-blood Mohawk, his father a Jewish radical, some kind of environmental activist. Dandelion grew up in a place called Hamilton, which he said was like Canada's Pittsburgh. Spent summers with his grandma on an Indian reservation. He'd shown Andrew some kind of First Nations ID card and said he didn't have to pay taxes on cigarettes back home because he was an Indian.

"New Orleans," said Dandelion. "Everybody says that's where he's going."

Andrew nodded.

"I hooked up with some cool guys, we're heading straight there."

"You still believe in him, Dandelion?"

"Never did. But I didn't *not* believe in him either." Dandelion laughed. "Either way, something heavy is goin' down. Some mega-seismic cultural shift, ya know? History is being written, dude, and I want a front row seat." He hitched his backpack up a little higher on his shoulders. "Hey, you OK? You look a little out of it."

"Yes. I'm all right."

"Groovy. Well, I gotta run catch my ride. We'll be camping in Louis Armstrong Park. If you wanna hang with us, just look for the tent with the big yellow smiley face."

"I don't know. Maybe. Thanks, maybe I'll see you there."

Andrew turned without saying good-bye and wandered away, allowed himself to be drawn into the stream of people heading toward the street, like fans leaving the ballgame in the sixth inning of a blowout, each quietly carrying a piece of the team's shame, made heavier by the shame of the apostate.

He walked the seven blocks to his truck, and stopped short. What he saw made him sick.

The blue tarpaulin was gone. All his possessions, everything that had been secured under the blue tarpaulin, gone. The gas cap had been pried open and the gas siphoned out, a length of dirty garden hose left hanging from the gas tank like a dead snake.

This was not God's plan…

62:

Julia glanced down at the business cards in her hand: FBI Special Agents Steven Hillborn (the handsome one with the square jaw) and Gary Robertson (the intimidating one with the ice-blue eyes). To Agent Hillborn, she said, "Like everyone else in the world, I'm betting he's on the way to New Orleans. In fact, I'm flying there with my cameraman tonight. But it's only a guess. I can't tell you what I don't know."

"You broke the story. You've had inside information since the beginning," said Agent Hillborn. "And you've been in contact with him."

Ignoring the first part of his statement, Julia said, "Tim Trinity contacted me on Saturday afternoon. I'd left several messages with his staff, requesting an interview. He called me back and we spoke for about two minutes. He didn't agree to sit down with me, but said he'd consider it and get back to me. And that is the only time I've ever spoken with him." Every word was true…she just left Daniel out of it.

"You're not a lawyer, Ms. Rothman," said Hillborn, "so do us a favor and stop parsing language. Frankly, you suck at it. Trinity is in way over his head on this thing. We understand he's running scared—who wouldn't be?—but he can't outrun it, and he definitely can't outrun us. If he comes in to us, helps us, we can talk to the US Marshals about getting him into the WITSEC program. We're his best option for survival, I'm sure you can see that."

"I do see that," said Julia, "and I hope he takes you up on it. I'd be happy to put you on camera, help you get the offer out to him."

Special Agent Robertson slapped the table with his right palm. "Hey, Cleopatra. Wake up. We've got over 140 dead bodies. Two explosions inside a week—one at a site designated critical to national security—while our nation is at war. And you are now officially wasting our time."

Special Agent Hillborn reached inside a leather folio, pulled out a photo, and slid it across the table: Daniel and Trinity leaving the stage at the tent revival in Greenville. Hillborn pointed at the photo, stabbing Daniel with his finger. "You used your MasterCard to wire five hundred dollars to a Western Union in Gadsden, Arkansas."

Julia's indignation was blunted by the awareness that she was, in fact, obstructing the FBI in what was a clearly justified investigation. She felt her moral ground turning to quicksand. Better to focus on the indignation. "You're looking at my credit card records? May I please see the warrant?"

"Don't need one," said Agent Robertson. "If that bothers you, call your congressman and tell him to repeal the Patriot Act. Then listen to him laugh."

"The distance from Gadsden to Greenville," said Agent Hillborn, "is 173 miles. The money was picked up at ten fifteen a.m. by a Mr. Daniel Byrne. Trinity showed up, with this man, at the tent revival in Greenville just under four hours later." He shrugged. "Maybe they stopped for a sandwich." He pushed the photo closer and spoke with exaggerated calm. "We are done fucking around, Julia. You have two choices: Continue to obstruct our investigation, in which case tomorrow will find you not in New Orleans covering the biggest story of your life, but in a jail cell while your lawyer begs a federal judge for a bail hearing sometime in the next week." He handed Julia a printout of her own cell phone records. "Your other choice: Tell us what you know about Daniel Byrne and his business with Tim Trinity."

"It's Julia."

" 'Course it is." Daniel reached over and switched the radio off. "You're the only one with my number."

There was a pause on the line before Julia said, "I'm sorry."

"Who?"

"A couple of FBI agents, they leaned on me pretty hard. I couldn't legally refuse them…and anyway, they need to investigate this. I'm sorry," she repeated.

"It's OK, Julia."

"They had my cell records, they could be listening in on my calls, so I ran to a payphone as soon as they left."

"What did they say?"

"They think Trinity's gotten himself mixed up with some very bad people, and they're offering to get him into witness protection if he cooperates. They knew about the money I wired you, and they asked about your role in all this. I told them the basics: You're a Catholic priest sent by the Vatican to investigate, and you told me how to decode the tongues. I gave them your number, so—"

"So they'll use my cell as a tracker and probably listen to my calls until they catch up with us."

"Danny, they want you to turn yourselves in for questioning. The longer you run, the worse it's gonna look. Think about it. At least they could keep you safe. And if Trinity is innocent, then why—"

"We've already been on the phone too long," said Daniel. "I won't answer this number again, and I'm not gonna call your cell."

"How will I—"

"Remember our first date?"

"What?"

"Our first date, the first time we went out alone. Remember where we met?"

"Yes."

"OK, go there. Three o'clock in the afternoon. Every day. If I don't show up, try again the next day. I'll meet you there at three o'clock. Oh, and I promise to be my usual punctual self."

Julia's laugh was worried but warm. "I remember."

"Good. Thanks for the heads-up." He snapped the phone shut.

"What's the trouble," said Tim Trinity.

"FBI." Daniel pulled off the highway, into a truck stop.

"Lemme guess: They think I blew up the refinery and rigged the lotto."

"At the very least, they think you *know* who did."

"I do. God did. But what are my chances of convincing *them* of that?"

"Yeah," said Daniel. He pulled slowly alongside a black pickup truck parked at the pumps, tossed the cell phone into its payload, and drove away.

63:

Daniel gave New Orleans a wide berth, cutting north all the way around Lake Pontchartrain, and then south into Cajun Country, past LaPlace, past Houma, picking up a new prepaid cell phone and an LSU baseball cap at a gas station along the way. Back in the truck, he tossed the ball cap to Trinity.

"Go Tigers," said Trinity, putting the cap on.

They continued south, deeper into the bayou. The road narrowed and foliage thickened as the world became less about land and more about water. The air was heavy with it, hot and salty and vegetal. They rode with the windows down, and Trinity chain-smoked. Daniel didn't mind; both men were getting a little ripe, and the smoke smelled marginally better than they did.

He stopped on the shoulder and turned on the new phone.

Pat Wahlquist had given Daniel his business card four years ago, after Daniel had smuggled Pat out of Central America. "If the shit ever hits the fan harder than you can handle," he'd said as he pressed the card into Daniel's palm. Daniel hadn't looked at the card since, but he'd always kept it with him, just in case.

He opened his wallet, dug behind the false flap in the billfold section, and pulled out Pat's card. It read...

PAT WAHLQUIST

Slayer of Dragons

…and a phone number. Daniel dialed the number. Pat picked up on the second ring.

"Wahlquist."

"Pat, it's Daniel Byrne."

"Daniel, my brother from another mother. Long time, long time."

"Yeah. You said if I ever—"

Pat cut him off. "How can I help?"

"Need a safe place."

"You called the right number. Where y'at?"

"Just north of Dulac."

"Coming in hot?"

"No. My cell was compromised, but I got rid of it outside Slidell."

"Awright, keep on coming south on the Grand Caillou. Number 7244—restaurant on stilts, called Schmoopy's. I'll be in the parking lot in twenty. You can follow me in from there."

"Got it," said Daniel. "And Pat…"

"Don't you dare thank me," said Pat Wahlquist. He broke the connection.

"A mercenary driving a Subaru," said Tim Trinity as they followed the green Forester. "Now I've seen everything."

"Pat and I bulled our way from Honduras to Guatemala in one," said Daniel. "They're solid. And check it out, up there," he pointed, "it's got a snorkel, you could drive through four feet of water." He started to point out the crash bars and roof lights, but realized Trinity had just been bantering. He smiled back.

"Quite a ride," said Trinity. "Yesterday morning we were 2,500 feet up in the Blue Ridge Mountains, hanging out with the flying squirrels. And now we're below sea level in the Louisiana swamp, hanging with Mr. Allie Gator and his pals." His hand swept the scenery. They were no longer just in Bayou Country; they were now well and truly in the swamp.

Pat slowed and signaled, turned right onto a one-lane covered with oystershell gravel. Just a thin finger of land, maybe thirty yards across, moss-draped cedars and shrubs, surrounded by the mangroves and cypress trees that rose from the water on both sides. Their tires crunched on the gravel as they rolled slowly along the finger, toward a one-story ranch house, surprisingly modern for the setting, situated at the end of the narrow spit of land. About fifteen yards from the house, a thick cypress had fallen across the road.

Pat reached up to his visor and pressed on something like a garage door opener. An electric motor somewhere by the side of the road started, and the fallen tree slowly rose to standing. They pulled forward, past the tree, into a circular driveway. The tree came down behind them, once again blocking the road.

Doesn't matter if you run a barbershop, pharmacy, or gas station, remaining independent in today's America is an uphill slog and the hill gets steeper with each passing year.

Buddy had always taken great pride in his entrepreneurship, and he'd rejected all buyout offers from the multinational petroleum conglomerates. So the big guys did just what big guys do to mom-and-pops—they built a super-mega-store across the road and undercut his prices. In a few years, he'd be gone and they'd own the road.

To fight back, Buddy had put an oil drum smoker and some picnic tables out back, and Buddy's Gas Bar became Buddy's Gas Bar & Bar-B-Que. It helped, but it wasn't enough. So when the mob guys had come with their offer, Buddy added three video poker terminals to the place.

FOR ENTERTAINMENT PURPOSES ONLY

And for a stranger, that was true. Just a video game to waste your time and take your quarters. You could rack up credits for free games, and that's as far as it went. But for locals in the know, the game was real.

The mob guys had provided Buddy with a cashbox to pay out any winnings over twenty bucks, and they gave him a monthly rental fee for the floor space. Sure, it was illegal, but it was a common practice throughout the South, and Buddy needed the money. And the risk to his business license seemed minimal, since the guy they sent to empty the machines each week, Bam Price, was a sheriff's deputy.

Buddy watched Bam carry the three thick canvas bags out to his police cruiser. Bam locked the money in the trunk and returned to the gas station.

"How's the float, Buddy? Need topping up?"

"Naw, thanks," said Buddy. "No big payouts this week."

"OK." Bam put a photo on the counter. "Have a look."

Buddy looked. "Yup, I've seen 'em."

"You've seen them?"

"On the TV. Whole world's lookin' for them."

Bam chuckled. "Yeah, well, if you see 'em *not* on the TV, gimme a holler."

Buddy grabbed the reading glasses hanging from a chain around his neck, put them on his nose, and took a closer look at the picture. "I'll be damned," he said. "I seen the younger one just today."

"You sure?"

"Sure I'm sure. He bought a cell phone and a hat."

"When?"

"Couple hours ago. There was another man in his truck, but I didn't see him too good, don't know if it was the preacher. They left here heading south."

It cooled off some as evening fell. Pat Wahlquist made a crawfish boil, and they ate outdoors, piles of spicy crawdads and corncobs spread before them on newspapers covering the picnic table in the backyard. Half the yard was fenced off into a pen, about twenty feet square, ten feet tall, chain-link stretched over a steel pipe frame, even covering the top. Inside the fence, a doghouse, a soccer ball, an old tire, and some chew-toy made of knotted yellow rope.

"Edgar's playpen," said Pat, scratching his coonhound's ear. A handsome dog, splotches of black and white, with expressive brown eyebrows. Pat put a crawdad tail between his puckered lips, pushed his face forward, and Edgar gently took the crawdad with his teeth and ate it. "Who's my spoiled puppy?" Pat baby-talked. "Who's my baby?" Edgar licked him square on the mouth, then turned in a circle and lay at his master's feet. A nickel-plated .12-guage pump-action Mossberg leaned against Pat's leg on the other side.

Daniel broke open another crawfish, sucked the head, dropped it in the communal pail in the middle of the table, and drank some sweet tea. He looked up and was startled yet again by Trinity's new look.

Trinity had resisted the idea, but Pat assured him that it would wash out, so he'd reluctantly taken the bottle and dyed his hair brown. Daniel had given Pat the *Reader's Digest* version of their journey and told him the goal was to get Trinity into the French Quarter to see a woman, and back out again. The silver mane was Trinity's most identifiable feature, so it had to go. Pat had lent them some clothes, shown them to a guest room with double beds, and they'd freshened up while he made dinner.

With the dye job, Trinity more resembled the man Daniel lived with as a boy, and the effect on Daniel was almost surreal. Not altogether unpleasant, but profoundly strange, like he'd become unstuck in time, like Billy Pilgrim in that great Vonnegut novel Daniel loved as a teenager.

Daniel ate one more crawdad and, realizing how full he was, declared it his last.

"Make more sense for you guys to stay here," said Pat, his tone signaling a return to the business at hand. "I can go and get the woman, bring her to you."

"No way," said Trinity. "I'm telling you, it was a vision, me standing in front of her place. A vision. I have to go there."

Edgar sprang up, cocked his head at the waterline, and said, "Woof." His attention was focused just to the right of the dock, to the right of Pat's aluminum airboat, where the wake of a gator moved steadily toward shore.

"Stay," said Pat, and in one fluid motion, he stood and swept the shotgun into position, pumping a round into the chamber as he walked forward. He stopped about six feet from the water. The gator stopped about the same distance in the water, its snout and eyes just above the surface. They stared each other down.

"Keep comin' and your new name's gonna be Handbag," Pat told the gator. After a few seconds, the gator turned away and glided on down the bayou. "Tell your friends," Pat called after him. He clicked the safety back on, returned to the table. "Tim, I'm agnostic about the metaphysics of your predicament," he said. "Maybe you've been touched by God, maybe you've just gone batshit crazy. Not my area of expertise. My area of expertise is thwarting bad guys, and I'm telling you, it's poor tactics to go there if you don't have to."

"Not negotiable," said Trinity.

Pat looked to Daniel for help.

Daniel shrugged. "What can I say? That's the vision he had."

"All right, be that way." Pat turned to Trinity. "Can I assume that your vision doesn't prohibit me coming along to help protect you?"

Trinity smiled, started to speak.

"No," Daniel interrupted. "Pat, I didn't ask you—"

"Fuck off, man," said Pat. "I'd have been dead four years ago if not for you. So as long as it's OK with the Amazing Kreskin over here, I'm in."

After a few seconds Daniel said, "Fine. Thank you."

"Don't thank me."

64:

The bedside clock glowed 1:30. Tim Trinity still couldn't sleep. Daniel's snoring, while quiet by snoring standards, wasn't helping any. And there was the anarchic symphony of frogs and crickets and God knows how many other nocturnal swamp critters, just outside the window screen. Trinity stood, tiptoed to the door, and slipped out into the hallway. Light from the kitchen spilled into the hallway, enough so he could make his way along, the smell of coffee getting stronger as he went.

Pat sat at the kitchen table. The mug in his hand bore a US NAVY SEALS crest. Spread on the table, a street map of the downtown New Orleans, red marker lines indicating routes in and out of the French Quarter. On top of the map, a John le Carré novel.

"Can't sleep," said Trinity. Pat gestured to the chair across, and he sat. "Got any bourbon?"

Pat shook his head. "I don't drink."

"Really?"

"Never touch it."

"Now I *have* seen everything." Trinity chuckled. "A tee-totaling mercenary. Amazing."

Pat smiled. "If it helps my badass credentials, I do smoke a little reefer from time to time. Alcohol just doesn't agree with me." He stood and took his mug to the coffee maker. "Speaking of drugs, you want a cup? Or tea."

"What the hell, I'll take coffee, I'm not sleeping anyway," said Trinity. "Black, one sugar."

Pat filled a purple and gold LSU mug and handed it to Trinity as he sat.

Trinity sipped the coffee. It was strong and had chicory in it and tasted like home. "I'm guessing you don't believe in all this," he said. "I mean, that what's happening to me is coming from God."

"You're assuming I even believe in God. I've been all around the world, and all I've seen are reasons *not* to believe. Still keeping an eye out for him, mind you. But..."

"I don't know how you do it," said Trinity. "I'm not judging, I just don't understand. You kill people for a living. I can see how you could do that in service of a larger belief...but if you don't believe in anything..."

"I'm not a nihilist," said Pat. "I protect people for a living, and I kill anyone who makes an attempt on my clients. Sometimes the client is trying to change his government, other times the client *is* a government. Or there is no viable government, and I'm in the middle of a civil war. I don't care which, so long as the client's goal meets my criteria. Free and fair elections in a democracy limited by a constitution that caps the power of the state and protects dissent. That's what I believe in."

"That's gotta limit your job opportunities."

"It surely does," said Pat with a smile. "But I'm very expensive, so I can be choosy."

"And that's it, that's your criteria?"

"Hey, it's the American ideal. I've been around enough to know we don't live up to it, but it should always be our aim. See, I don't need God to tell me about basic human rights. Reason does the job just fine."

"Thin line between reason and rationalization," said Trinity. "People step over it all the time."

"True 'nuff," said Pat. He sipped his coffee. "Look, man, I grew up in these swamps. Both my grandfathers were Cajun Catholics, one grandma was a Choctaw Indian, the other a half-black half-Indian who practiced a kind of swamp spiritualism somewhat akin to Hoodoo. They were all believers, and you know what belief did for them? It helped them accept their lot in life. Thing is, their lot in life was getting shit on by the ruling class. To me, that's what religion is. A philosophy of coping. It may bring comfort to the dispossessed, but comfort isn't good for the dispossessed. The dispossessed need to stay pissed off so things can change for the better."

Trinity hadn't intended to hit a nerve. He raised his hands in mock surrender and sent Pat a friendly smile. "Well, I haven't been a believer very long myself. Preaching was always just a grift for me."

Pat smiled back at him. "You and every other preacher on TV."

"Can't speak for all of them but, yeah, it's an exceedingly profitable business," said Trinity. "Anyway, Danny walked out on me barely in his teens…and I suppose I gave him every reason to."

"You two seem to be gettin' along OK."

"It's good to have him home," Trinity said. "But I don't want to rush things with him, you know?" He sipped some coffee.

"Ah, I get it. You want me to tell you about Honduras."

Trinity nodded.

"Just remember," said Pat, "there's three sides to every story: yours, mine, and the truth. I can only give you mine."

"I'd be much obliged."

Pat sipped some coffee. As he spoke, his eyes became unfocused, looking back in time. "My client was an economics professor, running for the Honduran National Congress. An anti-corruption do-gooder campaigning on electoral reform." He smiled. "My kind of guy. His popularity was growing fast, he was a threat to the status quo. He had supporters everywhere, and word leaked out to us that Battalion 3-16—that's the CIA-trained Gestapo down there—was planning to cancel his ticket while he slept. I drove him up to a small mountain village where the local priest, Father Pedro, was a supporter. One of those political priests, you know, the liberation theology guys, but he wasn't a Marxist like some of them. He just thought Jesus meant it when he instructed us to feed the hungry and care for the sick and visit the imprisoned. Anyway, Father Pedro was brave, he walked the walk, ya know? He hid us in the basement of his church as a couple jeeps pulled into town, six soldiers hopped out and started interrogating the locals. The padre told them we'd stopped to eat a meal, and then we'd left heading north. But somebody must've talked, 'cause they posted a few soldiers outside the church, front and back, round the clock." He shook his head at the memory. "The longer we hid in that basement, the more frustrated the goon squad outside got, but there was no way to slip past them. The military in El Salvador had murdered a couple of political agitator priests, and it was easy to believe the practice might be spreading."

From a dog bed on the floor, Edgar let out a melodramatic sigh.

"You said it, partner," Pat said to the dog.

"I think I see how Daniel got involved," nudged Trinity. "You couldn't get out, so you figured to bring the world to you. Fastest way is to run a con. Some kind of fake miracle to get the world's attention."

"No flies on you," said Pat. "Father Pedro put the word out, and one by one the village patriarchs came by, and he told them the plan. Next thing you know, old ladies and men are coming to church with various maladies."

"Spontaneous healings! A classic," said Trinity, "never gets old."

Pat nodded. "They confess their sins to Father Pedro, tell him their ailments, and emerge from the confession booth babbling excitedly about how they felt electricity running through their bodies when Pedro forgave their sins. Their various maladies miraculously vanished. It got the Vatican's attention all right. Within forty-eight hours, Daniel arrived to investigate."

"Danny'd never fall for that scam," Trinity said.

"He didn't, he was on to us right away. But Father Pedro brought him down to the basement and explained the situation. Daniel wouldn't certify a fake miracle, but he offered to conduct the investigation in slow motion, buy us some time. Once the news crews arrived, I'd be able to get the professor out. The goon squad would just have to pick another time to try and ice the guy."

"Sounds like a good plan."

"It was the best we had. But it didn't work. The bad guys realized time was no longer on their side, and they made their assault late that night. Daniel was in the basement with me and the professor, and the basement was one large room with a staircase at either end. We heard the spray of automatic gunfire upstairs. I couldn't cover both stairwells myself, and the

SEAN CHERCOVER

professor's brain was short-circuiting—he was rigid with fear, completely frozen. I shoved a pistol in Daniel's hand, and we each killed three soldiers as they came blazing down the stairs."

"Jesus."

"Yeah." Pat smiled grimly. "And the capper to the story, the real kick in the head…the professor dropped dead of a massive heart attack while we were saving his life."

"God does have a sense of humor," said Trinity.

"God needs one," said Pat. "Father Pedro was upstairs, dead at the altar. They'd cut him in half. We'd just killed six soldiers, and I was known as the professor's bodyguard. Daniel gave me a priest's uniform, and we drove cross-country to Guatemala, where he arranged a private plane to get us stateside."

"That's a hell of a story."

"A day at the office. Like you said, I kill people for a living." Pat drank some coffee. "Daniel had never killed anyone, so it was…it was an adjustment for him. But I tell you, he kept his shit together like a pro."

65:

D aniel woke with a start, a rough hand clasped over his mouth.

"We gotta move, brother," Pat whispered in his ear. "Visitors on the way." Daniel sat up as Pat woke Tim Trinity. "You guys get dressed, meet me in the kitchen. Leave the lights off." He disappeared into the darkened hallway.

Daniel and Trinity scrambled into their clothes and made their way to the kitchen by the dim blue light of dawn filtering through the windows. Pat stood at the kitchen table, shoving items into a backpack. He wore a pistol on his belt, an assault rifle slung over one shoulder. Edgar stood at attention by his side.

"I don't hear anyone," said Trinity.

"Motion detector at the end of the road," said Pat. "They'll be here in a minute." He zipped up the backpack, tossed it to Daniel, and led them to the back door. "Wait for me in the boat, I gotta set the system." He left them there and headed for the front entrance hall.

Trinity snapped his fingers. "Shit. Be right back." He started back toward the bedrooms. "Gotta get my Bible."

"Leave it," Daniel called after him, "I'll buy you a new one." Trinity didn't stop, but he was back quickly, blue Bible in hand.

They ran down to the dock and Trinity scrambled into the airboat. Daniel tossed him the backpack, then unwound the line from the cleat and held the boat in place. He could now hear a vehicle crunching along the gravel road on the other side of the house.

Pat emerged from the house, Edgar at his side. He paused to lock the door, then jogged down to the boat, picking up a long aluminum pole beside the dock. "Hop in," he said, and Edgar jumped into the boat, followed by Daniel and Pat.

Pat used the long pole like a Venetian gondolier, pushing them silently through the water, down to the end of the spit and around, staying close to cypress trees with roots that rose from the water like skinny legs with bulbous arthritic knees. Spanish moss hung down from the branches just above their heads.

"Eyes upward, Tim," said Pat. "You're on snake watch."

"Got it," said Trinity.

Daniel resisted the urge to look up as well. He shot a quick glance back from his position in the bow, just to satisfy himself that his uncle was scanning the branches, and then focused his attention forward.

A car's engine shut off and its doors went: *thunk…thunk-thunk, thunk.* At least four men. Gliding silently around the other side of the house, they could now see it. A shiny black Chevy Suburban, parked just past the fallen tree that blocked the driveway. A white man stood next to the driver's door. Mid-forties, built like a light heavyweight, wearing black chinos and a short-sleeved Cuban shirt that didn't do much to hide his gun.

They crouched low as Pat moved the airboat forward slowly, careful to avoid bumping the aluminum hull against a tree. They were within earshot; such a mistake would be fatal.

The man standing by the Suburban lit a cigarette.

"He don't look like a cop," said Trinity in a stage whisper.

"And those aren't government plates," said Daniel.

From the stern, Pat said, "Can you see my front door?"

"Just a little further," said Daniel. "OK, stop."

Pat jammed the long pole deep in the muck, held the boat fast.

There was a man crouched below Pat's living room window, gun in hand. Two more men stood by the front door. The white guy holding a pistol, the black guy a tactical shotgun.

The black guy was Samson Turner.

"Shit," Trinity whispered to Pat, "that's the guy who tried to kill us. Let's get the hell out of here!"

Pat shook his head. His face was unnaturally calm. "They're already dead, they just don't know it yet."

Trinity's eyes were wide with fear. He whispered, "No, no, we should just leave."

"And they'll just come after you again," said Pat. He handed the pole to Trinity. "Now shut up, take this, hold us in place." Then he gestured to Daniel. "Switch with me."

As Daniel crept to the stern, Pat knelt in the bow and brought his assault rifle into position, clicked off the safety, and looked down the sight. He spoke under his breath, "Come on, look in the window, you know you want to..." The man crouching beneath the living room window started to raise his left arm. "That's it, just pull yourself up for a little peek..."

The man started to rise, reached up to grab the security bars outside the window. He jerked against the bars, convulsing violently as a high-voltage crackle shattered the quiet. He convulsed again, his mouth open in a silent scream, and finally let go of the bars and collapsed to the ground, smoke rising from his dead hand.

The white guy on the porch said, "What the fuck?" and squared his body to the front door. He lifted his right leg and pivoted on his left foot and kicked the door handle. After a quarter-second of silence, there was a muffled *pop* and a thin metal blade two feet wide shot out from the door and embedded itself in the man's abdomen. His guts came out in a shower of blood.

Pap! One shot from Pat's rifle and Samson Turner's head exploded. He shifted his aim to the man by the car before Turner's body even hit the ground.

Pap! The man's brains splattered against the black SUV.

Pat clicked the safety on, handed the gun to Daniel, and took the helm, cranking the airboat's motor to life.

"Leave it," he said to Trinity, and Trinity let go of the aluminum pole that was holding them in place. Pat gunned the throttle and they took off down the bayou, the flat hull of the airboat skimming over thick vegetation, Daniel and Trinity holding onto the gunwales with each turn, wind whipping their hair.

A few minutes later, Pat cut the throttle and pulled up to another narrow spit of land, this one overgrown foliage and a rickety old cedar-shingle fishing cabin that listed to one side, braced from falling by three four-by-four beams that angled up from the ground.

Edgar jumped ashore first, followed by the men. Pat tied the boat to the exposed root of a cypress and led them to the cabin. "My safe house," he said.

"Doesn't look so safe," said Trinity.

"That's the whole point," said Pat, digging a key ring out of his pocket. He put out a hand and stopped Trinity. "Wait." He pressed a button on the key fob remote, and the entire front wall of the cabin began to rise like a garage door.

Behind the decrepit façade was a cinderblock structure with a metal garage door. Inside, another green Subaru Forester. Large metal cabinets lined one wall, and a Fort Knox gun safe stood in the corner.

Pat tossed the keys to Daniel. "You'll find clothes and bottled water in the cabinets. I'll go home and clean up the mess, meet you in New Orleans tomorrow."

"There could be another guy or two waiting for you. We didn't see if someone went around back."

"Be dead by now. Once I set the defense system, nobody gets off my property alive." Pat let out a grim smile. "Gotta go feed the gators."

"OK. I'll call your cell."

Pat took the pistol off his belt, handed it to Daniel. "You've shot this one before, you know how it works."

Daniel stared at the gun in his hand. The same gun he'd killed three men with in Honduras.

It felt better in his hand than it should have.

66:

"Tim, there hasn't been another car on the road for eight miles," said Daniel. "Put it in the glove box."

"Oh," Trinity sounded distracted, "OK, good idea." But he didn't.

"Or keep fidgeting with it until you accidentally shoot one of us."

"Right. OK." This time he put the gun away. "Sorry. Guess I'm a little rattled, now it's sinking in. That was...that was pretty close back there."

"Yes it was."

Trinity lit a cigarette. "Those men sure died ugly."

"Yes they did."

They rode in silence for a while. Trinity turned on the radio and found a talk station.

...and the Tim Trinity sightings just keep on pouring into 9-1-1 centers and newsrooms across the nation. The latest one, believe it or not, from Anchorage, Alaska. Elvis Presley, watch your back, I'm tellin' ya... The radio jock chuckled at his own joke. *Speaking of the King, a blurry YouTube video that some jogger in Memphis claims to be of Reverend Trinity has gone absolutely viral on the Interwebs and is now drawing so-called "pilgrims" to Tennessee by the tens of thousands...*

Trinity turned the radio off, shaking his head. "Memphis? What the hell would I be doing in Memphis?"

"Hey, it's good news," said Daniel. "The more people think you're in Memphis, the better."

They fell back into silence for a minute. Trinity shifted in his seat. "Danny, I, uh..." He gestured to the glove box. "I asked Pat about Honduras."

"He tell you?" Daniel kept his eye on the road, but caught Trinity's nod in his peripheral. "Good. Not my favorite story to tell. He tell you I freaked out?"

"He said you kept your shit together like a pro, and he wouldn't have survived without your help."

Daniel smiled. "Yeah, I did all that. And then I freaked out."

"Probably a healthy reaction," said Trinity, "certainly a normal one. You were almost killed."

"Wasn't that kind of freak-out."

"Moral crisis?"

"Identity crisis," said Daniel. "When it happened I was terrified of course, and the killing was horrible..."

"But?"

"But beyond the normal stress reaction, I was actually OK with it. I couldn't convince myself that I'd done wrong."

"You hadn't," said Trinity. "What, you're supposed to turn the other cheek?

"Yes."

"That's ridiculous."

"I was a priest. We're supposed to emulate Jesus."

"Even if it means dying."

"Especially if it means dying."

Trinity threw his hands up. "What can I say? You Catholics have some crazy ideas."

"Everybody's got crazy ideas, Tim."

"True." He gave Daniel an avuncular wink.

"Anyway, it's in the past where it belongs. But you were right, what you said before in Atlanta. I was a priest for the wrong reasons...and I've known it a long time. But every morning I woke up and made the decision to be a priest. And now...Now I just can't keep making that decision anymore.

They rode in silence a while, but this time it was an easier silence.

"She's not married, is she?" said Trinity.

"Nope."

"You think she'll have you back?"

"I don't know," Daniel said. "But I aim to find out."

As the skyline of New Orleans grew large before them, Trinity said, "Been home since Katrina?"

Daniel shook his head. "You?"

"No."

"You rode out the storm, huh?"

"Not my finest hour." Trinity stared out the window. With the baseball cap and sunglasses, his face was unreadable, and Daniel decided not to press him for details. So many things had happened, in both their lives. So many years had flowed past. It wasn't a matter of *getting caught up.*

Everything was different now. *They* were different now.

Trinity pressed the heel of his hand against his forehead and squeezed his eyes shut. "Christ, I got a headache..."

"I'll stop and pick up some aspirin."

"No, it's—*ackba*—" His hand flew up and punched the roof liner, a shower of sparks raining down from the cigarette between his fingers, "—*backala*—Shit, it's comin' on strong—*abebeh reeadalla...*" His left leg jerked up, slamming his knee against the bottom of the dash. "Fuck!" His entire body spasmed and his head snapped to the right, sending out a loud crack as it hit the doorframe.

The tongues were upon him.

On television, it had looked ridiculous. From the back row of the audience, disturbing. But up close it was a horror show. Chills ran up and down Daniel's arms as he quickly exited the highway, tires squealing in protest on the off-ramp, Trinity babbling and thrashing beside him.

He screeched to a stop on the service road, threw the truck in park, and grabbed his uncle's shoulders, struggling to hold him down and prevent further injury.

The next thirty seconds felt like they would never end. But then, finally, the tongues stopped and Trinity's body relaxed and his eyes regained their focus.

"I'm OK, I'm all right...It's over." Trinity blew out a long breath and sat back upright. "Man, that one came on fast." He wiped the beads of perspiration from his face and forced a smile.

"It looks painful," said Daniel.

"Thank you, Captain Obvious." Trinity chuckled, lighting a new cigarette. "Yeah, it ain't exactly a day at the beach." He dragged on his smoke, shook his head. "It is what it is. Anyway, it's over. Let's go."

"All right." Daniel put the car in gear. He didn't want to dwell on it either.

67:

Diamondhead, Mississippi...

They were five of the nation's top Christian evangelists, boasting congregations in the tens of thousands, highly rated television programs, bestselling books. One had even been a spiritual advisor to presidents.

They did not, however, all preach the same gospel. Three preached salvation and prosperity in equal measure (but they called it "abundance" and took pains to include the non-financial rewards of "abundant relationships" and "abundant health"). The other two had no interest in abundance of any sort. They preached that the End Times are upon us and the only thing that matters is getting right with Jesus in time to catch the Rapture and avoid being here for the living nightmare that will soon torment those left behind.

Despite their differences, they'd come together for a live roundtable discussion on television, to present a dire and urgent warning to the world:

Reverend Tim Trinity is not a servant of the Lord, and his followers are being led away from righteousness and salvation and straight to eternal damnation in hell.

That was the message. The case they were making to the world. They quoted a ton of scripture and carefully explained how each quote helped make the case. And they frequently returned to the warning, repeating it exactly the same, word for word, each time.

Andrew Thibodeaux sat at the Formica counter, absently stirring sugar into his eighth cup of coffee while starting at the television. He'd stopped at the Chevron next door to gas up, had almost fallen asleep standing at the pump, and realized how hungry he was when his eyes snapped open and the familiar yellow aluminum siding with the glossy black letters came into focus.

WAFFLE HOUSE

Two words that spelled *oasis* across the Southland. Even the red, white, and blue banner spanning the top of the menu provided comfort, assurance. Tim Trinity was not the Messiah and nothing made sense anymore, but a Waffle House was still a Waffle House, buttermilk biscuits were still buttermilk biscuits, and America was still America.

Andrew needed that assurance. Needed it badly.

But it wasn't enough.

The End Times preachers on the television weren't satisfied with warning everyone what Tim Trinity was *not* and moved the conversation to what Trinity *might be.*

Pastor Billy Danforth made their case. "Please understand, I'm not saying that Tim Trinity is the Antichrist. I'm saying he *could* be, and failure to look at the evidence is an abandonment of our pastoral duty…"

The waitress who smelled of old lady perfume stopped by to collect Andrew's empty plates and said something about all the coffee he was drinking. He wasn't listening, but she laughed and he realized she'd made some kind of joke, so he smiled at her and made a laughing sound before turning back to the television.

"…The prophecies in scripture provide characteristics of the Son of Perdition, and you can't deny a good number describe Trinity. Does he not present himself as an apostle of Jesus while preaching a different Jesus? Does he not make war with the saints and seek to change God's law? In his last televised sermon he said, *Paul was wrong.* If that isn't making war with the saints, pray tell me what is…"

Andrew remembered to stop stirring his coffee, put the spoon down.

"…Does he not speak great things and tongues, and understand dark sentences, and does the whole world not wonder after him? Indeed, has he not deceived millions into thinking he is the returning Messiah?"

Andrew remembered to drink some coffee, noticed it was cold.

"The Antichrist shall rise up out of the water," said the other End Times preacher, deftly taking the baton. "And this man's career rose up to new heights from the floodwaters of Hurricane Katrina. And I find it ominous that we know absolutely nothing of Tim Granger—that's his real name, I refuse to call him Trinity—we know nothing of Granger's bloodline on his father's side..."

Andrew Thibodeaux swallowed the rest of his coffee, signaled the waitress for a refill, and returned to the screen.

68:

New Orleans, Louisiana...

As they drove into the city, Daniel was struck by the number of rooftops still covered with blue tarpaulin, Dumpsters in driveways, portable storage containers on front lawns. Six years after Katrina, and New Orleans—the cultural womb of the South, the city that gave America much of its soul—was still struggling to her feet.

It's a *shanda*, he thought, recalling the Yiddish word Julia once taught him. He turned onto South Carrolton, and as they rose to higher ground, the blue tarpaulins disappeared and the city looked more like her old self.

He drove in on Magazine Street, and as they passed Bordeaux he felt a smile invade his face. Le Bon Temps was still in business and, aside from a fresh coat of paint, looked the same as when he drank and danced in the place with Julia and her friends on Friday nights...fourteen years ago.

Would she take him back?

Casamento's was also open. Under different circumstances Daniel would've suggested they stop for some gumbo and an oyster loaf, but just seeing the place was enough to make him happy. He switched the radio on, set the tuner for 90.7 FM.

"The mighty O.Z.," said Trinity. "Greatest radio station in the world. I've missed it."

"I stream it on the Internet."

"Thought you guys all sat around listening to Gregorian chants."

"Please," said Daniel. He turned up the volume. Louis Armstrong and Louis Jordan belting out *I'll Be Glad When You're Dead, You Rascal You*.

"Perfect!" Trinity laughed.

They continued past cafés and art galleries, hair salons and tattoo parlors, pawnbrokers and auto body shops as Satch assured them he'd be glad when they were dead.

It felt like coming home.

Daniel could see himself making a life with Julia here in New Orleans. Even if she wouldn't have him back, this was home. And despite Katrina, despite having been abandoned by the rest of America, New Orleans was rebuilding.

A good place to rebuild his life…assuming he lived through this strange odyssey he was on with his uncle.

The disc jockey thanked Big Easy Scooters, the Ra Shop, and Harrah's Casino for their sponsorship, and then played a beautiful Trombone Shorty song about falling in love. The song ended as they passed under the 90, and Daniel slowed and shut off the radio. He found a parking spot on Peters, just a block from Canal, the French Quarter beyond. Despite the muggy heat, he slipped into a windbreaker he'd borrowed from Pat's clothing stash. He reached across Trinity, opened the glove box, and put the gun in his waistband, under his shirt.

"Here's how this is going to work," he said. "Keep the hat and glasses on, and walk at a relaxed pace. I'll be about ten paces back, on the opposite sidewalk. Don't look for me, I'll be there. And don't look around to see if anyone recognizes you—that's my job. Your job is to be casual. Remember, you're just another tourist. Don't strut—"

"I do *not* strut," said Trinity indignantly. Daniel couldn't tell if he was serious.

"You have a distinctive walk, let's put it that way, and the point here is to blend in. Oh, and go ahead and smoke—nobody's ever seen you smoking on television, so it'll help to disassociate you from your public image. Just walk to the address on Dumaine—"

"Number 633…in case we get separated."

"Don't worry," said Daniel.

"OK." Trinity reached for the door handle.

"Wait." Daniel pulled Pat's map from the backpack, followed the red line with his finger. "Take Bienville to Charters, then stay on Charters all the way in to Dumaine."

"Bienville, Charters, Dumaine. Got it." Trinity climbed out and shut the door. He lit a cigarette, returned the Zippo to his pocket, and started walking. Daniel let him get some distance, then followed.

People usually try too hard when changing their appearance, thought Daniel, and end up calling more attention to themselves. Trinity's disguise wasn't perfect, but the points of reference for his slick public persona had all been removed. Jeans and a plain cotton shirt had replaced the silk suit. The silver hair was now brown and mostly covered by a ball cap, and shades covered his eyes. He was smoking, and the trademark swagger was gone from his walk. His gait was a little too stiff at first, almost lurching, like his quads were sore after a long run. But after a couple of blocks, he eased into it.

All in all, it was a pretty good disguise. Except for those damn cowboy boots. *Shit.* Daniel had intended to stop and buy Trinity some plain shoes, but with all the excitement that morning, he'd forgotten. Well, they were pretty dirty now, almost gray, not the gleaming white boots people saw on television. And it was too late to call Trinity back. Daniel said a silent prayer and hoped for the best.

The sidewalks were busy enough but not congested, so following was easy. Pat's route had them walking always on one-way streets, with the direction of traffic, so cars were passing from behind and motorists couldn't easily see Trinity's face. Daniel scanned the pedestrians as he followed. Nobody seemed to pay any mind to the man with the brown hair and baseball cap, walking stiffly down Rue Charters and puffing on a coffin nail.

As Trinity turned the corner onto Dumane, Daniel closed the distance between them and followed at five paces until Trinity crossed the street and stopped in front of a small, white, one-story house with a gray slate roof, green shutters on the windows, and a matching green door.

Exactly as Trinity had described it from his vision. Daniel felt weightless as he crossed the street.

It was a shop. A small red neon sign in the window glowed: OPEN. Trinity stood motionless, staring at something else in the window. Daniel came to a stop beside him. Next to the neon sign, a larger, hand-painted sign hung in the window:

AYIZAN VODOU TEMPLE OF SPIRITUAL LIGHT
AND GIFT SHOP
ANGELICA ORY, MAMBO

Daniel's heart sank. "Are you kidding me? A voodoo shop? That's what we came here for? That's what we dodged bullets to get to?"

But Trinity wasn't staring at the sign. "Look." He pointed to a laminated newspaper article in the window. "That's her. The woman from my dream."

The newspaper headline read, PRIESTESS ORY SEES BRIGHT FUTURE FOR CRESCENT CITY TOURISM, and the black woman in the photo was beautiful, her features as Trinity had described them.

"This can't be happening." Daniel shook his head.

Trinity tossed his cigarette in the gutter. "Well, we're here, and that's her," he said, reaching for the doorknob. "Come on." He opened the door and a bell jangled above their heads, announcing their arrival as they stepped inside the shop.

"Be right with you," called a woman's voice from behind a beaded curtain at the back of the room.

The shop was exactly what Daniel expected, and feared, from the sign in the window. A tourist trap, full of vigil candles and anointing oils, plastic statues of various saints, gris-gris bags and voodoo dolls, necklaces made from chicken feet and alligator teeth, new age books and meditation CDs, even cartoon voodoo zombie postcards to send back to the folks in Iowa. A sign behind the counter displayed a price list for services ranging from jinx removals to tarot readings. The place smelled of patchouli and frankincense.

Angelica Ory stepped through the beaded curtain, a coffee cup in her hand, saying, "Sorry to keep you waiting. How can I help—"

She gasped and her eyes went wide—piercing green eyes, rendered almost hypnotic by the contrast with her deep chestnut complexion—and she dropped the cup. It broke on the floor, splashing coffee across the hardwood. "I–it can't be," she stammered, pointing a finger. "It's *you*." She turned and darted back through the beads, disappearing into the room beyond.

Daniel looked at his uncle. "That was weird."

"She didn't even glance my way, much less recognize me," said Trinity. "She was pointing at you."

Daniel turned the deadbolt, locking the shop's front door. He switched off the neon sign in the window and walked gingerly to the beaded curtain at the back of the room.

Through the beads, he could see a sitting room furnished in carved mahogany, upholstered in rough silk, an antique oriental rug covering the floor. A mix of folk art and fine oil canvases, all depicting religious imagery—some Voodoo, some Catholic. In one corner, an altar. On the altar, burning candles and joss sticks shared space with various fetishes. An egg in a bowl of cornmeal…a black chicken's foot hanging on a leather string…three oranges…an open bottle of Barbancourt rum…a corncob pipe…a scattering of divination shells…a Saint John the Conqueror root…a small bottle of Florida Water cologne…the skull of a baby alligator. The altar was backed by a framed mirror and a carved mahogany crucifix.

Ory stood at the counter of the kitchenette along one wall. Her back was to Daniel.

"Are you OK?"

She turned to face him, a small sherry glass in her hand. She forced a smile. "I'm sorry, I'm being very rude," gesturing to the couch. "Please, come in, and bring your friend. May I offer you a glass of port?"

"Yes, ma'am," said Trinity. "Thank you, that would be very nice." He passed Daniel and sat on the couch.

Ory's eyes never left Daniel's face. She seemed to be cataloging his features. "It's Daniel, isn't it?"

"How did you—"

"You won't believe me," she said.

"I will," said Trinity.

Ory's hand trembled slightly as she refilled her sherry glass and poured two more. "I dreamed of you last night, Daniel," she said. "And I woke up with your name on my lips. I know, it must sound crazy…"

Daniel felt lightheaded. He said, "In this dream, did I say anything? Did we speak?"

Ory nodded. "You walked into the shop and called me by name. You said, 'Angelica, I need you to understand, we're on this road together,' and I said something like, 'What road?' and 'Who are you?' but you just smiled, and then you turned and left the shop. And I woke up. That's it." She stared at him for a few seconds. "It's truly incredible, you look *exactly* like you did in the dream."

69:

Tennessee Williams Suite – Hotel Monteleone...

William Lamech had sent the men on a kill mission, with strict instructions to report every three hours. The last text from Samson Turner had come just before dawn: STAGE 2 UNDERWAY. They'd located the truck and were moving in for the kill.

Not a word since. Lamech glanced at his watch. They'd now missed three scheduled reports. If they'd been arrested, he'd have heard about it. If the mission had gone wrong and any one of them had survived, he'd have gotten a report.

Lamech didn't get this far in life by lying to himself, and he wasn't going to start now. The men were dead.

He scrolled through the contacts in his cell phone and stopped at the direct line of *Eric Murphy, Esq.* Murphy was a senior partner at a blueblood Canadian law firm with offices in the historic district of Old Montreal and at least one former prime minister on the payroll. Lamech had been paying the firm half a million dollars per year for the last five years. The invoices read *legal consulting*, but that was a fiction. In truth, the money was just a retainer. It bought him access, should he ever need it, to the services of a man named Lucien Drapeau. The only way to contact Drapeau was through Eric Murphy, and keeping that conduit open was worth $500K a year. If you actually used Drapeau, it cost you an additional five million.

Lucien Drapeau was the most expensive assassin in the western hemisphere. It was said that he'd never botched an assignment.

But William Lamech was not disturbed by either the price or the possibility of failure. He was disturbed—deeply disturbed—by Drapeau's complete independence. Drapeau was a specter. The law firm's clients didn't know where he lived or what he looked like or how he traveled. Terms were simple: half up front, half upon death of the target. No meetings, no details, and no future promises. You could pay him five million to kill a guy, and when the job was done, he was free to take five million from the guy's widow to come back and kill you. The half-a-mil you paid to the firm each year bought you a place on the client list, but it didn't buy you Drapeau's loyalty.

William Lamech didn't like it, but the men he'd sent were capable professionals, and they were dead.

Now he would use the specter.

70:

When Tim Trinity took off his hat and sunglasses, Priestess Ory immediately recognized him. She sat in stunned silence as he told her of *his* dream, and how he awoke with the vision of her storefront.

He summed up with, "So I had a vision of you, and you had a vision of Daniel. I think it's safe to conclude that God has brought us three together. The question is, why?"

"I have no idea," she said. "I'm still trying to process the thing."

"Danny? Any ideas?"

Daniel was still stuck on *God has brought us three together.* She had dreamed of *him*, not of Trinity. And with that, his place at Trinity's side was no longer a leap of faith.

He was *supposed* to be here.

But that didn't answer the question. *Why here? And why her?* He looked from Ory to Trinity, shook his head. "Priestess Ory, do you know anyone who goes by Papa Legba?"

"Papa Legba is the guardian of the crossroads."

"I don't mean the *loa*. I mean, a person using it as a nickname."

"Of course not. It would be very disrespectful, and," she smiled, "nobody wants to get on Papa Legba's bad side. Legba can be temperamental, and you'll get nothing done without him."

Daniel turned to Trinity. "Well, I'm out of ideas. I don't know why the hell we're here."

They sat in silence for a moment. Priestess Ory said, "Following Tim's line of thought: The divine brought you here. To me. Maybe the intent is for you to receive what it is that I provide."

"Somehow I don't think he brought Tim here for a tarot reading," said Daniel.

Ory shot him a stern look. "Yes, I sell trinkets to tourists. I fail to see how that's different than the thousands of plastic-Jesus gift shops in cathedrals around the world."

"She's got you there, son," said Trinity.

"I apologize," said Daniel. "I didn't mean any disrespect."

"Yes you did," her tone still sharp. "I see how you got the wrong impression, but once you get past the gift shop, this really is a house of worship. We hold weekly services in the courtyard out back, and once a month we have a larger ceremony at my sister's house. For the record, I take my religion seriously."

"Priestess Ory, I believe you. Truce, OK? Friends?"

She smiled, regaining her poise. "All right. But my friends call me Mama Anne."

Trinity said, "Let's say God does want me to receive what you provide, Mama Anne. What does that look like? You gonna slaughter a chicken over my head or—not judging—I just want to know what I'm lettin' myself in for…"

Priestess Ory laughed. "I'm a vegetarian. In my *ounfo*, my congregation, all our sacrifices are *mange sec*."

"Dry meal?"

"Yes. It means that our offerings to the *loa* are without blood."

Daniel pointed to the altar. "Tell that to the rooster who left his foot over there." He meant it with good humor, and she didn't seem to take offense.

"Like all religions, we are not without our little hypocrisies. But I don't sacrifice animals at our rituals."

"You said 'the divine' brought Tim to you, instead of 'God.'" Daniel made sure his tone was curious, not challenging. "Why is that?"

"I received my Mambo training and ordination in Haiti, where the Vodou tradition does not include the neo-paganism that you see creeping into a lot of American Voodoo. We believe that God—*Bon Dieu Bon*—is somewhat distant and perhaps a little busy to deal with our day-to-day problems. So it wouldn't be God, directly, who brought you here but those spirits we call the invisibles—the *loa* and *orisha*—who do have direct influence on our daily lives. And it will be them who will help us understand why. As Catholics pray to various saints for intercession, so we pray to the invisibles. But instead of just lighting a candle, we make offerings of food and drink, incense, music, dance. We invite them to possess our bodies, so they can briefly experience the physical plane. In exchange, they help us on our journey through life. We look after their needs, and they look after ours."

"Right, but I thought possession rituals were usually reserved for initiates," said Trinity.

She nodded. "I'll be the vessel for the possession trance and act as an intermediary on your behalf. You'll probably feel the presence of the *loa*, feel them knocking at your door, but they won't enter uninvited. Don't worry, it's not an unpleasant feeling at all. It's actually comforting to know we're not alone." She smiled and put her hand on Trinity's knee. "You'll see."

It was two hours past sunset when Daniel pulled to a stop across the street from Trinity's old mansion in Lakeview. He'd insisted they at least wait for the cover of darkness. Coming here at all was a significant risk—*seriously bad tactics*, Pat would've said—but Priestess Ory had declared it an essential part of the ritual.

Ory had explained what would happen at the ceremony in general terms and said that in order to know which of the invisibles to call on for assistance, she had to know Trinity's history.

She served coffee and beignets, and Trinity talked for over two hours. He told her of his childhood, his career as a tent revival Holy Roller and his rise to riches as a prosperity preacher on TV, his experience of Katrina, rebuilding his business in Atlanta, the voices, the tongues, and Daniel's return with news of prophecies. He told of his failed attempts to warn the oil refinery and his conversion to belief in the aftermath, the attempts on his life, and his sincere desire to understand and do God's will.

"You have been at war with yourself, and now you are at war with the forces of darkness," said Priestess Ory. "Shango is the *loa* most helpful both in matters of personal transformation and in battle. We will summon Shango tonight." Then she gave them directions to her sister's house in the Ninth Ward, told them to be there at midnight. And she instructed them to obtain a cup of earth from the property of Trinity's old mansion in Lakeview.

Daniel scanned the block as they got out of the car. Lights burned behind the windows of some houses, but the street was empty, save for Daniel and Trinity. All the other homes had been restored to their pre-Katrina splendor, but Trinity's was in a state of mid-renovation, a Dumpster in the driveway and a small tractor parked in the dirt yard. They crossed the street, Trinity carrying a mason jar and Daniel resting his hand on the butt of his pistol, under his shirt.

Daniel watched as his uncle wandered from one mound of dirt to another. He checked the street again—all clear—and filled his lungs with warm, moist air, perfumed by a large magnolia tree that had survived Katrina and still stood in the yard.

Trinity came to a stop between two large mounds of dirt. "Which one?" he said.

"I don't think it matters, Tim."

"Yeah, I guess not." Trinity bent down, scooped some dirt into the mason jar. "Think that's a cup?"

"Just fill it. She can measure out a cup later." Headlights swept around the corner as a car turned onto the street, heading in their direction. *Damn.* Daniel pulled the gun from his waistband but kept it under the shirt. "Hurry up."

Trinity straightened up and screwed the lid on the now-full jar. "Got it."

The car was just four houses away, slowing as it approached. They couldn't cross the street unseen, and with the headlights, Daniel couldn't tell how many were in the car.

He pointed and said, "Take cover," and brought the gun out as they ducked behind the Dumpster.

He took a deep breath and blew it out, getting his heart rate down. He peeked around the corner. The car was now two houses away, slowing to a crawl. Then a turn signal flashed, and the car turned up the neighboring driveway and out of sight.

He pulled back and listened. The engine stopped, two doors opened, and two people stepped onto the driveway and both doors slammed shut.

A man's angry voice said, "Well maybe we could stay longer if you didn't drink so damn much."

A woman slurred a response. "Yeah, well maybe I wouldn't drink so much if you didn't hit on every woman in the fucking room."

"And maybe if you didn't drink so fucking much, I'd be hitting on *you*. Ever think of that?"

"Jesus Christ, you really are a bastard."

"That's just the Andersens," Trinity whispered. "They been having that same conversation for ten years."

Daniel tucked the gun away as the Andersens quarreled their way up the steps and into the house. When the front door slammed shut, he nodded at Trinity and they strode back to the car and got in.

As Daniel cranked the engine to life, he noticed Trinity staring back at the mansion with a haunted look on his face. "What's wrong?"

"Just remembering," said Trinity. "Remembering the man I was. And you know what? I'm ashamed."

71:

Conrad Winter pulled to a stop outside an unremarkable Catholic church in an unremarkable suburb just west of New Orleans. He'd left Father Doug in the Sazerac Bar back at the Roosevelt and come alone for this.

The parish priest here, Father Peter, had called the regional HQ with a lead, of sorts. Some young man had arrived in a state of severe psychological and spiritual distress, babbling about Reverend Tim Trinity and begging for guidance.

Probably not much of a lead, but perhaps an opportunity just the same. The young man sounded like a lost sheep, and lost sheep can be useful in the right situation. Throughout history, the men competing to shape the future had collected lost sheep to use as pawns in their game, cannon fodder in their wars. Conrad knew he was one of those men, in this age. He was in the game, a shaper of the future, and this particular lost sheep might be just what he needed.

As he locked the car and walked up the path to the church, Conrad congratulated himself on how well he'd played his hand. When he learned that Trinity and Daniel had survived the bombing at the TV studio, he'd guessed they would return home like salmon swimming upriver to spawn. Whoever planted that bomb had done Conrad a huge favor, and he'd immediately spotted the best play.

He'd called Cardinal Allodi, and Allodi had quietly come to New Orleans while sending Nick to the command center in Atlanta, where Nick could lead the official operation, unaware that he'd actually been removed from the game.

It was perfect.

Conrad entered the church and crossed himself, walked up the aisle, genuflected and crossed himself again when he reached the altar, and turned to face the disheveled young man reading a Bible in the front pew.

Father Peter approached and nervously introduced himself. He led Conrad to one side and spoke in a low voice. "I'm very sorry for bringing you all the way here, Father. I've spent some time with him, and I don't think he has any idea where Trinity is. In fact, I think he may be insane."

Definitely a lost sheep. Conrad smiled. "That's quite all right, I'm glad you called. And I'll be happy to minister to the young man."

"But sir, my call seems to have set off alarm bells in the council."

Conrad put a finger to his lips. "We will not speak of the council."

"No, of course, I'm sorry, sir. I—it's just, I'm pretty new at this, and…" His voice dropped to a whisper, "there's a *cardinal* in my office."

"I know there is." Conrad put a reassuring hand on the nervous priest's forearm. "Perhaps you'll be good enough to tell His Eminence I'll join him in a few minutes, after I talk with the young man."

"Yes, of course. Right away." Father Peter scurried away.

Conrad turned and approached the front pew. He smiled gently, put his hand on the young man's shoulder, and spoke with the voice of a shepherd.

✢ ✢ ✢

The lost sheep was not insane, but was clearly headed down that road, Conrad decided. Unmoored from his former self and now drifting, desperately searching for solid ground upon which to construct a new identity.

"I think I can work with him," he told Cardinal Allodi, after Father Peter left the office to sit with the young man. "He was Junior Army ROTC in high school, he responds well to authority. I can whip him into shape for it."

"I don't like it," said Allodi. "The risk of exposure is too high, too many variables you can't control."

"Well I don't really like it either," said Conrad, thinking: *"Yes, but…" always works better than "no."* "But I'll do everything I can to minimize the risk, tie off loose ends. And if it isn't coming together as planned, I'll scrub the mission." He closed with, "Sir, the council has made Trinity a top priority, and we're running out of options." Then he shut up to let Cardinal Allodi think about that.

After a full minute, Allodi said, "All right. You have a tentative green light. On two conditions. First, Father Nick must never, ever catch even a hint of this. If he had any inkling of the council's inroads into the Holy See..." Allodi didn't need to finish the sentence. They both understood what was at stake.

"Yes, sir." He waited to hear the second condition.

Cardinal Allodi reached inside a leather briefcase and pulled out a file folder. He handed the folder across to Conrad.

It was a personnel file. Conrad read the tab: FR. DANIEL BYRNE.

"You'll find details of his contacts at the seminary, his life in New Orleans before coming to Rome," said Allodi. "You need to find him and present Father Nick's offer, before going ahead with this operation."

"He'll reject it."

"That's not for you to pre-judge, that's for him to decide. If he takes the deal, we can avoid the risk of exposure entirely. If he doesn't, then you may proceed. Is that understood?"

"Yes, Eminence."

72:

Lower Ninth Ward – New Orleans...

Tim Trinity peered into the darkness. "Got any idea where we're at?"

"Not precisely," said Daniel. "I'll stop next time we see a street sign standing." There was still no electricity in this part of the Ninth Ward, and Daniel couldn't see past the beam of their headlights.

What he did see made him feel sick to his stomach. Piles of splintered wood and smashed windows, twisted metal and scattered shingles, broken furniture and rotted mattresses. The ruins of small houses. The ruins of blue-collar lives. Row upon row of them, block after shameful block. No sign of rebuilding.

As if reading his thoughts, Trinity said, "Looks like the aftermath of a three-day kegger in hell."

Ory's sister lived in a neighborhood that was rebuilding, if slowly. Maybe four in ten houses rebuilt, three in mid-renovation, and three still in ruins. This block had electricity, and a third of the streetlights were actually working.

Priestess Ory greeted them at the curb. In her shop, she'd been dressed very colorfully, but now she was wearing a simple white dress and white head-wrap. Her feet were bare. She led them beside the house to a gate in the privacy fence surrounding the backyard.

"Welcome to our peristyle," she said.

Inside was a courtyard, covered by a corrugated tin roof on stilts. The inside walls of the fence were painted green with red and yellow trim, and black drawings of the *veve* symbols of various *loa*, alongside snakes and roosters and crosses and coffins, and a large portrait of Marie Laveau, the nineteenth-century Queen of Voodoo. About a dozen tiki torches provided the lighting, augmented by twice as many flickering red and white candles scattered about the place.

In the center of it all stood a striped pole, surrounded by an altar that would give Ory's store altar an inferiority complex. A magnificent collection of fetishes and offerings, bottles of rum and perfume and sarsaparilla, plates and bowls overflowing with yams, plantain, apples, peppers, nuts, figs, and hard candy. Two framed portraits—Saint Peter and Saint Barbara—were propped up against the altar, behind the offerings.

Priestess Ory brought a couple of mugs to Daniel and Trinity. "Legba and Shango both love rum. We drink to honor them."

Trinity winked at her, said, "L'Chaim," and downed his in one swallow.

"Oy vey," Daniel deadpanned.

Priestess Ory let out a good-humored laugh, then took Daniel's hand in hers and turned serious. "You have a skeptical mind, and I respect that," she said. "I'm not asking you to believe anything, I simply ask that you clear your mind of preconceptions and be open to your feelings. You may not believe in the *loa*, but please do not disrespect them." She smiled and gave his hand a squeeze. "They can turn ugly if they feel mocked."

Daniel felt the ghost of an ice cube slide down his spine. "I'll behave myself. Promise." He drank the rum.

"Thank you," she said. "This is a *Rada* gathering—the invisibles we're working with tonight are very benevolent and not aggressive. They won't take possession unless you give them permission. So be sure that you don't, unless you're willing to be mounted. Just stand over here and relax. And if you get the urge to dance or sing along with us, feel free."

"My peppermint twist is a little rusty," said Trinity, "but you should see my watusi."

"He's just nervous," said Daniel.

"I know," said Priestess Ory. She turned to the back door of the house, and called, *"Tambours!"*

The screen door opened and a white man and two black men stepped into the courtyard. All three were shirtless and shoeless, wore white pants, and each carried an African drum. They set the drums up along the east wall, sat behind them on stools.

The drummers began beating out a compelling rhythm with their hands. The screen door opened again and an older black man came out, carrying a wicker basket, followed by five black women and two white women, all dressed like Ory, the youngest about twenty-five, the oldest in her sixties. Three of the women carried colorful sequined flags.

The drumming grew, both in complexity and volume. The old man put the basket down, picked a conch shell off the altar, lifted it to his mouth, and blew a long note through it.

Priestess Ory called out, *"Annonce, annonce, annonce!"* and the group sang out the same in response. She poured a thin line of Florida Water cologne from the back door to the center pole, then from side to side, creating a crossroads. The old man faced Ory, and they made three formal pirouettes and then exchanged a double-handshake, making crossroads with their forearms. The other women did the same, and then swayed with the drums as the old man took two handfuls of cornmeal from the altar and used the cornmeal to "paint" a *veve* on the ground. He leaned forward and kissed the *veve* three times.

Priestess Ory reached into the wicker basket as the group sang, *"Damballah Wedo, Damballah Wedo, Damballah Wedo..."* She lifted a young boa constrictor, about four feet in length, from the basket, held it above her head, and danced backwards around the center pole, pausing so each participant could touch the snake. Ory sang, *"Damballah Wedo... Nous sommes les sevite... Ti Ginen."* She returned the snake gently to the basket and closed the lid, then danced with a beaded gourd in her hands as the intensity of the drumming climbed ever higher, growing into a hypnotic polyrhythm.

Ory chanted…

Odu Legba, Papa Legba,

Open the door, your children are waiting.

Papa Legba, open the door,

Your children await.

Ago! Legba! Ago-e!

And the congregation responded…

Ayibobo!

The old man lit a corncob pipe and made the sign of the crossroads in the air with its smoke, then lifted the plates of food offerings for Legba and passed them through the center, inviting Papa Legba to take possession, reciting in French: "*Legba, qui guarde la porte. Mystere des carrefours, source de communication entre le visible et l'invisible. Acceptez nos offrandes. Entrez dans nos bras, dans nos jambes, dans nos coeurs. Entrez ici.*"

Ory took a swig of rum straight from the bottle and sprayed it from her mouth, soaking Legba's cornmeal *veve*. She then whirled around the pole, shaking the gourd over each initiate, and they joined the whirling dance, around and around, intentionally scattering Legba's *veve* with their feet as they passed. Ory picked up a handful of the rum-soaked cornmeal, daubing it on the forehead of each, except for the old man, who she touched on the back of the neck.

The old man closed his eyes and stood stock still for a few seconds, jerked spasmodically, threw his head back, and laughed very loud. He snatched a bottle from the altar, took a large swig, then poured the rest of the rum over his head, over his face, and even into his open eyes with no sign of discomfort. He then grabbed a carved walking stick and the smoldering corncob pipe and danced around the pole, twirling the stick and puffing madly on the pipe, sending up clouds of cherry-flavored smoke, dancing faster still as the drummers jacked up the tempo and the initiates sang praises to Papa Legba.

Priestess Ory came over and took up Daniel and Trinity's mugs. "Papa Legba has opened the crossroads to us," she explained. "We drink once more to his honor, and then I will paint Shango's *veve* and invite him to take possession of my body. If he speaks directly to you, don't be alarmed. His voice may come from my mouth or it may manifest in your mind's ear, so listen for it."

But there was something wrong about the way she said it. Daniel had seen a lot of religious grifters over the years, had grown up with one of the best, and until a minute ago Ory had seemed completely sincere. But that last line, about Shango speaking directly to Trinity...she seemed to be *selling* it.

He stole a glance at his uncle as Ory took their mugs to the altar. Trinity was moving with the drumbeat, a serene smile on his face, like everything was right with the world.

And now there was something wrong about the way Ory refilled their mugs at the altar, the way she turned her back to them...like she was purposely blocking their view.

Daniel shifted to his left in order to see.

The rum bottle was in her right hand...but something else was concealed in her left, hovering over Trinity's mug.

An eyedropper.

Daniel's heart filled with despair. Had he really seen that? Was she really spiking Trinity's drink with something?

Damn. He really had, and she really was.

Priestess Ory returned with the mugs and handed them over. She raised her own mug. *"To Legba!"* She drank.

Daniel slapped the mug out of Trinity's hand just before it reached his mouth.

73:

The drumming followed from the backyard as Daniel stormed through the gate and toward the car, digging the keys from his pocket.

"I don't know what you're so riled over," said Tim Trinity from behind. "It wasn't poison, she put it in her own drink as well."

Daniel stopped in the middle of the front lawn and spun around. "You knew?"

"Hey, remember who you're talkin' to, son. I've seen all the moves." Trinity smiled. "I may play a yokel on TV, but very little gets by me."

"But you were gonna drink it."

"Why not?"

"Because it's a con, that's why. Because the woman is just another grifter."

Angelica Ory stepped out from behind Trinity. "Watch your mouth, boy. *Grifter*? Did I ever once ask you for money? Did I even mention money?"

"Mama Anne, let me apologize for my nephew," said Trinity.

"Excuse me?" said Daniel. "I didn't slip drugs in your drink, I have nothing to apologize for."

"Before you make an even bigger ass of yourself," said Priestess Ory, handing him a small tincture bottle. "Extracts of passionflower, mugwort, kava-kava, and wormwood. All natural ingredients used by indigenous root doctors for thousands of years."

"And hallucinogenic," he said.

"Sure, if you drink about a cup of the stuff. We use about twenty drops. At most, it enhances your sense of connectedness to the world, boosts your awareness of your own mental imagery, and causes a slight numbing of the tongue."

"*Loa-in-a-bottle*," said Daniel, handing it back to her. "Very clever."

"It is an aid to spiritual insight. It does not render that insight false." She sighed deeply. "We agreed that the goal was for Tim to receive what I provide. You may not like it, but this is it."

"Exactly right," said Trinity. "You can wait in the car. I'm going back in for my date with Mr. Shango."

Ory shook her head. "I'm sorry, Tim. You left the peristyle in the middle of a possession. You walked out on Papa Legba. The crossroads are no longer open to you tonight…and I don't think he'll open them again to you any time soon, after such disrespect."

Daniel could not detect any insincerity in her at all. He didn't know what to think. He said, "So you actually believe that old man in there is possessed by Legba?"

"What does it matter? He believes it, and I believe he gets something of value from it. Daniel, you're looking for absolute knowledge about the ultimate reality of the universe. I don't have that knowledge. Nobody does. What I have is faith. And what I *do* know is, people have an inborn need to believe in the spirit, and ritual helps sustain that belief. And that is what I provide."

Daniel gestured toward the sound of the drums. "So all this is just a ritual to sustain belief in something we can't understand. That seems pretty hollow to me."

"Not hollow at all," said Priestess Ory. "It's healing, and it's very human. Listen, I didn't come up in Voodoo, I was raised a good Catholic girl, but I always knew I wanted to be a healer of some kind. I tried the conventional route, got a PhD in clinical psychology at Loyola, spent fifteen years as a therapist. Fifteen years of frustration…successes were too few and too fleeting. Then I found Voodoo, and it just spoke to me. And I'll tell you, I've helped more people by waving a chicken's foot over their heads than I ever did in endless discussions of how their daddies were mean to them as children. I don't deny there's an element of performance in the ritual, just as there is for a priest giving communion, just as there is in all human ritual. But whatever the ultimate reality behind it, the bottom line is, it works." From the backyard, the drums changed tempo and the singing stopped. Priestess Ory glanced toward the gate. "I must get back to my *ounfo*." She turned and walked away.

Trinity stepped forward and snatched the car keys from Daniel's hand. "Walk with me." He marched off down the middle of the street.

Daniel caught up and fell in beside him. Trinity kept marching in silence. Daniel said, "I know you're angry, but wandering around the Lower Nine in the middle of the night is a very bad plan. Let's at least get the car."

"I'm not angry, I'm thinking. I always think better at a brisk walk. Be quiet a minute so I can hear my thoughts."

The skyline of downtown New Orleans glowed faintly in the distance, and the sound of drums faded away as they walked the empty streets, Trinity listening to his thoughts and Daniel listening to their footsteps and watching for trouble among the ruins.

They reached an intersection and Trinity turned right. Daniel stopped him. "Not that way. No streetlights." So they turned left instead.

A few blocks later, Trinity stopped walking. "Can you find the way back to the car?" he said.

"I think so." Daniel pointed down the next block.

"Let's go."

And as they walked, Trinity shared his thoughts. "I'm not angry with you...I actually think everything happened tonight exactly the way it was supposed to. Think about it: We all react to things according to the people we are. God knows who you are, and he brought you into this knowing you'd react exactly as you did. I wasn't led here to commune with Shango at all, I was supposed to experience this night just as it happened." His hand swept across the devastation all around. "I was supposed to see all this." Even in the dim light, Daniel caught the glint of his smile. "Nothing tonight happened by accident. And I'm beginning to understand what it means." He stopped at the intersection, looked around. "God, I wish there were some street signs. Which way?"

Dawn was now breaking, and everything looked different bathed in its dim blue light. "Right, I think. No, wait." Daniel scanned for something recognizable, came up empty. "Damn. I don't know."

Trinity dug into his pocket, pulled out a quarter. "Heads it's right, tails left." He flipped the coin, caught it, and slapped it on the back of his hand. "Tails." He turned left and resumed walking. A foghorn moaned somewhere in the distance.

Halfway down the block, Trinity came to an abrupt stop, his mouth hanging open.

Daniel reached for the gun. "What?"

"Oh my…will you look at that!" Trinity ran toward the ruins of a single-story commercial building. The cinderblock structure was still in one piece, but the glass double-doors and all the windows were gone, and the sign was smashed. "You see?" he said. "This proves it."

Daniel looked to where he was pointing, to the smashed sign above the entrance.

T__ TRIN__Y WORD OF GOD MIN_____ NUTRIT_____
CENTER

The sign jolted his memory, and he recognized the place from a photograph he'd seen on Trinity's website. It was his uncle's old soup kitchen.

Nothing tonight happened by accident…

Trinity sat on the curb. "Now I can see it clearly."

Daniel sat beside him. "Tell me."

"OK…all my life I was a grifter, religion just a con, I didn't even believe in God. But I *did* build schools and clean-water wells in Africa and a medical clinic in Haiti, and I *did* fund the largest soup kitchen in Louisiana. Sure, I did it just to keep the IRS off my back, but that's not the point, just like my lack of belief wasn't the point. The point is I was doing good works, whatever the reason. But after Katrina, I abandoned the very people who made me rich. When this city desperately needed some good works, I ran off to Atlanta and revved up the money machine again. And then the voices started. And the tongues." Trinity looked back to the sign. "Remember that last sermon, before the bomb went off? I thought God left me up on stage looking like an idiot with nothing to say, but I was wrong. He said everything. It was the only time he's ever spoken through me clearly, no backwards tongues, just straight out. And he said: *Faith without works is dead.*"

"But you're saying more than that. You're saying faith is irrelevant."

"Of course faith is irrelevant. God brought together a Catholic priest, a Voodoo mambo, and a total unbeliever. I don't think He cares what the hell we believe—or even *if* we believe—as long as we live the word. Think of it this way: In my dream, Mama Anne said, 'There's only one God—everything else is metaphor.' Now, strip away all the metaphors, and what is the one single commandment common to every decent religion ever known?"

"Do unto others as you would have them do unto you."

"Exactly. Every religion in human history has had a variation of it, but why do so few people live by it? Because of all the other crap, because of the metaphors. Jew or Muslim or Christian or Hindu or Voodoo, everybody's trying to connect to the same fundamental truth, but they're confusing themselves, taking the metaphors literally. They've all got their checklists—*I don't work on the Sabbath, I don't take the Lord's name in vain, I don't eat pork, I don't drink, I don't commit murder, whatever*—but in the meantime, they treat each other like shit. Taking the metaphors literally gives them a free pass to duck out of the real heavy lifting. Hell, look around." Trinity gestured to the street. "And I don't just mean this, I mean look at the state of the whole world. People do the easy stuff, they run around bragging about their faith in God and their love of their fellow man…but easy to say ain't easy to do. And love is a verb. It carries obligation."

Love is a verb. The weight of it hit Daniel with an almost physical force. It was the very foundation of Jesus's message to the world. *I give you a new commandment, that you love one another. Just as I have loved you, you should also love one another.* It was also the Catholic prayer for the holy day of Corpus Christi…now just two days away.

Daniel stood and faced the old soup kitchen. "I've spent the last fourteen years searching for a miracle," he said, "searching for evidence that God is present in the world. But you know, I think what I was really looking for was that feeling I had as a kid…when you were God's messenger and I was His messenger's companion. The feeling that I was living in a state of grace."

"That feeling came from your belief that we were helping people," said his uncle. "I think you've spent the last fourteen years looking in the wrong places, son. It isn't about miracles or proof or having God on speed dial. You want to be close to God? Reach down and help your neighbor. Faith without works is dead…and maybe in the end, works is *all* that matters." Trinity stood and put his hand on Daniel's shoulder. "It is God's *only* commandment."

PART 3

74:

Daniel danced around the heavy bag, snapping off left jabs and pounding home right hooks, left uppercuts, the bag rattling its chains, sweat pouring down his brow.

The Saint Sebastian's Boys Athletic Club hadn't changed a bit. When Daniel rang the doorbell just after sunrise, Father Henri had welcomed him with a hug and a pat on the head. The old priest set up a couple of cots for Daniel and Trinity in the back rooms and then handed Daniel a key to the front door. No questions asked.

Daniel reversed his footwork and pounded the bag with another newly remembered combination, amazed by how being in the old gym melted the years away, brought it all back.

Trinity had his brisk walks, Daniel had this.

It wasn't just the boxing exercises flooding back. He remembered himself as eighteen-year-old Danny Byrne, remembered how it felt to be that kid. Soon-to-be New Orleans Golden Gloves Welterweight Champion. Living with the fathers and more than a little relieved that these particular priests in this particular parish didn't seem to have a thing for teenage boys. Good student, and street-smart as hell, courtesy of a childhood spent with the Reverend Tim Trinity, grifter-at-large. Enough swagger to carry on a relationship with a beautiful and smart college grad and drink with her friends in bars that catered to grownups.

But scheduled to enter the seminary after his next birthday. Scheduled to become a priest. On a mission to find a miracle.

He had told himself that it was a great way to get a free university education. He had told himself he'd find a miracle before his twenty-sixth birthday and still be a young man with his whole life ahead of him, an advanced degree on his resume, and the stain of the con man washed clean.

He had told himself a lot of things. He had even told himself that, *if it was meant to be*, he might still end up with Julia.

He was a smart kid. He could rationalize anything.

But he couldn't face the truth. Truth was, Daniel was an angry young man, and more than just angry. Trinity's betrayal of his boyhood trust had provided a perfect channel for it, but truth was, the anger had always been with him, a deep rage that rushed like ocean currents far below the surface calm. Rage for a mother who died in childbirth and, worse, a father who chose to kill himself rather than stay and raise his newborn son.

And rage for himself. Because, underneath it all, in the silent stillness of his innermost self, this thought was always waiting for him: *I killed my parents.*

At the seminary, Daniel had worked on it with church therapists, and in time he came to accept his personal history with not much more emotional baggage than most people carry through life. And he had learned to be honest with himself, most of the time, which he figured was about as much as anyone can ask for.

He shuffled his feet, switched to southpaw, right jabs and left hooks.

If it was meant to be... Would he end up with Julia after all? While Trinity was still sleeping, Daniel had only managed five hours, jolted awake by the realization that today he would go to the prearranged meeting place.

Today he would see her again.

And then what?

No use getting ahead of himself. He had more practical matters to focus on. Like keeping his uncle alive.

Trinity had vowed to resume preaching in public and to share the tongues whenever they came upon him. He'd also vowed to share what he'd learned about what he was calling *God's Only Commandment.*

Daniel told him it was suicide and suggested that Trinity send his messages to the world on television, from a secure location. "You don't deliver a sermon on love from the safety of a bunker," Trinity had insisted, "you do it out in the open, embracing the world." He would not be dissuaded.

Worse, he planned to announce the time and place of his next sermon in advance, during an interview with Julia on CNN. Daniel was happy to be able to make good on his promise of an exclusive to Julia, but the announcement was not going to make the task of keeping his uncle alive any easier.

*Keeping Trinity alive...*But how, when they didn't even know the source of the threat? Samson Turner had worked for a large, high-end security company. That told them nothing about who was behind the attacks. It could be any well-heeled entity with a vested interest in maintaining the status quo.

And what about the Vatican? What would be their next move? Father Nick would never sanction murder, but was it beyond Conrad Winter? Was there any line Conrad wouldn't cross for *the greater good* as he saw it? Hard to say.

Daniel unleashed a flurry on the heavy bag as Father Henri walked into the gym.

"You're still dropping your left," said Father Henri, as if Daniel had only been gone a week. "How many times I gotta tell ya?"

Daniel grabbed the big leather bag, bringing it to rest. "Never woulda won the Golden Gloves without you," he said.

"You got that right," said Father Henri.

This meeting with Julia wasn't a date, but you couldn't tell that by the butterflies in Daniel's stomach. Pat had arrived in New Orleans and was looking after Trinity at the athletic club, and Father Henri had been getting ready to serve them leftover red beans and rice as Daniel headed out to the French Quarter, freshly showered and shaved, dressed in clean clothes, chewing on minty gum.

Daniel entered the Quarter off Rampart, walking down Conti and then turning left onto Bourbon Street. The crowds on Bourbon would help him get lost if he were being tailed. He crossed the street every block or so, checking behind, but didn't spot a tail.

Walking down Bourbon, heading for this non-date with Julia, felt like walking backwards through time…

Their first real date did not begin well. In those days, Daniel's relationship to time was somewhat loose, and he was usually ten or fifteen minutes late for anything. When he arrived at the bar where they'd arranged to meet, he spotted Julia at a table in back, scowling into a book. As he approached, she took a long look at her watch and said, "An *hour and fifteen minutes*, Daniel. You better have a hell of an excuse."

She'd misremembered their agreed meeting time and had been sitting in the bar for an hour and a half. He protested, she checked her planner, and they'd finally laughed about it. The date was salvaged.

It became a private joke between them. Whenever Daniel arrived slightly late, and he usually did, Julia would glare at her watch, add an hour to his lateness, and say, "An hour and eight minutes, Daniel. Your usual punctual self."

So when Daniel told Julia to meet him at the location of their first date at three o'clock and said he'd be his usual punctual self, they both knew he meant four o'clock at The Abbey bar. Unlikely that the FBI had tapped his cell phone so quickly, but better to be safe, so he'd used the code only she would understand.

He turned right on Governor Nicholls, circled the block to be absolutely sure he wasn't being tailed, and then headed on down to Decatur.

He ducked inside the darkened bar. Dusty old stained glass windows lined one wall, and the little Christmas tree lights on the ceiling fought to cut through the cigarette smoke.

Julia was sitting at a table near the back wall—the same table where she'd been sitting on their first date—and as Daniel approached, she looked at her watch. And frowned.

"You're on time," she said. "I don't get to say my line."

"I've changed," he said.

She stood and hugged him hard, whispered in his ear, "I've been so worried about you." She kissed his cheek and they sat. There were two drinks on the table. "Ordered Sazeracs," she said, "for old times."

"Here's looking up your old address," said Daniel. They clinked their glasses together and drank.

He told her about the journey from Atlanta to New Orleans. He didn't go into detail about what happened at Pat's place, simply said that there'd been another attempt on Trinity's life, and they'd gotten away unscathed. And he told her about their astonishing meeting with Angelica Ory, the voodoo ritual, and Trinity's epiphany of *God's only commandment* at the ruins of his soup kitchen in the Lower Nine.

Julia smiled. "That's what secular humanists have been saying for ages, minus the God part."

Daniel smiled back at her. "Well, you can ask Tim all about it. On camera."

Her eyes went wide and she let out a small gasp. "Really? When?"

Daniel knew how important this story was to her, felt a thrill at being able to deliver it. "He wants to sit down with you for an interview, as soon as you can arrange it."

"Oh my God." Her face flushed and she looked a bit embarrassed, perhaps at having revealed such naked ambition, such elation at the prospect of bagging her prey. She put her hand on his. "Thank you."

Daniel's excitement turned decidedly sexual, and he didn't know exactly what to do with it. *This is not a date,* he reminded himself, crossing his legs. "I told you you'd get the scoop," he said. "But he won't tape it. It has to go out live."

"Not a problem." She picked up her cell phone, dialed. "Kathy, Julia. Great news. I've got Trinity."

75:

"Put that in your wallet," said Pat, handing Daniel a card key. "If the shit hits the fan and we gotta split up, we rendezvous at the Pelican Motel on the Westbank Expressway across the river in Gretna. Room 104. It's booked for the next three nights."

"Got it," said Daniel.

"You know I think this whole thing is a terrible idea."

"I know."

"I tried to talk him out of it," said Pat. "Got nowhere."

"He's committed to this. He knows we can't do much to protect him at a public rally. He just doesn't care." Daniel tucked the card key away. "All we can do is our best."

"We gonna have to get very lucky, brother."

"I know." Daniel checked his watch. "Julia's gonna be there with her cameraman in an hour. We should get going."

The door from one of the back rooms opened and Tim Trinity stepped into the gym. He wore a new silk suit, royal blue to match his Bible, crisp white shirt, matching pink silk tie and pocket square. His boots gleamed white. His hair was back to silver.

"How do I look?" Trinity grinned. "Ready for prime time?" He straightened his tie, shot his cuffs. "Couldn't believe it, Ozzy still works at Rubensteins. Still had my measurements on file, even remembered: long-point collar, French cuffs. Now *that's* customer service."

✦ ✦ ✦

Julia and Shooter drove out to Parran's Po-Boys in Metairie and parked in front, as per Daniel's instructions. They arrived early, split a seafood muffuletta for dinner. Shooter went back out to the news van to make sure the satellite uplink was working, and Julia stayed in the restaurant, reviewing the questions she'd written for the most important interview of her life.

She'd written her questions on index cards. Now she put the cards in three separate stacks, according to importance. She had forty-seven cards—enough for a ten-hour conversation—but only one hour of airtime with Trinity.

She pushed the two "less important" stacks aside and shuffled through the questions in the "essential" stack. She'd still only have time for half of them, even if Trinity was succinct in his answers. And once the conversation got rolling, she'd need time for follow-ups and redirects.

Damn, it was hard to choose. If the interview went well, she'd ask him to stick around and continue the conversation on tape, for airing later, so it was important to get him relaxed, but she wasn't going to resort to lobbing him softballs. It was a popular "bonding technique" used by many television reporters, but she'd always considered it disrespectful of the viewers' time and trust.

And besides, her professional ego would not allow it. She'd worked too hard to be taken seriously in this job, and she was damned if she'd allow herself to be made "soft" by the pressures of television.

Her phone rang, and she answered it. It was Daniel.

"We're in a motel a few blocks from you," he said. "There's a green Forester parked beside your van. The man inside is a friend, Pat Wahlquist. He'll lead you here."

Shooter angled a couple of chairs toward each other and wired a microphone to Tim Trinity's lapel, then switched on two powerful lights and stood behind the camera. He donned a headset as Julia gestured to one of the chairs and Trinity sat.

She took her chair, straightened her jacket, and spoke into the mic for a sound check. Shooter gave her a thumbs-up. Daniel and his friend Pat Wahlquist stood over to one side, in the darkness behind the lights. She could just make out Daniel's smile, and she nodded back at him.

Trinity leaned forward, touched her knee. "I think Danny's sweet on you," he said. "You should give him another chance. You make a good couple."

"Tim, please," said Daniel from out of the darkness.

Julia suppressed a smile, cleared her throat. She inserted her earpiece and listened to the director in Atlanta.

She nodded to Trinity and said, "We're on after this break," and shuffled through her index cards again, rearranging them, trying to clear her mind.

Just another interview, she told herself, *no big deal...*

Shooter said, "Quiet, everybody. We're on in ten..." He held one hand up high.

Through her earpiece, Julia listened to Anderson Cooper intro the segment. Cooper was saying, "Forget about Waldo, the question the entire world has been asking since Sunday is *Where is Reverend Tim Trinity?* Well, Julia Rothman of the *New Orleans Time-Picayune* found him, and he agreed to sit down with her for this live interview, exclusively on CNN. I, for one, can't wait to hear what he has to say. Take it away, Julia."

OK, here we go...

Shooter brought his hand down and pointed at her.

"Thanks, Anderson," she said, looking into the camera's shiny black eye, thinking: *No big deal, just another interview...* "We're in a motel in the New Orleans area with, as you say, the man *everyone* has been looking for." She turned to Trinity. "Reverend Trinity, thank you for being with us tonight."

"My pleasure, Julia," said Trinity. "Thanks for having me."

She'd already memorized her first five questions, didn't even need to glance at the index card. She said, "Please tell us—"

"Excuse me." Trinity held up a hand. "Pardon me for interrupting. I'd like to make a statement." He turned to face the camera. "On Thursday afternoon at one o'clock, I will be in front of Saint Louis Cathedral in Jackson

Square. At that time, I will share with the world what I've just recently come to understand. I hope you'll all join me. Thank you." Trinity smiled at Julia and said, "Thanks again for having me." He stood up, took the microphone off, and walked out the door. A second later, Pat followed after him.

Julia glanced at Daniel as he shrugged a bewildered apology.

She turned back to the camera, her cheeks burning.

76:

Within an hour of the broadcast, Trinity's Pilgrims were gathering in Jackson Square. Within two hours they were crowding out the tourists and pissing off the merchants.

According to news reports, the pilgrims had left a wake of destruction in Atlanta, and nobody wanted a repeat performance in New Orleans. At midnight the mayor gave the order, and the NOPD sent cops in on foot and on horseback to disperse the crowd with as much force as necessary. Which they did. A few hippies bloodied, a couple of bikers pepper-sprayed, but no serious injuries.

The crowd pulled back to the tent city that was now filling Louis Armstrong Park, and to Lafayette Square and Lee Circle, which were soon teeming.

At nine o'clock the next morning, twenty-eight hours before Trinity was scheduled to give his speech, the mayor made a statement to the press: Reverend Tim Trinity did not have an event permit and would not be allowed to hold a rally in or near the Vieux Carré. If Reverend Trinity wished to apply for a permit, he was free to do so, but it would not be approved by the following day, and there was no guarantee it would be approved at all. The NOPD and the Orleans Parish Sheriff's Office were putting all available officers on double shifts until further notice.

This did not go down well with Trinity's Pilgrims, and the scene in the parks was starting to look more like protest than pilgrimage.

Still they kept coming. By late morning Audubon Park was starting to fill up. At noon, the mayor's office announced that a press conference would be held at three p.m.

The press conference took place at four. This time the mayor was joined by the city police commissioner, parish sheriff, the governor, and United States Senator Paul Guyot. Senator Guyot spoke for the group while the mayor stood in the background looking like he'd swallowed a handful of nails.

Senator Guyot said he was delighted to announce that an agreement had been reached between federal, state, and local governments, allowing Reverend Trinity to hold his rally the following day as originally planned. The front steps of Saint Louis Cathedral were private property, but a stage would be set up on the public sidewalk directly in front for Trinity's use. The Louisiana National Guard was being mobilized to assist local and state authorities with crowd management. He said Reverend Trinity's First Amendment rights were not negated by the fact that so many Americans wanted to hear him in person, and that the government's goal was neither to restrict Trinity's right to free speech nor the right of Americans to peacefully assemble, but simply to do everything possible to ensure public safety.

"Uh-oh," said Pat, looking over Daniel's shoulder at the entrance of Vaughan's Lounge. "We got trouble."

Daniel turned away from the television and toward the open doorway in time to see two athletic men in blue suits and short haircuts close the doors of an unmarked gray sedan. The men peered into the darkened bar.

"They ain't local yokels, neither," Pat added, laying his hands on the table, open and relaxed. "These cats are the real deal. We don't wanna put them on edge, man. Keep your hands visible."

Daniel lifted the hand that had fallen in his lap, now hyper-aware of the gun on his hip, for which he most certainly did not have a concealed carry permit.

The taller man wore an expensive suit cut to help conceal his side-arm. The other man apparently didn't give a shit if anyone knew he was carrying. The taller man made eye contact and nodded as they reached the table. "Good afternoon, Mr. Byrne." He pulled out the chair next to Daniel and flashed his badge as he sat. "We're from the FBI, I'm Special Agent Hillborn, and," he gestured at the other man, "this is Special Agent

Robertson. Perhaps your friend Ms. Rothman mentioned that we were eager to speak with you." A smile, neither friendly nor menacing. Strictly professional. Hillborn turned to Pat. "And you are?"

"Pat Wahlquist. I'm an executive protection specialist, under the employ of Mr. Byrne. If you'd like to see my papers, I'll have to reach into my back pocket."

Hillborn waved it off. "I believe you." Back to Daniel. "We're investigating the bombing at your uncle's church in Atlanta." He signaled to the bartender, "Two Abitas here, and whatever these men are drinking." Back to Daniel. "Funny thing, Ms. Rothman neglected to tell us that Trinity is your uncle. Must've slipped her mind. But I spoke at length with a representative of the Vatican who was very helpful. He said that you seem to have walked off the job, said you are no longer operating under the direction or authority of the Holy See."

"That's correct," said Daniel.

The bartender deposited their drinks on the table and Hillborn dropped a twenty on the bartender's tray and waved him away. He took a swig of beer. "You understand, then, that you no longer have diplomatic immunity."

"I'm an American citizen in the process of moving back to my hometown." The gun was growing itchy against his side. "I'm not involved in criminal activity. I have no need for immunity, diplomatic or otherwise."

"If you're keeping us from meeting with Reverend Trinity—"

"I'm not," said Daniel. "The whole world knows where he's going to be." He gestured at the television over the bar, "And he'll be happy to meet with you after his public address tomorrow."

"Mr. Byrne. The bombing at your uncle's church was a very professional operation, and the people behind it are not lacking in resources. Do you really think, after going to all that effort, they'll just shrug their shoulders and forget all about it?"

Images from the bayou flashed in Daniel's mind…The man lighting a cigarette by the Suburban in front of Pat's house, the other man jerking against the window bars as electricity fried his body, the fine mist of blood that hung in the air where Samson Turner's head had been a second earlier...

Hillborn turned to Pat. "Let's hear your opinion, Mr. Wahlquist. As an *executive protection specialist*, I mean. How do you estimate your chances of keeping Reverend Trinity alive tomorrow?"

"Our chances? I honestly don't like them a whole bunch," said Pat. He sipped his root beer and looked straight at Daniel.

"Hire a professional, you should take his advice," said Hillborn. He took another swig of Abita. "Look, Daniel, I'm sure you're trying to do what you think is best, but your good intentions are going to get your uncle killed. You too, in all likelihood. You're a smart guy, you must be able to see the truth of that. *Twenty* professional bodyguards couldn't keep him alive at a public rally. Face it: you can't protect him. We can."

Daniel couldn't think of anything to say, so he took a long pull from his bottle and waited for the pitch he knew was coming.

It came. "You can still save your uncle," said Hillborn, "by convincing him to turn himself over to us. We're offering a way out."

"And what happens to him?" said Daniel.

"Well, after we debrief him, he'll get a new name, a new identity. The US Marshals will protect him, set him up in a new location. We'll let him keep enough of his fraudulently earned wealth that he'll be able to live out the rest of his life in the lap of luxury. Best of everything. Of course he'll never preach again, never get anywhere near a television camera, he'll have to stay completely under radar." Hillborn smiled. "But he will get to live."

Daniel shook his head. "He won't take that deal. See, the thing you guys don't understand...he's not running a con. I know, I know," he held up a hand, "I felt the same way not so long ago. But he sincerely believes that God is using him to bring something important into the world, and for what it's worth, I've also come to believe it. Regardless, he fully understands the risks and he'd rather die than turn his back on his obligation to see it through. I'm sorry, but you're gonna have to wait and talk to him after the speech."

"If he's still alive."

"Yes."

Hillborn and Robertson exchanged a look.

Agent Robertson fixed Daniel with a piercing stare and said, "Special Agent Hillborn has shown you the carrot. I'll show you the stick: Tim Trinity was involved in the deadly bombing of an oil refinery and the rigging of the Georgia State Lottery, and that's just in the last week. We will prosecute him in federal court and he will spend the rest of his life in a Supermax prison in the middle of Bumfuck, Minnesota, where he will be confined to an eight-by-eight windowless cell, all alone, twenty-three-and-a-half hours a day, every day, for the rest of his life."

"He had no part in the refinery accident, or the lottery. None. He'll beat it in court."

"Don't be dense," snapped Robertson. "Trinity stood in front of the cameras in Arkansas and freely admitted to being a con artist for the last forty years. He's been running a massive fraud scheme to the tune of millions. He will be convicted of multiple felonies, and he *will* go to prison. We'll see to it. And he will never come out again. Ever. That's the stick. If I were you, I'd take the carrot."

"In case you haven't been watching the news," said Agent Hillborn, "Atlanta is in tatters. At last count, 167 dead bodies in the parks and on the streets, well over a thousand assaults, 323 rapes and God knows how many more unreported, property damage in the tens of millions. So far. Next year's budget for schools and homeless shelters, wiped out. And you think God wants Tim Trinity to bring all that to New Orleans?" He shook his head. "Hasn't this place seen enough tragedy? Bottom line: your uncle is a walking public disturbance, and we are not having it any longer."

"Senator Guyot said—"

"Senator Guyot wants to be president, he can say whatever he likes. I'm telling you: Tim Trinity will not be making any more public speeches, tomorrow or the next day or next week or next year." He put a business card on the table. "I could arrest you right now, Daniel, but that wouldn't save your uncle, and more importantly, it wouldn't save New Orleans." He drank the last of his beer. "Think about what we've said, and take our offer to him." He stood up. "If we don't hear from you by midnight, the carrot goes away and all he gets is the stick."

They sat in silence for a few minutes after the FBI agents left. Finally Pat said, "I'd bet dollars to donuts there's now a GPS tracker on our car, courtesy of our new friends from the Justice Department. I'll drop you at a bus stop, dump the car in a lot somewhere, and we'll meet back at the ranch later."

"OK." Daniel drank some beer and they sat in silence some more. The silence was growing heavy, uncomfortable. Daniel said, "Go ahead, hit me."

"I know you don't want to hear it."

"When did that ever stop you?"

"Fine. If the government decides to put him away for life, he'll go away for life. Believe me, I know how these guys work—they'll find a charge and make it stick." Daniel didn't answer. Pat sipped his root beer. "You need to convince your uncle to take their offer."

Daniel shook his head. "That dog won't hunt, man. Forget it. He's willing to die tomorrow, you think prison is gonna scare him? I already told him, I made it abundantly clear we're playing exceptionally long odds. He understands."

"What'd he say?"

"Said just do our best to get him to the podium, and whatever happens after that is exactly what's supposed to happen. He's gone all fatalist on me. And the truth is, after everything that's gone down, I can't say he's wrong."

"But what's to be gained? Even if nobody puts a bullet in his head, the feds will snatch him up before he gets to the podium."

"Well, I'm just gonna make sure that doesn't happen."

"And how you gonna do that?" said Pat.

Daniel signaled the bartender for the check. "I have no idea."

77:

The bell jangled above Daniel's head as he opened the door and stepped inside the voodoo shop. Priestess Ory was behind the cash register, ringing up a nervous Yankee couple. She glanced his way, then turned her attention back to her customers and gave the young man his change. "Use it in good health," she said.

The young woman holding the paper bag said, "Thank you, we will," and punctuated it with an unnecessary giggle.

Daniel passed them as they left the store. The bell jangled and the door closed, and they were alone.

"May I interest you in a tarot reading, sir?" Ory deadpanned. "Some love potion perhaps? Money-drawing powder? A protection-from-enemies mojo?"

He deserved that, and acknowledged it with a nod of his head. "Fair enough," he said. "Guilty as charged, Your Honor." His smile went unreciprocated. But she looked more troubled than angry.

"Been near a television in the last hour?" she said.

"What is it this time? Another prediction come true?"

"No, it's Memphis. The tent city in Riverside Park. After Tim went on CNN last night and announced he was in New Orleans, the mood in Memphis fell pretty low. And when the heat rose today, it turned to anger and…well, things turned ugly. Then the police moved in, in full riot gear, and proceeded to make the '68 Chicago convention look like a love-in."

"Jesus."

Ory shuddered visibly. "Way it looked on television, it was almost a pleasant surprise to hear that the dead only numbered in the teens."

Agent Hillborn's promise rang in Daniel's ears: *Tim Trinity will not be making any more public speeches, tomorrow or the next day or next week or next year.*

"I realize I'm not in any position to ask you for favors, Mama Anne," he said. "But we really do need your help."

Ory looked at him for a few seconds and then offered a gracious smile that showed only a little reluctance around the edges. "We're on this road together," she said. "In my dream, you told me to remember that." Her smile warmed. "I haven't forgotten, and neither should you."

The sidewalks were as packed as midtown Manhattan at the height of rush hour. The police kept everyone moving along, but this being the Southland, everyone still shuffled at a pace that would drive any self-respecting New Yorker to murder.

The sun was sinking in the western sky, but it still must've been ninety-five degrees with the additional heat generated by so many bodies. And Daniel couldn't take off his windbreaker without exposing the gun. So he just kept pressing onward, sweating his way out of the Quarter as quickly as the crush of pedestrians would allow.

He stopped at the Everything Shoppe on Canal Street and cooled off while picking up supplies. Sandwiches and Zapp's chips for dinner, cigarettes for Trinity, a bottle of red wine, and some energy drinks for morning. Stepping back outside with his groceries felt like walking into a hot, wet blanket.

He spotted a man unlike anyone else on the sidewalk, watching him from under a palmetto. The man was in his late sixties, with thinning hair, perfect posture, and a Savile Row suit that easily cost eight thousand dollars but didn't need to brag about it. A silver and black Rolls Royce Phantom sat idling at the curb behind him.

The man approached, and Daniel caught a hint of his cologne as he got close. He smelled like old money. What some people still insisted on calling *good breeding*. He said, "Congratulations. You've kept to the path, and I daresay you'll know the truth before much longer."

You've kept to the path…you'll know the truth. The words resonated in Daniel's ears like an echo. *Walk the path, find the truth.* The note that had been waiting for him at the Westin, written in an elegant hand on expensive stationery.

"Papa Legba, I presume."

The man smiled. "Quite." He gestured to the Rolls. "Allow me to offer you a lift back to Saint Sebastian's. It's cool inside, and we can chat along the way. You must be very uncomfortable in that jacket."

The man poured thirty-year-old Macallan Single Malt into a couple of crystal glasses, handed one to Daniel, and settled back into the deep green leather seat as the Rolls Royce gently rocked into motion. He said, "We've been most impressed by you, Daniel. You've shown all the makings of a top field operative." His accent was maddeningly neutral. Probably an American who'd spent many years living in England and, to a lesser extent, continental Europe. Or maybe a Brit who'd moved to America decades ago and purposely lost the boarding school accent of his youth.

"Who's *we*?" said Daniel. "And for that matter, who the hell are you? I think Legba wants his name back."

The man's smile was utterly confident. A smile that would seem arrogant on a younger man, but on this man signaled the calm perspective that comes with a lifetime of wide experience. "We are an organization you've never heard of: the Fleur-de-Lis Foundation. My name is Carter Ames, and I'm the managing director. And as you already know, we've been your ally from the start."

Daniel tasted the scotch. It went down like liquid silk. "Why? What's your interest here?"

"The mission of the Fleur-de-Lis Foundation is to bring the truth to light, so the public can make informed choices about our civilization's future," said Carter Ames. "Unfortunately, there are other people, equally powerful, who do not trust the public with the truth. So we struggle against each other. It is a game we've been playing for many years, a game that may never end. But it must be played, lest we lose what's left of our freedoms."

"Do they have a name, these powerful people you're struggling against?"

"Indeed. They call themselves the Council for World Peace. But don't let the name fool you." He sipped his scotch. "Oh, they might accept world peace, but only on their terms, under their control. Peace without freedom. For us, that is too high a price. We do not consider slavery, however peaceful, to be a viable future."

"Slavery? Come on."

"Of course they don't see it as such. They prefer words like *security* and *stability*. But it all comes down to control, in the end. The council's roots—and the foundation's, for that matter—go back to the Middle Ages, albeit both under different names. The council began simply as a network of spies—a freelance espionage agency, if you will—gathering intelligence around Europe and the eastern trade routes and selling what they learned to monarchs and popes and wealthy merchant families, greasing the wheels of commerce. But over time their actions went far beyond intelligence gathering. They grew ever more powerful and became their own biggest client, really."

"And how did the foundation begin?" asked Daniel.

"We were one of their clients—a huge merchant shipping dynasty, with interests spread across the civilized world—one of the most powerful families in France at the time. But this family held some sense of *noblesse oblige*, and as the heirs saw what the council was becoming, how it was concentrating power into fewer and fewer hands, they established the Fleur-de-Lis Foundation to thwart the council."

"And what the hell does this have to do with my uncle?"

Carter Ames shook his head. "What's happening with your uncle, as significant as it is, is but one more battlefront in a war that has been raging for centuries. There have always been people who think like us and people who think like them, fighting behind the scenes of world events. What I'm trying to tell you, Daniel, is that the world as you know it is just what you're allowed to see. The council and the foundation have left their fingerprints on almost any major world event you care to mention. The Kennedy assassination? Sure, but also his rise to the presidency. The alliance between the United States and Russia to stop Hitler? Yes, but also the alliance between Hitler and Hirohito. Even the American Revolution. I'm saying that *history*, as you know it, is just the edited version."

"OK, thanks for the drink, Mr. Ames," said Daniel, "but that sounds all kinds of crazy. You expect me to believe that these two organizations have been shaping history, and the world has never even heard of them? I don't buy it."

Carter Ames smiled placidly. "I don't expect you to, not yet. But consider this: if you'd done the job the Vatican had sent you to do, the world would never have known about the Trinity Phenomenon. And that would just be one more piece of history kept secret."

The truth of it hit Daniel like a gut punch. If he'd not discovered the alterations of the transcripts Nick had given him, the world would never have known. How many other world events, what other strange phenomenon had been successfully covered up and kept secret from the public? He felt like a door had just been cracked open to another world, and the opening was too narrow to see more than a sliver of what lay beyond.

"I need more," he said. "What's the bigger picture, the truth you're trying to expose?"

"You're not quite there yet, Daniel," said Carter Ames. "If and when you do get there, I think you will want to join us, but it isn't something to be taken lightly. While the hours are brutal, the pay is excellent and the job comes with a first-class expense account. You will likely not live to see old age, but you might. And whenever you die, you'll die knowing that you've helped save the world from another Dark Ages." His face darkened as he spoke. "That's why I became involved. I wanted to be able to look my granddaughter in the eye knowing I'd done everything I could, on my watch, to make things better. Or at least to hold back the darkness."

Hold back the darkness... The words sent a chill through Daniel.

Carter Ames put his glass down and reached into his breast pocket. "At any rate, let's not get ahead of ourselves. Right now you need to focus your attention on keeping your uncle alive."

"Is Father Nick part of this?" He had to know.

"At most, he may have helped them unwittingly," said Carter Ames. "He's not a member of the council. But Conrad Winter is. And we know they have others in the Vatican." He pulled a photograph from his breast pocket and handed it across. "Anyway, this is the man you need to focus on." The man in the picture was bald, muscular, probably in his late thirties, with humorless eyes and thin lips. "It was taken at the airport yesterday. We spotted him coming off a flight from Montreal, kept him under surveillance until this afternoon. He slipped away from our operatives a couple hours ago. Just melted into the crowds. We have no leads on his location."

"Who is he?"

"Ask your friend Pat." The car came to a stop at the curb in front of the Saint Sebastian's Boys Athletic Club. The driver got out and opened the coach door for Daniel.

"Wait a second," said Daniel. "You know Pat?"

"Oh, Pat's been in the game for years," said Carter Ames. "As an ally, thankfully. We were very pleased when you brought him into this. Do give him my regards."

Daniel locked the door behind him and stepped into the empty gym. He dropped the keys in his pocket and began spreading the groceries out on the edge of the boxing ring.

Pat entered the gym from one of the back rooms and made straight for the potato chips. "Jalapeño," he said, ripping the bag open and inhaling. "My favorite."

"We need to talk," said Daniel, reaching into his back pocket for the photo Carter Ames had given him.

"Sure, what's up?"

Tim Trinity came in from the changing rooms, wearing only boxer shorts, socks, and a bulletproof vest. "You're right, it's not too bad," he said to Pat, "practically disappears under my shirt." He stopped when he spotted the groceries on the boxing ring. "Oh good, I'm starved." He grabbed a sandwich and took a big bite.

Pat said, "It won't stop a bullet aimed at your head, Tim."

"Don't start that again." Trinity groaned with a smile and turned to Daniel. "Our friend is in danger of becoming a nattering nabob of negativism." He took another bite and chewed. "Great sandwich. Thanks."

Daniel tucked the photo back into his pocket and picked up a sandwich while Trinity resumed the banter, teasing Pat about the health benefits of keeping a positive attitude.

After cheerfully wolfing down a couple of sandwiches and a handful of chips, Trinity announced he was turning in early to finish writing tomorrow's sermon and get a good night's sleep.

As soon as he was gone, Daniel turned to Pat and said, "Carter Ames sends his regards."

"What?"

"You saying you don't know who Carter Ames is?"

"Yeah, I know him. Just surprised you do."

"We only just met."

Pat thought for a second, then laughed through his nose. "I shoulda figured he'd show up in all this. Seems a little late to the party, though."

"He's been in it from the start. Remember I told you about the help I was getting from someone named Papa Legba?"

"Ah," Pat smiled. "Crafty old bastard."

"So what's this Fleur-de-Lis Foundation you guys work for?"

"He said I worked for the FDL?"

"He called you an ally."

"That's true enough. But I don't work *for* them, I'm independent."

"Who are they?"

Pat shook his head. "Carter Ames is playing us. He gave you a little glimpse, now he wants me to recruit you. I won't do it."

"But you believe in what they're doing."

"Yeah, and it'll get me killed eventually. You too, if you join up. Look, man, when this thing with Tim is over, just ride off into the sunset with Julia and enjoy the rest of your life. You've earned it."

"I'm not joining up. I just want to understand—"

"No, brother. You only think you do. I'm telling you, you really don't want to know what's going on out there." Pat stuffed some chips in his mouth and chewed. "Anyway, you want to hear the sales pitch, you gonna have to ask Ames. You won't hear it from me. Next subject."

There was no use pressing him. Daniel pulled the photograph from his back pocket and handed it to Pat. "He gave me this. Said you—"

"Holy shit." Pat stopped chewing. "What exactly did he say?"

"He said this guy came in on a flight from Montreal yesterday, but they lost track of him this afternoon. And he said you'd tell me about him."

"His name is Lucien Drapeau, and he is a very bad man." Pat handed the photo back to Daniel. "Pretty safe guess he's here to kill your uncle."

"An assassin?"

"Best in the world, maybe. They say he's a fanatic for precision, never misses. I've crossed paths with him a few times over the years, but we've never gone head to head."

"But he plays for the other team," said Daniel, "the Council for World Peace or whatever it is."

Pat shook his head. "Lucien Drapeau doesn't play for any team. He's all about the money." He pointed at the photo in Daniel's hand. "You need to memorize that face. Note the details…"

Daniel looked hard at the face. Eyes very close together, square jaw, small ears, and a dome shaped like a bullet, with a ridge running from front to back, right in the middle.

"How tall?"

"A smidge taller than me. About six-four, I'd say."

Daniel looked back to the face in the photograph. "Weird," he said, "the guy's got no eyebrows."

"No hair at all," said Pat, "anywhere on his body. He removes it."

"Some kind of kink?"

"No, he's just that committed to his craft. No hair, no DNA evidence trail. The man is uncompromising about his work." Pat put the bag of potato chips down on the boxing ring. "With Drapeau in the game, our chances of keeping Tim alive just went from slim to very-fucking-slim indeed. Wish I could tell you different, but that's the truth, Ruth."

78:

Julia called just after ten o'clock. "Got your messages," she said. "All five of them. Sorry, it's been a little hectic around here. What's up?"

"Come have a drink with me," said Daniel.

After a second of silence, she said, "That would be nice, really, but not tonight, Danny. We've got a big day tomorrow."

"We've been having a lot of big days lately." He could hear her laugh through the phone. It was a warm laugh. "Julia, I realize we've all got a lot on our plates right now, and tomorrow's gonna be crazy. I just want to call a brief time-out, a couple of hours, just you and me and a bottle of wine." *Stop talking*, he told himself. But he didn't. "You know, don't think of it as a date. I just, I need to focus all my attention on security tomorrow, and I can't afford to be thinking about things left unsaid."

"Geez, it sounded a lot more fun when I thought of it as a date," said Julia, a smile in her voice. "OK, tell me where you are and I'll come over and drink your wine while you leave nothing unsaid."

"Cut me a little slack, would ya? It's been a while since I asked a girl out."

When Daniel was eighteen, Father Henri let him have a key to the place so he could lock up or open the gym in the morning, and he'd brought Julia here a few times late at night to sit up on the roof and watch the world go by.

But fourteen years have gone by since she was last up here. Fourteen years. Man.

And now he was about to ask her to just forget about that. He would tell her that, this time, he would not run away chasing ghosts and dreams. He would tell her that, this time, she was his dream.

He would ask her to make that dream come true.

After she'd agreed to come over, he'd come to the roof and set up a couple of folding lawn chairs and a small table he took from the office, a portable radio, the wine, and two plastic cups.

And now she was here again, standing with him on the roof, the skyline of downtown New Orleans glittering behind her in the night, her black hair fluttering in the hot, thick summer breeze, her olive skin shimmering, slightly moist, a glass of red wine in her slender hand.

He was tongue-tied by this woman. He switched on the radio, tuned it to WWOZ. A jazz tune he didn't know, but it was sultry and slow and perfect.

"Julia, I-I have so many things…" He searched for the right words. "I want a second chance with you. I have thought of you every day for the last fourteen years, and I want you back."

She smiled and sipped her wine. "Every day?" she said.

"Well, not *all* day, every day. But yeah." He drank some wine. "Every day. I guess that sounds a little desperate."

Any answer—even *Yes, that sounds desperate*—anything at all, would've been easier than the silence that followed as she sipped her wine and thought her private thoughts. Daniel struggled to hide the tension that felt like it was about to rip him in half. He noticed his own hand shaking as he sipped his wine, hoped she didn't notice it too.

Waiting…his heart pounding out the seconds that passed in silence.

Waiting…and reminding himself to breathe.

Waiting…each second a lifetime.

Finally Julia approached with an expression he couldn't read and put her palm flat on his chest and said, "OK, but you can't just walk back into my life and claim me as your girlfriend. If we do this, we take it slow. We go out on dates. If we like it, we go on more dates. And who knows? Maybe it leads to a relationship. Maybe it leads to forever. But we don't just pick up where we left off fourteen years ago. We start anew."

Daniel clinked his plastic cup against hers. "I'll drink to that."

As they drank, the radio DJ said, "And this one goes out to all the broken-hearted lovers in the Crescent City. Leroy Jones, with *Mood Indigo*."

Daniel turned up the volume, put his wine down on the table. "Dance with me," he said.

They danced, her hands behind his head, his hands on her waist. And as they danced, they kissed. Soft, inquisitive *getting to know you* kisses that became stronger, declarative *I remember you* kisses and finally grew into passionate, demanding *I want you right here right now* kisses.

Coming up for air, Julia said, "Wow."

"Wow, indeed," said Daniel.

She reached for her glass, drank some wine, and shared some with him from her mouth. "Can I ask you something?" she said.

He smiled and rolled his eyes. "Yes, I've really been celibate for fourteen years."

"Gawd am I in trouble," she laughed. She drank some more wine and they kissed again. "Say, do they still have that horrible yellow tartan fold-out couch in the office downstairs?"

They did.

✢ ✢ ✢

Daniel woke by the light of morning, on the fold-out couch in the office, limbs intertwined with Julia. He kissed the top of her head and smelled her hair, and she purred against his chest.

"Mmm, what time is it?"

He looked at his watch. "Eight thirty."

"Oh my God." She jumped naked out of bed and scrambled around the room, collecting scattered articles of clothing and putting them on. "I gotta run." She paused at his side, leaned in for a quick kiss. "Don't take it the wrong way, that was wonderful, really. I'm late for work."

Daniel stood and got into his pants. "So, just to be clear: while we're starting anew and taking it slow and going on dates and then more dates if we like the first dates," he gestured at the bed, "we still get to do that again, right?"

Julia looked up from fastening her bra. "Oh, fuck yeah."

They grinned at each other for a second. "Good," he said. He put on his shirt.

"But maybe next time we'll try some place that doesn't smell like liniment and sweat socks," she said.

She finished dressing, and he walked her out through the gym and down to the front door.

"See you later," she said.

"I'm counting on it." A quick kiss, and he unlocked the door, and she stepped out into the bright sunlight.

He watched her walk away until she turned the corner.

A tall blond priest walked by him and into the gym, saying, "Hello, Daniel," as he passed.

Oh shit. Conrad…

Daniel ran in after him.

79:

Conrad wrinkled his nose and made a face. "My God, Daniel. You still reek of the woman."

"What are you doing here?"

"You're a priest," said Conrad.

"Not anymore. Didn't Nick tell you?"

"There's a protocol to be followed. You can't just walk away from it."

"Yeah, well, I did." Daniel crossed the gym to the fridge, opened an energy drink. "You guys go on and hold a trial in absentia, find me guilty, declare me the spawn of Satan, do whatever you're gonna do. I'm out, and I'm not coming back."

"And what? You're going to live happily ever after with Jezebel?"

"Fuck you, Conrad."

Conrad Winter let out a melodramatic sigh. "Father Nick is sick over this, you know. I tell you, the old man is heartbroken."

"Tell him I'm sorry," said Daniel. He meant it.

"He actually got Cardinal Allodi to sign on to a full pardon for you, if you come back in contrition."

"Tell him thanks but no thanks." Daniel sipped his energy drink. "If there's nothing else, I'll see you out."

Conrad nodded, like he'd expected the rejection and couldn't be bothered to argue the point. Daniel walked him back through the gym. Along the way, Conrad said, "You don't want to be a priest anymore, you want to break your vows, that's between you and God. And I understand Trinity's your uncle, but for the sake of everything holy, pause to think about what you're doing by helping him. Think about the consequences. He could be the *Antichrist* for all you know."

"Spare me." Daniel walked him down the stairs to the door.

"If you let him make the speech today," said Conrad, "you will only buy yourself a world of heartache. Fair warning, Daniel."

"Fine," Daniel unlocked the door, "fair warning." He gestured to the street. "Have a nice life."

Walking back to his car, Conrad dialed the number he'd just recently added to his cell phone and waited for his lost sheep to answer.

They'd been working on the young man for three days straight. Three days straight, in a windowless room with bright lights shining around the clock; sleep limited to one hour in every twenty-four; sustenance limited to high-fat, high-carb, low-nutrition, low-fiber fast food garbage and high-sugar sodas, wreaking havoc with the body's insulin levels; choral music playing the entire time, without interruption; a crucifix on every wall, and a near-constant stream of religious talk from a priest in a clerical collar.

It was a remarkably simple thing to push an already lost sheep deeper into the dark woods and over the edge of insanity. It just took the will to do it.

The young man answered the phone, finally.

"It's Father Carmine calling," said Conrad. "Yes, the Lord's shepherd, that's right. Do you remember what we discussed last night?"

He unlocked the car and got in.

"It has now become necessary, my son. The Lord needs your help."

He closed the door, stuck the key in the ignition.

"You know, in a way I envy you. You're a very privileged young man, very special. Of all His children, the Lord has chosen you. Everyone needs God, but it is the rare soul who is needed *by* Him."

He started the ignition.

"That's right, this afternoon. You remember where? Apartment 301, key under the mat. Everything you need is waiting there. Just like we talked about. Remember, it must be at one thirty, not before."

He pulled away from the curb.

"You are truly blessed, my son. You have God's grace upon you, and your reward will be great in heaven."

He broke the connection and tossed the phone on the empty passenger seat, thinking: *ALEA IACTA EST.*

The die is cast.

80:

Daniel sat in the passenger seat, staring at the photo of Lucien Drapeau he'd taped to the dashboard, committing every detail to memory, visualizing what that face would look like from different angles. He tried to listen as Trinity made small talk from behind and Pat bantered back from behind the wheel. He caught enough of it to toss a line in now and then and help keep the mood light for his uncle, but it was a struggle.

Last night, with Julia, he'd seen the full promise of his future self. There was a life ahead, a life to be lived in the world, outside the authority of the Church, a relationship with God more directly felt, if less clearly defined. The life of a free man, and all the uncertainty and responsibility that comes with it.

He wanted that life. He wanted the chance to discover what kind of man he could be in that new world.

He'd found it all, just in time to risk it all.

There was a crowd gathered under the blazing sun, on the boulevard's neutral ground directly in front of the Ninth Ward Bethel African Methodist Episcopal Church. About 120 people in all, young and old, drunk and sober, some in their Sunday best, some in dirty jeans and threadbare shirts, others dressed like they'd just dropped in from a voodoo ceremony.

Daniel looked out at the crowd as Pat pulled to a stop at the curb and threw it in park. It wasn't a huge crowd, but it was enough to start.

Most impressive of all were the costumed Mardi Gras Indians—a riot of color, a blur of green and yellow and red and blue, pink and purple, glittering sequins and shiny beads—dancing and spinning through the crowd, making the children laugh, with huge feathered headdresses waving in the humid breeze.

Tim Trinity hopped out of the back seat and Priestess Ory welcomed him with a hug and led him toward the crowd.

Pat pulled the keys from the ignition. "Last chance to back out of this cockamamie plan."

Daniel watched the scene through the windshield. His uncle was dancing with a Mardi Gras Indian chief, making faces at two small boys who convulsed with laughter at the sight. "Don't want to," he said.

"OK." Pat grabbed his backpack and handed Daniel a walkie-talkie wired to an earpiece. He pointed at a button on the top. "Push to talk, flip the switch to lock it in talk mode if you need both hands." Daniel clipped the unit to his belt on the opposite side of his gun and inserted the earpiece. Pat pressed the button on his own walkie-talkie. "Read me?"

Daniel nodded. "Very loud."

"Good." Pat pointed at the photo taped to the dashboard. "Take a minute," he said. "Tim's life depends on you being able to recognize this asshole."

Daniel had been staring at it the whole way from Saint Sebastian's. That's why he'd asked Pat to do the driving. But he took another minute now to examine the face of the man who'd come in from Montreal to murder his uncle.

He nodded to himself, snatched the photo off the dashboard, stuck it in his pocket, and put his sunglasses on.

Pat donned his own sunglasses, then pulled a lime-green plastic bowler hat from his backpack and put it on his head. He said, "Tell me true now, does my butt look big in this?"

Daniel couldn't help but smile. "Not at all," he said, "very slimming."

"It'll help you spot me in the crowd, brother." Pat opened the car door. "Let's go do this."

✦ ✦ ✦

Reverend Tim Trinity and Mambo Angelica Ory started walking together, and the people walked with them, down Caffin Avenue, passing one- and two-story homes, some mid-renovation with camping trailers parked in their driveways or on their lawns, others still boarded up, still bearing the spray-painted symbols left behind by soldiers after the flood waters receded, the number at the bottom of each symbol indicating how many bodies were found inside.

Veves of the damned.

But other homes told a better story, one of endurance and rebirth, of stubborn faith in the possibility that tomorrow can be made better than today. Those houses stood up straight and their windows sparkled and they wore new coats of paint and pride.

And as the crowd walked, so did it grow. People came down off porches and out of trailers, children ran from their yards, and by the time the parade passed Fats Domino's yellow house with the big star above the door and the gold-tipped iron fence, the crowd was more than two hundred strong.

Still not enough, but getting better.

On St. Claude Avenue even more joined their ranks, teenagers from the KFC and women from the Family Dollar parking lot, men from barbershops and bars. Shopkeepers looked out from doorways and people in the crowd called them to join with Reverend Tim, and OPEN signs turned to CLOSED in the doors of their shops, and the crowd grew even stronger.

As they passed the Gasco, a brass band fell in and started playing "Saints," and soon as many in the crowd were dancing as walking, many others singing along, the mood rising above festive, on the way to joyful.

But not for Daniel. He kept about ten feet to his uncle's left, Pat on the other side, scanning the crowd for the face of an assassin. White folks made up only about a quarter of the crowd, an advantage since he was looking for a white face. His eyes never stopped roaming, scanning the crowd, scanning windows and doorways, occupants of passing cars, cataloging white faces, dismissing black faces, moving on to the next. But the crowd was growing fast, and the task would only get harder as they got closer to the French Quarter.

They crossed Reynes, the drawbridge ahead, now clearly visible through the heat haze hanging in the air.

Daniel's earpiece crackled and Pat said, "OK, approaching the first choke point, and I smell bacon."

"Think they've had time to find us?"

"Yup. No cars coming over the bridge, and I don't think it's just a lull in traffic. Be ready."

A large sign with red letters stood in the neutral ground…

```
DANGER
NO PEDESTRIANS
BEYOND THIS POINT
```

…but nobody stopped. Daniel glanced at his watch, pressed the talk button. "We're bang on schedule."

Pat said, "Let's hope everyone is."

As Daniel glanced at the cloudless blue sky, two gray sedans came over the bridge side by side and stopped at an angle, blocking both sides of the road. Special Agents Hillborn and Robertson and six other hard-looking feds got out and strode forward. The bells sounded and the bridge began to rise behind them.

The parade stopped. The brass band fell silent. Then, as the FBI men approached, the crowd coalesced around Trinity. An angry black man with a gray beard and dreadlocks called out to them, "Yeah, *now* you come down to the Lower Nine, where the fuck were you when we needed you?"

"That's right," said a young woman in the crowd. "And why you ain't investigatin' them rich folk who made off with the money, what was supposed to be payin' for the levees, huh? What about that?"

Shit. This was not going to help.

Daniel separated himself from the crowd and walked directly to Hillborn and said, "Hi."

"*Hi?* That's what you're bringing to the party?" said Hillborn. "*Hi?* You fucking moron, did you really think we were going to let you do this?"

"You're not taking him from me," said Daniel.

"Actually, we are."

Daniel smiled as the sound of rotor blades grew louder and Hillborn glanced skyward. The news chopper had arrived. "CNN. The world is watching, Agent Hillborn."

Hillborn glared at Daniel, then shook his head. "Oh, you silly man, you are just determined to make things worse, aren't you?"

"With respect, you're just flat-out wrong here," said Daniel. "Our elected representatives are on record supporting Trinity's right to speak. Do you really want to be the government thug-in-a-suit who slaps cuffs on him and shoves him into a car, and then he's never heard from again? That's what the secret police do in places like Iran. You really want to be that guy?" He glanced up at the news chopper, adding, "I'm sure it'll make good television."

Daniel stopped talking and watched Hillborn think over his options. After what felt like a week, Hillborn said, "Stay put a minute. I'll get back to you." He turned and walked back to his car and sat in it, talking on his radio.

Daniel's earpiece crackled again and Pat said, "Hang tight."

"Where are you?" said Daniel, scanning the crowd. "I can't see you."

"Just working the room, checking out new arrivals," said Pat. "Speaking of which, your view is about to improve. In five…four…three…two…"

Julia came up fast and put a hand on Daniel's forearm, "Sorry we're late. Lost the satellite for a few minutes, but Shooter got it fixed."

Daniel looked toward the back of the crowd, saw Shooter approaching from the CNN news van with a camera on his shoulder. "Aside from giving me a minor heart attack," said Daniel, "your timing is actually perfect."

"Hi, Daniel," Shooter said, handing Julia a microphone and stepping back with his camera. "We're on in sixty seconds."

Hillborn's conversation became visibly more animated after Julia and Shooter arrived. Finally he tossed the radio mic on the seat, got out of the car, and crooked his finger at Daniel.

"Good luck," said Julia.

Daniel walked through the thick, muggy air, careful not to rush, past assorted FBI agents, all the way to Hillborn. Along the way he flipped the switch, putting his walkie-talkie into transmit mode for Pat to listen in.

Hillborn said, "The FBI's position is as follows: Considering the bombing at his church in Atlanta, we strenuously advise Reverend Trinity against any public appearances at this time. We believe that he is acting with reckless disregard for his own life, and we are not equipped to provide for his safety. If he chooses to go forward, we will not stop him, but neither can we protect him. The only assistance we can reasonably provide is to help divert traffic ahead of the parade route."

"Reverend Trinity certainly appreciates the help," said Daniel with a smile.

Hillborn signaled to the other agents, and the drawbridge bells clanged and the bridge started coming back down as the agents returned to their cars. He let out a derisive snort. "Understand: you haven't won anything at all. If by some miracle he's still alive when this day is over, you're both going to prison. I promise."

Daniel shrugged. "And I promised I'd get him to the podium. That's exactly what I'm going to do."

"We'll see."

Daniel flipped the walkie-talkie off transmit as he walked back toward the front of the crowd, looking for Pat's green bowler hat. Pat's voice crackled in his ear. "Nice job with the feds. Meet me in front."

Daniel wiped the sweat from his brow and walked closer as the green hat appeared in the crowd, bobbing forward. They came together at the front line and Pat said, "Full props to the man with the cockamamie plan."

"Thank you."

"Now shake it off and get your energy back up." He broke eye contact and scanned the crowd behind Daniel. "Drapeau is still out here somewhere. We don't find him before we get to the podium, Tim dies."

As the feds disappeared over the bridge, a trumpet blared and a huge cheer erupted from the crowd. Tim Trinity emerged from the protection of the throng to lead them forward, the brass band launched into "Didn't He Ramble," and the party resumed.

81:

Atlanta, Georgia...

After the call came in from Conrad Winter, Father Nick had no choice but to pull the plug on the operation. He summoned all of Conrad's men back to the command center, canceled any further investigation, and ordered all Trinity files wiped from the hard drives.

He thanked the young men working the command center for their efforts, sent upstairs for a few bottles of good brandy, and made sure everyone who wanted a drink had one.

Then he sat back with his snifter and watched CNN.

As far as the Vatican was concerned, the Trinity game was over. It was time to cut their losses. To Nick, the most painful loss was Daniel Byrne. A good man, gone.

A good man, gone wrong.

Nick told himself to stop speculating about how it all happened. No doubt Conrad was truthful about presenting his amnesty offer to Daniel. Nick had successfully sold Cardinal Allodi on the idea, and no way Conrad would disobey a direct order from Allodi. Anyway, Conrad was returning to Atlanta on a one thirty flight from New Orleans, and he would hear all the details soon enough.

Conrad had told Nick that Daniel turned him down flat. Whatever the details, they wouldn't change that basic fact. Nick would just have to accept it and move on.

He sipped some brandy and focused his attention on the television screen. An aerial view of well over a thousand people walking down the middle of a wide street, through an intersection and past a large building that seemed an impossibly bright shade of pink. Then the screen changed to a ground-level view from a handheld camera moving with the crowd.

And there was Reverend Tim Trinity, wearing his shiny silk suit, waving his famous blue Bible, flashing his perfect fake teeth, leading a parade of uneducated misfits, drunks, and hippies, dancing and singing through the streets like it was Mardi Gras day.

It would've been funny if it weren't so fucking tragic.

Tim Trinity, tent revival Holy Roller, charismatic faith healer, cable TV prosperity preacher…master con man. P.T. Barnum for the new age.

And, undeniably, some kind of prophet. But there was no way to know what kind, and the risk was too great, and so he would be stopped. If the Nevada mob didn't get him, the FBI surely would. Trinity's voices, whatever their origin, would not be allowed to change the world, when nobody who mattered really wanted the world changed. On that, you could bet the farm. It was all over but for the gnashing of teeth.

The camera stopped moving and focused on Julia Rothman, the ex-girlfriend reporter Daniel had brought into this case, thereby setting in motion the chain of events that led to this…disaster. Rothman cupped a hand over one ear and raised her voice to speak over the sound of a brass band marching by behind her.

Nick picked up the remote and turned up the volume.

"…just past Elysian Fields, and it's hard to estimate the size of the crowd, but it is definitely growing more rapidly now, and as you can see, the atmosphere is very lively. Impromptu street parades are part of the fabric of daily life in the Crescent City, and most of the people behind me are not religious followers of Reverend Tim Trinity but local residents, simply come out to pass a good time…"

As if to prove her point, a couple of drag queens paused behind her, vamping and blowing kisses at the camera before dancing off with the rest of the crowd.

"The real test will come when we reach Esplanade, where a much larger crowd awaits. I'm told the crowd assembled there numbers over ten thousand, packing Rampart Street all the way back to Louis Armstrong Park, but the National Guard is blocking the street, refusing to let them move forward…"

82:

Tennessee Williams Suite – Hotel Monteleone…

William Lamech muted the television and dialed room service.

"Yes, send up a cup of turtle soup, two dozen oysters on the half shell, and a bottle of…" he scanned the wine list, "Bollinger R.D., 1990. Thank you."

Let the rock stars have their Cristal, Lamech thought as he brought the television's volume back up. When the second-best is truly excellent, the key factor to consider becomes best *value*. The Cristal was superlative, but to his mind, the 1990 Bollinger was plenty excellent, for a lot less money. That's why so many rock stars ended up broke, while he had built a legacy that would make his progeny comfortable for generations to come.

It's a funny old world; if you live long enough, you'll see things you could never have imagined. He remembered that sunny day three weeks ago, when he first brought the news of Tim Trinity's predictions to his colleagues and had to convince them that it wasn't a joke. If you'd told him then that it would cost five million dollars to end Trinity's life, he'd have laughed you right out of Nevada. And if you'd told him that, in just three weeks, "Reverend Tim" would lead a march of over ten thousand people through the streets of New Orleans, carried on live television around the globe, he'd have thought you completely insane.

A lot can change in three weeks, and by God, had it ever.

And considering what Trinity had become in that brief time, five million dollars was very good value indeed. There are times when the second-best just isn't good enough.

He shifted his gaze from the television across the room to the laptop computer open on the coffee table in front of him. What a beautiful example of cause and effect in its purest form: Trinity dies on the television screen, and I press a button on the computer. I press a button on the computer, and money moves from a bank account in the Bahamas to a bank account in Switzerland.

William Lamech had no doubt it would be accomplished. He just hoped Lucien Drapeau wouldn't pull the trigger until the champagne arrived.

83:

"This is impossible," said Daniel, bulling his way between a couple of stoned surfer dudes, pushing through the crush of the mob.

His earpiece crackled and Pat said, "Roger that. Move closer to Tim and look for my hat. Can't see you, but I'm guessing I'm somewhere around your two o'clock."

Daniel got around a woman pushing a stroller, worked his way forward, looking slightly to his right. It was wall-to-wall people, the entire width of Esplanade, covering sidewalks, roadway, and neutral ground.

And here, on the edge of the French Quarter, the crowd had to navigate around the huge old oaks in the center of the road and the thinner trees planted at regular intervals along the sidewalks. The oaks provided a much-needed umbrella for shade—many in the crowd were verging on sunstroke as they arrived—but the same umbrella of branches and leaves also blocked Daniel's view of the second-floor balconies, packed with people, many leaning out over the wrought iron railings to cheer the parade on and shower the revelers with colorful plastic beads.

Lucien Drapeau could lob a grenade down from above and there'd be nothing anyone could do. But that didn't sound like the kind of precision Pat had talked about. Daniel hoped Pat was right.

He spotted the plastic green bowler and worked his way through the chaos up to Pat, walking a dozen feet ahead of Trinity, who had several men from Priestess Ory's congregation and the angry man with the dreadlocks walking in formation, forming a protective box around him.

Pat put a hand on Daniel's shoulder and spoke directly into his ear as they walked. "Need to change tactics. Drapeau wouldn't try to get up close in this crowd. He's a professional, not a kamikaze." He gestured toward the men surrounding Trinity and Ory. "We gonna have to take the chance that these guys will protect him from any crazies and focus on where Drapeau is most likely to be."

Daniel nodded. "Fine. You said Drapeau was a sniper." He started walking faster.

"Used to be."

"What's the range? How far are we talking about?" Daniel broke into a jog, leaving the parade behind, and Pat stayed with him.

"He could make the shot from twelve, fifteen-hundred meters, maybe more."

"We gotta get out from under the trees." Daniel pointed at the sidewalk on the uptown side. "You take the buildings on that side." He jogged over to the sidewalk on the left and continued toward the end of the road, toward the Mississippi River.

The sidewalk was still crowded with spectators, but not packed the way it was in the midst of the parade, and Daniel could maintain a quick walk, weaving around people, keeping his eyes up, scanning the balconies as best he could.

He pressed the talk button. "Got nothing here, almost at the last block—"

His gaze stopped on the profile of a man, about six-four, wearing running shoes, jogging shorts, and a red mesh muscle shirt, terrycloth wristbands and headband. Bald head. He quickened his pace, lost sight of the jogger, pushed his way around a fat man and through a group of college kids...and found the jogger again, a little farther down the street.

Daniel broke into a fast walk. "Pat, I think I see Drapeau. Head my way." Closer now, he could see the man's head had that distinctive bullet shape and his ears were small. The man turned his way. No eyebrows.

They locked eyes. Lucien Drapeau's expression remained dispassionate, not even a twitch of emotion, but Daniel could see the spark of recognition, and then something in Drapeau's eyes went out, like a switch had been flipped in his head, and he took off at a dead run.

Daniel took off after him. His earpiece came alive and Pat said, "I see him! Hauling ass down Barry Street, away from the Quarter, red tank top!"

"I know," yelled Daniel, not bothering with the radio. They converged at Barry Street and got past the spectators and ran flat out, down the center of the street.

Drapeau's lead was just half a block, but he darted right, disappearing from view, into the courtyard of the Melrose Housing Project.

Two rectangular redbrick apartment buildings, each four stories tall, faced each other across the courtyard, and a third formed a back wall to the compound. The buildings had never reopened after Katrina and were awaiting demolition. The government had installed metal shutters over all the ground-floor windows and padlocked the doors.

Daniel and Pat tore into the courtyard, drawing their guns.

In the center of the courtyard, four old men sat on crates, listening to a portable radio and passing a bottle in a paper bag. One of the old men turned his bleary gaze toward Daniel and, without saying a word, pointed his finger at the building at the back of the lot.

Daniel nodded his thanks as they ran past the men, and he caught a newscaster's voice from the portable radio: "…It's very slow going, but Reverend Tim Trinity has now entered the French Quarter, and police are clearing a path along Rue Chartres for him…"

He's gonna make it…

Daniel surged even faster, cutting around the corner of the building. Drapeau was dead ahead, running straight at the apartment building, with nowhere to go. Daniel could hear Pat just behind him and to his right. He angled to his left, Pat to the right, boxing Drapeau in. But Drapeau ran right up the front steps, opened the door, and disappeared into the building.

As they came together at the door, Pat picked up the padlock from the ground. It had been cut through with a hacksaw.

"He set it up ahead of time," said Daniel. "He could have a rifle waiting on the roof."

Pat put out an arm to stop him. "Take a breath. We go quickly but carefully. He knows the layout, we don't." He lifted his arm. "Sunglasses off."

They entered the darkened hallway with their guns out, keeping their footfalls quiet as they went. The hallway was dank, and Daniel's nostrils filled with the smell of mold and rot. They paused just long enough for their eyes to adjust, then moved forward.

The hallway had a staircase at either end. Pat pointed one way, then went the other. Daniel took the stairs two at a time, stopping on the landing to listen. He heard the echo of distant footfalls—Pat on the other stairwell. Then nothing.

He ran up the next flight of stairs, entered the second-floor hallway, listened. Footfalls, directly above. He turned back toward the stairwell, pushing the talk button. "Third floor," he said.

"Already there," said Pat's voice in his ear.

But as Daniel ran up the stairs, he heard a mighty crash and splintering of wood and scuffling in his earpiece, the smack of a fist against skin, and more grappling. He ran faster, pounding up the stairs.

Then a single gunshot—*bam!*—and a heavy thud. Pat yelled, "Fuck!" in Daniel's ear. Daniel flew up the remaining stairs, reached the third floor, and found Pat down in the hallway.

"Goddamnit," said Pat, pulling his belt from his pants. There was a hole in his upper thigh and the blood was coming fast. "Motherfucker had a pistol stashed behind the radiator."

Daniel knelt down, "Let me help—"

"I got this," Pat snapped as he struggled to tie the belt around his leg. He gave a sharp nod toward the roof. "Go." Daniel didn't move. Pat said, "Go. I'll take care of me."

Daniel tore up the next two flights, gun in hand. At the top of the stairs was a landing and a metal door leading out to the roof. It was open a crack. Drapeau was probably on the other side, aiming at the door. Or maybe he was at the edge of the roof, aiming at Trinity.

Time to find out which.

Daniel took a few steps back on the landing. He got a running start and launched himself into the air, crashing the door open with his shoulder.

A burst of gunfire—four rounds—ricocheted off metal and brick as Daniel flew through the air, tucked and rolled onto the rooftop, cutting his elbows on the gravel, rolling to a stop behind a rust-colored exhaust vent.

Another shot. The bullet from Drapeau's gun careened off the vent.

Daniel peeked around and returned fire twice—and pulled back just as fast as Drapeau unloaded another round off the vent.

He took a deep breath, and took stock. He wasn't hit, yet. The quick glimpse he'd gotten told him Drapeau had superior cover, behind the elevator maintenance shed.

He flattened out on the hot gravel and chanced another peek around the vent.

Nothing. Just the maintenance shed and empty rooftop. No Drapeau. And behind the shed was the edge of the building facing the French Quarter, facing Jackson Square, seven blocks away.

About one thousand meters.

Fuck. Drapeau might be setting up the rifle to shoot Trinity right now, or he might be standing with his pistol up waiting to shoot Daniel as soon as he came around the corner of the shed.

No way to know.

Daniel got up into a crouch, moved to the edge of the building, and looked to his left. Just past the maintenance shed, around the corner of the building, a metal pole extended straight out, horizontally from the roof. A flagpole or a lightning rod, probably brought down by Katrina's winds. If he could get to the corner of the building and around, he could grab that pole and haul himself back up on Drapeau's blind side. That is, if there was a ledge to stand on, and if the pole didn't break.

Two big *ifs*. He scanned the rooftop for other options. There were none.

He leaned out over the parapet and looked down. It was a dead drop eighty feet straight down to the concrete sidewalk below.

He got the tingle.

He forced his eyes away from the sidewalk and focused on the wall directly below. There was a narrow decorative ledge in the brickwork that ran horizontally above the top-floor windows. The ledge was about five feet below the roof—he would have to lower himself down to it blindly. Worse, it was only a few inches deep.

It would have to be enough.

He tucked the gun away, swung his legs out over the edge, and lowered himself, facing the building, his pointed toes feeling for the ledge, his heart pounding in his chest, pulse throbbing in his ears.

He found the ledge with his toes, lowered himself further, switching his handholds to the underside of the parapet.

He paused, forehead against the wall. Took a deep breath, and another, controlling his heart rate. It was one thing to lean against a balcony railing or stand at the edge of Stone Mountain, but this was not the same. God, the ledge was only a few inches deep, barely enough to accommodate the balls of his feet, and he had to move fast.

Fuck it. Go...

He shuffled his feet along the ledge and slid his hands along the rough brick, almost at a jog, keeping his pelvis forward, fighting to keep his center of gravity close to the wall, the red brickwork just an inch from his nose, not stopping until he reached the corner of the building, his hands raw and bleeding, fingers grasping the edges of bricks.

Now came the fun part, getting around the corner. He reached his right hand around the edge and slapped blindly at the wall, trying to find the ridge in the brickwork. No good, not enough reach, and his center of gravity was moving away from the wall each time he swung his arm. He pulled his hand back and anchored himself in place again, his adrenaline surging.

OK. A simple matter of physics...

He had to throw both hand and foot around the corner at the same time. Blindly. And if he missed the ledge, he'd fall.

One chance.

He blew out a breath, got in position, lifted his foot, and swung his body, flailing his arm along with his leg around the corner.

He got a toehold, caught hold of a brick, and pulled. Smacked his mouth against the corner and was rewarded with the metallic taste of his own blood, but he made it around the corner, his head swimming, the world spinning.

He stopped and held tight and this time allowed himself three deep breaths. Once the world stopped spinning, he moved a few feet forward and was now directly below the metal pole.

Would it hold? Time to find out.

He wiped the blood off his hands onto his jeans, reached up and grabbed the pole, and swung his legs out into the abyss. Swung his legs back for momentum once, twice, and then forward, hauling himself up, and swung his legs and body right over the parapet.

He let go of the pole and drew his gun as he rolled onto the roof.

The assassin was fifteen feet to his left, hunched over the rifle. But as Daniel hit the roof, Drapeau dropped into a crouch and scooped up the pistol at his feet.

Daniel jerked the trigger.

Drapeau froze in place with a confused look on his face and blood spurting out of his neck. He clasped his free hand over the hole, blood still spurting between his fingers, and raised the pistol.

Daniel jerked the trigger again. And again. And again.

Lucien Drapeau convulsed as bullets tore into his chest. He dropped the pistol and then, in slow motion, his body crumpled to the rooftop.

Daniel lay back on the gravel roof, utterly exhausted. He just lay there for a minute, staring at the sky, thinking of nothing, listening to his own breathing.

Then the sound of cheering, the cheering of thousands, rose up from Jackson Square and reached Daniel's ears. Wild, euphoric cheering.

He made it...

Daniel stood and wiped his bloody hands on his shirt. His legs felt like rubber bands as he walked to the edge of the roof. He found the rifle's safety and engaged it. Then uncoupled the scope from the rifle, dropped the rifle on the rooftop, braced his elbows on the ledge, and looked through the scope.

His uncle stood on the stage in front of the blazing white façade of Saint Louis Cathedral, smiling and waving at the multitudes packing Jackson Square. He raised his arms and made a gesture for quiet, and the crowd went silent.

He made it!

Daniel felt an incredible swelling in his chest, felt his face break into a wide grin. He put his eye back to the lens. His uncle placed his blue Bible on the podium, leaned toward the microphones, smiled once more, and began speaking to the world.

And then the front of Tim Trinity's shirt turned bright red.

A mist of blood filled the air in front of his chest, sparkling in the sunlight like a million tiny rubies.

People scattered, screaming, in all directions as Trinity collapsed to the stage.

Daniel dropped the scope and started running.

84:

Andrew Thibodeaux stepped back from the rifle on the table and listened to the pandemonium outside with a sort of calm detachment. He looked at the hole the bullet had ripped in the window sheers. Of course there would be a hole, but he was surprised to see it there. The hole looked odd to him, he didn't know why.

His mind echoed with instructions from the Lord's Shepherd. There was still one thing left to do. Killing the Deceiver was the most important thing, and it was accomplished, but Andrew's task wasn't finished.

He stepped back to the bed and stared at the pistol.

He didn't like this part.

Normally this would be a sin, but the Shepherd had explained. God needed Andrew's help, and so this was not a sin, not this time.

Divine dispensation for divine assistance, the Shepherd had called it.

He was God's most faithful servant now, God's special son, and when this last thing was done, he would be carried to paradise on the wings of angels.

He would be welcomed as a hero in heaven, and he would dine at the same table with Jesus and the Apostles.

Andrew Thibodeaux sat on the edge of the bed, picked up the gun, and put the barrel in his mouth, knowing he would be there soon.

Daniel leapt onto the stage where three paramedics worked furiously on his uncle. Trinity's shirt was open, his chest covered in blood, and a square of clear plastic was taped over the bullet hole. Daniel dropped to his knees and took his uncle's hand as one of the medics said, "Losing him…" and another said, "Pressure dropping…too much blood…"

Daniel squeezed his uncle's hand. "God, please don't die…" He could feel hot tears streaming down his face. "Hang on…stay with me…"

Tim Trinity's eyelids fluttered and he looked straight up. "Can't see you." Daniel put his face right above Trinity's. Trinity let out a small smile.

"Why, Tim? Why didn't you wear the vest?"

"God didn't want me to." Trinity's fingers tightened around Daniel's hand. "It's OK, Danny, everything happened exactly as it was supposed to." Trinity's eyelids closed for a few seconds, fluttered open again. His free hand struggled to lift the Bible it was holding. "Take this…"

Daniel reached across his uncle's chest and took the blue Bible and held onto it. "I've got it."

Trinity's smile grew as his eyes became more unfocused. "Quite a ride," he said. "Quite a ride…"

"I love you, Pops."

"I love you, son." Tim Trinity closed his eyes slowly.

He let out a very long breath and did not breathe again.

85:

Conrad Winter had just signaled the flight attendant for another Bloody Mary when the pilot came over the PA.

"Ladies and gentlemen, this is your captain speaking. We've just received some disturbing news from back in New Orleans. I'm sorry to report that, shortly after arriving in Jackson Square, Reverend Tim Trinity was shot, and has died." Several horrified gasps filtered up from the economy section. The flight attendant pulled the curtain closed as the captain continued. *"You'll find CNN on channel four of your personal in-flight monitors, should you wish further updates."*

Conrad put his headset on and tuned to CNN. Trinity had been shot at 1:34, safely after the plane was in the air. Always good to have an alibi.

And then came the news that assured Conrad an alibi would never be needed for this one. Police had just found the man who killed Trinity, dead of a self-inflicted gunshot, in the apartment block across from Saint Louis Cathedral. According to the Louisiana driver's license found on the body, his name was Andrew Thibodeaux. He had been twenty-three years old.

The lost sheep had fulfilled his duty, and the world was safe from what-ever upheaval Tim Trinity might have wrought. And Father Nick would never know about the involvement of the council in Vatican affairs.

Conrad turned off the monitor and removed the headset as the flight attendant arrived with his drink.

✣ ✣ ✣

The nearest hospital was Tulane, and Daniel found Pat there. But Pat was still in surgery, so Daniel used the opportunity to get the cuts in his hands stitched up and a butterfly bandage on his split lip where he'd banged it against the wall.

He left Tulane and walked numbly down the block to a diner. He was running on empty, knew he needed sustenance, so he forced himself to eat, even though he had no appetite and couldn't taste anything.

He wandered back to the hospital. Pat was now in a recovery room, asleep.

Daniel pulled a chair beside the bed and sat with his uncle's blue Bible in his lap. He noticed the red splatters on the cover, which made his chest ache. He took the Bible to the bathroom and washed the blood off. As he was drying the cover with a paper towel, the book fell open in his hands.

There was an envelope taped inside the front cover. It was full of photographs, snapshots of him as a boy and his uncle as a younger man. Fishing together in a river somewhere in Mississippi…sunbathing on top of the Winnebago…eating chilidogs at the Varsity.

Daniel wept.

It was late when the cab dropped him back at the Saint Sebastian's Boys Athletic Club. He used his key to open the door and headed straight for the office couch.

But he couldn't sleep. He switched the light back on, left the office, and went to the room where Trinity had slept.

On the cot was the bulletproof vest Trinity had chosen not to wear without telling anyone. On top of the vest, a piece of paper.

Daniel picked it up and read his uncle's handwriting…

LAST WILL AND TESTAMENT
OF REVEREND TIM TRINTIY
(Born Timothy Granger, New Orleans)

I'm not big on long goodbyes, so I'll be as brief as I know how. I realize a lot of people think I'm crazy, but I do declare that as I write these words I am of sound mind and body.

I hereby appoint my nephew, Daniel Byrne (Hi Danny!) as the sole executor of my estate. He'll make sure it gets done right. He's reliable that way.

Now, I got a lot of money. Don't know how much, really, it's been coming in so fast of late. Last I checked we were crossing one hundred and fifty million, ($150,000,000) if you can believe that. That's a right smart number of zeros.

Well, here's what I want done with it:

Take a third of the money and put it to use in the small towns where I preached in tents all those years (Danny will remember). Just spend it on whatever those towns need.

For the general welfare, as the saying goes.

Take the rest of the money, two-thirds of it, and use it to help rebuild the parts of New Orleans that need it the most.

That's it, folks. Short and sweet, as promised. Now I gotta go and meet my maker. It's time.

Be good to each other.

Love,

Tim

Epilogue:

New Orleans, Louisiana – four weeks later...

An autopsy revealed that Tim Trinity had been carrying a tumor the size of a small quince in his head. Atheists said the tumor meant that the Trinity Phenomenon was not evidence of a God. Believers said the tumor was God's instrument.

And since nobody could explain how the predictions worked, most folks just went on believing, or not believing, whatever they believed, or didn't, before the whole thing began.

Daniel was getting on with the business of grieving, and he was grateful for the grief. Of all the miracles he'd witnessed in the past two months, perhaps the greatest of all was that he'd reconnected with his uncle. This is what the grief taught him, and the pain of this loss was better than the emptiness he'd felt when they were estranged.

He felt like he'd found *himself* again. He felt truly blessed.

He made it down to Dulac once a week, and on the last visit was surprised to see that Pat had already lost the crutches. Having taken a bullet for the cause, Pat didn't even complain when Daniel said thank you.

Julia had become quite a sensation in the world of journalism. She still wrote for the *Times-Picayune* but also traveled on joint assignment with CNN. Daniel was living with her—until he found an apartment, they said—but she was away as much as she was home these days.

He missed her when she was away, but he didn't begrudge her making the most of the opportunity. And when he drove her to the airport last week, she'd said that maybe it was time for him to stop pretending to look for an apartment. So the early signs for the relationship were all good. He was happy to stop pretending to look for an apartment and was looking forward to her return later that afternoon.

He was sitting in the sunshine on Julia's back deck reading a novel when the package arrived. He heard the doorbell, walked through the house, and signed for the FedEx driver, who handed him a box.

He took the box to the dining room, cut the tape, and opened it.

Inside he found an aluminum laptop computer and a note from Carter Ames on Fleur-de-Lis Foundation letterhead.

> *Daniel:*
> *I once told you that if you walked the path, I would show you the truth about your uncle.*
>> *Your uncle was not the only one. The world is full of miracles.*
>> *– Carter Ames, managing director*

Daniel put the note down and looked at the laptop.

He went to the kitchen, tossed ice cubes in a glass, and poured some amber rum over the ice. He took the drink out to the back deck, sat in the sun, and closed his eyes.

He heard a key turn in the front door lock, heard Julia's heels on the hardwood in the living room.

"Out on the deck," he called.

Deep down, Daniel knew that he would open that computer and examine the truths Carter Ames wanted to share.

But not today.

Author's Note:

Everybody knows the great city of New Orleans was devastated by Hurricane Katrina and the flooding that followed, but many have assumed it has fully recovered. Not so. There are large parts of the city still struggling, and they sure could use our help. The Make It Right Foundation is doing heroic work in the Ninth Ward, and I hope you'll join me in supporting their efforts. If interested, you can find more information and a link on the *Good Works* page of my website, www.chercover.com. Thanks.

Speaking of New Orleans, I did take dramatic license near the end of the novel by moving a housing project a few blocks from where it actually stands. I signaled this by giving both the project and the street fictional names.

Biblical quotations in THE TRINITY GAME come from the New Revised Standard Version. According to most scholars, the NRSV is the second-most accurate translation, when compared to earliest known documents. The *most* accurate is the NASB '95. But the Catholic Church does not use the NASB, whereas the NRSV is accepted by both Catholics and Protestants and could be a Bible common to both Tim Trinity and Daniel Byrne.

The work of religious historian Bart D. Ehrman and theoretical physicist Benjamin Schumacher aided my research immeasurably. I first discovered them through their excellent DVD courses at The Great Courses, and I've enjoyed their books as well. .

I had a total blast writing this book, and I hope you enjoyed reading it. If you did, I hope you'll tell your friends and neighbors and booksellers and librarians, both in person and wherever you hang out online. I appreciate the boost.

Thanks and Praises:

Dan Conaway: Incredible agent, even better friend, and the idiot who told me to write this book when most said don't. Also Stephen Barr, Simon Lipskar, and the whole gang at Writers House.

Marjorie Braman: Editor extraordinaire, who brought fresh eyes and keen intellect and who definitely made this a better book.

Andy Bartlett, Daphne Durham, Jacque Ben-Zekry, Katie Finch, Justin Golenbock, Leslie LaRue, Renee Johnson, and the entire Thomas & Mercer team.

Barbara Chercover: Mom, friend, and first-reader without equal. Her fingerprints are all over this book.

Marcus Sakey: My road dog and collaborator, who repeatedly talked me off the writing ledge. Marcus is responsible for the fact that this book contains no Jesuit assassins or sea nymphs.

My other early readers: Agent 99 (more on her later), Jane Cornett, John Purcell. All gave valuable feedback.

Dana Kaye: Great friend and awesome publicist.

The crime fiction community: Readers, writers, librarians, booksellers, reviewers, editors, bloggers, publicists, agents…fellow crime fiction geeks. *My tribe.* Wish I could name you all, but you know who you are. Representative sample: Jon & Ruth Jordan, Jennifer Jordan, Judy Bobalik, Jenn Forbus, JD Singh, Marian Misters, Rick Kogan, Robin & Jamie Agnew, Mike Bursaw, Don Longmuir, McKenna Jordan, Richard Katz, Linda Brown, Bobby McCue, Marjorie Flax, Penny Halle, Sue Freemire…and Ben LeRoy, who makes the publishing world—and the world—a better place. One Love, y'all.

Clergy: Father Dave, Father Michael, and Father Ken, for their insight and openness. Mambos Ava Kay Jones, Sallie Ann Glassman, and Miriam Chimani, for accentuating the positive.

Finally, to the love of my life, Agent 99. Words fail. And to my son, a.k.a the Mouse, a.k.a Thunder Dragon, a.k.a Fire Dog. You are the two best things that ever happened to me. Don't know what I did to deserve you.

About the Author

Photograph by Iden Ford, 2011

Sean Chercover is a former private detective turned novelist and screenwriter. A native of Toronto, he has held a motley assortment of jobs over the years, including video editor, scuba diver, nightclub magician, encyclopedia salesman, and truck driver. He is the author of two award-winning novels featuring Chicago private investigator Ray Dudgeon: *Big City, Bad Blood* and *Trigger City*. After living in Chicago; New Orleans; and Columbia, South Carolina, Sean has returned to Toronto where he lives with his wife and son. His fiction has won the Anthony, Shamus, CWA Dagger, Dilys, and Crimespree awards, and been shortlisted for the Edgar, Barry, Macavity, Arthur Ellis and ITW Thriller awards.

www.chercover.com